Donated
by the
FRIENDS
of
Pickens Library

D1384690

THE TIME SEAM

BLACKSTON GOLD, BOOK TWO

THE TIME SEAM

SYLVIA KELSO

FIVE STAR
A part of Gale, Cengage Learning

Detroit • New York • San Francisco • New Haven, Conn • Waterville, Maine • London

GALE
CENGAGE Learning™

LIBRARY OF CONGRESS CATALOGING-IN-PUBLICATION DATA

Kelso, Sylvia.
    The time seam / Sylvia Kelso. — 1st ed.
      p. cm. — (Blackston gold ; bk. 2)
    ISBN-13: 978-1-4328-2547-8 (hardcover)
    ISBN-10: 1-4328-2547-X (hardcover)
    1. Time travel—Fiction. 2. Gold mines and mining—Fiction. 3.
Australia—Fiction. I. Title.
PR9619.4.K456T56 2011
823'.92—dc22   2011025024

First Edition. First Printing: October 2011.
Published in 2011 in conjunction with Tekno Books.

Printed in the United States of America
1 2 3 4 5 6 7 15 14 13 12 11

For my paternal aunts,
Ethel and Doris,
who didn't often tell yarns,
but who did write poetry.
Thanks for the genes.

ACKNOWLEDGMENTS

Thanks to Lois Bujold, Vreni and Peter Murphy, and Anne Roberts for reading this manuscript in process, and offering good comments as well as encouragement, to Rosaleen Love for wip reading and also for first remarking on the quartz graves, and to Pat Wrede for suggesting *The Time Seam* as a title.

I would also like to thank the following people who supplied vital information in special areas. Any errors remaining are my mistakes, or deliberate divergences from what they said.

Narelle Houston, for helping construct the law firm of Lewis and Cotton, and general legal advice.

Pat Crawley, of Cookstown, County Tyrone, for his great generosity to a stranger, particularly in showing me around the area, and in filling out Jimmy's backstory.

Les Scully, of Industrial Pumps Townsville, for assistance with the layout and details of Ben Morar, and stories about small Australian mines in general.

The female officer of the Queensland Police who supplied information on police procedure at serious traffic accidents, and whose name I have most reprehensibly lost.

Senior Constable Peter Shelton of the Queensland Police, who sketched out police procedure for major non-traffic accidents, and who suggested the Superintendent's BBQ.

Leith Golding, for IT advice, especially on the ins and outs of CDs.

And Mike Rubenach, for a wealth of data on geology, geologists and gold mines, but most for telling me the yarn that became the centre of Chris's story and the trigger for this book.

SYNOPSIS OF BOOK ONE

Dorian Wild is a junior partner in the law firm of Lewis and Cotton in the North Australian town of Ibisville. She is happy with her job and her partner Chris Keogh, senior geologist at the Ben Morar gold mine outside the old goldfield town of Blackston. Then a figure in nineteenth-century prospector's clothes walks out of the floor in her building elevator and balances a panning dish on her head before he disappears.

His further appearances involve Dorian's friends and fellow partners Laura McFadden and Anne Lee as they search for a link with problems at Ben Morar, where Chris has found a rich new goldfield with his revolutionary statistical analysis model. The firm is under threat of takeover. When Chris is killed in a suspicious car accident Dorian and her partners confront the mining megacorporation Pan-Auric, whose plans for his new field had made Chris resign in protest, asking Dorian to find a good environmental lawyer.

As threats and dangers escalate, Dorian finds herself falling through the "fold in time" which Chris thinks has brought the "ghost" into her world. A harrowing experience in nineteenth-century Blackston leaves her ready to abandon the project, but the "ghost" keeps appearing, and similar circumstances produce a bond between them. When Dorian goes to Blackston to confront George Richards, the Ben Morar mine manager, the ghost appears in daylight during a historical pageant. This time, it seems, he has come into Dorian's world for good.

Dorian learns that the "ghost" is actually Jimmy Keenighan, Northern Irish Catholic activist first for Land Rights, then for Trade Unionism. He was a compositor and reporter on the Blackston newspaper, *The North Queensland Miner,* at whose office both have crossed the "fold in time." The bond they have previously felt strengthens to attraction as they try to understand why Jimmy is there, then to stop Pan-Auric's plan for the new field, which, they find, is right under Blackston, "on top" of the famous old deep mine, the Solitaire.

CHAPTER 1

Dorian phased slowly back to wakefulness: where am I, when, how. Why?

Blackston. The Park Street Motel. Coming up to see George, confront him about Ben Morar. Screw him down, find out definitively: why did he sell out, and now, what does Pan-Auric plan? Where is this damn mine Chris found?

Did he sack Chris or not?

I sent the report. Memory rushed back with almost the original rage. I got nothing useful out of him and I sent the report to Dani, I talked to Anne and Laura, then I went uptown for lunch. And in the street . . .

The historical pageant. People dressed like the old times, like that time. Old Blackston, where the time-fold took me. But it was here and now. This time, old Blackston came to me.

Now I'm in bed in the Park Street Motel, and he's in the room across from me. Breathing. Talking. Living flesh and blood. Not just a ghost, a time-collision any longer. Jimmy. Jimmy Keenighan. A name, a life, a connection I never expected. Now I do know why we kept colliding. I do know, why me.

Physical answers, a bruising recollection. And then the cause of that strange split in her inner landscape, half lingering sweetness, half painful as a day-old bruise.

I kissed someone last night. He wanted it, and I wanted it. Whatever happened then.

And it's only five weeks since Chris . . .

11

Was I unfaithful to Chris?

No. The answer came without need to think. Chris gave himself whole to whatever he did: he'd have taken us to the limit too. Living together, kids. Marriage, probably. But he'd never expect—he'd never want to hold me, once that tie was gone.

"What, hang around years playing widow for me?" She could hear every nuance, every turn of phrase. "If someone else turns up, don't dither about old times, kid. Just go for it."

I'll do that, Chris.

That is, memory qualified ruefully, if you get a chance.

That *was* blackmail, she admitted, last night. I was too mad and hurt and—scared—to do better. To get past the knee jerk at that blasted outworn Catholic morality and try to explain. Just because you kissed me and you were drunk, it doesn't have to be guilt and panic and rejection. And *I* have a say in it. Things are different now.

She relived the sulfurous hush that had seen them through the bathroom dance and the final getting to bed. And lying there, tired out, twice-over aching, listening to him not breathe, trying not to do it herself. Can we ever get past that? Ever get the old understanding back?

It'll take a lot of time. And care. From both of us.

She opened her eyes and found the bed next to the window empty, sheets flung back in the full morning light.

Dorian sat up like a jack-in-a-box and that deep alien voice said wryly, "I've no' run away."

He looked down at her across the counter. Over her laptop, open between them. A half memory assembled: barest dawn, a persistent shaking hand, a bodiless voice demanding that she log on. "I need y'r wee machine," it had insisted. "I canna sleep, an' there's things I need to know."

"Ah. Erh." Oh. I showed him how to Search, last night. And I logged on, who knows how long ago? She found her watch face. Eight-ten. Two hours at least. He looked hollow-eyed and a little pale. That could be hangover, or exhaustion, or—something else. But there was a visible pinch around his mouth.

Their eyes locked. The silence teetered, this time with a different tension, the fraught moment of reencounter in a quarrel's wake. And neither of us, she understood with instant certainty, knows what to do. What to say. How not to relight the fuses—or even whether we *want* to light the fuses again.

Should I try to explain? Or just apologize?

No. What happened last night was too deep-based, too sensitive to drag out so baldly. He won't, and I shouldn't. Not yet. But he did speak. And I do need to respond. Make a less loaded, more neutral overture.

"Did you find what you were looking for?"

Her voice sounded too high, too brusque. But after a moment he said, "Aye."

I found, the inflection added, far too much.

He's talking to me. Or at me. And he mightn't want to deal with last night either. But he does need—that inflection's signaling it—he does need something else.

"What did you find?"

He rubbed a hand up his forehead, a motion that spoke more than weariness. "I found what happened here."

Blackston's history. Maybe more? "You didn't find . . . !"

He shook his head. The look said he had understood: Did you find Michael and Patsy and the wake of sabotage?

"Mind ye, I canna be sure. I couldna find the *Miner*'s back issues or suchlike, the way big papers have. Just a wee local history. But if there'd been—a bad—" She understood, a catastrophic accident, serious sabotage. "—surely, it'd be there."

In double relief Dorian slumped down and grabbed a pillow

for security. "So, what *did* you find?" Adrenaline kicked her own wits in. "The gold, the deep reef, it did fail: when?"

"Ah. In the nineties, Peep o'Day, the Solitaire, they were the richest mines in the colonies." His hand made a little gesture, as if history itself were water in his fingers, dripping away. "A decade, an' the lodes failed. Nineteen twenty, they'd leveled the mills. Pulled down the poppet-heads." Bleak now, the present image of desolation. His Blackston, his own future, being stripped away.

Do I say I'm sorry, yet again? More crows were calling in the park. Dorian let go the pillow and began thinking how to get out of bed. Glanced back, and stopped.

In a moment she said, "What else did you find?"

He studied the window too. "I asked for the history o' Queensland," he said.

"Oh. So, you know about Federation, and Australia being a nation, and all that?"

He nodded. The stare looked darker than ever, somber, impenetrable.

What else would he ask, with the Net, the world's history open, how he didn't glitch it a hundred times over I'll never know, but he must have—oh.

"You asked about—Ireland."

His mouth twisted. He looked away and did not turn back.

"So you know about—" She was resurrecting TV headlines, images. "The—Troubles, didn't they say?"

"Trrrroubles." This time the "r" was an explosion. "Trroubles, aye. They've cut Erin apart!"

"Eh?"

"The Orangemen. The bluidy *Protestants!* Marchin' an' drillin' and bleatin' about Union . . . *Union!* Wi' the *Crown!* Bringin' in arms! Stirrin' the nationalists, save us, this IRA, they're worse than Fenians. Bombs an' murders an' English troops again, all over Ulster. God be good to us. Parnell, an' O'Connell, an' Fitzgerald, an' all the Wild Geese that ever flew—all the blood they shed—the battles they fought—the battles *we* fought, for Erin—" The pain was raw in his voice. " 'Tis all come to this."

The last words dropped to nothing. It was a moment before Dorian dared speak.

"But I thought—wasn't it settled? They're at peace?"

The lift of his hand needed no words to expand. Ireland cut in two, half an English province? Every ideal, every dream generations worked and fought and died for, travestied? This is peace?

"An' it came so close . . ."

The tone of that brought her out of bed before she thought, around the counter, hand on his shoulder, trying to see his face. "What came so close? How?"

The stone wall had shorn away along with that self-aware irony. He looked raw, hurt. Desolate. But he had not pulled back. She was intensely, momentarily aware of his shoulder under her fingers, solid bone and muscle through the new white shirt. Then she thought, To hell with that.

"Tell me," she said.

He looked down at the screen. "I doubt ye'll understand the half." He paused, gathering thoughts. Probably, she thought without resentment, simplifying them. "In my time, we—Erin, all Erin—had MPs in Parliament. The British Parliament. An' for years an' years, right up into the nineteen hundreds, they campaigned for Home Rule. *Irish* Home Rule." His fingers rattled a tattoo on the countertop. "See this wee man Asquith, then, a Liberal Prime Minister. An' he's no' got a majority. So he comes cap in hand to the Irish, sayin', Help me form a Government. An' Redmond, that's their leader, *he* says, Aye. So ye give us a Home Rule Bill."

Dorian blinked. He looked up briefly and nodded as if she

had understood. "What we'd been after for years. Independence. Legal. Legislated."

"And it worked?"

He gave his usual wry snort. "The House o' Lords vetoed it."

"Oh." And then the rest began? The Fenians, the Orangemen, the IRA? Her hand relaxed, but he looked up and the twist had caught his mouth again.

"But Asquith still needed his majority, aye? So when Redmond put the screws to him, he changed the law. A bill the Commons pass three times, the Lords canna scuttle it."

"So even if the Lords refused again, it went through!" The look on his face broke her excitement in the egg. "It would have gone through . . . ?"

The droop of his head had answered already. "It would ha' gone through, aye. But that was in nineteen thirteen."

"Nineteen thirteen? But what . . . ? Oh. World War I started? But that shouldn't have made any difference!"

"They suspend legislature," he answered somberly, "for the first year o' a war. But that wasna the real block."

"What, then?"

"In nineteen fourteen." He dragged in a long, long breath. "In nineteen fourteen, they all thought the war'd end by Christmas." So, Dorian filled in, the bill would go ahead. "An' the Unionists, the Ulster Unionists, had a proper panic. They thought, in two more years they'd be out o' British hands." The tone went satiric. "A true part o' Erin. An' "—now it was savage—"get a taste o' their own medicine. Be trod under the heel o' Popery."

"What? Oh." History lessons became reality, the root of his defiance when she had said, "You're a Catholic." Centuries of prejudice and bias and outright oppression visited on Catholics in England and English possessions, after Henry VIII made the state religion Protestant.

"Aye." He still sounded more savage than ironic. "So they went beyond drillin' an' marchin' an' bellowin', an' bought guns. So then, o' course, the nationalists, down south, they did the same."

Dorian shut her eyes as the disastrous prospect merged with her own knowledge: the 1916 rising, the English reprisals. World War I over, the Irish Free State, and open war between the Irish factions, with British troops in the midst. On and on down the century, to the images of her childhood, terrorists in balaclavas, bombs and pub shootings, British troops with gas-helmets and automatic weapons in the Belfast streets.

And the worst is, it's all over and done. The future he believed and campaigned and worked to make so different is already lost. Already history.

Under her hand his shoulder was rock-hard. Rock-motionless. He had bowed his head again, as if he were holding a vigil. As if the laptop were the image, or the reality, of a cenotaph.

Then, faintly, huskily, he said, "An' the worst . . ."

There's a worse? She felt her own hand flinch.

"The worst is . . . it could all ha' been settled . . . twenty years before. There could ha' *been* a bill. Presented. Passed. In Gladstone's time."

The crows were still calling. Downstairs trays rattled as the motel came back to life.

He dropped his head in his hands, saying it in something like a groan. "How could he . . . how *could* he have . . ."

Dorian tried not to move, to breathe. But silence must have been its own questioning.

"Parnell." He brought it out as if lifting a stone. "Parnell. God be good to us, the man that started the Land League. That led the Home Rule party. That united Erin. That sat in that Parliament an' hounded Willie Gladstone, aye, hounded him, wi' an Irish block vote that could break his majority. An' we thought . . . I thought . . . out here, I read the papers an' followed the debates an' I knew—we all knew! 'Twas but a matter o' time!"

For a minute she thought she should withdraw, leave the rest in decent obscurity. She tensed to shift and he drew his head up and looked full in her face. His eyes were almost black. She thought they might be red as well.

"Then," he said with fearful calmness, "he couldna keep his trousers buttoned. An' he had to choose a married woman."

Oh, God, Dorian thought, as it burst on her like an artillery shell. Nothing, for you, could be a greater betrayal than that.

"No' just once." The calm was stony now. "A whole ten years. Wi' the husband shuttin' his eyes an' the party lookin' everywhere but 'twixt the bedsheets. An' then the wee fool files for divorce!"

With memories of promiscuous US presidents, she could imagine the result all too well.

"They impeached Parnell. Aye. The scandal finished him in politics." He put his head in his hands. "It finished the Home Rule party, for the rest o' the century. An' when they did rally—with Asquith, that they could twist wi' another weak government—it was nineteen thirteen. An' the Unionists past arguin'."

He stopped altogether. It was the muteness of desolation. Of a loss beyond defeat. Even Bridget's funeral couldn't have been quite like this.

And I can't hug you this time either. Not after last night. Not in a T-shirt and just out of bed.

Not now, above all. Not in the shadow of Parnell's adultery.

Dorian bit her tongue. Then, very slowly, lifted her hand away. He did not move. His face was still hidden, and the curve of his back said, Leave it. There's nothing that you, that anyone can do.

Except he did tell me. He wanted to tell me. I could do that much. And if *I* can't do more—there's still something that might.

Dorian put her hand back. Very gently, she said, "Let's go to Mass."

I do have a hat, she thought, staring in the bathroom mirror at the white blouse and peasant skirt. I've never worn one to Mass, but my grandmother was paranoid about it. So he probably will be too. It gripes me to regress, but he's already had a pretty hard time today. And it will put off the real upset, at least till we're in church.

She hesitated, gritted her teeth. Plunked the straw hat on her head.

When she had deposited the laptop downstairs they stepped out into the sun together. She thought, Make a little more time. Ease things. "I thought you might like to walk," she said.

He stopped. The stare was withdrawn again, closed and fenced. But she felt the hesitation, if she could not guess the terms of the debate. Then he made up his mind. Slowly, but not at all awkwardly, he offered her an elbow, slightly crooked, hand held waist-high.

Sliding her fingers into his arm, feeling body warmth under the shirt, the way he automatically drew her hand against his side, trying not to feel cherished and not at all superfluously protected, she told herself firmly, It's no more than an answer to your truce flag. A courtesy, a ritual gesture. He'd do it to anyone.

He was silent as they walked. The stare was dark as ever, but he looked tired, she thought. More than tired. Dispirited. She wanted to squeeze his arm, to let that say silently, I understand. You're not alone. Prudence—experience—restrained her. We're going to Mass. He'll be preparing himself for that now. Distraction's the last thing he needs.

Especially, the memory of last night added, from you.

19

"Saint Columba's Catholic church in Blackston has a nine-A.M. Mass," the recorded voice had said on the Catholic Information line. The map said, the corner of Church and Landers Street. When he aimed them along the park she hesitated, and he gave her one brief glance. "We'll go down to Church Street an' turn," he said. In another minute she worked it out.

Going this way, we avoid Landers Street. And the *Miner*'s office as well.

The church was evidently where he expected, though the pause as he took in its wooden, high-pointed Gothic-arch facade, the miniature poppet-head of the freestanding bell tower, and the Infants' School on the opposite side, said a good deal else had changed. Steering for the door, Dorian thought, Just don't let him clap eyes on a woman till we're in.

Consensus pointed them into a back pew. And the twitch as he surveyed the congregation told her the reaction would be all she had feared.

Ye didna say ye go bareheaded to Mass! She could feel The Look tattooing it on her skin. Not just trousers—women uncovered before the Lord!

Her neck cringed. If he's going to yell at me, let him keep it quiet. Or just not stalk out.

He leant sidelong to her ear. She tried not to flinch. But the general noise of assembly matched his undertone, and the voice was soft. Almost resigned.

"I suppose this is the custom in y'r day?"

She tried to nod without patent relief.

He straightened slowly. His profile spoke a tiredness that was not physical fatigue. Then he folded carefully down on his knees and bent his head.

Settling beside him, Dorian thought, He didn't fuss. Maybe he's just too battered from the Irish stuff. Then, with hope and relief: maybe he's starting to adjust, to make allowances. Then, recalling tradition, she thought, I hope so, because it won't be the only shock in here.

He did twitch when the priest moved to the altar, and the first words in English brought a splutter in his throat. He'd be used to Latin, she thought. And probably, in his day the priest didn't face the congregation, either. Oh, damn it, can I find anything that's still the same?

But as the service went forward she found herself drawn back into its progress, the easingly familiar patterns of ritual, as if she had slid into a quiet, buoying lake. When she glanced sideways, his stance, the line of his profile spoke a softening too.

If it does this for me, and I'm not a practicing believer, what must it mean to him?

He had already found a stray prayer book under the pew. When that deep voice with its alien accent began to murmur, then with increasing surety to join the responses, she felt gratitude move beyond relief. There's *something* here that works for him.

But when she rose to take communion he answered her look with a startled, almost scandalized head-shake. "I canna," he muttered, when she slid down again beside him. "I'm no' confessed."

Dorian was betrayed into another stare. He kept his face averted but she saw the line of his mouth. " 'Twas Thursday when . . ."

When his reality folded. And, Dorian remembered, Friday's always the day for reconciliation: confession, they used to say.

You can take communion without confession nowadays. Dorian opened her mouth and shut it again, and worked her way out of the pew.

Not really enough, she thought, as they dodged the post-service gatherings and started back down Church Street. Not to balance the past—his present—just torn away, and the future spoiled. More than spoiled. His hopes for Ireland broken. The mess with us. Even the comfort of Mass left incomplete.

"I'm sorry," she said on the thought's impulse. "Everything here's been so, so hard for you, so—wrong—it isn't fair, whatever it's supposed to do!"

He had been silent, that bruised, brooding quiet that had hushed her on the way to church. But now he scanned the wide street with its restored houses, the untrafficked bitumen framed in the green height of trees, the pure, dustless morning sunlight heightening its Sunday quiet.

" 'Tis no' all bad," he said slowly. "This: this is—better. The smoke . . . an' the din . . . an' the filth. I can do without them, ye know." The note was very near surprise. "An' that." He nodded to the park's spread of clipped, tended green. "That wasna here at all. Just a dirty great sawmill lot, an' tree-stumps. An' ruined—bush." He said "bush" as if it were still an exotic word. "That's very . . . fine." He glanced at her again, and now, at last, came a glint of that composed, ironic smile. "An' there's the machines. Y'r . . . electricity." The irony came uppermost. "If I have to bear wi' women barin' their legs an' 'football' on the telly-vision"—he made two words of it—"an' Mass wi' no Latin, I daresay I'll manage. Somehow."

All that, she thought, trying not to hug his arm against her, you can talk about. Even approve. But you won't—can't—talk about Ireland.

Though you like the park. Because it's green. Like Erin? Like home?

Her throat locked and her eyes swam. But he was talking again, a careful, almost tentative inflection. "Ye did say, ye're a lawyer?"

Dorian managed an "Mmm?"

"Then so are other . . . other women?"

Her throat unlocked. "Yes, women can be lawyers." With another surge of gratitude she realized, He's thinking again. "And"—suddenly she felt the pride inherited from generations of feminists—"women can be doctors and dentists and accountants and engineers and geologists and even judges, if they want it hard enough." With a bit of luck, she fudged, dodging the topic of glass ceilings and constantly lower women's wages. "And"—the time-gap recurred, the women's goal that would have been paramount in his day—"we've got the vote."

He stopped dead, swinging round. "Women can vote?"

"In Australia, since nineteen oh-three," she boasted, grateful for her mother's feminist histories. If he's a true activist, he'll be overjoyed.

"Aye?" The surprise was brightening into delight. "Since nineteen oh-three?" And now at last came a full open grin. "No wonder ye think ye can wear the trousers too."

Oh, she thought, trying to get her wind. That was a joke. A real, unmalicious joke. And that wasn't a grin either, even a sunrise. That was a lightning bolt.

She managed a sort of laugh. A press on his arm. He responded instinctively, beginning to walk on. Before she recovered words he spoke again.

"Ye said . . . even engineers?"

It was very close to wistfulness. "If they choose," she said. And let the *why?* ask itself.

"Bridgie," he said in a moment. "If she'd been a boy, she'd ha' been an engineer. She'd've fettled engines, could she get near a poppet-head. She was into all the wee stuff round the pub. Bar taps. Keg spears. Kitchen pumps. Let it go wrong an' Bridgie'd pull it apart an' sort it, no time at all."

"At the *pub?*" Dorian could not help herself. And you talk about decent women to me?

"No' in the bar!" He very nearly turned red. "When she came she was at the Royal, aye, an upstairs maid. Till she met Patsy. Then he—we—found her a place in the dispensary. The Medical Aid Dispensary. For miners an' the like." A hint of pride. "She ran the register, but there was nothin' much to fix. When she an' Patsy wed, an' we took the house, she'd do it there. She was ever at me to help wi' the press, but Dinny'd ha' had a fit. The mine engines, though, the big stuff, was what she really wanted." The too-even note wavered. "An' here . . ."

Here she could have been a mechanic, or a mechanical engineer, even a mining engineer. Dorian felt the bite of lost chances, lives scanted by the luck of history. I'm sorry? What use is that?

She tightened her fingers on his arm. It gripped in answer, pressing her hand to his side. Easier, truer speech, she thought, with gratitude. And in that, now, he's really talking to me.

They were halfway down the park. Open air, a less loaded setting, quiet, no distractions. As easy as we've ever been. The time I was hoping for.

"Um." She bit back a gulp. "Ah, I didn't mean to, uh, blackmail you last night."

His arm jumped. But he did not pull away. He even produced a half-encouraging, half-winded sort of grunt.

"I was angry. I was—hurt. You said, Yes, and I said, Yes, and then—I felt like you'd led me on and turned me down and—"

"I did lead ye on!" His ear was red. "I should ne'er have—!"

"No, listen. Nowadays it isn't like that."

"What isna 'like that'?"

"It's not all up to you! I'm a grown woman and—and—" How do I say, I'm not a virgin, without dishing both of us? "I make up my own mind. And I said, Yes!"

He stopped short again, half swinging around. But his arm had clenched tighter than before. He's very definitely not turning me loose.

"Ye said"—his ear was still red—"yes?"

"Yes! And"—she suddenly remembered lessons about Victorian morality—"nowadays, women can do that. It's not wrong. It's not a sin, it's not shameful. It's our right!"

He had her hand in a vice lock, but his breath was coming noticeably fast. "Ye can—do that. Talk about it—an' no'—no'—"

He looked away, over the park, anywhere but at her. She had never so vividly comprehended belonging to the twenty-first century. Henry Ford was nothing. How do I get the sexual revolution, freedom of choice, the pill, the rights of women, into a hundred words?

Then she remembered. Some of it he's seen for himself.

"Not be ashamed, no." Her voice was almost steady. "Any more than I was with Chris."

He very nearly threw her fingers like a red-hot coal. He did make a strangled noise and jerk his face away. But she could see the blaze of color down his cheek.

At the corner a family had crossed into the park: parents, stroller, toddlers, circling dog. Barking, children's shouts. She ignored them, trying to keep her fingers firm but not clinging on his arm. To let that language say, Yes. You saw us. That wasn't shame, that was freedom. Mutual assent. Comfort. Joy. That was what *we* call love.

"I didna forget." When he spoke it was just audible. "I *couldna* forget." His hand made a little jump against his side. "I thought . . . times . . . it might be—a vision. Temptation. Or—a warnin'—but I couldna see . . . I'm no' married. But I didna—I havena gone wi'—wi'—" He was scarlet beyond the ears this time. "I couldna see *why* . . ."

Why I should merit unnecessary divine warnings against resorting to whores, when every other man on the field was do-ing it.

Abruptly he pulled his chin up. "An' then . . . I said, it *wasna* temptation. I will no' say so. I will no' confess an', an' make it a—"

A thing for shame. A message from the devil. Her throat tightened. He wouldn't forget, and he wouldn't condemn us either. Not just defiance of his faith's rules. Near apostasy.

"An' ye say now, last night—*that* was why ye were angry wi' me?"

Not that I kissed you, Dorian translated frantically, but that I stopped at that? But, no, her own memory supplemented, that wasn't everything.

"Because you said, Yes, and then, No?" She looked up in his face. He was watching her now, straight and intently, the flush almost gone. "That was part of it, yes. But the rest was: you decided without thinking—without asking what *I'd* want."

Though her hand was still in his arm they had stopped and turned almost to face each other. She watched him think it through. Carefully, without the excitement he gave technology, but now without shame or protest or bewilderment.

You aren't just a weaker vessel, or a forbidden desire, or a dichotomy, outside marriage, of virgin and whore. Most of all, you're not the good passive Victorian woman. You have your own desires, you follow them without shame, and you expect them attended to.

In a minute he said, "Oh."

But he isn't taken aback, she realized. And then, so giddily she almost began laughing, she thought, He isn't scared, either. He's not going to run like a monk from a scarlet woman. He's just—taking it in.

Then he looked at her and there was a glint in that dark stare she had not seen before. "I'll remember that," he said.

Now *I* have to try not to blush. Or seem like I'm making an advance myself. She turned a little, shifting her fingers on his arm, and with relief felt him accept the signal, their feet crunching in unison on the road's pebbled edge.

A dozen strides, twenty. Then he suddenly glanced aside and lifted his free hand to just touch the brim of her hat. "But ye wore that," he said softly, "for—because I was wi' you."

"Well . . . yes." I can't say, I thought you'd already been upset enough. "It seemed—it was—one thing I could do."

To soften this world's impact, to make some gesture to your principles, your customs, some compromise with what I did last night, with the image of what a woman should be. For you.

In both senses of that phrase, she realized wryly, even as her mind completed the sentence he had altered: You wore that for me.

Very slightly, his arm tightened again. He was looking straight ahead, and the profile was forbidding as ever. But this time she felt the tremor when she tightened her fingers in response.

And whatever he did or said last night, that's not just courtesy.

Dorian lifted her eyes and the four-square bulk of the Park Street Motel loomed at them. Instantly her stomach grumbled and she heard his smothered snort.

"Ye're no'," he asked with spurious mildness, "hungry again?"

Now he's actually teasing me. "Ten-twenty on a Sunday morning? D'ye think," she imitated both his accent and idiom and won a definite half laugh, "I slipped out for brandy an' truffles at midnight? I'm ravenous." Suddenly it was true. The park was freshly green, the sun lucent, she hardly felt the rising upland heat. "Come on, they can't have taken breakfast off yet, surely?"

The remaining constraint dispelled over his first encounter with waffles—" 'Tis just a fancy name for pancake!" They were down to her coffee and his tea—"None o' that American pap f'r breakfast, d'ye mind?" when he gave her a thoughtful look, and said, "Mind ye, there's somethin' odd about y'r history."

He *can* talk about it, now. She tried to look noncommital. "Oh?"

"Ye've forgot the United Irishmen." He read her look. "Fitzgerald an' Wolfe Tone an' all. The big rising in seventeen ninety-eight. The biggest, before this at the Dublin Post Office. Well, maybe, risings. Ah, well, more like confusion than rebellion, what wi' three different tries an' French landin's fizzlin' out an' all the rest. But 'tis famous." He frowned. "An' on y'r Net I couldna find a word."

"That's . . . odd." Dorian sought some tactful way of saying, I never heard of it either, but then, you know I don't know much Irish history. "Did you check more than one—"

"I checked three—what are they, sites? Aye, it's odd. But I'll tell ye what's odder. Ye've lost Ned Kelly."

"Who?"

His eyebrows shot up and he set his cup down with a clunk.

"Ned Kelly, girl! The colonies'—Australia's most famous bushranger! Fought the polis all his life. Made himself armor and shot it out with 'em at the siege o' Glenrowan. Got hung in eighteen eighty. D'ye know nothin' about y'r own country either?"

"I *do* know about Australia. And bushrangers! Ben Hall and his gang, he robbed coaches and held up towns and died in a shoot-out saying, Don't let them take me alive!"

"Ben Hall, aye, he was older than Ned. But Kelly was more famous . . ."

"Not here he wasn't. I never heard of him."

He shut his mouth and stared.

"And," she added unwarily, as wits overcame umbrage, "if you can't find him on the Net . . ."

His brows drew down and the stone wall grew formidable. "Are ye sayin' . . . ?"

"No." She caught up with his meaning then. "No, I'm just saying this is really weird. I'm not lying. Why should you be? It's just weird, that's all. It's as if—as if—there was some kind of"—a phrase Chris had once used recurred to her—"alternate history."

The stare sharpened as if honed. "A different history? That would mean, a different past? Then—it could be a different future too."

Dorian's head did the proverbial backstroke. "You mean—this mightn't be *your* future—at all?"

He let out a grunt. He sounded winded himself. "Save us. That means . . ."

That means that our newspapers mightn't mention sabotage at Blackston in your time because it isn't your time they're reporting. It's mine.

"No," Dorian heard herself say while the small iron tables and lattice roof and overhanging greenery revolved slowly round her. "No, that's crazy. That's—impossible. I could, I could cope with this fold thing being a time-jump and I'm in your future, but! You're here! I'm here! Paddy Wild was here! Blackston was here and the Solitaire and—"

"An' no' Wolfe Tone. No' Ned Kelly," he said.

"How can some things be here and not others? If it was a different future how could all the rest fit? How could I be Paddy Wild's descendant and you have known him then and . . ."

"Ye said, alternate history."

"Yes, but so many overlaps, so many matches—that would mean anything could change! And if that's so, there might be other alternates, there might—oh, it isn't possible! I can't deal with this!"

He set a firm hand over hers. "We dinna have to deal wi' it. Not yet." Damn, she thought, with mingled wrath and laughter, he's gone into reassurance mode. He thinks I'm doing the

29

hysterical female thing. "In my time . . ." A jagged pause. "Whatever happened there, 'tis over. Whether we know or not. But before anythin' else, we've y'r 'megacorp' to settle." The stare grappled hers. "Today, we've to get out to y'r mine. While there's no one there."

"Yes." Dorian fastened herself back to priorities. *He's right. If he does make me feel like a fluttering flapper, he's still right.* "And it's already half-eleven." She reached for her bag and the keys, and the most notable omission of her morning struck home.

"Oh, heavens! Oh, lord! I've had my phone turned off!"

She jumped in her chair, he jumped in his. The waitress circulating past nearly jumped as well. Dorian twitched the cell phone from her bag and switched it on and it rang instantly.

"Dor! For God's sake, are you all right? Where are you? What's happened? What are you *doing?*"

"Ah, ah, I'm having breakfast—in the hotel restaurant." Dorian almost stammered. "Sorry, I had the phone off—"

"Jeez, Dor, of all the loony—! But you're okay? Nothing's happened? You're all right?"

"I—well—I'm okay." Suddenly the rest was too much to introduce yet. *The best defense is an offense.* "Has something happened down there?"

"Happened!" Laura's squawk made the waitress spin right round. Laura must have caught the motion in the holoscreen, she said rapidly, "Not here, somewhere quieter, your room?"

"My room, yes." *Anything to give her wits marshalling space.* "Five minutes, I'll call you, okay?" Across the table, he was already getting to his feet.

"That was Laura. My friend." He was on the stairs behind her, a heavier tread, but smooth and agile as a cat's. "You saw her—in my office, when you took the, the pencils." *Easier to use* his term than try another compressed history to make sense of a BIC. "Something's happened, down in Ibisville." Suddenly her heart sped up, has P-A moved, what have they done, is Anne all right? But Laura would have said. If Anne or Sam or the kids had been hurt, Laura would have looked worse than that.

"Ibisville? She—ye're both from Ibisville?"

"Yes, the same firm, she's another lawyer." She unlocked her door, and stopped. "I'll have to tell her. Sometime now, I'll have to tell her about you."

He waited. The pause answered, Of course. Aloud he said, "Best sort this first."

Laura too had gathered her composure. When the holoscreen came up she opened crisply, "You're okay, that's the main thing. You haven't had any trouble up there?" And when Dorian shook her head, incapable of qualifying "trouble" yet, Laura said, "Lewis and Cotton had a break-in last night.

"Somebody jumped the security man," she went on as Dorian gulped. "Knocked him out, tied him up. Disabled the Perp-Insurance alarm. Picked our front lock. Tried to get in the safe." It deepened to a growl. "And they went through your files and got the contract and the model copies, and tried to get in Dani's office as well."

Dorian's gasp came out a grunt. "The safe! My files! The *security man!*" Not just her own territory, the firm's territory invaded, but a known, innocent person hurt: she saw the gray hair, the kindly face. The next, too-predictable casualty in the enemy's track.

Then a sharper stab went home. "Your files! Anne's! Did they get—?"

"Anne thinks they didn't know." Laura flashed it back in her full-brain-engaged, courtroom voice. "She says otherwise they'd have tried us next. But there's an alarm on Dani's record safe, it alerted the cops. So they probably did your room and tried her safe, and then had to run."

Dorian was so angry she had no room for fear. No room for anything but rage and a vindictive pleasure. "Well, they only got one copy and now we do have evidence. Burglary, break and enter with violence. And a specific target! If that doesn't label P-A!"

"Except we have to get the perp."

"Well, the door video, it'll show—"

"It was disabled too." Laura spoke through her teeth. "That *bloody* Troy Sorenson. You can bet your life."

"Oh." A sophisticated security man might do that, yes.

"Wait a minute." They were back in the Sandbar, Anne tapping her glass on the tabletop. "How did he know where to go, what to look for—*how did he find out?* Laura, what if he's tapped our phones! We shouldn't even be talking like this!"

Laura bared her teeth. "Dani gave me an L&C conference phone. With the interference device, you know? She said, if someone's trying to bug the call, you can tell."

"Oh." Dorian's breath went out in relief. Well, let's hope Sorenson hasn't figured an answer to that yet. But Laura's look had already changed.

She said, "Dani thinks it isn't that."

"Dani thinks . . ." Dorian stopped short. "Dani thinks, what?"

Laura took a visible breath. "Dani thinks," she said, too evenly, "that George phoned."

Phoned who? Dorian's brain asked, caught in the spotlight of Laura's over-meaningful stare. P-A? About me? Dani said he would, as soon as I left. Then her own wits caught up and she snapped her mouth shut at Laura's glare.

P-A reacted. They broke in. Yes. But how did they know about the files? The safe?

Moira. It fell on her inevitably as a loose bucket down a

shaft. Dani gave Moira a précis, at some point. Or George phoned Moira too, some pretext, huh, an outright complaint about Lewis and Cotton staff hazing him, what else? So Moira skated off to Dani, and Dani would have to brief her, then.

God be good to us—she hardly noticed whose expression she had filched—Moira probably bleated it all back to George to make up for the nasty girl pestering him at home. And George spilled it straight to P-A. He'd be desperate to redeem his own mistakes.

"Yes," she said, and held Laura's eyes. "Yes, that would be right."

Laura nodded in warning as well as visible relief: don't spell it out. Dorian nodded too. The leak, the inevitable Lewis and Cotton leak.

But it mightn't cover the next step. My going to Ben Morar. Dani wouldn't spill that.

Unless the phones *were* bugged. Then P-A know I'm going, from our conferences yesterday. Can I expect an ambush at Ben Morar tomorrow?

Or a preemptive strike today?

Fist to fist with a megacorp, this soon, that rough? I'm not ready, I'm not equipped!

Her eyes slid to that dark stare beyond the holoscreen and deeper panic spurted. I've already jeopardized Anne and Laura and hurt a security man. Jimmy might be Union and an activist but he's not an ex-Army goon, it's not his time, he won't know the tricks or the weapons or—he could get more than hurt.

Her knuckles were over her mouth. Laura was staring, frowning, in a moment she would ask, What else is wrong?

"Yes," Dorian managed. "Sorry. I got a bit ahead there." Her mind started to function again. "Does Dani think I should check in with the cops? Up here?" After all, I do have something concrete now, a break-in and assault and files taken, and I'm here on the same case. Should I go to Ben Morar at all?

"Or does she think I should come back?"

Laura grimaced. "Dani says we need a conference and you have the final say. She suggested three this afternoon. But she says, in your place, she'd go on. Because if you do, it should be as soon as possible."

Before P-A do fiddle the contract, maybe forge a termination letter? Get it through the office staff before I can arrive?

"But she definitely doesn't think you should do it alone." Laura's jaw squared. "So I said I'd go with you."

The best Dorian could manage, in another thirty seconds, was a sort of exhaled "Oh."

Laura leant suddenly into the holoscreen. "Dor, what is it? What's wrong?" The voice went more than sharp. "There's not some other problem, somebody there with you *now*, you're not—"

Already captured, under coercion, in Pan-Auric or the goons' hands? Dorian shook her head vehemently and got out, "No. No. Nothing like that."

"What is it then? *Something's* wrong! Dor—!"

There isn't any other way. Dorian picked up the phone and moved so its input covered them both. "Laura," she cut in, trying to sound calm. "Something else did happen. This—this is Jimmy—Seamus—Keenighan."

The silence went so deep the crows in the park sounded like drums. Laura's mouth made a perfect, lasting O.

Then she said, just audibly, "You're real."

He had made to rise, to acknowledge the half introduction, and paused as his image slid off the input screen. Now, the stone wall solid but not impenetrable, he said, "Aye."

Laura jumped. "You can talk!"

This time a mouth corner twitched. "Aye."

"You're not—you're not going to disappear!"

The mouth corner went straight. "No."

"I—you—Dor, when did this happen, what, how . . . God, Dor, *explain!*"

Explain? Dorian yanked her hair. "Look," she went for the baldest and simplest version. "The historical pageant. The, the reality fold did work. Jimmy—Seamus—walked out the *Miner's* door, and this time *he* fell through."

For once Laura had been struck dumb. Dorian saw the questions boil to critical mass and dived before they burst.

"That was yesterday afternoon. I showed him the map and he figured where the mine is. Chris's mine. And we know why Chris blew his stack, it's the site, it's right here under Blackston and if they use an open-cut mine they'll destroy the town. And I met Ralston and he says Ben Morar's shut down. Temporarily—"

"Dor!" It came out a positive bellow. "Never mind all that! Did you find out why?"

"Why what?"

"For heaven's sake! Why it's all happening! The reality fold! What's the connection, you gotta know that by now! Why him? Why you!"

Dorian stopped dead. From the input screen his image looked back at her, dourly silent, while their exchanges flared across her memory. Paddy Wild, the hat story, things I mightn't want to tell anyone. Bridget and Patsy Burke and Michael and people back in Dungannon. His past, things *he* mightn't want to tell anyone. His religion. The Land League. The Unions. Parnell.

Why he thinks he's here.

The other things that happened here and almost now. Just last night.

She could feel herself blush. With nightmare helplessness she watched Laura's face change, she knew the deductions were whipping into line and suddenly she was almost praying, Don't let her blurt out, So you're sharing the motel room, you've both been here overnight, oh, my, just what *have* you been up to? Don't do the usual innuendoes, Laura, please!

"There is a connection." She sounded too cool, too loud. "We figured out—in his Blackston, Jimmy knew my great-great-grandfather."

Laura fell back in some chair with a skirl of triumph. "I *knew* it had to be something like that! What grandfather, how, what happened, go on!"

He was watching Dorian in the input screen as closely as she was watching him. She could feel the tension in his shoulder, close to her side. She concentrated on the words, edging amid landmines of omission and summary.

"He—my, uh, ancestor"—how weird that sounds—"was manager for the Solitaire. The first Solitaire, it was a big deep mine." Laura's yelp said she had already remembered Solitaire Two. "He"—she braced herself—"wasn't much on safety. Or wages. And there were no unions." Laura was ahead of her, she could see deductions replaying about the men in the pub. "So yes, Jimmy put something in the *Miner* about it. That's when his house was wrecked."

Forgive me saying that so baldly, she thought, but Laura knows it happened, if I don't make some explanation she'll ask. And then the rest will come out. And you won't want me to mention Michael and the Fenians, that I do know.

"So we figure"—I hope he goes along with this as well—"the fold's something to do with the, the two Solitaires—and problems with a mine. And"—now the logic opened, the way neither of them of them had spelt it out, but in terms that Laura would find made perfect sense—"maybe we're connected because last time"—she tried not to wince—"the problem couldn't be fixed. So we're both here now. With Chris's mine.

To—try again."

Dorian could see it all racing down a bypass built in Laura's terms. Karma, reincarnations, pasts replayed until bygone crimes and sins are put right, in a minute she'll figure either he did something bad or Paddy Wild did, and I can't handle either one. "I don't *know* that's what it is, but he—Jimmy—Seamus— says he'll help me. And"—don't, she threatened herself, don't you dare blush again—"I'm hiring him. Dani said, I need a bodyguard."

She menaced Laura with her eyes, with the weight of six years friendship and mutual experience. Don't you dare make one wisecrack! Don't even ask what use a nineteenth-century newspaper guy'll be as a bodyguard! Especially against P-A and Goonboy—Brodie—and Sorenson.

The glare had partially worked. Laura looked like a boiler with the pressure gauge stuck. Hellfire and damnation, Dorian cursed, why's she have to know me so *well?*

"Okay." Laura sounded positively faint. I have to think about this, said the waving hand. I need time to digest it all. The expression repeated with just the inflection Dorian feared: *Bodyguard!* "That's a—an info-dump, and no mistake." Then her mouth opened and the ribaldry was gone. "What are we gonna tell Dani!"

"Oh, heavens!" Dorian wanted to clutch her hair.

"I said we should have told her when we first came clean—"

"No, there was too much already—"

"Yes, but now—!"

"Whoa. Who's this 'Dani'?"

His deep voice brought them both up short. How come, Dorian's mind postscripted indignantly, guys can get away with that?

"Dani's our boss," she said hurriedly. "The senior partner, she said I should come up, look for evidence." Remember, she

37

tried to make her look add, what I said about pinning a crime charge on P-A?

"*She?*" Then he manifestly did his own catching up. "Aye. But if that's so, why d'we have to tell her anythin'? We dinna need this 'conference.' If y'r megacorp's fetched the shillelaghs we havena time to waste." He ducked his head briefly to Laura. "An' thank ye for the offer, miss, but ye're in Ibisville, are ye not? We're here. We can be out the mine today, an' pass the word back after." A mouth corner twitched. "The whole box an' dice."

I bet that's how you handled Dinny, she thought. Bypass permission and risk the uproar, just get what you wanted done first. Hand Dani a—time traveler, reality jumper? as a postscript on whatever we might turn up at the mine, and let shocks cancel out.

She looked at Laura and Laura said, "*What* was all that?"

"Eh?"

"I got 'conference' and 'megacorp' and 'box' and the rest was Net-chaff." She eyed Jimmy with visible dismay. "Does—um—is it Jimmy or is it Seamus? Does—oh, hell, do you always talk like that?"

"He's from County Tyrone," Dorian cut in in a rush. What did you expect, she wanted to shout, Oxbridge English? You wanted an exotic, that's what you've got! "He—oh, lord." She gave up herself. "I never did introduce you properly. This is Laura McFadden. Do you want to be Jimmy or Seamus with her?"

The stone wall had solidified with forbidding speed, but that gave him pause. Then he stood up, heedless of the input screen, inclined his head and said, "Pleased t' meet ye, miss." His look flicked to Dorian and evidently read more than she thought. Suddenly both mouth corners twitched. "I'd feel a right fool," he said, to her alone, "wi' one o' ye sayin' Jimmy-this an' Jimmy-that, an' t'other not."

So she can call me Jimmy, that look added, because you do.

Dorian looked hurriedly back to Laura and hoped her own ears would not heat. "Did you get that? Call him Jimmy, he said."

"Okay." Laura still looked somewhat as if a lab specimen had come to life. "Well—now, can one of you translate? What else did, er, Jimmy say?"

And it's another decision point, Dorian realized at thought's nanospeed. I can jump in and "translate" and the future can go one way, with him stuck in a ghetto, an alien we have to talk across as if his mind's impaired. Or I can have him repeat it and her try to understand it and—we go somewhere else.

"Can you say it again?" She tried to sound temperate. "A bit slower, maybe. Laura doesn't have an Irish background . . ."

The stare, dark, solid, but worlds from stupid, said, I see what you're doing. Then it flickered. He slid back into his seat to look directly at Laura, and said, more slowly, but with a glint in his eye, " 'McFadden's Handsome Daughter.' That's a tune, ye know. I see 'twas named ahead o' time."

Laura very nearly lost composure. And as Dorian thought, You devil, you've done it to her as well, he solemnly, slowly repeated what he had said.

Laura decoded it with a steadily gathering frown. "Okay," she said at last. "You're saying, you want to skip the conference with Dani. I stay here. You two go out to the mine. Today. Because they've stopped work, and you can look around."

He nodded. "Aye."

"How come you understand *me* no problem? Anyway. It's Sunday. The office'll be closed."

"Aye."

"But Dorian's got to see the contract. And that's in the office."

"Aye."

Laura stared. He stared back. Still blank-faced, he watched Laura's expression change, and Dorian felt her stomach churn. He means, If the office is closed, it doesn't matter. He's prepared to get in anyway.

A runnel of ice went down her spine. Reporter, compositor, Land Leaguer, Union man. What sort of activist have I hired?

Laura was looking daunted too. She began to speak and stopped. No, Dorian thought, don't spell out, You mean, you're prepared to break and enter too?

"Ah—" No need to ask, You think you can do that? It's all too clear that he does. "Do you—are you equipped? Do you know anything about, ah, security?"

Modern-day security, Dorian filled in, and shared the alarm rising in Laura's face. Alarm systems and door videos and all the other stuff. Does he expect me to disable them? I know they exist, and that's all. What could *he* know about all that?

"Equipped?" he was saying, double-dryly. "Security? Beyond a fella wi' a shillelagh an' a bluidy great dog?" Fleetingly, very wryly, the mouth corners twitched again. "Aye, I could wish y'r 'reality fold'd' brought m' Colt along. If only for the blacks. But I've done wi'out before. I can do it again."

"Colt?" Laura's look was well beyond alarm. "You mean a gun? You've got—you had—For the *blacks?*"

"The myalls, ye know? If we're goin' bush there'll be myalls. The wild blacks." He stopped, reading her face. "D'ye no' have blackfellas here?"

"Uh—we have—there are, there are, indigenes, yes, but they, they're not wild, they don't, we don't—" Laura turned almost wildly. Help, her look signaled, I didn't realize time travel threw up things like this.

"No' anymore?" He had already forestalled her. At least I don't have to say, We don't shoot them nowadays, Dorian thought. "Aye, but there's y'r megacorp, all the same."

"I know there is! Dorian?" Are you going along with this, Laura's look demanded, will you turn this cannon loose, with his experience and his evident predilections and his lack of expertise? "Shouldn't we wait? Try the police? And what do we tell Dani?"

"Miss." The note had the same effect as standing up. "Ye've one day—one half day—to run y'r eye over that mine. Ye canna get down the shaft wi' the hoists off, and they'd no' let ye near the face if ye could. But ye can see the stockpiles an' the amalgamation retorts an' the smelters, an' that's all ye need. Are the stockpiles low? Have they shut down the stampers? Are the wood heaps gone? That'll tell ye, has the lode dried, or is it somethin' else? Aye, the office has the contract, but wi' a bit o' thought ye can have that too."

When Laura only looked at Dorian his voice hardened. "Ye said y'r wee manager's already hangin' on the whistle rope. D'ye think, if ye wait till tomorrow, ye'll find *anythin'*?"

The thought hit Dorian like a cattle prod in the back. Of course George hasn't waited, he must have called P-A yesterday and they've had twenty-four hours to react—and they don't wait, haven't you understood that yet? Her limbs jolted involuntarily and a strangled voice was already breaking from her throat.

"Oh, God—no, we can't wait!"

Laura bolted up in her chair. "But, Dor!" It's too sudden, you don't have the right gear or expertise or help, it's too dangerous! Dorian could fill in everything. And the only answer is the one he's already made. The gear and the skills don't matter. We go now or we don't go at all.

"The cops," Laura was babbling. "You could get the cops—"

He looked from her to Dorian and back and the shift in his stance, slight but unmistakable, told her he knew her choice.

But he answered Laura politely, though the mouth corner's lift was too wry to be a quirk.

"We could take the polis, aye. But remember, they're *supposed* to play by the rules."

CHAPTER 2

I got stampeded into this, Dorian told herself, as the tall green highway sign saying, Beef Road, Clermont, slid past, and the Blackston hills parted upon smoke-blue western levels, with small peaks sticking through the haze. Laura was right: what on earth can she tell Dani, I should have better backup, I can't expect Jimmy to cope with it all. But, she admitted, he's right too. If the alternative's to squat in that motel room waiting for P-A to come after us, there's no choice.

We did get another tire iron at that petrol station and a cap and navy sweatshirt—I thought only a peacock would care about dirtying white shirts, till he said, "I'll not *ask* to get picked off." And I realized what he meant.

But I managed to get into jeans and sneakers without a major uproar. And brief him on Brodie and Sorenson and Laura's phone call. And do a half-hour Net surf to cover Mining 101. Or more like, Mining 302. I know about extracting gold with cyanide and running them both through leaching mats, but this stuff about SAG mills and flotation and pregnant solutions is beyond me. Though not beyond him, by the way he ended up bouncing round going, "Aye—aye! I *see!*" I'm still not sure this isn't some kind of tourist trip to him.

But the profile in the passenger seat said anything but Tourist. And I doubt, she added reluctantly, it's "blackfellas" he's thinking about.

The mine turnoff was twenty or so kilometers from Blackston. By then well-leafed timber had begun to mask the ridges' undulation, and despite reviewing Chris's occasional comments, she nearly missed the small, neglected sign. The turn itself was wide, well-worn as the gravel road beyond. Trucks, she thought, slowing as stones and corrugations made the car teeter like an unstable shoe. A lot of trucks, for years and years.

Beside her Jimmy said, "Pull up." When she obeyed, he slid out and went a few rapid paces up the road.

"Nothin' here the last few days." He sounded crisp and suddenly almost aloof. His eyes flicked once up the rise, with its strip of yellow-dun road shut in unkempt grass and dust-filmed shrubby trees. Then he shut the door, clicked the seat belt, and jerked his beard. "Drive on."

Thirty kilometers southwest of Blackston must be as the crow flies, Dorian decided, as the road unwound and unwound, stony and potholed through awkward curves and single-lane bridges with fleeting vistas atop each ridge. This is where Chris drove, memory added, talking to me on the phone. Only Chris could have done it, at that speed, on a road like this.

Then a tall metal chimney rose like a silver straw from the skyline and he said sharply, "Whoa."

"But we're not there yet—"

"Will ye roll in the front gate singin' 'Erin Go Bragh'?" He was scanning the verge, quick, sharp glances to and fro. "Can this 'car' o' yours go off the road?"

"It depends." She eyed the ditch and the grass-grown roll of dirt atop its rim.

"Bide a moment, then." He was out again, off the road with three heron-like strides, into the trees. "Try up there," he ordered, reappearing at her window. "By the cocky-apples." A reappraising glance. "Where I'll show ye."

"But why are we stopping here? And like this?" Dorian checked the hand brake, gathered hat, bag and keys, carefully did not slam the door, and looked across the roof at that absorbed, tense expression, on the verge of a frown. "No one's supposed to be here."

"Aye." He came round the front of the car, pulling on his cap. He had the sweatshirt on already and she saw with a jump of the heart that the tire iron was under it, thrust into his belt. "But 'supposed' and 'is' are no' the same." He flicked a glance into her face. "Y'r megacorp doesna shilly-shally. 'Suppose' they're out here already. Or 'suppose' we're just in the gate an' y'r wee manager drives up?"

"Oh." Dorian's heart sped up again. I was trying not to think about that. To tell myself it would be just a quick reconnaissance. "But if we just drove off the road?"

"Metal." Another flick of a glance. "A gun barrel, just a trooper's button'll catch the sun an' flash for miles. An' that . . ." The gesture finished, A gun's a lot smaller than that car.

"Oh." I don't like this, this isn't what I do, it's all jumped a gear far too fast, this is like burglary or, or army raids or something, this is—this is preparing for violence. I'm just a lawyer. I don't do this sort of thing.

She looked at his face, expectant, somberly alert, and thought, But I hired him. And he does.

The actual site was surprisingly small. Hardly an acre, Dorian estimated, staring down the long ridge to patches of silver galvanized roof, white prefab building walls, mounds of massive machinery like the propulsion end of a spaceship, all rising through trees beyond a substantial creek. I suppose that's where the tailings dam leaked.

And it's so quiet. Too quiet, she realized. When the mine's running there'd be trucks along here all the time. And cars, and people, and the machinery. There were crows in Lister Park, right in town. Here even the crows are quiet.

She moved closer to Jimmy's back just as he stopped. A second road was running in on the right. From Quandong lode, Dorian realized, recalling Chris again. They truck the ore here, he had said.

Jimmy said, "The mine track, aye?" They had found a Ben Morar site map on the Net. "Careful, then." They crossed, hopping kangaroo-like from rock patch to rock. "Mebbe y'r manager canna read tracks, but we've left more than enough."

The main road dipped into the creek's depression, with a makeshift causeway over the actual bed. Topping the further bank, they saw wide double gates in a metal-mesh fence.

"Open," Dorian breathed at last. "They've just left it all."

"Maybe." His hand held her firmly to the shade of a big paperbark. "An' maybe they've other visitors."

"Oh." Her ears seemed to have stretched an inch in the brooding quiet. "I can't hear anything."

"Ye might not."

With equal caution he reconnoitered ahead. It was another ten minutes, Dorian estimated, before they virtually tiptoed into the compound itself.

"That'll be y'r office." He jerked an elbow to single-story buildings nearest the fence. "An' probably the warehouse. An' that"—he stopped and stared—"that's the ore chute. But 'tis upside down."

Dorian stared herself at the pylon and steel-beam skeleton with its broad black chute running up the center like a giant slippery slide. "Upside . . . ?" Then the details meshed with scraps of Chris's acrid litany, *yield figures late, bloody conveyor glitched again,* and she understood.

"Oh. That's a conveyor belt. They put the ore on and pull it up—"

"A belt?" He looked startled. "Like a drivin' belt? On an engine? An' ye *load* things on it?"

"More electricity, I guess." I don't have time for Elementary Mechanics either, if I did know enough to explain. And my neck's prickling. "Can we just—"

"They didna have *that* on y'r Web." But at her shift he moved in turn, striding down the pylons' side. "So the ore goes up, an' not down from the poppet-head?" His eyes checked and narrowed like a pointed gun. "But here's the stockpile, aye."

Pile? Dorian thought. It's a mountain. A volcano, an unsquared pyramid whose summit almost touched the top of the conveyor belt, a hundred feet high and three hundred across, a massively squatted heap of loose, shattered, dun-gold, yellow-brown rock.

"That's—the ore?"

"Straight from the face."

"So is it right? Can you tell?"

"I'd need the yield figures to be sure. But wi' that much here, either they've shut down in full run, or they're workin', an' the yield's near petered out."

"That's not," Dorian said reluctantly, "a lot of use."

"The rest'll tell us." He glanced back to the hypothetical warehouse, a double-length building with several doors and a shallow loading bay. "I doubt that's all locked up. An' no point leavin' extra tracks. On wi' us then, an' find the mills an' leachin' stuff."

Dorian found only more daunting piles of machinery, but these he seemed to decipher readily. "This here's the main crusher, see the jaws? We had stampers, but this is better. An' this must be the SAG mill. We used ball mills, but no' like this." Catching the note of near-respect, eyeing what looked like the side-tilted bowl of an enormous old-style Mixmaster, Dorian thought, Men. They're all suckers for toys.

"They grind the ore in here. An' they must make the slurry as well." He was examining the huge connecting pipes. "Run a ton o' water through these. An' here's the sump."

"The what? I thought sumps were on cars."

"Maybe, but this one's where the stuff sits till they pump it off to the cyclone . . ." He noticed her face and absorption became the old wry grin. "Will I start talkin' English, then? All this," he swept a hand round the tangle of machines and pipes, like some monstrous malignant growth, Dorian thought sourly, spreading huge metal veins. "All this is just for gettin' the ore ground fine. Much finer than we could, aye. That's why they can use low-grade stuff. An' it comes out in solution—slurry— for the leachin' plant. That's where they put in the cyanide."

"Oh."

"But if the mine was down, they'd ha' drained this." He tapped the metal bulge, and it gave a muted note close to middle C. "I dinna think it is."

"What does that mean?" She trotted after him, feeling like a schoolchild on a tour, as he threaded from one mechanical conglomerate to the next. Tanks, she thought, in some relief. Not Mills from Mars this time, just huge metal tanks. "What if the sump's not drained?"

"Then they stopped untoward, an' they didna clean up, the way y'r Net says they do." His own voice stopped abruptly. "An' we'll have a time findin' why."

He ran like a sailor up the ladder on the nearest tank and she thought, He's done this before. He leant gingerly over, took a small sniff, and recoiled, almost scuttling down. "Arrh!" He half coughed, waving hands. "If it isna mercury, that stuff must be nigh as bad."

"Then it's full?"

"Well, it isna drained." He half turned, staring down the line of tanks to the concrete-block building beyond. "Those should be the smelter, an' all that electrolytic stuff. An' the gold room. Not that there'll be anythin' in there, whyever they stopped . . ."

And he stopped, in mid-phrase.

The silence rang in Dorian's ears. Not a crow, not any sort of bird, not a breath of breeze to mourn through the maze of pipes stewing in high afternoon sun. She opened her mouth and he made one quick gesture. Wait.

Her stomach churned. She strained her ears.

Distant, hardly more than a breeze's draw, but never confusable with wind. Never mistakable for anything but itself. A car engine's muttering purr.

"Shouldn't we have got—further in?"

Dorian panted against the heated side of the loading bay. His shoulder jerked and the hand that had towed her full pace from the tanks clamped her wrist. Two hundred yards if it's a step, she thought, half resentful, half terrified, I'm not a sprinter, dammit. She moved to free herself. The hand pulled her closer. From a mouth corner he said, barely audible, "Never lose y'r out."

Don't get trapped, she translated, at last. Don't hide with the enemy your side of your exit point.

He made a dart to the bay's opposite wall and leant cautiously to the edge. She followed. Looking somewhere under his arm she saw the car, parked casually aslant, their side of the second building's central doorway, with its wheelchair ramp. A dust-coated, four-wheel-drive sedan.

"That's"—her heart did a quick loop—"that's George—the manager's car."

The response was a little audible breath. Then, "He didna lock it like you do. He's gone in there. The office, aye?"

"He wouldn't bother to lock it here. But why would he *be* here?" Her heart was tapping steadily at her breastbone. "Oh. Ohmigod."

The hand went tight. The undervoice said with urgent

emphasis, "Aye?"

"They are going to fiddle the contract. George is going to do it himself. Today, with no one here. Of course!" She wanted to smack her forehead. "He has to re-sign it, too."

She could hear the frown. "Chris's name? Can he sign that?"

"I don't know. I wouldn't think George could do forgeries, but—"

His hand clenched. "What's that?"

Her teeth snapped shut. Her heart leapt. What? she began. And heard it too.

Distant still, eerily directionless, sibilant and resonant and growing louder by the instant, familiar world over from countless TV war coverages: *whop, whop, whop, whop* . . .

"That's a helicopter," she breathed.

"A *what?*"

"Oh, God." And there just *isn't* time for a history of flight. "It . . . it's . . . a way to fly." She herself grabbed his other wrist and jerked: Keep quiet. "Yes, they have machines to do it, I can't explain now. This one—has no wings." She shook his wrist again. His mouth was hanging at far more than half cock. "Just a big rotor, a, a set of, of, like paddles, oars, they go round so fast the thing can lift off the ground and move." A helicopter, air surveillance, over-ground vision, we can't run, we can't hide—oh, thank *God* he was paranoid enough to cover the car. "It can go backwards. Forwards. It can hover. It—it—"

It's the ultimate weapon against people on the ground. And if they spot our tracks . . .

Oh, God, he'll never cope with the thing, let alone what it means for us. I should never have let him come, I have to get him—us—out of here.

"Hold yer fire. Girl. Dorian. Hsshhht!" He was shaking her in earnest. By the shoulders, hauling her up against him in the eighteen inches' shade of the loading bay overhang. "Hsssh."

Something curt and acrid in Gaelic. *"Quiet."*

Her own mind gripped. She caught half a dozen breaths and tried not to hyperventilate, not to press herself into him like a possum against a tree. "Okay," she managed in a moment. "Okay."

His hands relaxed. His head cocked. The rotor noise was deafening, dust was sweeping by outside, it's nearly down—when he does see it he'll probably stampede like that myall from the engine whistle, she took a handful of sleeve for both their sakes. The din crescendoed. Altered pitch, slowed.

After another minute the engine cut off. The only sound was the faint hissing whop of rotor blades.

Inch by inch he leant to the corner again, with Dorian peering under his arm. The helicopter stood like some monstrous science-fiction insect, its skids planted midway between the office and the miscellaneous buildings that fronted the leaching tanks. A small helicopter, without a logo. Its rotors were just slowing to a halt.

She felt rather than heard him inhale. She could picture, too clearly, his face. She had no time to help. The passenger—the pilot?—was already climbing down.

A tall, almost gaunt man in a greenish-brown windbreaker, flying helmet under an arm. He had a holster on one hip, a bag that was not a briefcase in the other hand. A sense of faint habitual tension in the head's poise, the eyes' orbiting scan. Over-conspicuous cheekbones, skin heavily lined. Gray hair, cropped to an Army fuzz.

Dorian's blood congealed. That's Brodie. Goonboy. In the flesh.

She only realized she had said some of it aloud when she sensed rather than felt Jimmy quiver beside her. Then the murmur at her ear said, "Aye."

Her skin was crawling, her neck cringed as if they were

already exposed. Never mind sight, there's scent, smell, ESP . . . Black Rider, squalled her ricocheting mind. Then reality bit. She tried not to squeak aloud. "He's got a gun!"

"So he has, the spalpeen."

Whatever shock he had felt was gone. He sounded calm. Ever so slightly irate. More incredibly, faintly amused.

"Jimmy . . ." Damn you, can't you panic worth tuppence? At least sound as if you weren't expecting it!

"Sssh."

Brodie's head continued its slight smooth turns. His long stride reached the ramp. Silent as a Ringwraith—sneakers, she cursed herself—he disappeared. Somewhere in the building, a door closed. A minute later Dorian jumped six inches as machinery gave a sucking intake whine.

Idiot, she cursed herself again. It isn't mine stuff, it's right at the office. An air conditioner.

Holed up in George's office with the air-conditioning. Chris said it, when P-A first arrived.

"They're in the office. The main office." She drew back, feeling muscles shake as they relaxed, the momentary reprieve almost more sapping than fear. Now, instinct shouted ignominiously, the coast's clear. Let's get the hell out.

"What're they doin', then?"

She stared a full thirty seconds before it sank in. He isn't panicked. He isn't going to run. Even if I suggested it.

"If they're out here today, the pair o' them mean mischief. In that office." The tension was back, slight as a vibration, the stare pinioned her. Come on, it berated. You're my expert. Think. "What're they doin'?"

God help me. If he isn't going to run, neither can I. I have to think instead.

Her brain started to leap in more than giant bounds. "It has to be the contract. But not just George. This is P-A. They've sent Goonboy—Brodie. To do the forgery. Or oversee it. No. They've coerced George. *He* wouldn't change it, he knows I'll know and he already vouched for the other one. He'd squat there and let it blow up in P-A's face. But he's a welsher, they have to know that now. Brodie's made him come out and help. Then he can't gab on them without pooling himself."

Then the other alternative sprang like a monster into her path.

At the crunch even complicity mightn't shut George up. What if P-A knows that? What if they're going for double? Involve him with the forgery, set him up for the rap—then silence him anyway?

An awkward witness eliminated for them, a vital one lost to us. But not a big step for them. If they could rig a car for Chris, what's another accident for George?

Or would they bother faking an accident?

What does Brodie have in that bag?

Half her mind was bawling, This is crazy, this is just a net of wild suppositions—the rest was shaking his arm with both hands as she panted, "Out, we have to get them out of there—he's going to knock off George!"

She expected confusion, argument, disbelief. His brows snapped together over one piercing stare. Then he shot out under his breath, "Make him sign an' off him? The office as well?"

"What?"

"D'ye think he'll shoot the man or just torch the lot?"

He knows Fenians. He's lived on a goldfield, he played— provocateur, guerrilla?—with British troops. Of course he'd follow your thought. Of course his worldview runs to extremes. Think, damn you, think!

"He—wait—he can't take out the office, the contract has to be in place. Intact. No. He has to get George outside. The car.

Or something else."

"Like Chris?" For a moment the stare blazed. Then his breath went in hard and he turned on his heel, one swift scything survey that fixed like a pointing gundog on George's sedan.

"There's a rifle in there."

"What?"

"In the car. D'ye see? Across the splashboard, the dash, aye." His muscles had compacted with the rest of him. He felt like a primed grenade.

"A gun? Oh—*what?* You're not going to, what are you going to—Jimmy, there's two of them and Brodie's got a gun and there's the chopper as well!"

"Shht, girl." The shoulder pat was almost peremptory. The eyes' blaze was still focused inward, scan, focus, plan—it reopened. "Ever handle a gun?"

She tried to silence herself. Not to make it a wail. "We can't—"

"If we dinna, nobody can." He said it harshly, abruptly and the stare left her nowhere to hide. "That's y'r contract an' y'r witness an' we havena time to blether. Can ye handle a gun?"

I don't, she tried to say as her mouth dried. I can't—I couldn't use a gun. Not on a human being. I don't know about, I can't do this stuff. What nightmare have you planned?

Decide, that dark stare retorted implacably. Say no and I'll find another way, but don't waste time trying to quibble now. And don't deny, later, that you turned your back on a halfway innocent if stupid man and tossed away Chris's vindication and came all this way . . . brought me all this way . . .

The breath seemed to sear her throat. The words wobbled, but they came. "My brother. We'd go rabbit shooting. Just a twenty-two . . ."

He seemed to snap out of a physical crouch. "Yerra, girl!" One quick pat. "Bide here and dinna squeak. We havena long."

And he was round the corner, bent double, slithering like a ferret for the car.

Dorian's legs made one abortive leap. Her mouth opened to shriek, What if they come out! Shut up, she ordered herself. They just got in there. They have to find the contract and then actually make the copy. And the car's not locked. You heard him say that.

The near-side back door inched open. He seemed to pour himself in, below the seat, a hand reaching for the rifle set in a kangaroo-shooter's mount across the dash.

And if George locked that?

She had both hands over her mouth. But the rifle was already out of sight.

A second's eternity. What's he *doing,* can't he get out? Then the door closed and he was skittering back across the dust.

"I canna tell the make or caliber," he twisted it quickly, expertly. "But ye can figure the chamber and the safety catch." He worked the bolt. "Aye, 'tis like a revolver. Nothin' in the chamber, but rounds in the magazine. An' I've more fro' that, what is it, glovebox?" He looked up. "Can ye deal wi' this?" The weight, heavy, steel and polished wood, redolent of oil and gunpowder and violence, slapped into her hands.

You don't have time for dithers or scruples now. Her hands moved almost as automatically, taking the load, turning the muzzle away from him, checking chamber and magazine. I can load this. I can cock it. I could menace someone with it.

Can I do anything more?

Don't ask that now. She looked up in those dark waiting eyes and said almost steadily, "What do you want me to do?"

"I'll see to—out here," the deep quick voice said in her ear. "You get in there. More than one room, aye? Plant where ye can see their door. When they come out, dinna mind the other.

55

Watch y'r chance, an' nobble George."

She tried to swallow. "Nobble George, how?"

"Bail him up'd be best. We want him to talk. Tie him up somewhere. If he'll no' stand, put a bullet in him." The tone never changed. "In the leg if ye can, in the gut if ye must." A little pause. How well weighed, the next words told her. "I'm relyin' on you."

Goad, menace, accolade: I'm risking my life on the chance that you can stalk and capture a man. That you won't panic. That at the worst you'll shoot. That you can draw him off and leave me with Brodie. Lesser odds than two men, and at the worst, two with guns.

When I have nothing at all.

She nearly spun round and grabbed him and cried, I can't, I can't do it, I can't let you risk yourself on this mad . . . ! But some other entity had already usurped her tongue. Was demanding, almost coolly, "What do you mean, 'when they come out'? What are you going to do?"

"Ye'll hear. Are ye set?"

Now or never. It's Dani's office again. This time for real.

She nodded. She could not speak.

There was a pause. A quick audible breath. Then his left arm went round her and he kissed her hard and fleetingly on the mouth corner with a twist to avoid the rifle, and the Tyrone accent said in her ear, "An I'll kill ye, if I dinna see ye again."

"Jimmy . . . !" But his hand was already in her back, pushing her toward the far warehouse corner, the best-covered approach to the office steps.

Corner, gap, office wall. A blind building end, safe. Front corner. One last glance, if they come out now . . .

Don't think about it, she told herself, and she made desperate strides for the outer door. Brodie left it open, remember, when he went in.

She risked one glance back, but Jimmy was already gone. Loping in that ferret's run for the stockpile, stooping swiftly, scooping up rocks.

Understanding burst like a bomb. She whipped inside.

Vestibule, receptionist's desk, twinned corridors. She went left, away from the air conditioner's hum, grabbing door handles, heart almost choking her. If they come out, for a file, the photocopier . . .

A handle moved. "Utility Room" said the plate on the door, sliding past her eyes. Long window panel, double-size room. Table, chairs, sink, coffeemaker, urn. A cornerful of buckets and brooms. Much further's too risky. Too far, anyway. And the door opens away from the vestibule.

With the gun against the wall and her eye to the crack she tried desperately to control her breathing. Not to think about what might happen, simply what should happen. The oldest trick in the Australian schoolboy's book, they must have used it on the goldfields too.

The crash was all and more than she had expected, a rock that size on the light prefab roof reverberated and bellowed like a veritable bomb. She bit her lip to blood to contain the scream. If that doesn't fetch them they're both dead. And now Brodie'll be hunting *you.*

She heard a door fly back. Voices, loud and startled and an American accent harsher than Jimmy's Tyrone. The ring of orders. Hurrying feet.

Brodie went past like a human hunting dog, stance an uncanny echo of Jimmy's run, slightly crouched and slinking with head lifted to swing like a radar scanner, gun already drawn. Behind him George shouted something and he flapped his left hand, irritation manifest, and shouted without looking round, "Goddamn it, c'mon!"

He was outside, on the ramp, gone. Her heart was choking

her and she had to forget it: keep your mind on George.

He came loping down the corridor at last and swung into the vestibule. She had the door open in a sweep and her own sneakers were silent on the cheap carpet. George had propped at the ramp head, staring left and right. Brodie was a blur of motion beyond him, past the helicopter, headed for the leaching tanks. She said, "Mr. Richards? Don't move."

He swung round in absolute disbelief and she snapped the safety catch off, louder than an actual shot.

His mouth opened and shut. Uh, he said, soundless, like a landed fish.

"In here." She took two steps right on the little porch and swung the rifle to compensate. "Hands up. Move."

"What the—what—Miss *Wild!* What the *hell* are you doing?"

"I'm holding you up." It was almost a liberation, to abandon fear and scruple at once. "Put up your hands."

"Where did you come from? What are you doing here!"

"None of your business." She tried to sound threatening. "I said, put up your hands."

"You won't—you can't—!"

"Get your hands up or I'll shoot."

"The—that's my rifle! You're not—this is ridiculous! Put that thing down, you won't shoot me, you don't even know how!"

He took a step toward her and the perennial insult condensed six weeks' rage and grief and newer terror in one pure lightning bolt. Her lips went back. Her shoulder braced against the butt and the muzzle dipped smoothly to sight square in his belly. To hell with the leg, this is the guy who let them murder Chris.

He stopped with one foot literally in the air. She saw the sudden pallor round his eyes.

"Don't call out."

I'm not purring. It sounds worse than that. For a moment she felt what it would be to experience true killer's madness and he seemed to shrink where he stood. I could just pull this trigger. Right now.

Somewhere behind them came a flat, smothered crack and a screaming whine.

He twitched. In that glorious, berserker's clarity not one of her muscles shook. She held his eyes and thought of her finger taking up the final pressure and when she minutely twitched the gun muzzle he moved with it like a marionette.

One step back. Two. Passing her in the doorway, as she pivoted with him and the rifle was an extension of her hands. Into the vestibule. Up against the wall.

"Turn around," she said, and saw his neck tremor. "Keys," that stranger's voice added and he made a move to his pocket. "Slow." The hand half froze. "Show me the master key." The hand came out. Sorted through the bunch. "Now drop them." The bunch rattled and clinked. Her brain whiplashed. "Your cell phone. Drop it too. Carefully . . ."

He groped in another pocket. Let the cell phone fall. Tie him up, Jimmy said, but there's nothing here. Outside the gun cracked again and her inner flesh shrank at the image of its bullet's path. No time, I have to get out there quick, quick.

"Down there." She hustled him into the corridor. "In there." The utility room. "Stop." He stood in mid-floor while she scanned frantically round. No big cupboards, no loose electric leads, no rope. Another ricochet screeched outside. And if there *was* something I'd have to put the gun down to tie him and he'd jump me, hand to hand I'd never have a chance. George's shoulders twitched and she snapped, "Still!" Oh, God, Jimmy, this won't work, I can't leave him and I have to get back out.

I *have* to get there. It hit so hard it nearly took her breath. If Brodie thinks twice and comes back for the helicopter, if he gets in the air . . . I'd never bring him down.

And Jimmy can't have a clue about air pursuit.

George fidgeted and she snapped, *"Still!"* The window, I can't just lock him in, he'd be through it like a ferret himself. I can't tie him and there's nothing to put him in.

No time, no other way. Not tied up but well and truly immobilized. The rifle barrel dipped, the sights steadied and the berserker in charge said, Now.

The trigger gave sweetly under her touch. The butt bucked less than the old twenty-two. The shot bellowed and George gave an animal scream and leapt and collapsed with both hands grabbing for the insignificant rent in the trouser leg behind his right thigh.

She slammed the door without a second thought and ran for the keys, found the master, shoved it in the lock. I'll hear the noise he's making for years. No time. Outside the other gun made that flat lethal crack again, she kicked George's cell phone under the desk and almost flew for the steps.

If I get in Jimmy's way I could kill him, if I get in Brodie's way I'll kill *him*—

Where are they, which way do I run? Her teeth had bared again, her head was swinging as Brodie's had, they've got to be in those tanks somewhere . . .

The helicopter. I have to stop him getting that. I can't get mixed in the main hunt but at the helicopter I can go any side and he daren't shoot at me for fear of hitting it.

She went down the steps in a spring and sprinted across the dust.

Left side, right? Behind, in front of the skid? Reload, idiot, don't leave that to the last minute. Her fingers slid, slippery with sweat, she swore in deadly fear she would let the magazine jam. The other gun spoke again and something cracked like a whip in reply. She jumped and clenched her teeth. You have to stay here. You can't run in there and get tangled in the mess.

Silence. Sullen, weighted, aching, silence, sweltering with

metal in the sun, closing like a vice on machinery, buildings, dust . . . I can't bear it. I'll have to move.

The gun cracked in a savage triple burst and she nearly screamed aloud. Shut up, shut *up,* you *have* to keep quiet, you *have* to wait, you can't go down there, you just have to pray Jimmy can stay ahead of him, get past him, get back up here, somehow.

Or that he comes back himself and gives you a shot—please, God, just one shot.

Another ringing *spanngggg* almost made her pull the trigger herself. Come *on,* Jimmy, please, you can't dodge forever, get back up here.

The gun spat again, *spannnggg, spanngg,* then something rang like a maddened gong. She was moving before she knew it, round the skid, along the cabin, there was just time to freeze before they came.

She never saw Jimmy at all. There was only a rattle and clatter somewhere near the mysterious bulk he called a crusher, an invisible panting gasp. Then Brodie burst from cover almost in front of her, slamming a fresh magazine in the gun, face a dull astounding purple, eyes staring like a maddened bull.

Not at me. She froze behind the skid strut. Hunted, hunter's instinct said, Keep still.

Brodie was panting, too, but every sense he had was on the quarry and he isn't just hunting, something told her, he's hunting crazy. Whatever happened has got him past thinking. All that's left is—bloodlust. He's—possessed.

Something clattered again. The gun whipped up like the proverbial striking snake and again metal *spannggged* with that human cry. Brodie made a noise too, a deep-chested whine. A hound on the scent. A killer at the end of the hunt.

And Jimmy's somewhere in there.

The rifle was down to target Brodie's back but he was moving too fast and erratically to hold the bead. Oh, Jimmy, where are you? What are you doing?

Navy blue flashed. Something hurtled from the crusher's rim compacted like a human ball and Brodie's gun snapped twice and Jimmy was gone to another splat and whine and a fountain of sparks at the stockpile's edge.

Brodie made the noise again and ran. Up to the stockpile's rocks. Left round the rocks. Back again. Stopping short at the rocks, swinging round, small against the stockpile's bulk. Adrenaline coursed through her like electric shock. I'm behind the chopper cabin. I can see the blur when he moves. If I don't move he can't see me.

I can't help if I don't move.

Blood was warm on her chin. The berserker in charge was saying relentlessly, You can't help him now if you do move, you can only put him in double jeopardy.

Brodie's shoulders heaved. Sweat patched the short-sleeved fawn shirt. He's dropped the windbreaker somewhere. His head was weaving, to and fro, to and fro. In a white-hot flash she understood.

The stockpile's not real cover. He can hunt Jimmy out, the way he couldn't—or why's he so livid? In among all that machinery and pipes. But if he runs one side, Jimmy'll go the other. And sometime, Jimmy can reach the warehouse. The office.

Whichever side Brodie goes.

Rock rattled. Brodie's body whipped like a prodded snake. But he did not move.

He knows. He knows it's a standoff and Jimmy's teasing him, and catching his breath with every second he waits.

If he hasn't—the sweat froze on her throat—if he hasn't been hit. If he isn't bleeding already. If Brodie only *has* to wait.

Her own blood congealed. Do *I* do something?

Move. Make a noise. A diversion. Draw Brodie's attention? No. He has the gun, Jimmy can't jump him. There's no way that can help.

Then do *I* shoot him? Adrenaline burnt like nausea in her throat.

While he's there? Out of cover? Unsuspecting?

In the back?

Again?

Then memory flashed on the other side of the stockpile, the conveyor gantry, if Brodie gets there he could climb up and shoot and it won't matter which way Jimmy runs.

She was moving before she knew. Up the cabin side. Round the skid. Level the gun. Draw a bead. The sights came up and steadied in the center of Brodie's sweat-patched back. Let's not try for fancy here either. Take the middle of the body and be done.

Safety off. Head down. Cheek to the butt. Take up the first pressure. Start to squeeze . . .

Brodie's head went out and down and he flew like the proverbial greased lightning straight up the stockpile's side.

For Dorian the rest remained a video collage. Human shape, human motion, blur of color and form in the reflected machinery's glare and torrid windless light, furred thump of footsteps become thud and grate on stone. And sudden as a trapdoor dropping, the stockpile's single roar.

The pyramid shattered as half a side avalanched, faster than a gunshot and catastrophic as a bomb. Dust exploded. Earth shuddered. Then the trapdoor shut.

Leaving a long new buttress stretched at the stockpile's base, tardy fragments still cascading down it, dust spreading outward from the U-shaped cirque carved into the pyramid above it. Over the place where Brodie had run.

CHAPTER 3

Dorian's jaw undid. Suddenly her legs wobbled. Then the rifle was sliding through her fingers and her teeth chattered while her mind repeated, He was there. Five seconds ago. He was there, and now he's gone. He was there. Five seconds ago. He was there. And now he's . . .

Someone gripped her arm. Someone grasped the rifle as its muzzle hit dirt. A voice said huskily, "Will ye let me do the safety catch?" Then the rifle went too. A hand lifted her chin. The voice said shakily, "Girl. Girl. Dorian. Can ye hear me? Do ye hear? 'Tis me. 'Tis all right."

He had one hand round the rifle and the other in her armpit, holding her up. The cap had gone, the cowlick stood on end, he was daubed with sweat and dirt and panting like a winded dog. One shoulder hunched as if he had a stitch, she had seen that wild white-out stare in Brodie's eyes. And blood was spreading on her sleeve, over her shoulder, seeping, trickling, down that supporting arm.

"I'm no' wrecked. Uh." His breath sucked as her muscles galvanized. "Uh!" It was short and concussive this time. "Dinna move—quite so fast. Let me put rifle . . ."

She took it out of his hand. Propped it on a skid strut. Then she all but flew at him gabbling, "You're hurt, he hit you, oh, God, how bad is it, let me see . . ."

"Only creased." His shoulder was still at an angle, though he had a hand on the helicopter cabin now, and the glaze in his

64

eyes had become a sort of smile. "De'il's own shot, the man. Once across the ribs." His right elbow made to gesture and stopped. "Once up the back o' the head . . . thought I'd got a dint wi' a red-hot iron. An' the deep one, 'cross the shoulder top. Hurt like Satan's kiss an' bled like Hennessy's pig."

"Oh, God." The adrenaline was still racing through her, she wanted to shake him till he rattled and simultaneously hug till she strangled him. "You fool, you madman, you howling maniac! You never even had a gun!"

"Aye." It was half laugh, half gasp. "Waved the iron at him . . . couple o' times. But he couldna be *sure* it was a bluff. So he couldna just rush me in the machinery. I'd only to move . . . an' rattle things. Every time he clipped me he thought 'twas done. An' when he found it wasna—he went ravin' mad."

"Mad?" Who was mad? Creased? Up the back of the head? A millimeter deeper and you could have died. If you weren't knocked out. Or knocked silly, for just too long. Brodie's crazed stare leapt back at her, the weaving head, the deep-set hunter's eyes. He could have run you down and *murdered* you!

"Aye, out o' his mind. If ye'd heard him swear—Ah! It's all *right*."

This time his arm was round her and her head was buried in his sound shoulder, her own arms strained high around his ribs. The misused sweatshirt smelt of dust and oil and furious effort. And fear. Pain, adrenaline, survival, triumph, all in that hurtful, uncontrollable ghost of a laugh.

"Dinna take on so. Only one o' him, after all. No' half a platoon. An' pipes're better than hedges, for stoppin' things. Eh—what did ye do wi' George?"

George? What? Who? Oh. She lifted her head.

"I shot him," she said.

"Ye *what?*"

"I shot him. In the leg. The back of the leg."

"Jaezus." It was barely breathed.

"I couldn't just leave him, there was a window. You said tie him, but there wasn't any rope. Or time. I could hear *him*— shooting at you."

"Ah."

"If he'd got to the chopper he'd have . . ." His shoulder flinched and she knew he had understood more about air surveillance than she thought. "But if I waited there I could keep him grounded and he couldn't shoot at me. When you went past he stopped. Over there." She could not look. She gestured with her chin. "I meant to shoot him. I had the trigger tight. Then he ran . . ."

He had gone queerly still. Now he got two fingers under her chin and made her look up. The glaze had cleared. His eyes were deep and somber, searching into her own.

"An' would ye ha' done it?"

The moment came back: the adrenaline charge, the berserker in control, the wholly unhesitating bloody-minded drive to protect what was her own.

"I'd have done it," she said.

The stare held. Then the mouth corner curved. Very softly, he said, "*Now* I can think ye kin to Paddy Wild."

No! Never! she almost cried. Don't say that about me!

But that dark gaze held her eyes. Not repulsion, she realized. Then, almost as softly, he said, "He was a pigheaded, bog-trottin' bla'guard—but he'd take hold like a bulldog, an' never let anyone back him down." A tiny pause. "Or touch anythin' that was his."

Metal ticked, air stirred, driven by the indifferent sun, while memory and emotions clashed inside her like icebergs in a thaw-time sea. *Anything that was his.* Anything—anyone—that's mine—oh, do you mean that, all the way through?

But I shot someone. I *shot* him and never hesitated. I would have shot the other one, I wouldn't have hesitated then either. I did stand here and see him . . . see him . . . disappear.

And I don't care if I'm a respectable lawyer out in the sticks with a gun, covered in dirt and blood like something out of *Deliverance.* Or that I can feel good—good! To have him say I'm like my villain ancestor.

I think, now, I might digest the shame. I might—she felt the berserker rouse, cold as Dani and ruthless in defense of her own—I might even find heritage to value, in Paddy Wild.

But that isn't what I should be thinking now, damn it, with Jimmy bent into a pretzel and a million other things ready to fall on us—

"God," she burst out, "you're still bleeding, come on, there must be a dispensary—"

He gave her a very odd, almost uncanny little smile. And shook his head.

"No' for me. Not yet."

She gaped.

"Find the dispensary, aye. See to George. One o' them shells through the leg—either he's dead, or he'll no' trouble ye. If he can hear—tell him the jig's up—wi' his mate. Do somethin' "— for an instant his face winced with pain that was not his own— "wi' his leg. Then come back."

"But you! What are you going to do?"

He looked past at the stockpile and she could just hear him. "He might—no' have died."

"*What?* But the rock—I saw it! You can see—!"

"Aye. But he wasna at the top. Ye can see that too. An' if he ended low enough . . . if he could still breathe . . ."

He looked back at her suddenly. "Times they've found 'em when a pile goes. Afterward. An' ye can tell—they didna die. No' straight away."

Not straight away. Alive, entombed as by an avalanche. Left

there, to smother. To . . .

Times they've found 'em when a pile goes.

"Did you know it would do that?"

His slightly crooked stance had tightened, his ribs have to be hurting like hell. But the voice was quiet. "I thought it might. An'—he didna know."

About mines, the way you do.

"So you led him there—deliberately?"

His mouth twisted. "I led him there, aye. 'Twas the last place I could go. We'd played Here We Go Round the Smelter House two-three times already, he wouldna let me do it again. I thought if 'twas Ring Around the Stockpile, I might get a run at the warehouse. The office. If ye couldna help, at least."

The hair crept on Dorian's neck. I would have been right to shoot. You did trust it all to me.

I *was* right to shoot. If I hadn't sidelined George, you'd have died. We'd both have died. Probably George as well. And P-A would have won and we'd all be just bodies in the bush.

He had read most of it, she knew, on her face. He made a careful, left-handed gesture. "See to George, will ye?" He started forward, with that twisted limp, and paused. "Then—come back, aye?"

She heard what he left unsaid: So I don't have to do this alone.

I didn't think there'd be that much blood, she thought, appalled.

It had spread on the linoleum in a murkily shining carmine film, it had dried in margins dark as spilt Coke over a silver tabletop. But the center was fresh and wet. Pooled about George, on the floor with his back to the sink and head sunk on his chest, one hand still clutching his leg, where what looked like a bloody piece of rope had got wound in a kitchen knife.

Tourniquet. He hasn't passed out. He even managed to do something for himself.

"Mr. Richards? Can you hear me?" Nobody could be insane enough to ask, Are you all right?

His head moved. His eyes had a different sort of glaze. Shock. Pain—I don't want to remember how he yelled. "Mr. Richards? Is there a dispensary here?" And why am I still calling him Mr. Richards when I've bailed him up and shot a hole in him? "Mr. Richards! George!"

The eyes focused. Briefly, the face blurred. Recognition, fury, impotence. Hate. No surprise in that.

"I can get stuff for your leg. Help you. If I know where?"

He licked at his lips. Dehydration, she guessed, doesn't that come with loss of blood? Then the free hand waved vaguely and he slurred. "Firs'-aid kit . . . there."

"There" seemed to be the next cupboard from the sink. First-aid kit, she thought, tugging the handle. A first-aid kit, where there can be accidents like what just happened outside?

At least it's big. There'll be dressings, scissors, a pressure bandage or something, like a paramedic would use.

Paramedic. Why am I trying to do first aid when I should be calling Emergency?

She put the kit in George's reach and grabbed the rifle as she babbled, "Do what you can, I'll be back." The phone's in my bag, in the loading bay, God grant it works out here. She shot into the vestibule and almost leveled Jimmy coming in.

"Oh, I'm sorry, I'm sorry, did I hit one of the—George is alive, I have to get the phone, call Emergency—"

"Phone?" He had his breath back from the involuntary grunt, and his balance as well. His hands were clamped on her upper arms and now there was dun-gold dust all over her shirt atop the blood. "Call what? What's emergency?"

"The cops, the SES, paramedics, they could have a chopper

here in half an hour—"

His brows came down hard. The adrenaline was wearing off. He was beginning to look thoroughly spent. Of course, he's been wounded, lost blood, he has to be in shock too.

"The polis? Half an hour?" He drew a quick breath and his lips pinched. "Get it then, right now—but dinna call anyone."

"But we have to, I don't know if George will make it—"

"If he's no' died yet he'll live." His muscles spoke curbed impatience. "The phone."

"But—!"

"I've found him," he said.

Her eyes flew back to his face. "Is he—"

"No' dead, no. Get y'r wee phone. Meet me out there. George can wait. First we'll try to have"—the bleakness grew starker—"a word wi' him."

When she did not move the stare intensified, almost black now, shadowed and hollow under his brows.

"Ye still dinna know for sure that he put away Chris? An' if 'twas orders or no'? An' ye canna tell what he—or y'r mega-corp—was plannin' here? Are plannin'? D'ye no' think this a prime chance o' findin' out?"

The words stuck on her lips. He's trapped in those rocks, he's got to be injured, maybe dying, we should be trying to get him out. Him and George both.

If we do that, her lawyer's experience replied with crystal clarity, they'll be whisked off into officialdom and cocooned in hospitals and procedures. We'll never get another chance to grill either of them, alone, face to face. And never in a situation like this.

Instead we—or I at least—may be facing charges, if George makes them, and he could. Trespassing. We have no feasible reason to be here. Wounding with intent, grievous bodily harm—

And what happens when they start routine inquiries? Right,

Mr. Keenighan, where do you live, what's your occupation, where's your ID? Driver's license, passport, credit card?

Her hands were clenched in her hair and she found she was shaking her head to and fro. I can't deal with all this, I can't *think* out all this, I can't play human chess this far ahead with three men all needing medical help, and one . . .

One who might have murdered—in cold blood, just rubbed out—Chris. Who would have shot Jimmy without a second thought, who nearly did shoot him three times, who would have shot me the same way.

Another who would have winked, maybe connived at murder, who has connived, under whatever coercion, at what was probably going to be a major fraud.

If we're to salvage anything from this we need proof there was dirty work. We have the break-in at L&C. We have Chris's message. But if we had a confession. Some sort of confession—

A word with him. It'll have to be more than a word. It'll be a real interrogation. You found it hard to pin down George. What will it take to crack Goonboy?

"Y'r phone." Those midnight eyes were still locked on her face. "Can ye no' keep things on it—'record'—the way Chris did that message for you?"

Of course. Not just talk to Brodie. Or get Brodie to talk, in the one place and state we might have a chance of cracking him. Record it as well.

That *would* be evidence.

And to hell with pleas that it'll be a confession under duress, invalid in court, as well as disgusting, immoral. It's the utility room over again. Necessity. One chance.

Her teeth clenched. Right, then. I want the truth this time. Straight from the stockpile's mouth.

Her muscles sprang to move. And froze. Not like this. Paddy

Wild or no Paddy Wild, Chris or no Chris. I just can't—*do it* like this.

She looked up. She did not know what her face said, but his head jerked. Then his brows came down like bars.

He said suddenly, harshly, "Half an hour?"

"What?"

"The polis? Ye said: mebbe half an hour?"

"It—I think—at least that . . . ?"

His nostrils whitened. She saw thought move at nanospeed and could not tell why. Then the rigidness broke. He said curtly, "Off wi' ye. Get y'r phone. Call the polis first."

Dorian ran without asking more.

She skidded into the loading bay, snatched up her bag. When the operator answered she found herself almost babbling, "I need the SES, rescue equipment—there's been an accident—"

"Police or fire, madam?"

"What?"

"We have no line to the SES. Police or fire or ambulance?"

"Police—I don't know! Rescue stuff! There's a man wounded in the leg and one trapped in a rockfall, I need—"

"Location, madam?"

"Ben Morar, it's a mine, thirty-five kilometres southwest of Blackston—"

"The Blackston police will respond, madam."

"But I don't just need the police, it's a rockfall! In a mine stockpile! We need somebody who knows how to—"

"The police will respond, madam. Please hold the line."

Dorian clutched the phone and tried not to curse. Clicks, beeps, ringing tone. More ringing. A female voice saying "Blackston police" with a dismaying waver underneath.

"My name's Dorian Wild." Determinedly, she suppressed the snap. "I'm at Ben Morar mine, thirty-five K southwest of you. I need help straight away. An accident, somebody shot, somebody caught in a stockpile fall, we need people and gear to move rock, paramedics, a helicopter—"

"Oh, oh, my husband, I mean, the sergeant, they're all out, there was a crash on the Greenvale bypass, a semi and two cars. And we don't have a helicopter anyway—"

"Then call someone who does! Ibisville, *somebody!* Oh, hell!" Should I call Laura or Dani, get them to light a fire under Emergency? Or Ibisville police? A motor ambulance would be useless without rock-shifting gear. They must have a chopper somewhere . . .

"I can call Ibisville Central," the voice was more agitated than before. "They can use the hospital helicopter but it'll have to fly up—"

"Do that, then." It's the best we can manage, she calculated, gritting her teeth. "Pass them this number, they can contact me."

She clicked the phone off and tried not to hurl it into the wall. Hospital helicopter, hurrah. That's if it's not out on some other call. And how long will they be?

As quick as they can, she told herself. She shoved the phone back in her bag and ran.

"He's not dead, you say." She swallowed, trotting at Jimmy's heels, rifle in one arm, phone in her other hand, now, switched, with a sickening sense of bridges burnt, to Message Bank On. "But how do we know he can—how do we get him to—talk?"

"I've ideas for that." He rounded the stockpile's flank with that crooked gait and came to a sharp halt.

"D'ye see the fall? The long bit stickin' out? He's in the angle there." His lip twisted. "Down low, near the edge. I canna tell what way up. He's alive, aye. But there's six good feet o' rock atop. Take a navvy gang half a day to have him out."

"We could try—"

"Aye, if ye've a bucket'll carry the sea. Half a day at least, for twenty men. An' by then . . ."

By then he could be dead. Just from the weight. Let alone injuries.

And would modern machinery be much faster? Especially with the lag time we already have.

"So I doubt he'll do much arguin'."

He said it entirely without expression and Dorian's blood ran cold as she understood. We *can* break him. Easier than you can imagine. Just a little coercion. Her nape crept, her back shuddered. Oh, God, this has nothing to do with the law.

But it has a lot to do with justice, the berserker retorted implacably.

She took in her breath. If we're going to do it, let's not waste time with protests and recriminations. Let's try to share the process. And the guilt.

"So we say"—she tried to sound steady—"we've got a phone here? But we haven't called Emergency? Not yet."

"Aye." This time that long-drawn cadence signaled thought. "I'm no' sure he should know the phone's here at all. Or you, either." He tightened his shoulders. "First, I've to get to him."

"But—"

"I heard the curses, walkin' round the heap. But he's no' in sight."

"That means . . . *you* have to go in there? You have to shift—shift the rocks!"

"Shhh. It'll be tricky, aye." He had straightened a little, and the abstracted note was back in his voice. "But I've seen—I helped—wi' a slide at the Worcester, one time. Ye mostly need a lot o' patience. An' time."

We don't have time and you're not mentioning the risk! What happens if you get it wrong and the thing slides again, that new fall has to be rickety as a house of cards—it might kill Brodie but it might get you as well!

She got her breath. Unclamped her hand from his arm. He's said he'll do it and he's had the experience. And if you want to go ahead with this, hysterics are no help.

Fairly steadily, she said, "What will I do?"

He turned his head to eye the phone. "How far away will that make messages?"

"You're supposed to be close. Oh." She tried not to bang her head. "I can film it. This phone's got a video facility. I mean, I can take moving pictures, like in the pub."

Even then, the marvel elicited an indrawn breath. "Can ye so?" Then he visibly recalled priorities. "Stay behind me, then. Try . . . if I get his head clear, try to stay from sight." He paused. "I heard him, down there in the pipes. I think . . . I know him now, sort of. I'll try to get him to talk. O' his own will. If that doesna work . . . I'll come away an'—we'll try the other thing."

Always supposing, her brain skidded back down the sequence, you can get his head free without killing him or yourself or both of you, and nobody arrives in the middle or . . .

That's all time-wasting. Irrelevant. She took a handful of sleeve and shook it slightly and tried to imitate his accent. "Remember, I'll kill ye, if I dinna see ye again."

It did bring a quick stifled laugh. He put a gingerly hand to his ribs and started forward. She found the video controls, turned up the microphone volume, and followed in his wake.

Dynamite, Dorian thought. Juggling dynamite, with the fuses lit.

Her arms, her neck, her teeth ached with the bare effort of standing still. Holding her breath every second minute or so. Simply waiting, while she watched him walk up to the heap, almost casually go on his knees, then crawl forward like a frog, all four limbs splayed, and begin inching himself, shift by laborious shift, up the trembling, quivering, grating, slithering rocks.

She had heard Brodie, once or twice. The first time almost stopped her heart, when the noise of footfalls must have reached him and sound came like a ghost's voice from the tomb. No intelligible words, but a too frantic inflection: Is anyone there?

Jimmy had answered as wordlessly, a sketch of, "Aye." By then he had been studying the slope. Once launched, he answered again, as briefly, to Brodie's calls. Dorian had the source almost pinpointed now. Four, maybe five feet up. In the angle of the new fall, in peril of a slip from both sides. As Jimmy was . . .

Stone slipped and clattered and her heart tried to jump through her teeth. Jimmy had frozen again. Another of the endless, heart-straining pauses while he waited for it all to regain equilibrium, while he assessed what rock he could move next and where, and how long to wait. Her head said, If it does come down he can run, he can jump. He's no more than ten feet away. If you were right there with him you'd be a hindrance, not a help. Her heart yelled, To hell with all that, I want him out, safe, with me!

What he intended when he began she had no idea. Now, fifteen, eighteen minutes later, she could see he was hollowing a dip into the slope. A wide, shallow dip, demanding what seemed an endless number of shifted rocks, waits, calculations, more shifts. And he has to be hurting too, having to keep still, spread-eagled like that, having to wait so long, to think so hard, to move so carefully. Oh, God, I think I'm going to die of suspense long before this is done.

Then he lifted, held, deposited one more rock, and under his arm a new color appeared. Not dun-gold or sulfur-brown but gray. Stippled gray, flecked with muddy red, a dome shape foreign to the rock's angular fracture planes.

Brodie's head.

She was closer without knowing it, directly behind, looking down at them: Jimmy flattened to the rock just to Brodie's right, using his own head and shoulders to pin part of the bowl. And obliquely below him, the top of Brodie's skull. He's on his back. Head outward. That big rock. That bigger rock hasn't fitted into the others round it, there's a gap. That must be why he can breathe. How a man can have such luck . . .

If you can call it luck, her heart quailed as she took in the height of rock above him and thought of the weight, the tons and tons of weight bearing down on human flesh and bone, and who knows what he already broke or damaged in the fall?

After another eternity the bigger rock came free. Jimmy eased it away. Paused, hand still on it. Lifted the hand, his own breathing tallying the effort to maintain control. He flattened his cheek a little closer to the stone, and past his shoulder she saw Brodie's face.

Blood, sweat, dust. A death mask that was not dead, for the grimy lashes lifted and the eyes looked up and across, washed-out ice-blue, colder than Dani's, even yet. With awareness waking in them. Recognition. A malevolence that blocked her throat.

She pressed *Record* just as Brodie said, on an almost voiceless breath, "You son of a bitch."

With absolutely no expression, hardly louder, Jimmy answered, "Aye."

Silence. Then, faintly, "You *knew.*"

"I reckoned, *perhaps.*"

Jimmy had not moved a muscle. His face was blank. But his voice held a weird note of complicity. Shared experience. Even the hint of a bizarre companionship.

You knew the rock would fall.

I thought it would, yes. Enemies, Dorian thought while her skin goose-pimpled. Enemies after battle have a bond, understand each other, are close to each other in ways . . . I don't even want to know about.

After a moment, Brodie spoke again.

". . . ha' got you. In Iraq." He pronounced it Ai-rack. "Semi-auto. Heat scope. Dead. Or . . . wing you. Then . . . in a cell." The dust-caked lips drew back. "Strip you. On your fucking knees—to me . . ." The last word faded into breathlessness. His lips writhed and his face distorted. He described what would happen in a cell until his breath ran out, while Dorian shuddered and tried not to stop her ears and Jimmy's face grew wholly expressionless.

"Aye," he said, when the catalog broke off. "Ye're the manky wee man, sure enough." It was soft, cold and cutting as broken glass. "Ye made a proper colander o' me."

Brodie half coughed, half choked. Jimmy's face was still blank as the rock. In that remote, dispassionate tone he said, "Ribs, shoulder, head. Ye'd no need of any 'Ay-rack.' "

Brodie was quiet. Then that wheezing half voice said, "Fucking Brit."

Jimmy's nostrils flared. But he still sounded calm. "Ye think?"

"Fucking Brit—parlor games. *Palantir.*"

With a little more volume it would have been a snarl. Dorian's breath stopped: the holdup. *Parlor games.* He said that to Chris.

"Got it past ye, did he?" Jimmy sounded casual to the point of sheer disinterest.

This time it was a definite snarl. The lips writhed again, the teeth bared. Even, white, smooth teeth, with blood caked in their grooves. "Fucked *him* over. Would have . . . *you* . . ."

"Ye did for him?" It was patent disbelief. Brodie's neck muscles contorted and Jimmy said with soft indifference, "If ye shift the rock'll come down. An' I'm no' sure, now, I'll bother gettin' ye out."

Brodie swore as long as his breath held. When it came back

he hissed, "Fixed him . . . sure as shit. Jigged that fucking—four-wheel drive. Off he went . . . hair up his ass. And straight off . . . range. Fuck, I laughed."

Keep the phone still. Dorian bit her tongue and let the tears run down into a red fog. Just keep the phone still, don't let the focus wobble, he's admitted it and you're recording it, you'll get all the revenge you want.

"Is that so?" Jimmy sounded almost disdainful. "An' o' course y'r boss was happy wi' that."

"No." It almost reached a growl. ". . . fucking smarter . . ."

"So ye never told him at all?"

The light, casual tone glossed, too stupid to report? Brodie hissed like a veritable snake. "Reinschildt said . . . get fucking math stuff. Laptop . . . 's all."

The pause stretched and stretched, filled with the struggle of Brodie's breath. The grate and creak of rocks. Dorian saw the lines deepen up from Jimmy's mouth. Then he said, "So ye did it all y'rself. Ye clever wee gombeen. An' never even thanked."

Brodie's face jerked. "He fucking smashed . . . laptop." It came in a raw-throated snarl. "Fucking . . . *fingerprint* . . . password. Didn't even—try—hack." Again the face contorted. "Could have got—fucking—math thing—no—fuss."

"A fine Jackeen himself?" As stupid, said the tone like the flick of a whip, as you?

Jimmy can't have a clue what this means, Dorian thought with her heart back behind her teeth, but my God, he can fence. And he's remembered everything I said I didn't know, did Brodie rig Chris's car, did he do it to orders or not. Go on, she urged, don't ask him to explain it, just keep going.

Brodie had run out of breath. Jimmy looked sidelong down at him, then up at the rock, letting the glance give his opinion of Brodie's fix. "An' y'r fine Reinschildt set up this caper too?"

Brodie's eyelids sank. The life sank with them, fading to leave the mask of a face. Jimmy's mouth set. But he waited, silent, until the whisper came.

"Reinschildt said . . . fix it. 'S all."

"Fix," Jimmy wondered indifferently, "what?"

"Papers . . . fuckup."

"What papers? 'Tis all fuckup to me."

Brodie snarled at him again. "Papers—fuckwit. Contract. Fucking—*math* stuff. Get . . . copies off . . . stupid bitch making fuss."

Jimmy's lips set like rock. But the voice was still tauntingly cool. "An ye couldna do it?"

Brodie literally spat. "*Will* get 'em! Know—where they are." The eyes narrowed poisonously. "Seen to that."

Jimmy rolled his own eyes round. "The way ye've seen to this?"

Brodie swore till his breath went again. "All fixed," he got out. "Without *you.*"

"Is that so?" Jimmy actually raised an eyebrow. "Ye havena got the copies or the—woman. Ye're stuck here in the bush wi' nothin' but y'r wee manager man. Just what were ye goin' to fix?"

Dorian felt her heart labor and stop. For an instant the rock pressed down on her own bones, her own flesh, her lungs struggled in time with Brodie's breath. He *can't* realize what Jimmy's doing, what he's saying, he must see it soon, he must shut up . . .

But the whistling, wheezing voice had resumed.

"Change . . . contract . . . 'course. Make—fucking Richards sign." It was still the half of a withering stare. "Give Reinschildt—legal . . . base. Whip their asses—in court."

"Aye." Jimmy sounded half skeptical, half indifferent. "An' who'll sign the other half?"

"Fake it . . . fuckwit." The bruised lip curled. You think, said the stare, I'm as stupid as you?

Jimmy stared back with his own scorn patent. "An' the first time somebody puts the screws on Richards he runs squallin' to turn Queen's Evidence? That'll work in court a proper treat."

Even under the dust and blood, spots of color came up on Brodie's cheeks. "*That* fucking . . . lily prick? Take care—him."

Jimmy let one eyebrow rise a little. "Just how"—the drawl was rich with irony—"will ye do that?"

Brodie snorted. It was almost full-voiced. "Think I'm . . . real sap, dontcha? Tell you . . . everything?" The eyes slitted, again the face almost convulsed. "Got me in here . . . fucked now. I know that. Can't feel . . . thing below . . . waist." The wheeze had taken more of his voice. "And rock . . . too much. Fucking Brit—*street boy*"—the lips writhed—"would've got you . . . one clear shot."

"But ye didna get it, did ye?" Jimmy said. The tone was equable, but his nostrils had a faint white rim. For the first time his eyes came away from Brodie. Lifted, and met Dorian's in one long, inscrutable stare.

She tried to make her own eyes say, That's enough. Leave it, we've got plenty of evidence and we can't push for any more. Not and face ourselves afterwards. Leave it. Now.

If he understood, it did not show. The eyes were dark and blank in more than a stone wall, a stillness that verged on inimical.

Then he looked back to Brodie and his voice went light and scathing, deliberate as the cut of a whip. "Pogue ma thóin," he said, "ye scabby wee toe rag. Ye *tried* to get me. Ye just werena fast enough."

Brodie bellowed like a hamstrung bull. The head jerked, the buried arms must have heaved and Jimmy came away in one long spring like a leaping frog as the new fall's balance gave and the buttress side fell in another gravel-pit roar.

Chapter 4

Dust boiled up in a choking dun-gold fog and Dorian ran for her life to open air. A last shred of sense pressed *Stop Record.* Then she smothered a scream and hurled herself back into the murk just as a dun-gold shadow exploded out at her bawling, "Dorian, Dorian, where are ye, are ye—!"

They collided and it cut off in a grunt. Something maybe Gaelic ended in "dheeah" and a long shuddering breath. He clutched her like a life buoy, wheezing, coughing, shaking from head to foot. "Ah, Dhia . . . I thought . . ."

"No." Her own arms were clamped like a vise. If it hurt his ribs he had not noticed. "No," her voice was quaking too. "I'm all right."

The dust rain eased. Neither of them let go. It isn't passion, she thought with her head buried in acridly dusty sweatshirt, it isn't even affection, it's—needing to feel another person. To be sure you're both still here. Still alive.

After witnessing that.

He took his cheek out of her hair at last. Sneezed. Gasp-grunted and made to hold his ribs, and she let go too. He half swung with his good arm still round her, staring back into the flank of the pile.

Presently, in a very small voice, she managed, "Is he—could he have—"

He answered without looking round. "No."

Dust soughed down to rest. Stone shifted and scraped and

grated, and her nerves twanged in reply. But it's just the pile settling. It's not—anything else.

"I shouldna—have done that." His voice wobbled like the rest. "I should—I ought—ah, the poor stupid gomeril, I called him dirty an' a fool an' a town jack an' he ne'er blinked an eye. I thought he hadna the Gaelic. Then he got my dander an' I lost m' head. An' he must've understood *that*."

"Understood what?" The dust rasped in Dorian's throat.

He looked down at her, the stone wall gone. Stunned, shaken out of himself. Regret, perhaps open guilt.

"I said—" Red darkened the dust on his cheek. "In Gaelic—I said, 'Kiss my'—" He wrenched his face away. "Ah, I canna say it. No' to you." He bowed his head, suddenly and completely as a ritual penitent. "I *shouldna* have said it. I ought ne'er to've fleered at him at all."

"You lost your temper? I thought—" Dorian stopped.

When she did not go on, his brows twitched. Making the prompt clear, he said, "Aye?"

She wiped vainly at her own face. He was waiting. She took another breath. If he didn't, he may never forgive me. But if he did . . .

Paddy Wild's descendant or not, maybe I can't forgive *him*.

"I thought," her throat croaked almost as Brodie's had. "I thought maybe—maybe—you'd meant—"

"Meant? Meant what?"

Then his face changed. His mouth opened. It was almost a silent cry.

"Ye thought I *intended* it! To have him stir the rock? Finish him off?"

"I didn't think, I couldn't tell, but the way you looked at him, the way you looked at me—!"

His face had gone beyond shocked. "God and the saints," he said, just audibly. "How could ye—"

He stopped. Every bone of his face had come through the dust as if they had been stripped.

"No," he said. "Ye dinna know me, after all. Ye canna know me. Not in day or so. An' there's been times—men—in Ireland—" He clenched his shoulders. "They'd do it, aye. To have the answers out o' him. An' leave all tidy. But I—I never—"

He rubbed the back of a hand up his face and left a daub of dust and sweat. Then his shoulders sagged to match the bow of his neck.

"I shouldna," he said bleakly, "ha' done any o' this. Ye'd called y'r SES. But there was stuff ye—we—needed." The voice flinched a little. "About Chris."

At her movement he twitched too and said hastily, "An' he was alive, an' . . . I thought . . ."

He balked altogether. Dorian tried to make herself not be there. Then, effortfully, slowly, he turned back to the heap. Bent his head. And more slowly, crossed himself.

Just audibly, he said, "I'll be needin' confession, aye. For plannin' this. For doin' it—how I did. For losin' my head wi' him. But as God sees me . . . no' for plannin' that."

"No, no, I believe you." Know you or not, nobody could plan that and then talk about it like this. Or counterfeit those last words, that little falter in mid-sentence, that . . .

She put both arms back round him and he drew a sharp small breath that was not pain and turned hard into her grasp.

The kiss grew out of the embrace as naturally as seed becomes plant. It tasted mostly of dust and the aftermath of adrenaline, and it was not passionate, Dorian thought, in the usual sense. A peace kiss, perhaps, but also not in the usual sense. A seal, maybe an affirmation. Of being alive, of having survived what we've survived, of acceptance. Of others' death. Of our complicity in that death. Of what we've found. In each other, as well as in ourselves.

Of being prepared to meet the consequences.

It seemed a long time before his grasp eased and their mouths relaxed, and she laid her forehead back against his shoulder and felt his fingers shift lightly in her hair. Before he sighed and she pulled her head up. And realized the phone was still clamped in her right hand.

"Aye," he said, that resigned cadence, and let his arms fall away. Plainly girding himself for the next stage, he added, "Did the—did it work?"

Dorian braced herself in turn and pressed *Replay*. The holo-screen came up, framing rock and Jimmy's profile and the upside-down view of Brodie's face, and that lizard-rasp voice said with less volume but undiluted malevolence, "You son of a bitch."

"It worked." She switched off in a hurry. "Now . . . first, we have to see to George."

"An' y'r polis?" He made to dive in a trouser pocket for his watch and stopped. "The time? When did ye 'call'?"

Dorian checked the Out file. "About, um, thirty-five minutes ago."

"Thirty-five! An' ye said a, a 'chopper' might be here in half an hour?" He jumped as if it were right overhead. "Come on then, quick."

"Quick what?" He had snatched up the rifle, caught her free hand and was yanking her toward the office. His hair stood on end, he was plastered with dust and sweat and blood like a bomb-blast survivor and he seemed to have forgotten even the pain in his ribs. Then her own brain cut in.

"The office, yes, we should have a look there and I have to check for messages, the cops must have called. But George—"

"Never ye mind George. Off wi' ye to that office, an' see can ye figure what they were doin'. Before the polis come an' claim it all. I'll no' be any use at that. I'll see to him. That," with a dour turn of the voice, "I've done before."

"Yes. Yes." Dorian began to hurry herself. There could be real evidence down there and once the police arrive it'll be out of bounds for us, they could even miss—destroy things. "Oh, heavens! Brodie's bag!"

"Leave that be." He spoke sharply. The cramped pose was returning, but he moved almost as fast as at the stockpile. "He'd take care o' George, he said. An' you said, No' in the office. Who knows what's in that de'il's poke? Leave it for the polis. Where did ye put George?"

Still carrying the rifle, he hurried out of the vestibule. Dorian turned the other way and stopped. Cops first, some sane part of her mind dictated. I can't hit the office till I do that.

When she keyed up Messages the holoscreen lit instantly. A nondescript wall caught in artificial light, distant mechanical noises, a fox-sharp blue-eyed face.

"Ms. Wild?" it said. "If you're the person who called Emergency about an accident at Ben Morar mine, please respond at once. This is Senior Sergeant Lancini from Ibisville Central Police. We're assembling a General Duty Crew to answer your call. We'll have medical support and we're using the hospital helicopter. If your phone doesn't keep call records, it's now three-twenty P.M. We've had to fuel up and collect the Area Superintendent, but we expect to be airborne by three forty-five. Our ETA at Ben Morar is four-ten, four-fifteen P.M. I repeat, please respond at once."

Dorian flicked a look at her watch. Three-forty P.M. She stared down the corridor and felt the heart sink in her chest.

Oh, God, I'm so tired. It hit now like another stockpile's weight. All I want is to lie down and curl up and just—just exist, till all this recedes a bit. And instead I have to think.

More than think, I have to make decisions that will fix a

watershed. Because we're on the official radar now. And everything I say in this call, like the pebble that starts an avalanche—at the simile she winced—will shape the outcome of it all.

Which can't, she acknowledged bleakly to the photos of anonymous mine sites on the corridor wall, ever be the unvarnished truth. Tell some hard-case cop like Gifford there was a fold in reality and you're out here chasing American ex-Army goons with a bodyguard from the nineteenth century?

She bit her lip and smothered the peals of incipient hysteria. You can't flake out. You have to answer this call, field their preliminary questions. Give them some reason, at the very least, for having the message bank on.

Paddy Wild, she wondered, feeling an absolute fool, where are you now?

What slid into her mind was one of Dani's rare aphorisms, in firm lore from the day Dorian arrived: *The best defense is the highest percentage truth.*

Dorian thumbed the *Return Call* button. The screen came up. The slightly familiar voice said curtly, "Lancini," and she said, "This is Dorian Wild."

"Ms. Wild—" He got a good look at her image, and his head jerked. "Are you hurt?"

"No, no, I'm okay, I just—" The blood's not mine. "I'm sorry the message bank was on. There's—there's been another rockfall and I think—I think the—the person trapped is—is probably—probably dead."

Don't say, *We* think, Don't say why the phone was off, let him assume you were out doing something about the rocks when they fell again, don't mention the recording or anything else. Just the facts, ma'am. Only, not *all* the facts.

His face had set. But the voice was no more than crisp. "The Superintendent's on his way. We'll be there by four-fifteen at the latest. Where are you now?"

"At the office. The mine office."

"Stay there. If they have the facilities, make a cup of strong, hot, sweet tea." Damn it, she thought, you and Anne must have taken the same first-aid course. "Any medical supplies?"

"There's a first-aid kit . . ."

The curl of his lip answered, Cowboy mining company. "Can you assist the wounded man?"

"I haven't done much yet . . ."

"Do what you can. Any complications or questions, call me back. We'll be with you as soon as possible, Ms. Wild."

"Thank you, Sergeant." The gratitude was real, despite everything.

She clicked the phone off and felt her lungs empty on a long thankful breath. First hurdle past. And it seemed to work. Tell the highest percent of truth. Enlist sympathy, be shell-shocked, because you are. Let the rest unfurl as you must, once they arrive.

Once they arrive, my God. Thirty, thirty-five minutes, and we're on stage. They're bringing a Superintendent, they've pulled all the stops out, I have to tell Jimmy what they'll do and who they are and, God, what he'll have to say just for their preliminary interview.

And I have to figure what I say. Where I *start,* for heaven's sake. Panic surged up and with a huge effort she cut it off.

Whatever I say depends on what George and Brodie did. I have to check that office. Now.

The door at the corridor end said, "G. Richards. Manager." Convenient that they left it open, Dorian thought, trying not to tiptoe. The air conditioner was still going. I can't touch that either. I can't leave my fingerprints in here. All I have to do is look.

Oh. But I could do more than that.

She checked the phone's camera facility. About fifteen MB left. I can take our own crime shots. And leave the actual stuff for the cops.

The room filled the building end, air conditioner in the outer wall, more window panels both sides, filing cabinets beneath. The obligatory manager's-family shots on the desk, other photos on the interior wall. George and a second man with guns pointed heraldically upward, feet planted on some black supine bulk she thought might be a wild pig. George and other men with machinery, perhaps a mine site. George and suits round a drilling rig?

A filing cabinet drawer stood open. Folders strewed the desk. The computer was up. No screensaver. Whatever George had been at work on when the rock landed was still there.

She walked round beside the black leather swivel chair and recognized the middle page of Chris's contract, the one she had read off her own screen.

Except this one said, "Regarding the mathematical model titled 'Christopher Keogh's Statistical Core-Log Analysis Model,' Ben Morar Mining Company shall have full rights to any finds made by use of this model. Fifty percent of the model's value as set by independent assessors shall remain the exclusive intellectual property of Christopher Brian Keogh."

For a minute it all swam behind a wave of red. You *shits,* she thought, locking her teeth, you little *shits.* Give Reinschildt a legal base, Brodie said. Oh, yes, indeed it will. George, you *worm.*

And of course the codicil about me as legatee won't be here.

She squinted at the phone's camera input. Cursed her meager experience, and pressed Shoot.

The phone flashed. With bated breath she stared at the holo-screen. Dark came up, turned to white. Some screen dazzle, print too small to read. But I can zoom it, she thought, suiting action to word.

And it's legible. And the date's on the bottom of the shot.

Trying not to punch her fist in the air, she scanned the desk.

Personnel folders, but no papers out. George must have known exactly where to find the computer file and set right to changing the wording. Else he couldn't have got this far so soon. Is there a printout, too?

She checked the work shelf, but the printer's tray was empty. Then she thought, What was Brodie doing?

She sighted the bag almost immediately, its details incised in her memory: floppy fake canvas, dusty Army green with a couple of patches that suggested camouflage, on the floor by a pair of easy chairs that bracketed a coffee table. Loose papers on its top.

A memo pad, a biro. A sheaf of stapled printed pages. Lord, it's the hard copy, the original Ben Morar contract. They did need the personnel folder after all.

It was open to the signature page. And . . . her heart jumped like a kangaroo . . . on the memo pad someone had written, several times over, each time closer to the original signature: "Christopher Brian Keogh."

The phone was in her hands without need to think. She took three pictures for surety, checking each one, wanting to yowl like a genuine berserker. You pair of sneaking, cheating bastards, Jimmy timed that rock better than he ever imagined. Oh, I'll give you legal bases now!

She hurried down the corridor with elation lifting her feet. But in the vestibule her mind leapfrogged again and yanked her to a stop.

I needn't wait for court to use this stuff. I can short-circuit George with it. Right here.

He could press charges, for what we—I—did. She remembered his face when he recognized her in the utility room. He almost certainly will. And if he does, there's no way I can keep Jimmy, at the very best, inconspicuous. If he gets fully into the legal system . . . Her mind swerved from the horror of getting a nineteenth-century time traveler even a legitimate ID.

But if George is fit to talk and think, and he knows what we've found . . .

The utility-room door stood ajar. She whisked round it and Jimmy jumped off his knees and caught his side before his stance eased and he wheezed, "Could ye no' light a cracker as well?"

He was waving his good hand before she managed to apologize. "I've found the bandages an' such, but I canna make head nor tail o' the rest. D'ye know what they use for laudanum?"

George was still propped against the sink, but a wide swathe had been wiped through the blood, his trouser leg was missing an arm's-length section, and a wad of bandage circled the leg itself. "The hole," Jimmy said with some respect, "goes clean through. But"—his eyes flicked, and a mouth corner curved—"ye made a bigger one in the wall."

Dorian followed his eye and gulped. "Oh, heavens! It's a miracle—"

A miracle I didn't kill him, if that rifle can leave a hole like that in things harder than flesh.

"So 'tis. I dinna think it'll bleed much more. But what he needs is laudanum."

The old version of morphine, Dorian's brain slowly translated. *Not heroin. Painkiller.*

"Oh." She hunkered over the first-aid kid. Antiseptic solution, did Jimmy know to use that? If not, the paramedics will. Aspirin. Panadeine, Nurofen. Nothing stronger. Doesn't aspirin stop blood clotting? Panadeine, then. It mightn't help but it shouldn't do much harm.

She shook out four capsules and tried to reach the sink without miring her shoes. Nothing, a side cell of her mind remarked wryly, like spreading the tracks of your barbarity.

George was glassy-eyed and gray under what had been a moderate bush tan, but when she dogged him with the glass he managed to lift a hand. She gave him the tablets one by one, trying to ignore disaster scenarios. Do you give tablets to people in shock? Can they choke if you do?

George survived. Jimmy took the glass and put it on the sink. Next to the rifle laid out on the cupboard tops: bizarre, her freewheeling brain said. Then it assessed George coldly and calculated, Ten, fifteen minutes, if those do work. He might think better then.

Or listen, anyway.

She picked up the first-aid kit and beckoned Jimmy to the table. "Now let's see to you."

The sweatshirt came off with relative ease. When she began unbuttoning the shirt he started a little, before he said ruefully, "Ruined. An' brand new." He grimaced at the rips and wide-soaked bloodstains, and twitched again when Dorian pulled at his old-fashioned sleeveless under-vest. But when she laid hands on his belt buckle, he skittered clean out of reach.

"What are ye doin'!"

"I can't," she said, not quite patiently, "get a dressing on that 'crease' over your ribs with your clothes in the way. You'll have to take off the singlet thing and undo your belt and, um, some buttons or something, and let your trousers down a bit."

She got The Look cubed. Oh, lord, she thought, he's probably never stripped even to the waist in front of a woman in his life. And I don't have the time or the strength to explain about infection and soothe outraged Victorian modesty now.

"Just do it," she commanded, and turned hurriedly to rum-

92

mage for cotton swabs. At least I can give him a pretense of privacy.

She found the antiseptic bottle and turned. The baleful silence had suggested the worst, but he had the vest off. The belt was undone, he was clutching his trousers with the waist an inch or so below his navel, like a Barbara Cartland heroine ready to defend her chastity.

"That'll do." She advanced on him, determinedly ignoring her own embarrassment. "This is going to sting."

It did more than sting, to judge by the gasps. She wiped off the surrounding gore, then seized a dressing. Just let me get this on and you can pull up your trousers, at least.

"There. If you sit down I can reach your shoulder." She lifted her eyes and for the first time actually looked at him.

His face and throat and forearms were the usual weathered bronze of skin exposed to Australian sun. His chest and midriff and the upper slope of his belly were pale as cream. Flawless as cream. Almost hairless, smooth as cream, with the distinct modeling of those long muscles she had already mapped in her own arms. Not an ounce of fat on him, said her mind, following the finely hollowed torso curves. Tall, long-boned, the muscle of somebody from an age when they did most work with their hands, and the extra slightness of people raised on deprivation's edge. His chest and hips rose from the dark clumsy trousers like some elegant human plant form from the sheath of its bud.

Oh, said somebody, very far away. Oh.

"Ye needna tell me." His torso had curled inward as defensively as the tone. "I was a skinny brat an' I'm skinny still. Long an' gangly as a drink o' water an' now gone to wire an' string. 'Twas bad enough before the holes."

He's a peacock, she thought helplessly. Right down to the skin.

"You're not . . . oh, lord." She stopped as the laughter nearly overtook her. He'll think I'm mocking, agreeing with him. She put the bottle down and reached him in a step, her hands going unthinkingly either side his waist. "You *aren't* skinny or stringy, you're . . ."

"Dinna *do* that . . . !"

He had gasped. She let go with a jolt. Her palms kept the contours of muscle, the texture of skin delicate as a baby's, slightly chilled from the outer air. "I'm sorry, I didn't mean—"

Mean to hurt you, her mind finished. And then postscripted: Or mean to do it at all?

He let his trousers go from one hand and grabbed at hers. There was a chasm of a pause.

Then he opened his fingers, inch by inch. She had expected he would pull away. Or grab his belt and buckle himself into partial security. She looked up willy-nilly with more words of apology and he was watching her.

"At least," he said, deliberately, "not if ye mean to stop at that."

Her brain took a moment to decode. Don't do it? No. Don't do it, if that's all you do?

The rest was in his stare. Dark, unwavering, but not the stone wall. Expectant. With a glint, a certain conscious intent she had seen before.

In a minute her lips moved. She said, "Oh."

The glint sharpened. Straight-faced, too straight-faced, he said, "Aye."

You told me modern women made their own choices. That you chose when to say yes. What will you do if I say yes, consciously this time, knowingly, to you?

It's reaction, it's foolery, it's the reflex human response to death. A bounce-back, extravagant but natural, from all the rest of this. It's a challenge, it's a joke.

Underneath, it's not a joke at all.

She looked straight back in his eyes and spoke as deliberately as he had. "Grow a whole skin, first."

His lashes flickered. Then he let her hand go, slowly, carefully. After another endless moment, as soberly as she had, he said, "Aye."

This time, she knew without question, it's a pledge.

The shoulder crease was high over the muscle's top, a bloody furrow inches from his neck. She dabbed and wiped and cleaned now without embarrassment, even with a kind of pleasure, that his stillness said he shared. A promise made, she thought. An envisaged future to fulfill. With quiet, with determined anticipation, not to be denied. As soon as we get through this.

The present crashed back. She had to consciously steady her hand.

"The cops," she said, trying not to gabble. "For a normal accident, they'd set up a perimeter. That means, put tape round the site. Make some sort of command post. Probably in the office." Oh, God. I *have* to tell them about the evidence.

And George, caution suddenly cut in. She whipped a glance behind. His head had fallen forward, his hands lay lax on the floor. He doesn't look fit to hear, let alone make sense of this. All the same . . .

She lowered her voice. "I haven't figured how much I'll have to explain about what's really going on. But we're witnesses, they will interview us, and probably alone." She felt his muscles twitch and understood. "Usually they'd just ask your name, date of birth, address, a contact number. God." Her brain felt as if it would overheat. "Your name's okay, your date of birth?"

"That," he said dryly, "would be eighteen fifty-six."

"Oh, heavens. Well, take your age off twenty twelve."

"Ah." His own voice said, This is surreal. "That would be— nineteen eighty-two."

"Okay." Thirty years old, her own brain tallied. Two years younger than me. "Your address." She took a deep breath. It's the only possibility. Don't even think about dead men's shoes. "You're staying at . . ." She recited Chris's unit address. "Can you memorize that? And the contact number's this."

His lips moved. His muscles had tensed again under her hands. "I have that." He sounds steady enough, she thought, half appalled, half relieved. Maybe he's had to do this before. Oh, what I'd give for a time-out here, just an hour, two hours, to sit down and let us both catch our breaths and think what we're doing.

But we don't have it. So what's Jimmy's overall story? You have to get it sorted before they separate you.

"I canna say I'm no' from Ireland. But do I say, Emigrant? An' when did I arrive?"

He had tensed and straightened but the deep voice was perfectly cool. He's thinking. I don't have to do this all by myself. She flattened the last sticking plaster on a gust of relief.

"Not an emigrant, a visitor, you came out—oh, six months ago. You—" Illumination burst, dazzling her. "You came to Blackston to follow up some family history—"

He gave a yelp and grabbed her hand, scissors and all. "I had a relative. A black sheep relative!"

"Oh, Jimmy, you did *not!*" She was laughing, he was laughing, quaking with it, stress overwound to another half-drunk release. Perfect, it's insane-perfect, he came looking for himself and if he has to know things about the past, he can. "And you were in Blackston for the historical weekend and you met me."

"An' found we'd both had kin—"

"Yes! At Blackston, in the rush." She shoveled scissors and loose dressings into the kit. Could it be better? The highest percent of truth. "I'm not touching your head, the paramedics can handle that. But, listen, unless the cops ask, don't tell them *anything*."

"Aye." The stare added, Teach your grandma to suck eggs. He reached for his under-vest. She scrabbled in the kit as her mind scrabbled at the list of priorities. "Here, take four of these Panadeine yourself, then come outside. I've got something else to tell you." And this I'm definitely not risking in front of George.

By the time her tale reached Brodie's counterfeits his elation almost equaled hers. "An' ye took pictures? We've proof?"

"And I want to use it. Now. With George. He could have us charged. Trespassing at the least. He could make claims about Brodie—"

"So we pull his teeth?" Lord, she thought, he's almost ahead of me again. "Ye'd best do the talkin', if it's legal stuff. D'ye want to 'record' this too?"

"Oh." He *is* ahead of me. "Yes." Once a weasel, always a weasel. If George does make any concessions, I'd like proof. "No. I have to show him those pictures on my phone, damn it. But wait." The lure was irresistible. "I could use his phone."

Her dubious look as the corollary struck her brought a quirk to his mouth. "If ye show me how to point the wee machine, I think I can play mouse." Something in the inflection made her wonder if he had witnessed this before too. Then he looked back through the doorway and his voice changed. "Right now, I'm perishin' for a cup o' tea."

There's just time, Dorian thought. And it might help George as well.

He was still slumped against the sink, but when she said, slow and clearly, "Mr. Richards? This is tea. Can you hold the cup?" His head inched up.

She helped him drink half of it. When she sat back on her

heels his eyes followed her. Blurrily but intelligibly he said, "Miss Wild?"

"I'm sorry I had to shoot you," she said.

She had fixed on it as an opening gambit. Let's give him a chance at reason, if not amiability. To ask why, at the very least.

There was a pause. Then, in slow motion, his upper lip lifted. He said, slow but clearly, "You'll be sorrier."

Very conscious of Jimmy behind her, she said, "Oh?"

"I'll sue you." He pronounced it carefully. With relish. "Every penny you have. And your job." With increasing if half-speed malice. "Moira—when I tell her," now with open vengeance, "you can kiss Lewis and Cotton good-bye, *Miss* Wild. You'll never work as a lawyer again."

"You think so?" The berserker roused and she pressed it down. She took her phone and clicked up the picture of his computer screen. "What do you think Moira will say, Mr. Richards, when I show her this?"

It took him a full minute to decipher it. Then he seemed to deflate where he sat, like a punctured tire.

"You know and I know, Mr. Richards," she spoke no more than dulcetly, "what that contract originally read. And I photographed this version in situ. You'll notice, it has the date."

He tried to pull his head up, but he could not yet manage words.

"And what do you think Moira will make of this?" Don't gloat, she exhorted herself. This recording may well be a trial exhibit. She clicked up the shot of the trial signatures.

His head jerked. His breath caught as the motion jarred his leg. Thick and furiously he said, "The bloody *fool.*" Then his wits cut in.

"I have no idea what that is. I had nothing to do with it." It was too labored for vehemence. "That—that's a complete fabrication."

"Indeed? I have something else to show you, Mr. Richards."
She braced herself and switched to video. "This is what your,
um, associate said."

She fast-forwarded. The holoscreen filled between them.
Brodie's breathless rasp said, "Change . . . contract . . . 'course.
Make—fucking Richards sign. Give Reinschildt—legal . . . base.
Whip their asses—in court."

"Aye." Jimmy said. "An' who'll sign the other half?"

"Fake it . . . fuckwit."

Brodie's lip curled again. With ice down her own spine Dorian
cut it off and looked at George.

For a moment she thought they had gone too far. He had
shrunk in on himself, his skin the color of lead, his whole face
sagged, Marlboro bones overridden as by the load of age, he
looked literally dead. She snatched his wrist to find the pulse.

The touch roused him. He tried feebly to pull away. Then
shock overrode hatred as well. "That . . . how did you get that?
Where? How?"

"Was that Mr. Brodie?" The honorific almost turned her
stomach. But this is a recording, be formal. "The P-A bodyguard?"

"That—yes. That—how did you get—*where* did you get—"

"When we disturbed you. The person who ran out of the office with a gun?"

He tried to wave that away. "Trespassers, he had a right—*how*
did you get that?"

"He chased my friend," Dorian said very clearly, "with his
gun. Wounded him three times. Then he tried to run over the
stockpile to do it again and the stockpile gave way. He was
buried in the rocks. But we were able to speak to him."

George was turning yellow under the gray. She watched him
with clinical attention, the berserker suppressing all pity. Will I
tell him we think Brodie's actually dead? Or would it be more

effective if he doesn't know?

George spared her the decision. He gathered himself up and broke into words.

"Brodie—Brodie made me—not *my* plan." He almost managed an exclamation. "He said . . . come after Connie and Beryl—!"

Dorian stared at him, thinking, Passing the blame again. Whining like a telltale kid. While someone else replied in counterpoint, Of course Brodie would. No wonder you buckled. To protect your sisters, at least you had that much decency.

"Brodie." George tried to pull at her. "It was him. Not me!"

He stared at her so Dorian clamped her lips and thought furiously, He's doing it again. In a jam and expecting a woman to get him out. All right, her other half mind retorted. Let's help him, then.

"You'd be prepared to testify to that?"

"Yes. Yes!"

Now the rest, she told herself, however it sticks in your throat. "And these charges. Will you go ahead with them?"

"No, no." His understanding was revoltingly quick. "No charges." Apart from anything else, she thought, if this came out in public, in a court, he'd never be able to face Beryl and Connie again. "No suing? No—representations to Moira?"

"No, no." But his hand was trying to paw her knee. "Brodie, Brodie did it all, he made me, he had the gun. He didn't want any witnesses—you've got the record there. If they charge *him* will you . . . ?"

Will you testify for me?

A perfect weasel, she thought, trying to contain her disgust. But he'll play along with what you want, and he's a live weasel. If he's alive, he can go back to Connie and Beryl. If he's alive, he can answer questions. And when it comes to P-A—if it comes to a court action over the mine—at the very least, he can testify for us.

"I can certainly make that recording available to a court." That's as close as I'll come on record. Plea bargains, barristers do it all the time, but in private. Not like this. "And I assume you'd be prepared to repeat your testimony about Brodie in court as well?"

"Yes, yes." He didn't even hesitate, she thought indignantly. Rat and weasel both. What happened to that Australian code about standing by your mates?

"That is, if I have protection . . ."

"I can't guarantee that, I'm not the police. Or even on a legal brief. But I think"—she could give him this much—"you may not need it. We think—we're fairly sure—Brodie's dead."

It took another minute to sink in. Then his lips parted. Huskily, tentative as a man reprieved on the gallows, he managed, "Dead?"

"We think so. The rock—fell again." He was looking less shocked than relieved and she could not manage her feelings any longer. "We called the police. They're bringing medical support. They'll be here in"—she checked her watch—"another quarter of an hour."

The hospital helicopter made itself heard a good ten minutes before it dipped abruptly from the northern trees. The light was already shifting to the golden register of late afternoon. Silhouetted against it the big double-rotor machine looked like a tilted, flying railway carriage, and his first clear look sent Jimmy backing for the office door. Dorian said in a hurry, "It's okay, it's like Brodie's, just bigger," but her own throat was uncomfortably tight.

Here they come. Now it is official. And so much unofficial but far more vital will depend on their personalities. Especially the Superintendent's. If we strike a stickler or a troublemaker or just somebody bloody-minded rather than calloused to efficiency . . .

She swallowed hard and touched Jimmy's elbow. "Let's get out where they can see us," she said.

"Ms. Wild?" The second man off the ramp was leading by the office steps. Two plainclothes men flanked him, the fox-sharp face to the left identifying Lancini, a couple of constables and the paramedics pressed behind. The leader said, "I'm Superintendent Childers," and took the steps in a stride.

He was as tall as Jimmy but much bulkier, solid build loaded with the weight of age. A typical long-term cop shape, she thought, probably middle fifties. Sandy clipped hair, light-blue eyes. The first-encounter police mask altered as her appearance registered so she said quickly, "I'm all right," before his eyes went past her and stopped.

"You said that the wounded man was shot in the leg?"

"That's someone else. This is Seamus Keenighan. A friend of mine. He was hurt during the, um, incident." If I ask for the paramedics to treat Jimmy, Childers may take it as encroachment. But if I don't?

She said, "The man with the leg wound's in here. My friend can show you?"

Childers' eyes traversed, definitely chillier than before. He said over his shoulder, "Dave, you and Frances see to that?"

One's a woman, Dorian had time to think as the paramedics surged past. There was no time to think of Jimmy, swept away on their flood. Childers was already saying, "Now, Ms. Wild, where's the other one?"

She led the way, biting down the urge to babble, anticipate, explain. Brodie's chopper, George's car, the evidence in the office, the whole story of what we're doing here, it doesn't matter yet. Just let it wait.

They passed the warehouse. The stockpile loomed. She halted and without intending drama pointed at the new fall and said, "He's under there."

The axe-fall hush, she realized later, was the sight's rating on the calamity-hardened police scale. For herself, the rock's newly outflung sprawl, the bite in the stockpile's flank above it, the summit still looming, had somewhere become numbed into usual.

"When it slid, he was halfway up. He ended on the edge of the, the fall. We, we cleared some of the rocks. He could talk. And breathe. Then he tried to move his arms and, and . . ."

She had not intended drama then either but abruptly Childers was very close beside her, the carrying but not abrasive Queensland voice saying, "Joe, start setting up here. Bob can help. Ms. Wild, come back inside now. You can tell Steve the full story when we've fixed the incident room."

"Yes, I—thank you." She had not meant it to wobble either, but the relief of moving away was disproportionate. Then the rest snapped back to consciousness. Incident room. They'll take the first office available, and if they do . . .

"Superintendent." I'll only have the one chance at this: be rational, be emphatic but not urgent. Nor conciliatory. "The main office is open, but the incident room might be better elsewhere. In the main office—I'd appreciate a moment to show you personally—there's some important and fragile evidence. That might be part of a criminal prosecution."

There, she thought, at the prickling hush behind her. You've really put the cat into the pigeons now. Time to establish what clout you may have, before you say anything more.

"I'm a junior partner," she said, over the crunch of police boots, "at Lewis and Cotton. This, um, event, involves me personally and professionally."

"Dani Lewis?" She got the full wattage of the senior police

stare this time, sidelong over a shoulder. Of course he'd know the firm. And he knows Dani at least in person. But the attitude? Friendly, hostile, somewhere in between?

"Show me the evidence," he said, jury still out. They were halfway to the office. "Keep the rest for Steve." He glanced aside. "Is that your car?"

"That belongs to Mr. Richards. The manager. He—"

"He's *here?*"

"He's the, um, other wounded man."

His look said, I *see*. Or at least, *I don't see*. "And the helicopter?"

"That was the, the other man's."

He was reading the nuances she could not wholly suppress. His own voice sounded extra flat. "Back there?"

She nodded. He glanced back once, lips folding, and then again, to the men behind them. "Steve, we'll need the office keys, the manager's down with the medics—" Dorian made a half gesture and he stopped.

"Ah, I have the master key here."

She had actually sent his eyebrows up. He said, "That'll be handy," and picked up speed for the steps.

CHAPTER 5

I'll scream, Dorian thought, if this guy says, "Tell me more about that," just once again.

Fluorescent light ricocheted off the Ben Morar publicity officer's desk into her stinging eyes. She itched in imagination and reality, her throat felt full of sand, and the strain of constantly abridging the story rather than yielding to that catch-cry was eroding endurance along with sense. I'd kill, she thought, and tried not to wince at the cliché, for coffee and a shower.

Across the desk the detective said in his mild, I'm-only-here-to-help voice, "Yes, Ms. Wild?"

His name-flash read, Stephen Demetrios. He was as dark as Lancini and Childers were fair, as patient and as implacable as Nemesis.

"Uh—where was I?" she said.

He flicked a glance at his notebook. He was taking shorthand despite the video filming on his phone. "You—ah—decided to shoot Mr. Richards," he said.

At least, she thought with idiot satisfaction, that did make him twitch. Even if nothing else rated better than that damn, *tell me more,* from him. From Chris and Ben Morar and the takeover to the break-ins, to the really high-wire omissive stuff. Why we hid the car, why we hid when George and Brodie arrived. Why we thought they'd forge the contract, even.

It must, she thought wearily, be long past dark. Outside the window floodlights met the fluorescent with a competing glare.

Now heavy machinery let out a preliminary roar and involuntarily she winced.

End-loaders. Childers said that: Whatever the odds, we can't make this a simple body recovery yet. We'll call for volunteer mine workers, turn on the night-shift lights, get straight to the stockpile. Can't risk that Brodie might—might—still be alive.

She shivered. Demetrios waited. But if there was no sign of rapport, let alone sympathy, neither had his body language hardened in any sort of antagonism.

After all, she thought, he was in the office when I showed Childers the computer screen. And the counterfeits. And he saw Jimmy. Jimmy's shirt. However bad shooting George sounds in cold blood, all that—pre-evidence—has to make me look less of an off-the-planet paranoid now.

"With Mr. Richards, I couldn't see another choice. He— Brodie—just ran out and started firing. Seamus didn't have a gun. I had to help. And I didn't know what Mr. Richards might do."

The medics had been outraged. "You could have killed him! Shattered his femur—cut the femoral artery—he'd have been dead in minutes, or lost the leg—*look* at the hole in that bloody wall!"

No chance to speak to Jimmy then, or when Frances dressed his head, after they got George on the gurney and ran it out to the helicopter. I only hope he—and George—remember what we arranged. God knows what Jimmy'll do with the bits we couldn't arrange, the two of ten questions no one can foresee.

The machine roar crescendoed and stopped. Rock rattled like a gravel slide under a splatter of shouts and Dorian's head whipped up before she could help herself.

Demetrios had half turned as fast. Their eyes met, saying too silently, Was that calamity? Or just routine? Then he looked back to his notebook again.

"Yes, Ms. Wild. Tell me more about that."

I will not throw anything, she resolved. Instead she remembered with perverse relish how Lancini had popped up as she and Childers left George's office, passing the room already half full of police paraphernalia—she had tried not to wince at that door, labeled "T. Ralston. Senior Geologist"—and Lancini's tone, sharper than his fox face, as he said, "Andy, this was in that chopper," and held it up across himself in both plastic-gloved hands.

Metal and plastic and the stink of gun oil, glistening evilly, with the sight's space-age apparatus to balance the heavy black sickle of the magazine. She had stood frozen, hearing Brodie's voice again. "Semiauto . . . heat scope."

In the helicopter.

She could remember thinking, I *was* in the right place. And far more vividly the tense hush. Before Lancini said, "Incident room?" And Childers nodded. Then added curtly, "Tell Blackston to call a bomb expert. There's a bag in the main office," and gave her a very different glance as he ushered her on down the corridor.

She tried not to rub her eyes. Demetrios was still waiting. She said baldly, "I didn't see the shooting. They ran in among the machinery. I was scared he—Brodie—would use the helicopter. And then, even the, a pistol would be enough."

For the first time something showed, however fleetingly, in Demetrios' face. He had seen the semiautomatic too.

"But they went to the stockpile instead."

I'm not saying Jimmy led him there. Too dangerous, too complex. Abridge, abridge.

"Then he—Brodie—tried to run up instead of round it and—the rock fell."

Outside the loader roared again, like a hunting dinosaur.

Dorian shut her eyes and tried not to clench her fists as Demetrios said, "Tell me more about that."

"There isn't any more." Feeling and calculation meshed. "It fell and he got caught, like I said out there. In the rock."

"And what happened then?"

The other catch-cry. She rubbed a hand over her face to give herself time. What happened while I was stuck in here waiting for this interview, drinking more tea, thank God, while you lot set up your incident room, and the other lot, the Occupational Health and Safety people, got in the act. Dividing the carcass—the site, the witness interviews. God help us, they'll probably want to do this all over again.

Until the Blackston cops finally arrived, so now the place is crawling with police, probably waiting for the bomb squad, with Jimmy still stuck somewhere, and some poor underling down at the gate to fend off visitors. Like, all too possibly, the media.

Oh, God, I don't even want coffee or a shower anymore, I just want out of here. To my car, to Blackston, into the motel room, be safe, be somewhere else, collapse.

And get Jimmy out.

Which means finishing this.

"Then," she said too evenly, "I came to see what I could do for—Mr. Richards—and Seamus looked round the fall. And I called Emergency."

"Tell me more about that."

She bit her tongue to suppress, but you *know* about that. Even if the Blackston section was ephemeral, the actual Emergency call has to have been taped. You'd all have heard it.

Outside the machinery din crescendoed and dropped, then altered pattern. There were two loaders now, she realized, working in alternation. Through each one's revving came the grumble of stone as the other dropped its load.

"We couldn't be sure"—she kept her eyes on the desk, to de-emphasize the point's importance—"that Brodie would—live—

till anyone came. That the rock wouldn't fall again. So we—
I—as the will's executor, as Lewis and Cotton's
representative—as *myself.* There were things I needed to know."

This time Demetrios had the sense to ask by keeping quiet.

"This is what happened."

She fished her own phone from the bag. They went through
the brief dance of recording that the evidence would here show
an insert. He switched his video off, she switched hers on.

As dun-gold dust finally mushroomed over the camera lens
she took the teeth out of her bottom lip and thankfully switched
off. There was an extended pause, while the loaders roared
outside. Then Demetrios said, "Tell me more about that."

You've got to be kidding. Doesn't it speak for itself?

"Seamus said, he thought he—Brodie—might talk to him."
She did lift her eyes then. "Well—you saw."

He could not quite keep the flicker from his own eyes, that
said, And on some level below police work, I understood.

"And you saw what happened at the end."

He was clearly torn between, Tell me more about that, and
the knowledge that the interview was already evidence.

"After—that," Dorian forestalled him, "we came back here. I
returned your call. Checked Mr. Richards' office. Photographed
the evidence. We did what we could for Mr. Richards. And
then . . . you people arrived."

There was relief in that thought, after all, as well as in reaching the end with so many gaping chasms overleapt. She sat back
in the spine-pinching chair and as a loader reached top pitch
again thought, I'm so tired.

But it isn't over yet. So stick to the rules. Answer what he
asks, but only what he asks. Wherever he gives you the chance,
abridge. And never, never, never volunteer.

The loaders bellowed at each other but no human shouts
intervened. Instead the little office vibrated as feet thumped

past, and voices rattled indistinguishably along the corridor. Jimmy, she thought. Did they leave him in with Frances when I left, did Dave come back with the chopper? Probably, in case they found Brodie and he actually was alive. Poor Jimmy, he must be ready to drop. I hope Lancini interviewed him. Then maybe, now, they might let both of us go.

Or will they keep us here, after what I've said, till the bitter end?

Demetrios reached out to his phone. "End of interview, seven twenty-five P.M., twelfth September twenty twelve, Ben Morar mine," he said, and clicked off the video.

"Thank you, Ms. Wild," he said, while she tried to straighten her back and not look as if she were ready to weep with thankfulness. He got stiffly out of the office chair. "Please wait here."

The loaders went on rumbling, the voices and feet continued their counterpoint. She was trying not to put her head down on the desk and simply pass out when an extra-noisy convoy terminated at the office door.

"Ms. Wild." Childers stepped inside with a neatness striking in so bulky a man. "You've been very cooperative." He read the look on her face and switched tones. "No. Nothing. Not yet."

"I didn't think so." Dorian tried to make herself sound anything but too numb to care.

"We've called for a sniffer dog. He just might pick up something." He sat down in Demetrios' place. Less intimidating, she thought, than towering over me. They're really playing this in kid gloves. At least, so far.

"I understand that your car's back along the road."

She nodded. It won't hurt to repeat this. "There are no 'Keep Out' signs, but we were unsure—how others might react." She met his eyes and let them both remember the blood on Jimmy's shirt.

"Well, the media have heard, they're at the gates right now. ABC, Ibisville local stations. Radio reporters, couple of TV crews. So the helicopter will take you and Mr. Keenighan into Blackston for the night. You have accommodation there?" Before she could say, Yes, ask, When, add, What about Jimmy's interview? he added a carefully calculated nod.

"Since your interview took some time, Sergeant Lancini's done the preliminary with Mr. Keenighan." She did not have to hide the gratitude that made her sag in the chair. "You can leave immediately."

"Thank you," Dorian said, meaning every word of it, and checked halfway to her feet.

"The computer." Not yet, first I have to protect that chain of evidence. "Mr. Richards' computer. That file. I don't want to interfere, but have you managed . . . ?"

"We've taken pictures. And fingerprints. Our forensic computer expert will be here tomorrow." He sounded neither affronted nor surprised. He must have expected me, as a lawyer, to think of that. "It's a little tricky preserving clean evidence on a live machine, so we're leaving that part to him."

Dorian felt her shoulder muscles release. They'll have the counterfeits, and George's fingerprints on the mouse, they have the actual wording, even if the machine does go down. They have Brodie's semiauto. They'll have an expert to undo that bag of his. George is in hospital. They'll probably interview him tomorrow. There's nothing I can do about that now, except hope he remembers what we said. Surely that's everything?

Not yet. She stifled a groan. "Do you"—it felt like offering to lop her arm—"do you want my phone? It has a recording that's pertinent. Sergeant Demetrios has seen it." Oh, God, she thought, remembering further. "There's one on Mr. Richards' phone too."

"Steve mentioned the recording. An interview with—" The pause was tiny but evident, is he hesitating between, Victim and, Perpetrator? "—Mr. Brodie?" He considered a moment, then gave another short nod. "You've been very careful with the evidence, Ms. Wild." In the garish light she was uncertain if that came with a glint of conscious ambiguity. "If you can last another quarter hour, I think we could take a copy of that. Then you can keep the phone."

"That's—extraordinarily kind." It's only temporary, she told herself, this is just the second hurdle, the really bad part's still ahead. But the thought of keeping her phone atop finally escaping Ben Morar was relief to the point of euphoria. "Thank you, Superintendent."

She did manage to get up this time. He rose too, with considerably more energy. "Of course," he said, "we'll have to ask you to stay in Blackston until further notice. We'll have more questions for you both."

The tone took her awareness of that for granted, but the hint of challenge brought her eyes up before she knew. And she heard the steel in her own voice as she answered, "I have no intention of leaving, Superintendent."

He watched her across the desk, a police scrutiny that held more than routine attention. Wariness? "Steve tells me," he said, "there's quite a story here."

And a personal involvement, his look added. As big an involvement as revenge? An active, shooting feud?

It's all going into the scales, for or against my innocence or my ruthlessness or whatever else shapes his assessment of what happened here and why. He's come himself, to deliver my dismissal, to make that assessment. Like all police on site, he's his own jury and judge, however the verdict comes out in a court of law.

"A long story, yes," she said, and held his eyes. "I won't take your time repeating it now. But"—suddenly she could hear the berserker in her voice, implacable as Paddy Wild—"you can rest assured, I'll be with this case to the end."

The loaders roared in a little space of indoor quiet. Then he inclined his head a fraction, and said, "There's a CD burner in the incident room."

The scene outside looked more than ever like a science-fiction movie, floodlight glare glinting off pipes and windscreens and the bubble sheen of helicopter cabins, limning car roofs, distant machinery hulks and webs of rotor blade, human figures moving in backlit haste while the loaders roared and shuttled at the illumination's heart. Dorian kept expecting a film camera crew to dolly past. Or a TV crew, she thought woozily, springing up right here by the helicopter ramp. But only a clutch of empty-handed figures materialized, three tall men together like a posse or an arrested man's escort—it's only Lancini, she told herself, as her heart jumped. And someone else, must be the pilot, he's got the flyer's helmet. And Jimmy, between them. At last.

Her next thought was, I feel how he looks. As they drew closer the half-light turned his face bloodless, and his eyes made a cave under his brows. The line of his mouth was invisible, but the droop of head and shoulders said enough. He's exhausted. Past exhausted, he probably isn't even tracking anymore. All those hours without food. The chase. Digging Brodie out. And now the interminable waiting, and that minefield of an interview.

He lifted his head briefly as they reached the ramp, but not even recognition showed. The pilot skipped inside. Lancini nodded to Demetrios, Dorian's escort. Demetrios said, "Ms. Wild?" and nodded her up the ramp.

I won't look back, she thought. I don't want to see any more. Not the loaders, not the other men. Not the stockpile, above all.

The helicopter's main cabin had seats in front of the medical section. The pilot gestured from his cockpit, helmet already on, talking, she thought, to air control. Sit down, the wave said. She fell into a seat, and a moment later Jimmy copied her.

It's probably just as well, she decided, as the rotors fired, that he is almost out to it. Else this might scare him clean out of his wits. His first time in the air, in a chopper, and at night. But anyone could need help with a helicopter seat belt, if I can't offer much else.

The rotors crescendoed into a single roar. The machine trembled, bounced, and lifted, unstable as a dragonfly, she had always thought, and she saw Jimmy's knuckles go white on the seat-belt buckle. Unable to help herself, she touched his arm. The cabin light gave her, just visible, his sidelong look. Then with gingerly care he lowered his head against the seat back, and she knew he had closed his eyes.

Barely ten minutes later they were back on the ground, on what Dorian discovered was the open field of the Blackston Hospital Reserve, stumbling down the ramp to confront one of the rare Blackston cabs. No sign of the media, she realized, too tired to admire the police security. Five minutes later, they were at the Park Street Motel.

A shower, Dorian vowed as she struggled upstairs. I'll call room service, then let God speak and the heavens fall, it won't keep me from the shower. Not even Jimmy's claim for first turn will keep me from that shower.

She dug feebly for the keys. Dropped them jingling on the veranda planks. Cursed aloud, and as she tried to find the lock, light blazed out at her side.

The lamp had come on over the neighboring door. Now the door itself opened. Someone came out and paused at the shadow's edge, and a voice said, "Is that you, Dorian?"

Dorian dropped the key again. She was vaguely aware of

Jimmy, shifting beside her with unwonted clumsiness. Of her own voice, groggy as he sounded, in sheer disbelief.

"Dani?"

In casual clothes Dani still looked immaculate, a buckskin-brown suede jacket over tailored jeans and boots. Colorados, remarked Dorian's skittering brain. What a well-off lawyer chooses to go bush. Her own face, she realized, was probably adding, What in God's name are you doing here?

"I thought," Dani said, "you might want some legal advice."

Dorian's first reaction was pure, blissful relief. Her second was, Oh, God. Not now.

Because now, she thought, all my sins of omission are coming home to roost at once. I'll have to tell her about Jimmy. All about Jimmy. Tonight.

Reflex produced a welcome respite. "How," she heard herself begin thickly, "did you get here—did you know . . . ?"

"When I'm at a barbecue with the Ibisville Area Superintendent, and his beeper goes off, and the call mentions an accident at Ben Morar, and one of our junior partners . . ."

"A barbecue!"

"Right out at Alligator Creek. Even with a siren, it took them thirty minutes to pick him up. He being"—she still sounded perfectly straight-faced—"well above the legal limit himself."

"Oh, heavens!" I'm definitely past it, Dorian registered. Otherwise I wouldn't be giggling and putting my hand over my mouth. "So that's why they took so long."

"Possibly. He was certainly determined to go." A wry ripple crossed even Dani's voice. "So, since police security, not to mention professional etiquette, forbade grilling him on the spot or lurking on the police wavelength, it seemed best to hear the story, and offer some resources, myself."

"Resources. Yes." Relief came uppermost. "I need all the

resources I can get." Don't ask what she's done with her own workload, don't exclaim at an L&C senior partner stuck in Blackston for the start of the working week. She's clearly given this case priority. This *is* her work.

"I . . ." The rest stuck in her throat. She did manage, "Thank you, Dani. Thanks."

And let's hope, she nearly groaned as the high water of gratitude passed, that I'm not going to put myself offside now for good.

Dani's eyes had already shifted. As she looked back from Jimmy's shadow her brows rose millimetrically. "Is this the friend Laura said you'd met?"

Blessings on your head, Laura, Dorian thought. At least I won't be starting completely cold.

"Ah—yes." I'm so sorry, Jimmy, she wanted to say. You're dropping, and so am I. But I have to tell Dani about you. And I have to tell her now.

"I think we'd better go inside," she said.

As the light came on, Dani's eyebrows rose, as rare and eloquent a comment, Dorian thought, as Childers' own. "We look a mess," she said, "but we're okay. Well, sort of. Well, anyhow. Dani, this is—Seamus—Keenighan. Jimmy, this is Danielle Lewis. My senior partner."

He had caught at least some of the nuances. He had already pulled himself upright. Now he inclined his head in something very near a bow and said gravely, "Ma'am."

Dani's reaction was far less legible than Laura's. The pause seemed to go forever. Then Dani turned her eyes back to Dorian and said, "How long since either of you ate?"

Dorian nearly gulped. "I thought, room service—"

"In Blackston, at eight-thirty on a Sunday night? Why don't you and Mr. Keenighan clean up, and I'll see what I can find."

116

The door closed gently. If she means to grill us, Dorian thought, at least she's going to feed us first.

She looked at Jimmy, who was looking at her. Looking literally gray, she thought with fierce compunction, and hurried round the bed. "You shower first," she said. "Can you wash round those dressings? Oh." Her eyes had dropped from the tattered windbreaker to his one pair of heavy, laced boots. "You'll never get those off, let me . . ."

"I can do it, I'm no' useless . . . ah." It had taken a mere touch to sit him down. And when he tried to reach his laces, his caught breath spoke for itself. Dorian swooped, hauling one boot up against her jeans' thigh. "Damn it, let *me.*"

He sank back, catching his weight on both hands. He caught his breath again too and stopped arguing.

She wrestled the knots undone, loosened laces. "You can push them off now." And we can both dodge comments on stinking socks. Lowering the second boot, she looked down at him a moment. Lord, he is wiped out. No wonder, after everything he did out there.

And so much of it for me.

In a surge part concern, part affection, part outright possession, she leant closer and said, "There you are, then." And set a firm hand on his thigh.

He twitched. She whipped the hand off. He snatched it in midair. "I'm sorry," she began hurriedly. Will I ever stop saying that? "I didn't mean—didn't think you'd mind—"

"I dinna mind." He was either exhausted or out of breath. " 'Tis just . . . surprise." His eyes lifted. "An' no' knowin'—no' expectin'—the things ye'll do."

Things no proper Victorian woman would. Like putting your hand on my leg in, sort of, public. Expecting me to strip in front of you. Talking about sex. Actively kissing me.

Their eyes had locked again, as firmly as their entwined

fingers. He still looked gray, but a spark had rekindled in that stare. Acknowledgment. A rueful, half-amused defiance. *I can't predict what you do, it said. It's shocking sometimes, unexpected. But I don't mind, now, being surprised.*

How, Dorian wondered, is there suddenly so much time? *I could stand here another five, ten minutes, with my hand in yours, your eyes holding mine, and not need anything more. Not a closer touch, not a kiss. Not even food. Even a bath.*

His mouth corner had pucked. A slight, weary twitch, but irrepressible. He murmured, "Will I do as I'm told, then?" And she undid her fingers, feeling her own mouth slide toward a smile. "Off with you," she said, trying for equal demureness. "And don't dawdle in that shower."

Dorian came out toweling her own hair just as Dani reappeared. Setting down a parcel that smelt delectably of toast and heated ham, she inspected them, nodded briefly, and put a bottle on the bench as well. The label said, Glenfiddich. Dani said, "This might help."

Well-off lawyers indeed, Dorian thought, trying to remember Glenfiddich's price in ordinary bottleshops. But on the nearer bed, Jimmy's droop into a doze had become dazzled relief.

"A drop o' the creatur," he murmured. "An'," devoutly, "what a creatur." He lurched to his feet. "Ye're a pearl among fossickers, ma'am."

Dani's eyebrow kicked up and Dorian wondered if she should flinch. *I'm too tired,* she decided, foraging for glasses. She said, "We should eat first."

Jimmy was beyond more than a half query about the nature of toasted sandwiches, but after a couple of lethargic bites he wolfed three quarters of the packet. When he finally took a long swig of whiskey and sank back, carefully tendering his right side, Dani said, "Dorian?"

There had been time to find an opening gambit. Dorian said, "I—we—got some evidence." When Dani waited she reached, yet again, for her phone.

She began with the contract and the counterfeit signature pictures. Backtracked over the now familiar incident trail, this time, with a weird relief, omitting nothing. Moved to the video.

When she switched it off, Dani said, "What are the police doing?"

Dorian tried not to gulp. It's Dani. Expect hard practicalities, essentials. Not exclamations, not commentary, not concern. About anyone.

"They—Childers said, they still have to take it as a rescue. They've got volunteers out to shift the rock. Try to find—"

"Do you think he's dead?"

Damn, Dorian thought, as her spine crept. This is more than acuity. This is single-minded focus, with Lewis and Cotton's welfare as its motor. Nothing more.

Jimmy said, "He's dead."

When they both jerked their heads round he said, more starkly, "He'd ha' died, whatever we did. Maybe before the polis came. Even if we'd never—could ye no' hear it? In his breathin'? He said it himself. Too much rock. Nothin' below the waist . . . he knew."

The room was so quiet Dorian thought she could hear her heartbeat. Then, as once before, she heard herself say, more than distant, "*You* knew."

He met her eyes. "When ye said—SES. Polis. I had to— decide. It was—" The sideways jerk of his chin added everything she had thought herself: immoral, illegal, ethically abhorrent. "But . . ."

But I did it. Because you needed it. Not so much the other stuff, Reinschildt, the laptop, even what Brodie planned for George. Because you needed to know about Chris.

Now, she thought, I understand those odd hesitations, after the second fall, in the loading bay. Another thing you really did for me.

Dani spoke across their eyes' entanglement. "You've unearthed a deal of evidence, but you've also left us a very unstable situation. Especially putting a bullet in George. Dorian, what were you thinking of?"

Dorian tried not to wince. That's not just Lewis and Cotton bias, she admonished herself, it's objective legal opinion. Even if I have told her the logic of shooting George. The rest, she knew, could not be spoken. Tell Dani about the berserker, about protecting my own? Reincarnating Paddy Wild?

Jimmy said, "That was my fault."

" 'Twas all my fault," he went on as Dani's eyes turned. "I was the one wanted—pushed to go out there today. I planned gettin' them out o' the office. An' I saw the rifle, an' I gave it to—Miss Wild. An' I said, Shoot him, if he willna stand still."

Even in the half-light, Dani's eyes were blank as ice. "You didn't *do* it," she said.

"Yes, but," Dorian's brain caught up. "We talked to George. We showed him the pictures, the contract, the signatures. He won't press charges. He said Brodie made him do it. He's agreed to say that in court. We recorded that as well. It's on his phone, but I mailed myself a copy, it'll be on my e-mail . . ."

I'm not liable to be charged with worse than trespass, or make scandal for Lewis and Cotton. And that'll be Dani's priority, she found herself adding, with the very first tinge of bitterness.

Ever so slightly, Dani's shoulders did relax. But she said, "That other—interview—is suspect, to put it mildly. Provocation. Leading the witness. Not to mention the circumstances. A halfway competent barrister will shred it in court."

"But the evidence will be there."

She locked eyes with Dani, knowing what both of them saw: a courtroom, the bullfight of opposing barristers, using every tactic from truth and logic to shameless grandstanding. All fought out before a jury who, however evidence is discredited, will remember what it said.

Dani frowned a little. Jimmy dropped his eyes and said heavily, "That was my fault too."

"Jimmy," Dorian began, and he moved a hand whose meaning was patent: let me finish this.

"I dinna know . . . if I can make ye see. But he lost his head, down in the pipes. He'd but to wait. Go back for his 'chopper.' Remember the rifle. But he kept missin' me. An' he couldna get past that. I think"—the note was almost wonder—"it never happened before."

Not with a semiautomatic, Dorian thought in sudden certainty, and a heat scope. Not in Iraqi streets and villages, with how many others round him. He and Sorenson must have moved through that war like the Four Horsemen, destroying, killing, unstoppable. Feeling themselves invincible.

"When ye deal wi' someone that way . . . ye have this—tie— like ye'd never have wi' anyone else." He was suddenly looking beyond them, into a black as well as distant past. I've felt that, his eyes said, before.

"So in the rocks . . . he talked to me. An' *I* knew—I gambled—he might."

His stare came back to Dani, dark and redoubtable as Dorian had felt it herself.

"So I got him in a, a—" he hesitated. Blushed ever so slightly. "What we'd call a slashin' match. Like, like . . . boys, in front o' a wall. An' because I'd beaten him, he was still crazy, an' he boasted o' things he'd ne'er've let out otherwise. Not if ye'd beaten the brains out o' him."

In the hush, Dorian could hear that malevolent, struggling

whisper, see that dust mask of a face.

"I had to lead him, aye." Jimmy's face was drawn to mask-point too. "An' tease him. An' then I let him fetch me, after all. *Street boy.*" His eyes flared. For one searing instant Dorian saw a lost world of foreign tyranny and adolescent rebellion, the rage of a weaponless boy against an army, the guns, the armed ranks, the conqueror's jibes. "I'm no' proud o' it. Any o' it. An' maybe a lawyer could smash it to smithereens. But whatever it comes to, none o' it was Dorian's—Miss Wild's fault."

He stared at Dani and she stared back. Her face was still blank as a judge's. He had tucked his chin down and was looking under his brows in a positive glower. The way he'd look at Dinny, Dorian thought, braving something out. But this isn't Dinny. Her mouth shot open and Dani's hand shift said, Not yet.

She said, "You defend her very nicely. Just how did you get involved?"

Oh, no, Dorian thought. Jimmy, visibly disconcerted, crumbled into an "Uh—ah" and a desperate glance at her. Dani snapped, "Wait, Dorian!" and Dorian shook her head.

"I think I have to explain this part," she said.

Dani paused. Flicked her glance between them. Seeing too much, Dorian felt uncomfortably. Evidently withholding judgment. "Well?" Dani said.

Despite the boost of food and whiskey and a sense of renewed circulation, Dorian's mouth was suddenly dry. "You'll think this is crazy—that I'm going mad—"

Dani gave a thoroughly inelegant snort. "If it's any crazier than Dorian Wild, model junior partner, out in the scrub with some hairy bushranger shooting holes in George Richards' backside, I *will* be surprised."

"Oh . . . !" Dorian reclaimed her balance. Model junior partner? She crossed mental fingers, and plunged.

"The first time I saw him," she said. "Jimmy. I thought he was a ghost."

As the train of incidents escalated she could feel Dani's silence growing more and more effortful. When she reached, "I saw these people dressed for the pageant . . . and there he was. He's been here ever since," Dani produced another definite snort.

"You're right," she said. "Preposterous. Lunatic. Utterly. So this is what you've been hedging over." Dorian felt her jaw drop. "If I hadn't seen—" Her eyes turned to Jimmy in something between outrage and disbelief. "This is—*impossible.*"

"Aye," he said, without heat. "Preposterous, ridiculous, crazy. But—here I am."

Both Dani's eyebrows reached for her hairline. Dorian said hastily, "We didn't tell you or Moira, it was just too crazy, and until this—episode—we didn't have a real reason, until Jimmy and I talked we didn't know what was happening or even if it was connected with Ben Morar, and I never expected anything like this, I couldn't warn you."

Dani's borderline scowl smoothed a little and Dorian felt her neck relax. *She's got a sense of justice after all.*

"No." It came with a delayed but decisive nod. "Just what is the connection, then?"

Dorian tried not to cringe. The most preposterous, irrational parts of all.

"Chris said he thought it must be a, a fold in reality. That our two times—overlapped. Laura thinks it's some sort of, of karma." She looked to see if she should explain, but Dani's long-suffering look said, *No.* "Jimmy," she glanced at him, seeking tacit permission. His face was expressionless, but his eyes said, *Go on.* "Jimmy thought—it might be—Providence."

I don't know if Dani's practicing or Catholic or even Christian. She pushed on with an effort. "So he might have been—

sent here—for a reason. And if there is one—it's to do with Chris's mine. You know Jimmy read the map for me?" Dani nodded. Dorian swallowed. "Well, back in—his Blackston—he was—involved with trouble in a mine. In the same place. And the—the other main player—was my great-great-grandfather."

There was another thoroughly pregnant pause. Then Dani folded her hands on the bench-end and let out a long-suffering sigh.

"Folds in reality. Time travel. Environmental crusaders"— now the tone held definite irony—"trying to right the past." In a gesture far too human for Dani, she rubbed both hands over her eyes. "But you can't tell the cops this. Ever. Even Andy Childers. Lord!"

"I know that. It's been the worst part of this whole mess, trying to figure what to do about Jimmy, what we could say in that first interview—" I'm babbling, Dorian realized. Mostly out of sheer relief. That Dani's not going to wipe the floor with me for sitting on this. That she's seen the biggest problem immediately. She bit her tongue on a yet more ingenuous, Now what'll we do? "Do you think, now, we have enough evidence for a case?"

Dani did not answer. Her eyes were back on Jimmy. After a moment she said, "They interviewed you both, of course. What did you say?"

He twitched, Dorian thought perhaps at the brusqueness. But her own heart lifted. She hasn't just seen the problem, she's going to act on it. She's already thinking practicalities.

"The polis—the polis feller kept sayin', Tell me more about that. I tried not to blether. What happened out there—I mostly said what Dor—Miss Wild—"

"Dorian." Dani allowed herself a hint of impatience. "You're using it anyhow."

Their eyes locked and Dorian thought Jimmy might blush. But he managed a very conscious "Aye. Ma'am."

"So you gave him the précis. And about talking to Brodie? What else?"

"I said what we set up: that I was lookin' for family history in Blackston, an' we met at the pageant, an' found we'd both kin here in the rush." Dani glanced at Dorian with something near respect. "An'—Dorian—asked me to go out there wi' her, me knowin' a bit about mines." He turned his eyes, dark but alert now, to Dorian. "We didna fix this part, but I said, six months out from Erin, aye, an' then, I'd been round the tin-scratchers in the Peninsula, because I'm by way o' bein' a journalist, an' thought mebbe to write a book. About Tyrone folks in the old mines."

Dorian found she actually had the energy to clap her hands. "Brilliant! I never thought how you were supposed to know about mining."

He did not preen. He did look very relieved. "There was other things, I didna—he asked, did I have a license, an' I said, No. I thought, he couldna expect me, in six months out here, to be runnin' a pub?" Dorian tried not to splutter at the look on Dani's face. "So then he said, do ye have y'r passport? I didna know what that was, but 'twas plain I should have it, so I said, No' here. But the birthdate, an' the contact stuff, that was all right."

"I told Jimmy they'd ask that," Dorian glossed to Dani. "I told him to take his age off this year's date. And for contact . . . I said, Use Chris's address."

Dani gave her another long, inscrutable stare. Dorian felt her own cheeks heat without knowing why.

Dani said, perhaps thoughtfully, "No." And looked away.

"Do you have," she asked Jimmy, "anything that could count as ID—as identification—at all?"

"D'ye mean, that I am who I say?"

"We have that," Dorian struck in. "Anne's friend Anthea sent me a picture of him. Outside the *North Queensland Miner's* office, the newspaper, in eighteen eighty-four."

Dani's brows shot up. But Jimmy was groping in his new trousers' pocket, clawing out what Dorian guessed was a wallet, nineteenth century style. "I've a letter," he said, "from Ma. Dated. April, eighteen eighty-six. An' m' old Miner's Right. An' these."

He laid them out on the counter. A much-folded sheet of paper with official watermark and stamp, a handful of coins, and a paper note.

A banknote, Dorian realized. A plain greenbacked banknote, uncannily like the modern British currency. But the monarch's head was very definitely not—

"That's," she heard herself blurt, "Queen Victoria."

"Aye." Jimmy's look said clearly, who else? "Oh." Evidently the Glenfiddich had kick-started his wits too. "Ye'd no' have British notes nowadays. After 'Federation,' an' all. An' . . ." His face shadowed. Too evenly he said, "An' if ye did, 'twouldn't be—"

The same monarch, no.

Dani, Dorian realized, is making the journey I did, watching him realize the mines were gone. Feeling time's distance for herself.

Being Dani, she recovered quickly. "Those are proof you do come from—eighteen eighty-six, is it?" I don't believe, said her brows' cant, I'm saying that. "But it wasn't what I meant." She paused, and Dorian realized she was conducting her own version of twenty twelve for the century-disadvantaged. "When they say license, they mean a driver's license. For a car. To get one, you need a birth certificate. They're both proof that you're a legal citizen. A passport does the same, internationally. It says, your country guarantees your identity. So you can enter other countries as well."

"Ye need one o' them to cross a border?" Jimmy was looking outright appalled. "Just to the colonies, from, from Liverpool, even?—I never had such a thing in m' life!"

Dorian felt her jaw sag. "You've never had a passport? When you emigrated?"

"I signed m'self on the ship's register an' paid the passage. I didna need any more!"

Dani's eyes met Dorian's. They probably, she thought, looked equally appalled.

No passport. No concept of, no need for one. Absolutely no shred of viable documentation for acquiring one. And with his story already in the cops' hands, it's only a matter of time till they ask.

Dorian put her head in her hands and groaned.

Jimmy did not burst out, What is it? There was merely a plummeting pause. When she looked up he was watching her like the bushranger Dani had called him, eyes shuttered, face stonewalled, his very body coiled back into the chair.

An activist, her mind said. An agitator. Somebody used to lawlessness and danger. To being an outlaw. On the run.

Then he said, very quietly, "Might be, I should head for the *Miner*. Now."

Go back, go home. Cut the Gordian knot in the simplest, most brutal way.

It would certainly be the best for him. It would make things a lot simpler for us. So why do I feel as if the bottom just fell out of the world?

Dani must have followed by ESP, Dorian thought. It was a bare half minute before she said, "That won't work."

"You do mean, try to go back? To eighteen eighty-six?" she went on as Jimmy stared. "It's too late. You're on record here. You've been in the thick if not the instigator of this incident at Ben Morar. If you just disappear the police at least will get very suspicious." She glanced briefly at Dorian. "I thought your long-term aims were to resolve this slur on Chris. Stop Pan-Auric, if necessary. By a prosecution, if necessary. How far will all that go, if one of two crucial witnesses for this crucial—incident—disappears?"

"Yes, but—Jimmy. His ID. If we don't have that, what can we do?"

Before Dani could answer, Jimmy had sunk his own head in his hands. "I canna go," he groaned into the countertop. "Bridgie. I canna go."

Dani said, *"What?"* Dorian's own heart fell into her shoes.

"But," she said desperately, "we don't know she's here."

He lifted his head. "If ye've a picture o' me, an' ye're here, an' Paddy Wild must ha' been here—or why d'ye know about the hat? Then she must be too."

Damn. He's still thinking, even now. Dani was looking more exasperated than baffled. Dorian said rapidly, "We think this isn't just time travel, we think, we think, there might actually be two, two alternate histories. Because in his Blackston they have this bushranger called Ned Kelly we don't even know about, and, and, Jimmy's sister died and was buried here—well, maybe here . . . in Blackston, I mean—in, in his time. And if P-A destroy the town, they'll raze the graves."

Dani's eyebrows gave up the fight. She rubbed her brow instead. " 'Two Blackstons,' she said, as if it meant, 'Two Satans.' " No, her posture added, that's enough.

"That at least," she said crisply, "we can handle. Check the old cemetery."

"Oh." God, Dorian wanted to say, I am a fool.

"And if she's not there?" Dani had shot it at Jimmy. He stared almost as blankly, though looking more distraught. "If she isn't there, will you still go?"

Dorian smothered a gulp. It makes sense either way. If he

goes it cuts the knot, if he stays we have a better chance in a prosecution. But that's not what's mattering to me.

"I dinna . . . I canna . . ." He was staring at Dani as if mesmerized. Now he pulled a hand through the cowlick and stood it on end. "How can I stay, even if she is? I havena this 'passport.' I canna get one, I dinna have, I couldna get a birth certificate."

Dani's lashes went down. She said slowly, to the countertop. "A driver's license might do. It's not an international matter yet, after all."

Dorian felt her breath stop. Am I, she thought dizzily, hearing what I think?

Jimmy looked bewildered. "But I'd still need a, a certificate?"

"Yes."

I am hearing what I think. The senior partner in Lewis and Cotton, the Terminator, is actually contemplating illegality. Shady deals, counterfeit ID. And she sounds as if she might know how to do it, as well.

Dorian's head spun slowly round, whether from shock or whiskey or fatigue she was uncertain. Before she recovered, Dani had slid from her seat and scooped up her bag.

"For the moment," she said, precise and ladylike as ever, "we all need a good night's sleep." Her glance turned to the bulk of dressings under Jimmy's old shirt. "Or as good as we can manage. Tomorrow we can expect the police again. And they'll almost certainly have made a statement to the media. Dorian, I'll update Laura and Anne." Dorian had no time to so much as look her gratitude. "I'll see you both at breakfast. Eight o'clock, downstairs."

Her Colorados thumped softly on the floorboards. Then her head came back round the closing door.

"Oh, yes," she said. "Good shot, Dorian."

CHAPTER 6

At seven-thirty the clock radio went off like the tocsin of wrath and ruin, and Dorian tried to tunnel through the bed head before she remembered where she was. She turned over, groaning. Then asked blearily, "Jimmy? Are you awake?"

The lump in the other bed struggled against the pillow over its head. Surfaced, tousled and red-eyed, made to sit up and groaned in such earnest that Dorian nearly dived on him.

" 'Tis all right." He was breathing very lightly, trying not to touch his ribs. "Ahh . . . I'm no' the jimp gossoon I was, rampagin' through hedgerows." He stopped to breathe, so reminiscent of Brodie that Dorian felt her skin chill. "But I'm awake, aye." He scowled at the window. "Fro' m' one decent sleep."

"I'm sorry. I thought it might be bad. Even with painkillers." Hardly a surprise, with creased ribs one side, creased shoulder the other, a third nick in the back of the head. "Ohh, God." She staggered up. "We have to meet Dani in half an hour, while I'm in here can you get dressed?"

"Aye." Then the mumble became a strangled yelp. She spun round. He had his original shirt out at arm's length with a look of pure calamity.

"I canna wear this! No' in public! No' to meet Herself!"

She tried not to explode, then not to crack up. Herself. Dani. Oh, yes. "You'll have to, there's nothing else, the shops won't be open." She reconsidered his face. "Oh, *God.*"

The receptionist, girded for Monday with ash-blonde tips on

her gel-spikes, opined that the paper shop would have opened at six A.M. "They might have souvenir T-shirts." The announcement that Dorian's unheralded male roommate had lost all his clothes left her so unmoved that Dorian hurried out wondering about other people's weekends. She discarded the topic along with Jimmy's protests—"I canna walk round in a miner's sark wi' the Stock Exchange painted on m' chest!"—and herded him into the restaurant only five minutes late.

Dani was already there, perfectly groomed if jacketless, menu propped before her. But when Dorian began apologizing she waved it away. "They've found him," she said.

"It was on the early news," she added, as they both slid mutely into chairs. "Unidentified man's body removed from stockpile at Ben Morar. Presumed accident on site." She paused. "No mention of George."

"No?" The ignominious relief passed—I won't have to defend myself just yet to the rest of the world, as well as Demetrios—and Dorian sat up. "Why wouldn't they—?"

"Andy Childers may want to interview him first. Or"—Dani sounded more than usually expressionless—"he may have other fish to fry."

The waitress orbited up. When Dani ordered fruit, cereal and toast, Jimmy darted a piteous glance at Dorian. Oh, she thought, he's used to a big workingman's breakfast. "You need a decent meal," she said, and he plunged thankfully into the arcana of mixed grills and hash browns. As the waitress left, Dorian said, "Other fish being us?"

Dani allowed herself a millimeter of frown. "You've given him a fine big box of tricks to open. He'll want time before he sees you again. More likely he's waiting on forensic reports. Sorting evidence. And, of course, considering Pan-Auric."

Dorian's heart went fast. "Deciding if there really is a case? A criminal case?"

The waitress bore down with orange juice. When she had gone, Dani said, "On the current evidence, there might be a case against Brodie. Assault with a weapon, intent to defraud. Possession of illegal weapons. Homicide, possibly." Her lashes flicked. "Over Chris. But that's the worst on the criminal side. And though there's a sort of confession, the perpetrator's dead." She picked up her glass, drank, set it down. "Even if Pan-Auric could be proved to have commissioned all that, it doesn't come to much more than discreditable publicity about personnel— now defunct."

"But!"

Dorian caught herself and sank back in her chair. It's the truth. The hard truth. Brodie's gone. And he cleared Reinschildt, sort of. The cops might not decide to prosecute. Even if they do, and succeed, it won't be more than a pinprick to the P-A elephant hide.

All that—terror—all that blood, and pain, and maybe now, the need for more and more deception. That death. For nothing. After all.

In a very small voice she said, "So we wasted our time."

The waitress was back with Dani's fruit. Dani eyed the plateful of melon balls and blatantly canned pineapple. With consummate dismissal, she said instead, "If it did reach court, as I said, a good barrister would shred that interview."

"Then . . . Jimmy can go." It was like a tent collapsing on her. "We don't need him. And I'll have to put together an environmental suit." She wondered how David would have felt if his sling broke at the first pull. The projected effort, the expenditure of time and spirit rose before her like a sheer-sided hill. An environmental lawsuit. Against P-A.

Dani was watching her, closely, gray eyes dispassionate but searching as a steel probe. "You'll try to stop the mine?"

"Of course I will, I have to, Chris intended to, he blew his stack at George and Reinschildt over it, he resigned over it, he—he died over it." She had to stop as the tears clogged in her throat. "I have to go on with that! If I didn't, I couldn't face myself."

Or Jimmy, she had time to think.

Dani was still watching her, unmoved as a Sphinx, yet with a palpable intensity. Then she shot at Jimmy, "Will you check the cemetery today?"

He twitched. There was a teetering pause. Then he said, "I've no need. I'll no' be goin'."

Dani's brows lifted. He held her stare.

"Whether or no Bridgie's here," he said, "I am. And if ye're right—if this that we've turned up willna stop y'r 'megacorp'— I'll no' be able to leave. Not till I finish—the job."

Providence's task, Dorian thought with another lump in her throat. Religious belief, sheer speculation, crazy as every other reason. And I could float up in the air with relief.

Dani considered him a moment longer. Then she turned back to Dorian.

"If you hadn't gone out yesterday," she said, "we'd now be facing a fait accompli. The contract altered. Brodie still at large. No evidence about anything he did, and nothing to implicate George. As it is . . . you've checkmated George. Brodie's eliminated." Dorian tried not to let her backbone chill. "What you found mightn't win a court case. But it could make Pan-Auric—very uncomfortable."

Jimmy let the waitress set his plate down unnoticed. Dorian herself ignored her toast. Something seemed to have ignited, like an oil-fed fire, under her breastbone. A jet of revived hope.

"You mean, we tell them what we've got and threaten a case? Then offer to settle out of court?"

"Something like that." Dani set aside her fruit. "If it's properly done, Pan-Auric should do the offering." She held

Dorian's stare. "You could reasonably ask a guarantee of personal immunity, for you and anyone connected with the— incidents. At the very least, that Pan-Auric exonerate Chris. A public announcement. You'll probably have to sacrifice the truth of the accident. You might ask for divulgence of Brodie's doings this time around."

"But I mightn't get it?"

"It's a bargain point."

A cede-able demand, Dorian thought. The sort you load on top when you haggle, to be sure of what you really want.

What I really want . . .

Chris cleared. Jimmy safe. My job again. All this over with.

And the mine? Blackston, Chris's crusade. Jimmy's— whatever it is that he's done. Bridget's grave?

"Do you think," it seemed to echo in her ears, "it would stop the mine?"

She knew the answer by the time Dani's passionless gray eyes considered her. Before she reached for her cereal and said evenly, "It might."

Jimmy had still not started to eat. Through the last exchanges he had been quite still, Dorian realized. The quiet, not of fear, but alertness, concentration. A hunter, rather than prey.

Now he said abruptly, "But ye think not."

"For the moment," Dani answered at length, "this is all just estimate. We don't know what else the police have already found. For example, on Brodie's phone."

"Yes!" Dorian exclaimed, recalled to minutiae. "He'd have that on him. And there's the bag in the office. And George."

"Who might well let out more about Pan-Auric than Brodie's plans," Dani agreed. As she glanced at Dorian the steel almost softened. "It's not a foregone conclusion yet. Either way."

"Oh." It took a moment to absorb that. "Then—what do we do now?"

Dani spooned up cereal. "I've updated Laura and Anne," she said. "I've told them both to take leave, and asked Laura to go out to Anne's place. I don't want her alone in that unit, and I don't want either of them in a public area. At least for the next couple of days. I'll drive you out to get your car, Dorian, but then I think you should both go to ground too. You might consider getting another room, or rooms, now the motel's emptied. It'll help stall the media. The police will find you when they're ready."

Get the car back, Dorian thought gratefully, and time for Jimmy to rest, and on the way through town I can find him some clothes. Though it all seems a bit excessive. "Anne and Laura?" she hazarded. "Surely the media won't go after them?"

"Perhaps not," Dani said, "but what about Brodie's associate?"

A bucket of ice landed in Dorian's stomach. She heard herself almost whisper, "Sorenson?"

Brodie's crony. The one who burgled our flats. Who knocked out the security man and broke in at L&C, while we were having dinner, Saturday night.

"I forgot him," Dorian gulped. "I just never thought—!"

"You've had," Dani murmured, straight-faced, "other things to think about."

"He's unlocated, yes." While Dorian spluttered, Dani went on. "We assume he's been in close contact with Brodie. He has no scruples about lawbreaking. If he's like Brodie, he has none about violence. He has the only loose copy of the model and contract. He may already have figured what happened to Brodie. And we don't know his connection. Associate, employee, friend? He's a wild card. He could do anything."

Dorian's mind replayed the *spannggg* of bullets on metal, and her spine shrank. "You think he might . . . come after us?"

"With you, that's reasonably unlikely. You're in Blackston, in the police limelight."

"Anne, then. Laura. We should get them protection!"

"The police won't have the resources, and I don't want to draw attention. Maybe give him ideas." She's thought this all out, Dorian realized. It's not just a stopgap measure, it's a calculated balance of risks. "Nothing might happen. But some precautions won't hurt."

The toast dried in Dorian's mouth. The restaurant noise seemed to wash in around them. Then Jimmy spoke.

"Ma'am? Could ye get me a gun?"

"A pistol'd do." They had both spun round, but he did not take his eyes from Dani. "If this boyo comes huntin', I wouldna be sat like another duck on a fair-shy—this time, I'd as soon start square."

Dorian shut her mouth on her first cry of, More guns, it's too risky, no. Damn it, she thought, will you leave him with nothing *again?* Sorenson might come after us, and if he does he *will* have a gun, he'll go for Jimmy first, and as surely Jimmy'll try to protect you.

"There's a gunsmith in Landers street," she said. "I could get something. Oh—but the license, and the permits, all the red tape. We'd never do it in time."

Jimmy's shoulders twitched. But he kept his eyes on Dani.

Dani, Dorian decided, was wearing what her father would call a very old-fashioned look. Seconds ticked by. Then she said, "Can you use a gun?"

"Aye."

He's trying, Dorian realized, to accommodate the twenty-first century. Not to roll his eyes.

"I carried a Colt twelve months in the bush, ma'am. An' a Winchester. There's no polis for a fossicker, if ye meet blacks, or a rough claim-jump. Or," the tone flexed, now definite irony, "a bushranger."

There's for your crack about his beard, Dani. Dorian tried to suppress a grin. "He figured out George's rifle," she said.

Dani added unknown pros and cons while Dorian worked to sit still. At least let us get out of this restaurant, she thought. Then Dani pushed her plate aside and said, "Finish your breakfast. I think we'll discuss that upstairs."

When they filed onto the veranda Dani headed straight for her own door, not bothering to add, Follow me. Trying not to gawk, Dorian thought, I've been to her house for firm dinners, a few parties, but really, this is the first time I've seen Dani at home.

The room was scrupulously tidy, apart from the unmade bed. A laptop on the counter, a squared heap of files, a carry-on-size bag on the suitcase stand. The suede jacket tucked in the wardrobe space, everything else closeted behind the bathroom door. Dani flicked the light on, leaving the outer curtains drawn, and opened her laptop carrier.

"I saw Gavin," she said, "before I came up. He has a lump on his head and he's extremely mortified. About the L&C break-in," she added to Jimmy, while Dorian realized she herself was expected to identify "Gavin" as the night security man. "He's also had to take four days' leave for work insurance. So he insisted on lending me this."

The stock gleamed as blackly as Brodie's semiautomatic, though the holster masked the rest. Dorian gulped and then tried not to whoop aloud. Damn it, she's equipped for everything!

Jimmy unbuttoned the holster. Slid the pistol out. Glanced round, pointed it into the corner adjoining their own room, and began to explore.

"Aye," he said, as they watched his hands, deft, assured, if yet unfamiliar with the exact model. " 'Tis smaller than a Colt, but the same system." He drew in a long sigh, controlled a wince, and reached for the holster. With a level look under his brows, he added, "Ye're more than a pearl among fossickers, ma'am."

This time Dani twitched both eyebrows down. "I can trust you not to use it, except in extreme emergency? You can't wear it openly, you're not accredited security. And if you go out with it hidden, you're carrying a concealed firearm."

"So I'll ward it like a miser, aye." He folded the belt rapidly round the holster, gave his T-shirt one disgusted look and turned to Dorian. "In y'r bag, d'ye mind, for now?" He turned back to Dani. "Now, ma'am. As soon as ye're ready to leave."

Protests and pleas that he rest had no effect at all. His sole response was an eye-corner glance at Dorian, and a flinty, "Ye said ye hired me. As a bodyguard. Fine use I'll be, squatted here feelin' m' sore spots while the pair o' ye's stravagin' round the bush alone."

"We won't be alone if we're with each other!" Dorian was still fuming when Dani shrugged minutely, took her jacket, and said, in a tone that added, On your head be it: "Let's go."

This time the Ben Morar road had been thoroughly trafficked. It did not need Jimmy's backseat comments for Dorian to identify airborne dust still smudging skylines ahead of them, or Dani's cautious driving to recall the imminent media. She was still concocting a reason for their own presence when Jimmy leant forward and said, "Pull up, ma'am. 'Tis just here."

Dorian finally identified her tire marks on the verge. Beyond the branches, with a surge of relief, she saw her car, leaf-dotted but otherwise untouched. Then Jimmy's hand shut on her arm.

"Bide a moment," he said curtly, and began scanning the ground.

When all else seemed undisturbed, he reluctantly admitted he would not be able to tell if, "y'r brake things are jiggered," and let her work out onto the road. Dani had leant from her own window for a final exchange when an engine roared behind them and another car topped the ridge in a cloud of dust.

Damn, damn, damn, Dorian thought, jumping out to grab Jimmy before he went into full gunslinger mode, we didn't hear it with our engines on. Dani was already maneuvering to the verge. Dorian stepped hastily against her car, pulling Jimmy's arm. He eased out of the half crouch, but his hand stayed at his hip and he wanted to step in front of her. Just go by, she thought, squinting in the dust, don't be anyone inquisitive, media, or cops, or—

But the dusty four-wheel drive had already stopped, and the driver was leaning out to call, "Dorian? Miss Wild!"

"Tom." Drat him, is he trailing me round Blackston? "What are you doing here?"

"The whole town's talking, supposed to be a big accident out here, somebody killed, then they called for loader drivers, it was in all the pubs last night. I just got back from Ibisville. Tried to phone George—Mr. Richards. His cell phone's off, I thought I should come out . . . but there's a cop on the gate and crime tape everywhere and—" His wits caught up with his nerves. "What are *you* doing here?"

"I, ah, we had business, but we couldn't get in either." She tried to step in front of Jimmy, but it was too late. Ralston's eyes had changed direction. Then his mouth made a small, startled *uh*.

"What happened to *him?*" His eyes went wide too. "They said there was shooting. Dorian, what the hell—"

"There was shooting, yes." I might as well admit it, with blood round every rent in that jacket, and he's already guessed that's what it is. "I, uh, can't say any more, it's all under police wraps." What police injunctions ever stopped a witness shooting off his mouth? "Tom, we have to go—"

139

"Wait!" He was out of the car with a bound. "What happened, you have to tell me, is it the mine? Did they find something—are they investigating—what's going *on?*"

She heard it then. More than employee anxiety, more than bystander's curiosity. As she stared at him the rainbow of response, reaction, an attempt to reclaim casualness flashed across his features like a switched-on sign.

"Uh—at least, you can't tell me, I may as well—"

"Wait!" Like a lethal sheepdog, Jimmy had already answered her tone. He was sidling to get behind Ralston, between him and his car. "What were you expecting them to find?"

It was a bow drawn by sheer intuition. The jerk of his hands said the shot had hit the gold.

"Come on, Tom." He tried to back up and she stepped after him, Stupid, I'm being reckless, but he's only a little fish, he'd probably never even dare swing at me, and he knows *something*. I can tell.

"Is it the shutdown?" Her own wits came up to speed. "Some dirty trick P-A's pulling with the mine? Saving wages, redundancy payments, not putting people right off?" His shocked look became indignation and then a sort of relief. No, not that. "The new mine, then?"

Compensation. George said, if news of the new mine gets out the compensation claims'll go up. But if the new mine's kept quiet, and the old one's not shut down, P-A can get their whole scheme set up without anyone smelling a rat, either over why Ben Morar closed, or why this big company's still poking around.

"They've suspended to keep the punters quiet," she said. Ralston gaped. "While they set up the new mine." He still looked lost. Not that either. But there's something he's twitchy over, something cops, a criminal investigation might find. Something that has to directly involve *him*.

The yield figures. Checked each week by the geologist. Chris's long-term bane. 'Ralston's cocked up the yield figures again.'—*The yield figures, I couldn't,* George said, in his home office, and suddenly cut it off. I thought he meant, he couldn't hide the falloff anymore.

But what if he was already hiding it?

No, she thought, feeling her own eyes pop, he couldn't fudge yield figures, monthly averages, annual returns, right up to a stockholders' meeting, auditors, he couldn't—while a small cynical voice retorted, CEO and chairman, a small local company, look at the other shonky practices, the first-aid kit, the tailings dam.

And once Chris was gone . . .

Ralston might have come face on with a witch. She considered him with less contempt than pity, thinking, Just a small fish, yes. George probably put it on him to rejink the figures after Chris saw them, *that's* why Chris was always having trouble, he'd do them, Ralston would jigger them, then Chris'd come back. Her throat shut on an impossible bubble of mirth. So then Ralston would have to redo them, maybe even get them back from George.

Until Chris was gone.

Ralston retreated almost into Jimmy's arms and recoiled. No, she thought, trying to set her face back to innocuous. George was shocked when he heard about Brodie's holdup. George can't have been in on Chris's car. And if George wasn't, this pip-squeak wasn't either.

Was he?

"Tom." To herself she sounded quite gentle, but Ralston twitched as he stood. "Did you know Brodie at all?"

"Who?" Nobody could act that confused. "Who's Brodie? What . . . ?"

"With Pan-Auric." She dropped each word like acid in a test

tube, watching every shift of his eyes.

"Oh. You mean the one Chris used to call the goon? The VP's whatever-he-was?" He realized he had spoken Chris's name and consternation came and went. "I don't think I ever talked to him. Why are you—"

No, ruled the berserker, assaying every inflection. *Of that, at least, he's innocent.*

Ralston's stance eased a fraction. Behind him, Jimmy's hand had eased open. *I really have to stop this Deadly Dora act,* she thought. *If I try it on someone like Childers he'll jail me on the spot.*

"Okay," she said. "I just wondered. Tell me, did George think of faking the yield figures, or did you come up with that yourself?"

Almost better, she thought, *than a bomb.* Ralston had squawked like a stepped-on frog, gone from brown to yellow to red, then begun gargling half words in his throat. *No,* she wanted to say, *I'm not a witch. Or a clairvoyant, though just lately I seem to be pulling far too many queens out of my sleeve. Terror,* she decided sardonically. *A wonderful concentrator for the thoughts.*

"Look, it's not my business. I have no interest in what happens to Ben Morar, except—" *except getting justice for Chris. But damn letting him right off the hook.*

"I'm not recording this, I won't use it against you. I just want to know."

He had gone halfway to yellow again. He eyed her with something like Jimmy's fascinated stare, as at an exotic snake. Then he pulled at his hat brim, and made up his mind.

"George—Mr. Richards said—have to keep the yields looking viable. Else it'd bankrupt the company. It's local. All local people. I know a few." *He would,* she thought, feeling sick. *The same story George tried on me.* "Just temporary, he said.

Chris'll find another lode, somewhere, with or without that model, it'll be okay in the long run. I didn't think . . ."

It would ever be found out. Just disappear into the general George-fudge. I should have left that weasel to Brodie after all.

But this damage would still have been done, too.

"Okay," she said. "I said, this isn't my affair. But for now— yes, there was an accident out here. And shooting. George is in hospital, that's why he's not answering his phone. I doubt the cops are looking at anything to do with you." Though a financial investigation could be another matter. "For the moment, I'd, I'd just go home. And"—illegal, wicked, I am learning so many bad habits over this—"think about resigning. Getting another job."

She stepped back. They both read her body language. Ralston's shoulders slid down in relief, and behind him Jimmy sidestepped like a ghost so Ralston could back away, stammering, "Sure, sure, if it's not, not urgent"—he gave her a thoroughly white-eyed look—"I'll, uh, see you around."

He disappeared like a rabbit down a hole. The four-wheel drive's engine coughed, turned over. It shot forward with a roar.

Jimmy turned a slitted eye back to Dorian. Then his mouth corner pucked. Just as Dani, still leaning out her car window, remarked conversationally, "Is that your usual style of witness interview?"

"Uh—oh! No, no, sorry." She swallowed. "I just thought, he might have known something. About Chris."

In a moment, still bland, Dani said, "I'm glad to hear that was an exception." She added, "Now, if you two start back . . ."

Dorian stopped in mid-step. "But you're coming? Where are you going?"

"I think I'll try the mine." Dani's stare was minutely overconscious. "Andy Childers is probably still there."

"Oh. You're going to ask what's happened? Get an update?"

He would see a senior partner, Dorian thought, when she herself would be sidelined as an expense of time. "That's, that's very, um, kind."

More like shrewd, she thought, and a further preemptive defense of Lewis and Cotton. But Dani was looking more conscious than ever. "Ah. Yes," she said. And put her car in gear, then reversed past them with a firmness more revealing than her face.

They were five kilometers down the road before remote and nearer pasts dovetailed. Then Dorian slapped the wheel and exclaimed, *"Oh!"* And Jimmy nearly clipped his head on the roof.

"Oh, *what?*" he spluttered.

"Dani. She said, 'At a barbecue with the Ibisville Area Superintendent.' She didn't say what sort of *With!*"

"Eh?"

"They weren't just at the same barbecue, she went there with him. They're an item! They're—oh, just wait till I tell Laura this!"

"What d'ye mean, an item?" Then he too extrapolated. "Ye mean, they're—they're—walkin' out?" His own voice rose. "Herself an' the head polis-man?"

"Yes! Heaven knows how long it's been going or who started it." Or what Dani's doing with a police officer, but what do I know about her taste in men? Except that it doesn't run to George. "But I bet that's it."

He considered. Then his mouth twitched. "Do y'r lawyers consort with the polis, here?"

"Not usually. But Dani makes her own rules."

"Aye." I can believe that, the tone added. A half smile flickered. "An' so do ye, mo cailín sidhe."

"What?"

"Did ye just make another o' them—guesses—back there? Like at the office wi' Brodie? Or did ye mean to scare that poor gossoon out o' his wits?"

"What?" She forgot the Gaelic or whatever it had been. "About the yield figures?" She felt her hands tauten on the wheel. "I suppose, it was a guess. But it was pretty obvious. Who'd drive out to check rumors of an accident at some place where he's already half laid off, if he didn't have a personal stake in it? He's a geologist. Yield figures are his business. He wouldn't be in on the forgery, he's too minor. And he was away, anyhow."

"An'," he said softly, when she stopped, feeling her teeth set, "he didna know anything about Chris an' Brodie. Ye made sure o' that."

"Yes. I—suppose I did."

The berserker, she thought. Or Paddy Wild, or whatever this force is that's suddenly surfaced, that will switch on, it seems, without my intent. That will do whatever it deems necessary, to protect what matters to me.

Beside her Jimmy slid the gun out from under his windcheater. I wish you wouldn't carry that stuck in your belt like a pirate, she thought, before logic retorted, Where else can he put it? Watching him check the magazine and safety catch, remembering the way he had moved round Ralston, she thought, something's changing in you too. Or resurfacing. The Land Leaguer, the wild boy in the hedgerows, running from the troops. Maybe doing more than run.

They both jumped as on the dash Dorian's phone lit up. She punched *Answer*. The holoscreen came up and Demetrios said mildly, "Ms. Wild? Could you call at the Blackston police station? We have a few more questions for you."

The Blackston station was on Landers Street, an old building that retained its high-peaked roof and ornamented brick facade, though the interior was all modernized. The desk sergeant pointed her to the first right-hand door off the ground-level veranda. And Jimmy subsided dourly into a reception-area chair.

He should go and get clothes, like I wanted, she fumed, *I could give him more money. At the very least he could rest. I don't need a watchdog in the cops' laps. But I might as well try shifting another railway sleeper as managing* him.

It was an office rather than a dedicated interview room, with a piled desk and notice-papered walls. Before she had time to examine anything Demetrios came in.

"Ms. Wild," he said, setting up a genuine recorder this time, dictating names and dates and place. He did not bother with amenities such as How are you? Instead he said, "The prosecutors have decided not to charge you. Over the gunshot wound."

After a winded moment, Dorian managed, "Oh."

"Given the—ah—circumstances, Andy—the Superintendent was already in two minds about it. Then we interviewed Mr. Richards this morning. And about the leg wound, he says, and says he'll repeat in court, it was an accident."

Despite my own admission making that a blatant lie. Trust the weasel, she thought, over her own relief, *to remember his vantage. If he lets me off, I owe him. Silence to Beryl and Connie about what he tried. Protection, maybe, against Pan-Auric. A definite legal debt against the consequences of that attempted forgery, and all his other shady goings-on.*

She said, "I see."

Demetrios gave her a level look across the paper piles. She could not tell if it held vexation or sympathy. *But let's not,* she thought, *let him quite control the information flow.*

"The bag. Brodie's bag. Did you get a bomb person?"

He nodded once. "The bag's been examined. It contained a number of, ah, unlicensed weapons." He considered her face, and plainly chose to go on. His own generosity, she wondered? Or that I'm a lawyer? Dani's influence? Something more devious? "They included a knuckle-duster. A silencer. Two electric antipersonnel devices." Stun guns? she thought, trying to translate the officialese. "And, ah, a timer with what seems to be an incendiary."

George's car. No chance at the steering this time, as he must have had with Chris's car. But an incendiary, in the backseat or under the bonnet. To explode, down the road some distance, or maybe just set fire . . .

She said, "Could it destroy a car?" And Demetrios gave her an almost Childers-level nod.

"The bomb guy—expert—thinks that's what it was for."

"Brodie said he'd fix George. Mr. Richards. On that, um, interview we recorded." No harm in reminding them, she thought, and earned another nod. Maybe that means I'm still on tolerance, so I can ask something more.

"The gun. Brodie's pistol. Was that—did that have anything—"

"Ballistics have collected a couple of bullets and spent shells. The gun hasn't turned up yet."

So we aren't out of the woods. It's not cast-iron solid that all the shots outside were fired from the same gun, and that it was in Brodie's hand. But they're still looking. A plus.

I can't ask about Brodie. How they found him, how he was. I don't want to hear. But one thing I do need to know. "Did they find his phone?"

He was too well-disciplined to show interest, but he answered at once, "He had a cell phone on him, and another in the helicopter."

"And have you . . ."

"There was a destructive safety device on the phone in his pocket. It had recorded calls, but it also had a password. When our phone expert bypassed that, the recordings erased."

Dorian tried not to curse aloud. What might he have had on there, calls to George, to Sorenson, almost certainly to Reinschildt—maybe something more specific than, *Fix it*—we could have nailed P-A maybe, or at least Reinschildt himself. She let her hopeful expression ask, Anything else? And his almost immediate response told her this was what they wanted to know.

"We did salvage the Address Directory. The Superintendent wanted to ask if you'd recognize any names. And what you know about them."

She sat back a little on the worn wooden chair. Blackston police station was almost as close-fisted as Ben Morar with office furnishings. "You have them there." No need to make it a question, she thought. He nodded, unearthed a piece of paper, and began to read.

The list was Christian names, almost all male. He could have used a surname occasionally, Dorian grumbled, as Dan and Harry and Gino and Jake tumbled past her, Cody, Al, Kurt, Troy—

"That's Sorenson!" Demetrios stopped short. "The guy Laura was seeing, the one we think did the break-in at the office—and burgled my flat!"

Demetrios had snapped alert. He scribbled on the paper. I can extrapolate, she thought, what he probably won't admit.

"You can locate him, can't you, from the position of his phone?" He gave her a police poker face, then must have remembered she was a lawyer, and conceded a nod. "Well, alert the Superintendent, or do that yourself. Because this guy . . . Dani—my senior partner's concerned about him."

She condensed Dani's points and precautions. By the end Demetrios' brows were down and he was making rapid notes. Then he said, "Do you have your friend's address?" He noted that too.

"Good moves," he observed. "Shifting rooms up here wouldn't hurt, either. Notify us where." He produced a card. "This is my cell phone. As soon as you're settled, call."

Dorian took it, feeling her mouth begin to dry. *He's taking it seriously.* She bit her tongue on, *What else did you want to ask?* In a moment he said, "You don't recognize any more?"

He finished the list, while she thought with exasperation, *Reinschildt's probably on there somewhere, if I just knew his first name . . . but I bet George does.* "You could try them on Mr. Richards," she said.

He nodded again. *They already thought of that,* she decided, and bit her tongue afresh. *If there's anything else he wants to know, he'll have to ask.*

He looked up from his notes. "It'll be a day or two till we're finished at the accident site. We'd like you and Mr. Keenighan to stay until then." *No extras like, Is this a problem?* He added interview details and switched off the recorder. "Thank you, Ms. Wild. We'll be in touch."

I bet you will, she riposted silently, heading for the door with a rising sense of relief. *Another time in and out of the lion's den, and no tricky questions yet. But I had ID on me at Ben Morar.* Her stomach squirmed. *How long before they start to tie up loose ends, and want Jimmy's confirmed?*

Check with Dani, she decided, *when I report again. I wonder if I'll interrupt a tête-à-tête at Ben Morar? Meanwhile, we should shift rooms at the Park. And, with a lightening sense of diversion, I can get Jimmy more clothes.*

By the time she talked him into a denim jacket, two pairs of jeans and some T-shirts—"look, if you don't wear what everybody wears traveling nowadays, the cops'll smell a rat"— argued him into accepting more cash to pay for them—"I've hired you, remember?"—and suffered not merely baleful comments on fitting rooms—"I canna lift an arm wi'out hittin' somethin', an' I'm sore as a bullocky's dog"—but protests at the need for more shoes, more underclothes, and a rucksack to carry it all—"I'm no' settin' up for a gambler wi' valet an' trunk!"—it was almost two o'clock. They fell into the Blackston version of a lunch bar, then headed for the motel.

With the race weekend past, there were rooms to spare. Dorian weighed the advantage of being upstairs against proximity to room twenty, and was about to say, "Fourteen and fifteen, are they cleaned yet?" when Jimmy's hand closed on her arm.

"What is it?" He had drawn her along the hall. His other arm was full of packages but he looked at once harassed and forbiddingly dour. "Did you see something?" Sorenson? She glanced hurriedly around.

"No' that, no." The harassment deepened. " 'Tis only—" He wavered, balked, and lunged. "Were ye askin' for one room—or two?"

"I thought two, I thought you'd want—" You made such a fuss about sharing before, surely you want to avoid it now?

"Aye, an' I would want. But I canna."

"What?"

He had started to blush. The red almost reached his ears. "Ye've hired me. Ye've made a fair song about it. An'—I've taken y'r hire. But if this other bla'guard comes callin', I'm as much use as ribbons on a windlass, stuck in a different room."

Dorian stared. The stone wall became an outright glower.

"I know, 'twill fair blast y'r reputation, however ye count that here. An' I'd ne'er say—I'd ne'er *think* o' sayin' such a thing if it wasna—if I wasna—if I didna have to keep ye safe!"

It ended on something near exasperation with a rising volume he could not quite suppress. Dorian felt her shoulders jerk as if someone had drawn a bead on them, could almost feel the receptionist turning their way.

"Okay, okay, okay." Not the time to say it'll hardly raise an eyebrow, let alone get into holts about my "reputation," and whether I give a damn for whatever that is. "Just let me tell the receptionist."

As soon as fourteen's door shut behind them Dorian unearthed her phone. Laura, she was thinking, Anne, I have to update them, and tell them about Dani and Childers, heavens! No, I should call the cops first. Or Dani, she's still not back—okay, the cops first.

Demetrios answered immediately. He took down the room number, but when she said, "I'll pass it on to my friends," he broke in, "Ms. Wild, I wouldn't do that."

"Isn't this Sorenson the one you think hacked your friend's phone?" he added. "It might be better"—he held her startled look—"not to contact them. Unless it's absolutely necessary."

Laura's cell phone, she remembered. Her organizer. Which must have had all our numbers, and our addresses, and . . . "Oh, my god, he's probably got Anne's address!"

She explained. Demetrios' own face sharpened. He said crisply, "I'll pass that on. In the meantime, don't call them—"

"But they should be warned!"

"We'll do that if necessary. Best you keep communications minimum. For all of you."

Because, her own skipping brain filled in, Sorenson might bug Anne's phone, if he can't get through Laura's firm phone, and he could have the same tech as the cops. And if by some chance he doesn't have her address, but he gets a location for either her or me . . .

Feeling far too breathless, she managed, "Please let me know as soon as it's safe." He nodded, looking officially blank, and the screen cut out.

"They'll be okay. This might all be just precautions. We don't know if Brodie means—meant—more to Sorenson than a hole in the ground. He mightn't have Anne's address. And he mightn't even think about any sort of—When he figures what's happened, he might just cut and run. Or slide back to his job. Anyhow, the cops'll keep an eye on them. They'll be okay. It's just a matter of waiting . . . where the hell is Dani?"

Jimmy had maneuvered a bed to face the door, and stretched out, shoulders gingerly settled on a heap of pillows against the wall. In new jeans and a gray-and-black Billabong overshirt, with a set of budget trainers crossed on the luckily plum-colored quilt, he was an anomalous blend of past and present. Except for the holster bulking ominously under the ample shirt front. And his hands, yet again deftly, delicately checking, nursing, dandling the gun.

The clothes say, average nerd. The hands, the eyes say, trouble. Danger. Not just criminal, but political, activist. Organized, undercover activist.

IRA.

She shoved the thought away stillborn. As she patrolled past him, he said, "Why d'ye no' 'call' her, then?"

"I could, uh, interrupt something." And not just a romantic interlude. "She must know we're back by now. If she's still at Ben Morar, the cops'll know where we are. Whatever she's doing, if she wants me to know, *she'd* call."

He watched her circle the room. As she came past again he said, very softly, "Would ye call the polis?"

"Oh. You mean, ask them where she is?" She felt a weird mixture of anxiety and relief. He knows enough to suggest it. But if I do? "Um. If she's okay, she'd scarify me. Junior L&C partner has ghost-kittens, senior partner gets tracked down by cops? Maybe out with their boss man, having a private lunch?"

Their eyes met. That dark stare was not quite the stone wall. It was too attentive, too alive to feelings as well as thoughts. He did not have to say aloud, And if she's not all right?

Dorian turned on her heel and went to the hotel phone.

"Your senior partner?" Demetrios looked a little taken aback. "I'll check with Ben Morar." *Click.* The holoscreen went to an AusTel logo. He could, she thought, have said, "I'll put you on hold."

Demetrios reappeared. "Ms. Lewis was at the mine from ten A.M. till midday. The Superintendent says she used our secure phones to confer with Lewis and Cotton." His official look went poker-faced. "Then they had lunch." Dorian restrained her own expression. "She's now back in Blackston. She called at one-thirty P.M. Consulting archives, the Superintendent thinks."

Dorian managed to press *Off* in good order, before she forgot to be sheepish and lost control of the laugh as well. " 'They had lunch'! How can she be so barefaced . . . ! And archives? What archives? What on earth can she want with archives here?"

"Does the *Miner* have them?" Jimmy said.

"Yes, but—oh." Is she looking for that picture of him? "But she believed us! She—"

"But she's no' in trouble." On the bedside table, the phone was close enough for him to reach her as she stood. His hand was big and warm, closing on her wrist. "She'll have her reasons. We'll hear them in good time. Be easy." The downward draw on her wrist was slight but insistent. "Take a pull y'self."

"Do *what?*"

"Take a pull. Stop. Bide a step. D'ye no' say that?" He looked resigned. Then he let her wrist go. With an odd sense of loss, she plumped down on her bed.

"You mean, rest?" I don't want to rest, she wanted to say. I want the cops to wind up their affairs and us to get out of here. Get it over. Know we can be—all of us can be—safe.

"God, how can you take this so quietly? You've got to be wiped out still—I know you're sore. How can you just sit there, and, and play with that gun and—"

And wait, as if it was all normal, just wait on the chance that somebody with another gun's going to come through that door?

He was looking sidelong at her, shifting his eyes only, that echo of Michael the Fenian in his own parlor. "The gun," he said in a moment, carefully casual, "makes that easier."

"You have—" She stopped. This is stupid. I don't need to know this. But her mouth had gone on already. "You have done this before."

"Aye."

The quiet spoke louder than the word.

"I—"

"Mo cailín. Let it be, aye? For today."

The implication said, One day I'll tell it. At least to you. The tone said, Right now, it's not something you need to hear.

"No. Maybe not." I've answered the sense again, she realized, and not the words. Then she remembered what else he had said.

"What was that word just then? Like, c'lleen, or something. You said it before. In the car. 'C'lleen sidhe.' What's that?"

"Oh. Ah." His hands had stilled. " 'Twas the gossoon. Y'r wee geologist. The way ye handled him, as if ye *was* fey."

"So what does it mean?"

"Ah, 'tis just . . . 'tis the word for 'girl,' that's all."

Cailín sidhe. Sidhe girl. Then, considering that slight residual tension, the eyes just averted, she thought, I bet it's more than just generic "girl." I bet it's like, My dear, or something. A mark of closeness. Of deepened affection. An emotional watershed.

And now I'm getting all conscious myself. It's *not* the time to remember what happened in the utility room, it mightn't ever be time to just throw myself on him, and, and—if I did that now, it would be a stopgap. A diversion. A way not to think.

I'm already using him enough. He's been wounded, he's sitting there ready to do it again for me.

He heaved himself up a little against the headboard. "I canna speak for you," he said, elaborately casual, "but I'm fair clemmed for a decent cup o' tea."

They had the tea. They wrangled over who most needed sleep, and substituted a session in what Dorian mentally termed Social Science 101. "If I went tin-scratchin', I need to know some o' the places, in y'r time. An' this passport. How do I use it? An' what else do I need?" They had moved to an hourly TV news with commentary—hers explicatory, his acid ("politicians, they're aye the bluidy same!")—when someone knocked.

Jimmy was off the bed in one convulsive leap. Into the bathroom, gun out, mouthing, Ask. Dorian gulped her heart back down, and managed, "Who's there?"

After a tiny pause the door returned, with no hint of surprise, "Dani."

"Sensible," Dani observed, with a judicious nod, as Dorian locked the door again and Jimmy reemerged. Although you could have registered under Lewis and Cotton, this time."

"The, ah, receptionist already knows me," Dorian managed at length. "And"—she censored, if I *had* thought of it—"Sorenson knows that too."

Dani omitted the nod. Instead she swung her laptop on the counter, set her bag beside it, and as she unzipped the bag's central compartment to reveal the Glenfiddich, allowed herself a tiny smile at Jimmy's face. "It's almost five-thirty. And I've some news before dinner," she said.

"The police said, archives." Dorian could not help leaping in, the instant the Scotch was distributed. "Ah, what archives, and ah—"

Dani eased her shoulders against the other bed's headboard in an echo of Jimmy's pose, and looked seraphic. "Actually, I needed a sterile Net connection."

"A—" A number and server and machine with no e-trail back to you or Lewis and Cotton? Dorian just managed not to burst out, For what?

"I wanted to contact a very smart young man in Hong Kong." She took a sip of Scotch and tossed the sentence after it. "Who specializes in IDs."

Dorian managed not to produce another parrot comment before her brain cartwheeled in her head. IDs. Hong Kong. Some kind of hacker, some specialist in ID production, ID faking, how in God's name did Dani ever find—IDs.

She's going to—she's doing something about Jimmy's ID.

Unsteadily, Dorian managed, "I see."

Dani gave her a tiny but genuine flash of smile that said, And you manage not to babble about it. Good.

"He surfaced in a case of mine, about three months ago. So he's probably still extant." And reticence earns another crumb of information, Dorian thought. But Dani had already turned to Jimmy. "A good story about where your passport is, and why, will soon be very helpful. For the moment, the police will accept you're who you say, and your good character, on my cognizance."

This time Dorian could not restrain the "uh!" Lewis and Cotton's senior partner risking her own and her firm's reputation, pulling all the favors that reputation, and maybe personal connections, could achieve, to cover a more-than-dubious, almost-total stranger. And embarking on shady dealings for him as well?

Jimmy had understood too. He got off the bed. Set his glass aside. Inclined his head, then made it a very near full-scale bow, and said with quiet more eloquent than any effusion, "Thank ye, ma'am." Squashing down her own effusions, Dorian thought, Seconded.

Dani read her face, and granted her another slight nod. "There's also news from Ben Morar." Jimmy sat down in his best approach to haste. "They've found the gun."

Dorian let out a long grateful sigh. "So at least we can prove that."

"As soon as Ballistics finish, yes." She glanced at Jimmy again. "Nowadays, if you have the gun, the shell and the bullet, you can prove which gun fired the shot." His mouth fell open and Dorian grinned to herself. We did miss Elementary Ballistics today. "And they have the file off George's computer. Officially franked, so admissible evidence. A most interesting comparison to the original hard copy." This time it was a very wintry smile. "George is already pleading coercion, but it's making him sing very small."

"And it'll implicate P-A"—Dorian bared her teeth—"through somebody who isn't dead."

"Partly, at least, since even if George is technically a Ben Morar employee, Pan-Auric *have* signed off on the takeover. So if the plan worked, the model would have come to them."

"They really have signed off? How did you—! Oh. Of course. Police access to financial records." And a personal connection to the case's chief officer. The suppressed grin faded as her own mind added, If she's getting this much from Childers, what's she giving him?

Dani's gray stare, cool again, retorted, What did you expect? She drank more Scotch and said evenly, "The other news isn't so good.

"The police had to contact Pan-Auric for Brodie's personnel records," she went on. "They couldn't get anything off his phones, even the one that didn't erase messages. His name and firm ID were in his wallet, but they had to call to find his next of kin."

"It's a wonder he even took his ID out there," Dorian said,

and Dani lifted her eyes with a glance like a blow.

"His stated next of kin," she said, "is Troy Sorenson."

Steps on the veranda approached and passed. Cars might have passed too. All Dorian heard was the hush that made a drum-tap of Jimmy's set-down glass.

"Then . . . then . . . he knows—he knows for certain now, the police have had to contact him."

And he's not just an associate. Laura's voice flashed back to her: *good ole boys stick together. I bet he's a personal friend!*

More than a friend. Someone trusted well enough to stand as kin. Claim Brodie's body. Arrange his funeral. Someone with a real personal stake in this.

She tried to keep her voice cool. "Do they know where he is?"

"Not at work." Dani's lips compressed. "The office say he's on leave. His home phone is on message bank. His cell phone's off. Or if not, he's screening calls and refusing any from the police."

"But do they know—"

Dani sighed just visibly and nodded. "The last location had him headed for Ibisville."

For an instant Dorian's hearing switched off. Then her muscles jumped as if she was trying to run three ways at once. "Then we have to—! He's going to—they've got to *stop him,* he is going after Laura and Anne!"

Panic launched her involuntarily for the door and Jimmy caught her as she flew past, his "Wait, wait" all but soundless with something else in Gaelic as he swung her deftly round into his grasp. Pressed hard into his chest, she could hear only the rush of his breath in her ear, his rapid half-voiced, "Wait, mo cailín, ye canna fly off into nowhere, listen, listen to me . . ."

Then Dani's hand was on her shoulder, and Dani was very near snapping, "You know the police can't detain a man on mere

158

suspicion. There's no proof he even committed the burglaries."

Dorian yanked her head back far enough to yell, "This is *Laura! Anne!*"

"Yes." Now it was a definite snap. "We've alerted the police. They've sent people to Baringal. The house is under surveillance, I've hired private security. If that's where he is going, he won't get in."

"Oh. Oh." She was shaking, she discovered, breathless as when she had run to the Ben Morar loading bay, and the *spanggg* of bullets on metal was back in her ears. "Oh, God, if that's where he *is* going, if he *does* get in—"

"It still won't help to panic about it here."

Dorian tried to whip round. Jimmy's grip tightened. Don't be crazy, it warned. Think who you're talking to. Stop and think.

She laid her head back against him and struggled for breath. Struggled not to see images of sieges and shoot-outs, Anne or Laura hurt, bleeding, dying on the beach-house floor . . .

Dani's hand tightened too. Quietly this time, she said, "All we can do is wait."

In a minute Jimmy's grip relaxed. When he let her go Dorian turned about, trying not to rub her eyes, not to shout aloud. Or to weep.

"Okay." Despite it all, her voice hardly shook. It takes a lot to break our composure, she thought. Us good Catholic girls. "Then what do we—what can we—"

"The police are tracking him." Dani sounded just a little too composed herself. "If anything happens, they'll be in touch immediately. Andy Childers will see to that. For the moment?" She gave a small shrug. "I suggest we finish our drinks. Have dinner. Change your registration. And go to bed."

In another hour, another half hour, another ten minutes, Dorian thought, I really will jump Jimmy. Just for some time when I don't have to think.

Her watch said four-twenty P.M. The window curtains said a fine sunny day. The TV, muted in the corner, cavorted to some afternoon pop show. On the counter her laptop brought up another list of Search results and Jimmy sighed and sat back, stretched his shoulders, and winced.

"Didn't they fix the dressings properly?" At least he got down to Out-patients with Dani this morning. While I was stuck here with a cop on the door.

" 'Tis just tender." He stood up, and despite the care his ribs still enforced it had a pent quality that was more than boredom. He's used to moving, of course. At work, he'd be setting print, maybe heaving piles of papers about. At home, he'd have to chop wood just to cook. He has to be feeling tetchier than me.

No use saying sorry again, she thought. We're confined to barracks, with room service, no outward calls, an actual cop on the door because we can't let on about Dani's gun. Now waiting's our only choice.

Dani says, Tonight. If nothing's happened by tonight, they'll ease off security. They ought to be finished at Ben Morar by then. Maybe then we can go home.

Jimmy sighed almost soundlessly and tweaked the curtain and she thought, Home? Ibisville. That's home for me. But for him?

Should I take him away from Blackston? Would he want to come? Shouldn't he stay here, in case, in case, the fold works again, and he just—goes?

But I can't leave him here. Not alone. She knuckled at her own eyes, feeling the aftermath of a sleeplessness terminated at three A.M. with a dose of Jimmy's painkillers. God, what's Sorenson *doing?*

Dani said, at lunchtime—lunch break—he's in Ibisville. In some motel, they think. But the phone hasn't moved since he arrived last night.

Is *he* waiting too?

Does he expect another news release, or word from somebody? Like Reinschildt? Does he even know what's happened yet? He must, he turned off that phone before the cops contacted him. Maybe someone passed it on from P-A, or maybe he knew beforehand about Ben Morar and then he heard the press release. Is he really after Anne and Laura or is there some other plan—oh, this is all just speculation, as useless as us sitting here.

She put her head in her hands. Beside her Jimmy drew an audible breath.

Then his own hands settled over her shoulders, palms cupping the shoulder's curve, thumbs almost reaching her shoulder blades, long fingers shaping themselves across her collarbones. The weight of bone and muscle and the warmth of flesh and blood rested on her like a coverlet in the chilly room.

She sighed a little, involuntarily, and he did close his hands then, drawing her to him almost as delicately as he had pulled on her wrist. She let her head follow the touch and suddenly she was leaning into him, propped against another solid, unyielding warmth. His hip, her thoughts said, going sideways. A leg. Living muscle through new denim. Half sideways in this stupid lounge chair, with the armrest in my ribs. Or it would be, if he wasn't so close.

And I don't want him to move.

The moment stretched like warm toffee, a sweet, impossible stasis whose end she would not think about. My back will hurt, or he'll get tired or—something else will happen. But not yet. This is too precious. Not yet.

He did not move either. He did begin to hum. And then croon, a slow, plaintive string of nonsense syllables, too irregular to call a melody, meandering just above a murmur in that deep remote voice. Almost despite herself, she felt her eyelids relax.

It's probably a kids' lullaby. Or he heard Bridget sing it over the ironing. She had an inexplicable certainty that Bridget had ironed. But it must be the fiddle-playing that taught him such a true, rich—beautiful—voice.

Her shoulders relaxed too. Her head felt heavier. Just a minute, just let me stay here another minute, and pretend everything's all right.

His hands no longer merely rested on her shoulders. The fingers had tightened to a definite grasp. The croon faltered, then faded away. They were both absolutely still.

Then he left one hand to steady her while he slid down beside her on his knees, and his other hand came under her chin, turning her face to him, so he could reach her mouth.

Not like the other night, Dorian's mind said as her body came back to life. No whiskey this time. No fumbling, either. She twisted about in the chair to reach more easily, and as his hold became an embrace she reached her own arms round his neck. To hell with the chair, in a minute we can get out of it. To hell with the bed, maybe, and the cop outside. To hell with Sorenson, and . . .

Her cell phone went off like a gunshot in the hush. Dorian squeaked and jumped as if she had been shot and Jimmy nearly jerked her on the floor as he plunged to his feet and she scrabbled dizzily to get up, reach the counter, the phone beside her bag.

Hope said, It's Anne or Laura, everything's okay. Habit ordered, press *Answer.* The electric prod of caution had hit before Jimmy grabbed the phone over her hand and hissed, "Bide . . . !" She pressed *Screen.*

The ID said, Laura's cell phone. The holoscreen did not come up.

At whatever her face or body said, Jimmy froze, hand clamped over hers.

Laura wouldn't blank a call. Not a call to me. Laura wouldn't *call* me, they have to have tight security down there too. Laura . . .

Oh God, oh God, oh God, oh God.

Her blood had solidified down her veins. She wondered how her fingers moved, punching, Call forward, punching, Dani, on the Quick-Call list, punching, Blank, for her own holoscreen even as her mouth hissed at Jimmy, "Keep back, stay out of pick-up range." And then, frantically, as Dani picked up on the third ring, "Dani, call forward, get the cops . . ."

He mightn't expect this. He might think I think it's Laura, even with the screen blanked.

The phone clicked in her ear. No one spoke.

Dani's smarter than to say anything.

The phone clicked again.

And the cops have to know better, God grant they know better than to butt in on this.

She bit her lip and drew in a long, long breath. Then she pressed *Accept,* and something like her own voice said, "Yes?"

The caller answered in a Midwest American drawl. "You Dorian Wild?"

CHAPTER 7

The driver stopped the siren and the police car slowed, then eased to a halt. Beyond the orange and white sawhorses that signaled a temporary roadblock, a wasps' nest of roof lights and randomly parked squad cars buzzed with fluorescent green police vests, occasional loud-hailers, blatant flak jackets. Over it all a Christmas tree of communication antennae stuck up into the watery lilac dusk.

"Forward command post," Demetrios said in Dorian's ear. "The house is just round that turn."

I know where the house is, she tried not to snap. Second from the corner, garden with clumps of palm and big hibiscus bushes, Mickey-Mouse hip-high front fence. Two steps to the door with living-room windows flush to the right and garage to the left. Conventional cream siding, ochre trim. Full-length vertical blinds, shrubs under the window edge. Higher side fences, backyard closed off for kids and the pool. A siege team's nightmare, with all those obstructions. The answer to a gunman's prayer.

She bit her lip and swallowed to clear her ears from the pressure shifts in the helicopter. Still going sideways, her mind ticked up the clusters of people loitering outside the barricade. Evacuees. They've cleared that block, both sides the street, the block behind. They'll be cursing us, dragged out kids and all, with no clothes or wallets, away from dinners and TV.

Two sawhorses had been pulled apart. The car edged forward.

The front-seat passenger used his radio mike, and from the wasps' nest a big, familiar figure emerged.

Childers. Oh. Yes. Dani said he left Ben Morar today. So he was in Ibisville for Sorenson's call.

It replayed yet again, vivider than her memory of Anne's house, incised in her brain. That impossible pause after Sorenson's first words, before she managed another, "Yes." The even longer pause, while her nerves and the connection hummed, before he spoke again.

"You got the cops on line?"

Do I say yes? Do I say no? Do I fudge for time? Do I not answer at all? Do I . . . Jimmy's eyes burning into her cheekbone and the silence spreading like acid, What do I say, oh, God, what do I . . .

Then she had to speak, before the silence did. She shut her eyes and croaked out, "Yes."

And the revolting, the obscene approval with which he said, "Smart donna. Cos I'm not gonna say this twice."

I couldn't speak at all then. Just feel my heart hammer, and watch Jimmy's knuckles go white on the counter edge.

"You know where I am."

Another pause, till I had to reply. Just getting it audible. "Yes."

"*Smart* bitch." With the little click of tongue on teeth I'm coming—I've come—to hate like poison itself. "Listen up, then."

And the all-too-recognizable slap of something hard against flesh, the strangled scream overriding a child's shriek. A woman's scream, a half intelligible ". . . him *alone!*" A hubbub of thumps and bumps under the child's cries, the rumble of a man's threat, subsidence into smothered, choking sobs.

Then the voice again. "You get that?"

I had to struggle, not to vomit down the phone.

"You've—got—the children."

"And your buddies." Click. "Both of 'em." Satisfaction, how much more obscene? "Your—security's—out the back. Dumb bastards, both."

"How did you get—"

Dani that time. Sharp as the draw of a knife.

"Never you mind how I got." Click. "This ain't one of your dumb TV shows. I'm not gonna yap about anything. Shut up."

A long, long pause, then, while I pictured Dani's face. Then him again, in that same drawling, overcasual tone, "You hear me, cop?"

The longer wait, while they must have made their own tactical decisions. Before the answer. Identifiable even on a phone. Childers' voice.

"We hear you, Sorenson."

Were they trying to faze him, letting him know they had his name? It could hardly have surprised him, by then.

"Okay, cop. Then you know what *your* surveillance is worth."

Another little pause, to drive home the gibe.

"Now I want that donna here muy pronto, hear me? That Wild bitch. You got an hour. That's five twenty-five"—with unctuous smugness—"Eastern Standard Time. Five twenty-five, I want you on this phone, you tell me you got her out there, got your roadblocks and sharpshooters set up, yeah, go right ahead." Click. "You get that bitch here, and you give her every copy of that fucking math thing and that fucking contract, and every copy of that recording the bitch made in the rocks with Ed . . ." For an instant the casualness wavered and there was red fury underneath. "Every copy, hear? You give 'em to her, and you point her straight in that front door."

Her stomach rolled over again at the memory. Simple physical terror. I couldn't have answered then. I couldn't answer now.

It was Childers who replied, icy but not hostile. Siege

protocols, I suppose. "We can't organize that in an hour. Ms. Wild isn't in Ibisville."

"She's in fucking Blackston, yeah." Click. "You throw her on that po-lice chopper and fly. Round up the fucking recordings before she arrives. Hear me? Five twenty-five." Click. "Because if she don't walk up that stoop by five-thirty—I'm gonna carve me a kid's ear."

It was sheer horror that wouldn't let me scream.

Anne. Laura. He must have them tied up, her brain had ratcheted on, while she stared numbly at the window blinds. If Anne wasn't tied she'd have killed him or died trying when he hit one of the kids.

That too was incised deep as a burn. Deeper than Childers' voice saying, "We don't have a police helicopter, we use the hospital chopper and it's on a call. We'll need at least an extra hour—"

Click.

It had been the connection that time. Bell-sharp in her ear, lost in Dani and Jimmy's double bellow of "She's not going!"—"Ye're not goin' in there!"

In there. Just round that corner, where he's waiting, where he wants me, me personally.

On her side opposite Demetrios, Jimmy shifted to press his shoulder against hers. A solid pressure, dourly determined as the look on his face. As his controlled but ferocious protests had been, down the phone to Childers and then Dani, face to face with Demetrios when the Blackston police car came scouring round to the motel. "I dinna care what that sod says, she isna goin'! No' to Ibisville! An' no' in there!"

But I had to go. For all Dani's equally fierce protests, the cops just kept saying, This is what he wants. What happens is unforeseeable. But we need you there, for contingencies.

They tried to leave Jimmy behind, and he wouldn't be left. "If ye take her, ye're takin' me!" Billabong shirt bulked over new dressings and concealed gun, cowlick on end and a bristle in the beard to match that glare. "She hired me f'r guard. An' ye've no' done such a job wi' the others as'll make me trust ye here!"

Dani said that too. To Childers himself, with a barb I never heard in her voice before. After she flatly told him to let Jimmy come, and then announced she was boarding the helicopter too. "If your protection works as well for Ms. Wild as it did with our colleagues, she'll need on-site legal advice."

Here, she meant. At the command post. Where the decisions will be made. Routine first. Block streets, evacuate bystanders, get sharpshooters up. Her mind reenvisioned those flak jackets, and her spine shrank all over again. Bring loudspeakers and negotiators, talk at if not to the gunman, try to reason with him, warn him about consequences, delay, quibble, impede. While they settle the crunch points. Do what he says—or not.

Storm the house. Risk the hostages. Or . . .

They can't expect me to go in.

Her hands flew up involuntarily and Jimmy caught and drew them down on his own knee. The grasp repeated clearer than words: whatever they say, *I* willna let ye do it. Ye're no' goin' in there.

Childers was almost at the car. Demetrios and the front-seat passenger slid out. They were waiting for her.

Dorian struggled across the seat, feeling her limbs stick as if glued. She was ignominiously grateful that Jimmy slid after her, close as a shadow at her back. Close as he's been since we left. In the first police car, on that flight to Ibisville, when God knows, he should have been panicking, out of his wits, airsick— and he didn't notice any of it.

"Ms. Wild."

Childers loomed over her. Backlit by the command post, he looked ten feet high. She managed a little noise in her throat.

"It's five forty-five."

I know that, she tried to say. Do you think I haven't watched the time clear from Blackston, close as a condemned man seeing his last minutes run?

"You've been kept informed?"

She produced a nod, aware of the car stopping behind theirs, the crunch of police shoes overridden by Dani's boots. Feeling Dani reach her other shoulder, a second bulwark, lowering almost as ferociously as she felt Jimmy was.

"Then you know he's currently using a revolver." The provisional tone warned: like Brodie, he might have a bigger weapon. "He has all the hostages in the living room. We still can't locate the two private security, but running our surveillance records, we've now found someone out here this afternoon in a meter reader's vest. And IbisElectric says he wasn't theirs."

So simple, she thought, feeling sick. For a patrolling police car, somebody going house to house in an official fluorescent vest would be invisible.

"The presumed scenario is that he went round the house. Disabled"—the tiny pause said they were both thinking, Maybe killed—"the security guards."

Then he could get inside. Even if the back door was locked, it wouldn't stop Sorenson.

"We estimate he arrived about three-thirty."

Afternoon, stasis in the suburbs, hardly anybody home. Except Anne and Laura. And, after playschool, the kids. With them there, subduing Anne, let alone Laura, would be a foregone conclusion. Just thank God Sam must have been at work.

The nausea boiled up so for a moment she lost track of Childers' words. When she could hear again the intonation said his update was almost done.

"The negotiators have kept telling him, we couldn't make his deadline, informing him where—the helicopter was. You do know . . ."

That he didn't cut anyone's ear off. That he just—just—hit one of the children again.

"The contract and model copies were couriered out from Lewis and Cotton and the bank. We have the copies of the Brodie interview." The police-announcement voice roughened. "Though if the stupid bastard thinks he's got it all he's crazier than they're saying." The humanity ironed out. "We've told him they're here."

A long pause. She already knew what he would say next. "We've told him—you're on the way."

The sentence end seemed to stab like glass. Beyond the simple physical terror her thoughts somersaulted crazily. What's the point of sending me in there, or the records either, if he's crazy he may not intend an exchange, he never has spelt that out. He might just want the records, me, Anne, Laura—a clean sweep. Images of other hostage bloodbaths washed over her, he mightn't even worry about escaping.

He might mean to die himself.

Jimmy's hand clamped on her left arm just as Dani gripped her right and Dani's voice, colder than frozen helium, snapped, "It will be illegal *and* tactical suicide to offer him another hostage. Let alone give him the records with her."

Childers' head snapped round. His posture said it was very near a glare. "We have to consider the number of lives—"

"You won't save them by risking more." She visibly bit back something else. "Have you asked, after he gets the records— what then?"

Childers' stance returned an equally bitten-back, What the hell do you think, we've sat here with our thumbs up our butts?

"He won't say."

"Then tell him flat out we don't go a step further, till he does."

She's still not saying, *when* I take them, Dorian thought, trying to unstick the tongue in her dry mouth. And I bet she's still got a whole salvo of other shots: tell him the records only come to the door, they'll only come with a cop, we want some hostages out first. Maybe she'll start pressuring for a diversion and back-door attack. Or something wholesale like gas grenades. Oh, God, there has to be some way to get them out.

Even if I do have to go in.

The personal terror closed over her again, choking as a hood. I'm so scared, and I may have to do it, I may have to walk in there, for my friends' sake, and have him do whatever he . . .

Dani and Childers were still glaring. The set of Dani's jaw said clearer than words, Forget the personal relationship. I'm a lawyer, and you're threatening physical harm, worse than physical harm, to my client.

The law just divided. Which side's justice? Or doesn't justice come into this anymore?

Childers said, "Steve, get them to the console. I'll see John." And turned away.

Amid the tangle of cars and personnel and electric leads the console was the command-post nerve center, two headset-wearing operators, a continuous crackle of incoming reports, microphones for individual response. When Demetrios navigated them in, the broadcasting voice held a tone Dorian instantly recognized, experience or not. Over-calm, determined patience, the conscious note of someone aware, overly aware of his audience.

"Ms. Wild's car is turning off the highway. We can send the records in, as soon as we have some idea what's supposed to happen next."

Silence, crackling over the connection. A PA hailer, she thought. He must be round in that street, right in front of the house. If Sorenson gets tetchy enough, full in the line of fire.

She looked toward the corner through the deepening dusk, and in her peripheral vision the amorphous hump of a fire hydrant or electrical housing shifted a fraction. Became a shoulder and helmet and line of rifle barrel, and the heart jumped in her throat.

Sharpshooters. Riflemen. They're probably right along the street.

"We may need some surety before the records come in. One or more of the children released. We also need to know your other requirements. If you request transport, and we have its type, the location and destination, we can keep the road clear of traffic. We want to get these people out as soon as we can."

More crackles. Nothing else. Then inside her bag, Dorian's phone went off.

Childers was there before she could move. He whipped the phone clear, pressed *Blank Screen,* jerked his head for a microphone. As the frenzy of switch-flipping subsided he held phone and microphone together, pressed *Answer,* and said, "Yes?"

"You got that donna, cop?"

"The car's headed in—"

"You *call* me. When it's here." Click. "Then you send her in."

"There are legal problems with that, Sorenson. Her lawyer's here. We can't legally compel anyone to—"

Click.

Right beside her, Demetrios said, *"Bastard,"* under his breath.

Childers switched the phone off. Handed it to Dorian. He did look at her for a fraction of a moment before his eyes went back to Dani.

"He's not going to negotiate."

"She's not going in."

Around them the subordinates, the peripheral actors had slowly begun to freeze.

"I have a responsibility to those people—"

"I have a responsibility to Ms. Wild."

"We can suggest, if he won't play ball about what happens later, she takes them to the door—"

"She's not going anywhere."

"Look, I don't like this any more than you do." The volume had dropped though the tone remained official ice. "You think any of us does? Grown men, standing about out here, sending a woman—"

"She's not going."

"*Somebody* has to! We have to respond to his demands, that's the law!"

Do you want some innocent police constable, the glare demanded, to carry the can for your client, the person who's really responsible for this whole—

I'll do it, Dorian tried to say. Yes, somebody has to. But all that came out was a sort of croak.

Dani and Childers both whipped on her, and from somewhere came coherent words.

"Call him back. Say—I'll come in. Once the others are out." And as they stared, "If he won't make terms—we can."

She felt Jimmy's whole body leap for some huge response— and stop. She did not look around. She stared back at Childers and thought, Go on, do it. Before I lose my nerve.

Childers took the phone, found Laura's number, and punched, *Call.*

"She there?" it said.

"We'll send her in," Childers said too evenly, "when two others have come out."

Click.

Childers swung to the console and grabbed the open microphone.

"Sorenson," it modulated in mid-word from outright rage. "You can switch the phone off as often as you like. Ms. Wild's lawyer has stated her legal rights. We can't send Ms. Wild in until you respond to these terms."

Dorian's phone rang. Childers slapped the *Answer* button and the sound burst out of the speaker at them, an agonized ear-drilling scream. A child. A child in ultimate pain.

Demetrios swore like a madman in Dorian's ear. Half the command post surged out of their seats. Childers hung onto the phone as if it were bucking in his hand.

The scream vanished in a boil of other shrieks, fragmentary words, crashes and thumps. Dorian almost catapulted herself past the console at the sound.

"I'll go," she could hear herself panting as the uproar ebbed. "I'll go, I'll go—" But as Childers slapped the phone off Dani yanked her physically backward and snapped, "You will not!"

"You *heard* that!" Childers yelled at her then. "Christ, woman, we can't—"

"We can't send anybody else in there! You've absolutely no guarantee he won't shoot the lot! Bring in gas, storm the place— it's still better odds than that!"

He'll send her away. At Childers' expression Dorian's backbone shrank. He'll tell her she's out of line in a police operation and send her away and then he'll make me go in . . .

Jimmy's hand shut on her shoulder, solid and warm in the chilling dusk. In her ear he said, *"Gas?"*

"Special gas." Police Tactics 101. A thought topic. She nearly cried with relief. "It knocks people out."

His comment was the audibly indrawn breath. She knew his

eyes had gone back to Dani and Childers, bristling at each other by the console operators' backs.

"Ms. Lewis." Childers was having to try for composure too. "We don't have to send *anyone* in there. If we tell him we will . . . if we get him to talk . . ."

"He won't talk. He's proved that." Despite the words, Dani had also softened her tone a fraction. "If you ask your psych people I'll bet they agree. That in there is not a domestic situation and that's not your normal gunman. He's not even an ordinary criminal. That's an ex–US Army security man. Maybe special ops. He won't talk and he won't scare. He has a high personal stake in this. And he's probably"—now, it held a slash of bitterness—"done it before."

Childers pulled in his lips. Someone at his elbow murmured, "I could contact Harry . . ."

Dani's frown tightened. Dorian felt her breath stop. Is Harry a psychologist? Or the gas detachment chief?

Childers turned his head. "Okay," he said curtly. And then, to Dani, "We'll call the psych unit. Get a second opinion."

At his elbow on the console, Dorian's phone went off.

Childers did spin round that time. He very nearly knocked the phone to the ground before he could blank the screen and hit *Answer.*

"Yes?"

The phone said, "You done arguing?"

Childers' upper lip pinched under its glisten of sweat. "I told you, we have a problem. Ms. Wild's legal rights—"

The phone screamed again. Childers almost threw it on top of the console. Dorian's hands flew without volition to her ears.

Again the uproar died. This time Dorian could hear the child's smothered, continuing sobs.

"Cop, I told *you.* Lawyer be fucked." The complacence had

become cold malevolence. "You send that donna in, or I'm gonna do more with this kid than hit it upside the head."

Dorian had jumped before she thought. Demetrios caught her elbow, Dani half sprang, Childers thrust out an equally reflex arm. He mouthed something. Dani, eyes blazing now, mouthed back. *No.*

There was a shuddering hush. And in the gap Jimmy stepped past Dorian and spoke, loudly enough to reach the still-live microphone.

"*I'll* bring y'r records, Yank." A tiny, precise pause. "That's if ye've nerve to face a man."

Childers' hand whipped out and Dani nearly leapt at him. Then they both froze.

As the lag time stretched and stretched. Still with no terminating *click.*

Before the phone said, "Who the hell are you?"

Fraction by fraction, Childers' hand relaxed. Dani took one long step halfway between him and Dorian where she could see Jimmy's face.

"*I'm* the one put y'r mate in the rocks." Jimmy's eyes were half-closed, empty. The words came overclearly, slower than usual. A public speech. A challenger's taunt, every phrase shaped and targeted like a blade.

"He couldna hit me, for all his shootin'. An' me wi' no gun at all." Another tiny, deliberate space. "An' *I'm* the one planned that interview. Got him talkin'. Aye. Y'r foul-mouthed scumbag spilled his guts to me. I'm no' a lawyer, an' I dinna care what the polis say. But *I* dinna hide behind women an' children. If ye've the nerve for it, say so. *I'll* bring y'r records in."

Childers opened his mouth with a more than white-hot glare, Demetrios came to lunging point. Dani hissed at them both in dumb show. Jimmy ignored it all.

The microphone crackled. Crackled again. Then the Midwest

drawl said, thick and deepened into savagery, "Fuck you, you piece of shit. Get your ass in here."

The connection went *click,* and Dorian seized Jimmy by two handfuls of shirt back and just managed not to scream like a genuine banshee, *"No!"*

"Mo cailín—ssh. Dorian, listen." When all else failed he hauled her hands loose and gripped her in front of him, shaking her, ignoring the rest of the uproar, that dark stare burning into her own eyes till he actually hissed between his teeth. *"Listen to me!*

"The polis canna send ye. They canna send a polis-man. The"—he used something Gaelic that spat like acid—"willna heed. An' I dinna care what y'r law says, *I'll* no let ye walk in there while I've a sound leg to m' name." He shook her in earnest then. "Now whisht an' *listen.* Ye're the only one'll follow this. Do ye no' understand? This—maybe this—is what I have to do."

Think, said that night-deep stare. Don't wail and curse and protest, think. I can't say this to anyone else, I can't say it more clearly. Perhaps even to you.

When she froze, staring up at him, he added right under his breath, "Maybe, 'tis why I'm here."

Providence. Folds in reality. Things that didn't go right last time and now . . .

And maybe he thinks he isn't going back, but this will do instead, he can walk in there and let Sorenson—and then it will all be fixed. Tallied up, sorted out. No anomalies, no ongoing impossible secret problems. In his world. Or here.

Her hands clamped in his shirt front and the scream welled up inside her. No. No!

You mustn't, she tried to let her eyes plead. If you can't let me go, I can't let you go for me. Not when you've already been dragged here and lost your world and got yourself hurt because of me, and—

And I can't bear it, if I lose you too.

He looked down at her in the chancy floodlight glare, somber as in that photograph. The set of mouth and chin said, Don't argue. The eyes, despite the stone wall, said, I understand. Don't say it.

Because it will do no good.

Then he detached her fingers and kissed her once very lightly on the forehead and said to Demetrios who had somehow got back to her shoulder, "See to her, will ye?" Before he looked past at Dani and added flatly, "Ma'am, will ye consider y'rself m' lawyer? Sort the polis then, if ye please. I'm ready to go."

God, Dorian thought. Whoever, whatever You are. Are You listening?

Because I'm making a promise here. Get them out of there, get *him* out of there, alive, and I'll never miss another Mass. As long as I live.

Her heart thumped and her teeth were clenched solid to keep the tears in her throat. Her fists ached, doubled to keep her still. I can't run out there, any more than I can break down and scream and weep and beg him all over again, Don't go.

At the street's center, Jimmy looked taller as he began to walk away. His running shoes made a mere scuffle on the bitumen. His shadow stretched behind him under the relentless floodlighting that had succeeded dusk, stretched and stretched again and she tried to keep the tears back so she could watch every moment.

In case I never see him alive again.

On the loud-hailer microphone Childers said with furious clarity, "Sorenson, our man's coming in."

I can't decide if I'm glad he won that fight or not. Twenty

178

minutes' furor with Childers actually bawling that he would not have any civilian preempt police decisions, threatening to arrest Jimmy on the spot, having another set-to with Dani over the rights of clients. Dani getting madder and madder till I thought I'd see the Lewis ice cliff crack at last. Everybody in range trying not to cower.

Jimmy himself just standing there, arms folded, head down, producing a world championship glare. Until he lost all patience and bawled at Childers, "Ye willna let me go for I'm no' polis, I'm 'civilian'—but ye'll bully a *female* 'civilian' into doin' y'r dirty work?"

I thought Childers would lose it completely then. He did start forward and Demetrios nearly turned himself inside out and Dani was going to throw herself between them.

When my phone went off.

And that obscene voice drawled, "You wiring up that piece of shit?"

They couldn't stall any longer then. They did make him sign a disclaimer, that he was doing it without duress, of his own volition, no responsibility of the police and state. And have a minor fracas over arming or armoring him before Jimmy undid his own holster and handed it to Dani and said, "I'm no' wearin' anythin'. D'ye take him for a whole eediot?" Then, when they actually stopped and stared, he added, with the first hint of a snap, "They're in there waitin'. Will ye gi' me the stuff or no'?"

The angle of Jimmy's shadow changed. The men around her tensed and she tried to swallow dust.

The corner. The last I'll see of him. In a minute . . .

Beside her at the chest-high barricade Dani said under her breath, distilled acid, "Men."

Who have to argue and delay and invent regulations. Who put ego and testosterone into every decision they make. Who can't be stopped—her own throat swelled uncontrollably—from

179

playing the hero—playing the damnfool hero—no matter what anyone says.

She made a strangled sound that held all she could have crammed into *Yes*.

Jimmy's shadow blurred. Her eyes watered, and when she blinked them clear he was gone.

"Coming round the corner now." The voice came from the console microphone, lowered as if Sorenson might hear. "No activity inside." Somebody at the actual corner, she thought, the forward forward witness. The scout.

"Approaching the gate."

Dorian took hold of the plastic barricade top, biting her fingers with its edges, and shut her eyes.

"Inside the gate."

Beyond the hum of microphones the command post was completely quiet.

"Approaching the door."

An infinity of a pause, when she felt her nerves slowly begin to shred.

"At the door. Said . . . something . . . 'open this or will I?' "

Dorian felt her lip give under a tooth.

"Something inside. I can't catch it. He's opening the door."

Silence again.

"He's in."

And I thought watching him walk away was bad.

Dorian dug her fingers at a new angle into the barricade and tried to remember to breathe. Not to curse aloud. Not to lose all control and start to scream.

"Ten minutes," Demetrios said under his breath beside her.

Ten minutes since Jimmy disappeared. Ten minutes, with no sign of life at all.

Oh, God, what is that bastard *doing?*

Red images cartwheeled before her inner eye, every atrocity from news and history, every vile refinement of cruelty that could be wreaked in ten silent minutes on an unarmed man.

Or—her breath stopped along with her heart. What if somehow—some miraculous how—with those streetboy reflexes, or that guerrilla experience, or just that scorpion tongue—Jimmy's turned the tables like he did with Brodie and got the jump on *him?*

The jet of hope almost made her physically sick. Another collage flew across her inner eye, Sorenson surprised, knocked out, disarmed, Jimmy untying Anne and Laura, reassuring the kids, any minute the door'll open and they'll be there, safe.

The kaleidoscope jammed. Relentless commonsense retorted, No unarmed man could jump that bastard without an A-Grade brawl.

The police surveillance picked it up when he hit the kids. They'd have picked up that.

Fifteen minutes. Oh, God, oh, God, what can the bastard be *doing?*

Then she thought her heart really had stopped at the shrill of her phone.

Childers snatched it off the console and pushed *Answer.* Dorian tried not to shake.

"Got some orders for you, cop." Click. The rage was gone. He sounded complacent again. Almost smug. "You clear your fuckwits out of that backstreet." Click. "Right out. Back to the end of the block."

Dani's hand was locked on Dorian's arm. Childers' face looked like the proverbial stone. "Give us five minutes," he said.

"If you get five minutes, you clear the front street as well." Click. "Put a plainclothes car round that far corner." Click. "Clear the roadblock. You got that much sense?"

Childers said flatly, "We hear."

"Then do what you're told." Click. "Cos I'm coming out that front door, and I'll have an escort. Little lady you know about." Click. "That car, cop? I'll check it for tracers. You put one on it, you know what'll happen to her?"

Childers' jaw muscles worked. But he sounded expressionless. "Where are you going? We can reroute traffic—"

"Never you mind. You park that car and get the fuck out. Understand?"

"We can—"

"Shut up. You got ten minutes, cop. Then I'm coming out." Click. "You give me shit, I'll give the lady shit. You do as I say and I'm out of here." Click.

"And you can have what's left."

Click.

"He'll take Laura. He'll know better than to untie Anne." The stress that burred everyone else's voice had turned Dani's to diamond ice. "He wants that backstreet cleared to keep him safe when he goes."

I don't care what he wants, Dorian tried not to shriek into the flurry of command-post action. All I want is Jimmy! Out!

And Anne and the kids and oh, God help us, Laura. Her stomach turned over yet again and she bit her knuckles to stem another sting of tears. Oh, Laura, Laura, what's he going to do to *you,* he'll take you with him but where's he going and where will he leave you and how?

Dani's hand shut yet again on her arm, and Dani spoke softly in her ear.

"Once he's out and moving, the odds are far better. Whatever he says, even at night, they can track the car. There's more chance of getting her clear." A little, dagger pause. "And now—"

She let Dorian finish for herself, the thought neither of them could voice. Now, there's only one life, not five, at risk.

Another surge of police pushed them into a corner. Dorian strained her eyes yet again down the empty street and tried incoherently to pray.

"Ten thirty. Forty. Fifty . . . activity in the house."

Even the microphone sounded less dispassionate. After the rush to shift roadblocks, position the car, withdraw street surveillance, the flurry of setting new lookouts, the command post seemed still as death.

Not a good simile, Dorian thought, forcing hysteria down. Don't make up stupid comparisons. Try not to think at all.

"Movement in the living room. Somebody at the blinds. White, male, armed."

Sorenson. Checking the street.

Dani's shoulder had settled against hers. There was comfort in Dani's iron stillness. Not Jimmy's warmth, but support.

Sorenson can't see much, if he does look. All those plants. The palm clumps. Her eyes, staring tearlessly down to the corner, seemed to blur so the landscape slid, and suddenly her heart jumped yet again behind her teeth.

There's a rifleman—a sharpshooter—up at the corner, diagonally across the corner, in the cover of those shrubs. They've cleared that street, yes. But he must be able to see clear into Anne's house.

"Blinds closed."

Another eternity, where she could only think, Come on, you bastard, get it over. Move.

"Movement at the door."

In unison, the command post breathed.

"Door opening."

Another excruciating pause.

"White, female subject coming out. Hands behind her." An

abrupt break. "Subject has rope—dog leash—round her neck."

Dorian felt her teeth grind instead of clench. If *I* only had a gun. Memory replayed the sweet give of the trigger and George's screaming leap.

Dani's hand tugged sharply at her arm. Don't lose it. Not now.

"Subject stopped at foot of steps. White male subject partly visible . . ."

Dorian shut and opened her eyes and forced herself to take a long, shaking breath.

"Female moving from steps."

Another endless pause. The command post, the connections, the ambient air had grown so still Dorian thought her ears would pop.

Before they rang to the bomb-loud crash.

Then a more remote muffled crash and a ripping triple gun-burst and suddenly half the command post was racing for the corner while the microphone bawled, "Noise in the house, male turned, female pulled away and dived, male fired . . . !"

The words vanished, swamped. But running with the others in the tow of Dani's biting grip Dorian saw the sharpshooter break cover to race cross-street ahead of them, and filled in the rest.

Something startled Sorenson. A noise—something fell?—in the house. He spun round before he could help himself and whoever he's got with him made the best of it. Better to chance getting shot there than let him get her in the car.

And when she dived, the sharpshooter had a clear bead.

They flew round the corner together. Men shouted, hands snatched. Dani ducked the nearest with a football forward's swerve and they were right behind the sharpshooter as they tore in Anne's front gate.

It was Laura, Dorian's brain said, distinguishing red-gold

184

hair in the fallen tangle of clothes and limbs and blood beyond the steps. It was Laura and he got her, oh no, oh no . . .

A hand rammed her back. Dani snarled in her ear, "Run!"

I'll see to this, Dorian translated with adrenaline's speed of light. You get inside. Find Anne and the kids. Find Jimmy as well.

Laura was ten feet from the door. Sorenson had been driven backward by the force of the shots and fallen half across the steps. Dorian never had to think, Should I wait, can he shoot again, is he still alive? The flashlight flares of light between plants and running men threw the image up at her as vividly as the scarlet of blood that had mixed with Laura's trailing hair. Gleam of revolver barrel. Red star growing on a plaid shirt front. Blood and other things spattered where a forehead had been.

Dorian hurdled the body in stride and flung herself in the door.

She bounced herself off the kitchen partition and the familiar living room seemed to fly at her. TV, sideboards, piles of computer magazines, big Chinese rug littered with toys . . . Anne tied hand and foot to a dining chair, Della having hysterics with head sunk in her mother's lap, Jonathon just beyond, eyes like a night bat's in a tiny wraith of face. And beside him, the overturned CD tower that had hit the wood floor loud enough to hear down the street, and the hail of disks strewn half across the room.

Dorian was almost over the rug when Anne screamed at her. "Pool! The pool!"

Her legs jammed. A squawk of a voice cried, "What?"

"The pool!" Anne nearly overturned the chair. "He took him out there—the *pool!*" It was a wildcat scream. *"Run!"*

Dorian's feet were halfway down the kitchen passage before her brains caught up. Jimmy. The pool. Twenty, thirty minutes ago, whatever that bastard did. Oh, God, oh, God, oh, God!

The kitchen lights were on. The laundry lights were on. Under Sam's tool bench her eye snagged two bulky shapes, rugs, why in God's name did he roll up rugs . . . ? The back door, on its spring to foil escaping children, was shut. She slammed it open and fell into the yard, under the house floods' glare.

Twenty feet of lawn. The metal-rod pool fence, childproof gate, floodlight-glow blazing from the little house pool, no more than four feet deep among its landscaped shrubs, giving the lights a refulgent turquoise response.

And refuse blotting it, a heap, a sprawl of sodden, water-dark clothes.

Dorian went over the edge before she had to think. Her feet hit bottom and skidded but her hands were there, snatching and heaving frantically at the first fistful of cloth. She screamed without knowing it and heaved upward and a shoulder surfaced with the drag of a dying whale.

His head came with it. She shoved her free arm under and braced her feet to pull up his face, her eyes catching but not yet understanding the unopened champagne bottle that dragged from the cord tied under his beard. She was already hauling toward the pool edge, gasping as if half drowned herself, silently screaming, Don't let him be dead, don't let him be dead.

Her back hit the poolside. With a convulsive heave she got his head over the six-inch rim. Hung on, choking, panting, turning his face sidelong. He could breathe like that but I need someone else to get him out.

She filled her own lungs and screamed with every grain of strength she had. "Heeelpp!"

Men shouted in the house. Feet thundered through the kitchen, thudded on the lawn. Curses and kicks opened the gate. As somebody leapt into the pool to grab Jimmy's legs and someone else snatched his shoulders she saw the two-liter Coke bottle, empty, tied to his ankle ropes.

Then they had him on the poolside. Had rolled him on his face. She saw the ropes on his wrists as well before someone was kneeling over him to begin CPR. And she heard the sound—God, she found herself praying, never let me forget that sound—of his first spluttering choke.

CHAPTER 8

"The hoor's melt told me . . . what he was goin' to do."

"Don't try to talk. Not yet."

The deep voice, the Tyrone accent itself had thinned to a husk. Too much water. Not enough air. CPR. Dorian took a firmer grip on his hand as the ambulance began to move. Through the side window the revolving flash threw a lighthouse flare, and a split second before their own siren burst into life she heard the ambulance ahead give a preliminary keen.

Laura. She squeezed her eyes shut on the memory, Laura strapped on a gurney with IV bags already hung above her, sheet-white and still under the blood-dribbled tangle of hair, the massive clot of temporary dressings masking her torso, medics still working furiously as the ambulance doors closed.

Another friend's damage to my account. At least let this be mendable. Not a loss, not a permanent disability. Not . . . another death, like Chris.

"Where're we . . . goin'?"

"Shhh."

"Let him talk," the paramedic at her side said curtly, working to loosen the soaked rib dressing. "Orient him."

Jimmy twisted his head to find her, eyes cavernous between sodden elflocks and the still dripping thicket of beard, and her hand clamped involuntarily on his. Of course he's out of it, out in ways this guy can't imagine.

"We're headed for the hospital." She could hear the wobble

in her own voice. "To Emergency."

His eyes clung to her face, but a hint of recognition showed. He knows the word, if not what it is. She felt the shock tremors in her own muscles, and he shivered with her, laid out on the ambulance bunk under a blanket and half-mast hospital gown, trying now to get up on an elbow as the medic swabbed at his ribs.

"Him . . . Sorenson?"

"He's dead. The cops shot him. At the door."

His arm relaxed. When the medic gently pushed him down, he went without demur. But then his face tautened back to a frown.

"Door?"

"He was trying to leave. He . . . had Laura. For hostage. And, and, he got distracted . . . she dived away. He hit her. But they got him."

Jimmy's eyes went huge and she almost gave him a real hug. "She's alive, they're working on her—" His lips clamped and she knew he was remembering George in the utility room. His one benchmark for a modern gunshot wound.

"That gun . . . 'twas a fair cannon."

"Right side," the medic interposed. "Through the shoulder blade. May be some lung damage. Heavy blood loss. She's on plasma now. She'll go straight to surgery."

Jimmy half relaxed. Then he winced at some touch, and Dorian found herself tallying debts again. Jimmy here. Laura, headed for Emergency. Anne, left in her living room, with Sam and the kids and the psych people, first-aid and painkillers and tranquilizers, oh, God, the memories we—I've given her.

And Della. And Jonathon. They'll never forget. Anne and Sam may not keep the house. They may never be able to live there again.

Her mind played inexorably back to Sorenson's body on the

steps, the broken-doll posture, the doorjambs spattered with blood and flesh. *I couldn't live there, remembering that.*

The ambulance vibrated, the siren wailed. Banshee, she thought, shivering afresh. We cringe inside too, when we hear it, knowing it presages crisis, injury, death. His time or ours. Nothing's really changed.

The medic came round to reach Jimmy's shoulder. Dorian shuttled down the opposite bunk, Jimmy reluctantly releasing her to let them trade. When she settled, he reclaimed her hand with palpable relief. His eyes were fixed on her face. Her stomach squirmed. *He wants, he needs to tell me something. Medic or no medic. Something . . .* she shifted her fingers, saying silently, *What, then?* And his mouth clenched.

"It wasna . . . the records. Ye know? All along . . . what the sod wanted . . . was you."

Dorian felt her lips shape, *Me?* Her neck crept and he tried to draw her nearer, fingers vice-tight on hers.

"Got inside . . . wi' the bluidy things. He knocked 'em—out o' my hand. He said . . ." He stopped. "Foulest mouth . . . outside a cesspit. What ye'll *say* around here . . ."

Dorian squeezed his hand hard and pointed with her eyes. He followed her gaze to the medic, and visibly checked himself.

"He said . . . the records was . . . bait. For *Harvey.* Whoever that is. An' . . . the cops. A way . . . for gettin' you."

Dorian's spine chilled as she reheard that voice over the phone. Drawling, casual, cold as a slow-moving snake. "But," she almost whispered. "Why me?"

"I said that. When I—after." He did not say after what. "I said, 'What d'ye have agin her?' " His mouth pulled down. "That started him. He was fair slaverin'."

Dorian stared at him, wanting to burst out like a child, *What did I ever do to him?*

His teeth gritted. "The things he called ye. I near claimed

him. Gun or no'. Before ye came, he said. Everythin' . . . green."
His brows corrugated. "I didna follow that. But then ye
started . . . trouble. Findin' the copy—the model." Another
grimace. "The language about that! Askin' questions. Roust-
in'—George." The tuck of brows marked more censorship. "An'
Harvey . . . an' then him—Brodie—havin' to fix it all . . . again."
Reinschildt said, Fix it. 'S all.

So Reinschildt's Harvey. Some corner of her mind cached
the information. The rest had been sucked back into memory's
dark, where Jimmy was going.

"Ben Morar . . . the stockpile . . . was worst. He was fair
daundered . . . about that stockpile. Kept talkin' . . . about Ai-
rack. Him an' Brodie, comin' through—a bunch o' weird talk.
Arab, I think. An' purple *hearts?* But . . . 'I'll no'—uh, I'll no'
see him offed,' he kept sayin' . . . 'by some—umm, some—
woman—in a bluidy backwoods mine. He wasna a . . .' somethin' or other. 'He should've got—Congress Medal'? No' gone—
like this . . ."

He turned his head carefully, and looked full at her, that dark
stare baffled as well as still half dazed. "I swear ye, mo cailín . . .
the Yanks here—all plain cracked."

Don't follow that up either, she thought, squeezing his hand
fiercely while history replayed before her into human lives. Iraq,
the wars, American troops trapped in a hostile occupation, like
Belfast, a long, bitter, miserably inglorious campaign. Brodie
and Sorenson, survivors as well as comrades, bonded by that
understanding even enemies could share.

Then the fighting done. Medals irrelevant. Maybe too old for
the army, taking what jobs their skills would fit. Even less glory
than a losing war.

To end, trapped like a rat in a mine stockpile, outwitted by a
woman and an unarmed man.

No wonder Sorenson wanted blood. No wonder he grabbed Anne and Laura, and didn't care about getting all the records. They *were* only bait. For Reinschildt. For the cops.

What did he want from Reinschildt, then?

And why did he take Jimmy, in my place?

"He said . . . 'But ye, ye'—I'll no' say that word—'ye did— hmph—*her*—dirty work. Ye'll be *bette*r than her.' "

He stopped very short this time. The ambulance slowed, Dorian guessed to run a red light. Accelerated. As the speed steadied, Jimmy breathed a little, and began again.

"He took me outside." He ducked his head, an odd, awkward movement, and the medic said sharply, "What's wrong?" Then his hand darted up behind Jimmy's ear and Jimmy flinched.

" 'Tis nothin'. Gun barrel. Knock me silly, while he tied m' hands . . ."

He stopped short as the medic began feeling delicately through his sodden hair. "There's a contusion, yeah. One end's been bleeding. I'll fix that, soon as I'm finished here."

Under his breath Jimmy muttered, " 'Twas nothin'. I said."

But it wasn't nothing, Dorian thought, what Sorenson did out there. She looked down at his wrist, where the weals stood viciously from water-softened, water-bleached skin, and felt her teeth grind. If I could have laid hands on *him* . . .

But I can do this, for Jimmy. A better recompense. She took his hand in both her own and said silently, Go on.

He looked back to her, eyes black in the overhead light.

"By the wee pond. Wi' these bottles. He said, I planned this for—her . . . an' he tied the empty bottle . . . to m' ankles. An' the full one . . . round m' neck."

The medic finished the shoulder dressing. Reached up to the overhead shelf for more swabs, and began on the contusion. Still silent, but Dorian thought, slower than before.

"He . . . said, 'Wi' y'r hands tied, ye canna swim. The full bottle'll no' . . . drag ye right down. But the empty one'll keep . . . pullin' up yr' feet. Ye can drown a man . . . in eight inches o' water . . . if ye just keep pullin' up his feet . . .' "

Dorian felt her blood run cold. And I thought the worst was over with.

He was staring at her, that darkness haunted now. He licked half involuntarily at his lips.

" 'Ye're a good strong . . . uh, man,' he said. 'Ye can get y'r head up . . . every now an' then. 'Twill be a while. Before ye get . . . tired. Longer . . . than *her*.' "

Dorian's skin crawled all over. Jimmy stared at her, those sunken eyes darker still.

"Draggin' me to the edge. He . . . said, 'Now ye'll find out . . . how 'twas for Ed.' "

Dorian shuddered and from the way his hand locked round hers knew he understood. He thought Brodie smothered, so he meant to drown you in revenge. Slowly. There's no plumbing the depths of human ingenuity. Human malevolence.

The medic's hands had stopped. The look on his face was pure disbelief.

"He planned that," Jimmy was barely whispering now. "First of all. 'Twas why he . . . went out . . . there. 'Let the'—ahem— 'let the polis come,' he said. 'So long as I get . . . her.' "

And if you hadn't stung him with that tongue of yours, hadn't claimed your part in Brodie's death, he could still have got me. Held out till the police decided I had to go. I could have been in that pool. Drowning, slowly, fighting for air, wearing myself out.

She shuddered again and the medic said softly, "Christ. The guy was a certified nut."

Jimmy leaned slowly, painfully back into the bunk. With his eyes closed he looked more exhausted than at Ben Morar. Haggard, she thought. Haunted. And not just by the close transit of his own death.

"I dinna think so," he said slowly. "He was thinkin' . . . well enough. He planned everythin'. Reckon . . . he had the women . . . tie each other up. Way he did. Wi' me. He had the little girl . . . hitched to his belt. Like a dog. 'Shoot off y'r mouth. Try somethin' . . . an' I won't hit *you*.' "

Of course he'd do it that way. Just as he would with Anne, she'd do whatever he said, with the kids there. And Jimmy, Jimmy'd never risk a child's life.

"He figured, he had a fifty-fifty chance . . . o' gettin' out. Me an' Ed, he said, we've beat worse odds. He wasna . . . crazy. Just . . . like t'other. Hadn't ne'er . . . been gainsaid. Always . . . run clean over, what tried to stop him. An' when somethin' did . . ."

He opened his eyes and looked remotely, wonderingly, at Dorian. "An' when someone did . . . like Brodie in the pipes . . . he couldna suffer it."

The medic sucked in his lips with an audible, disapproving smack. He gathered up the used swabs. Then he glanced down the line of Jimmy's back and frowned. "Turn over a moment."

Jimmy grimaced. The medic put a hand on his shoulder and pushed.

Dorian caught her breath. The medic said something that sounded like "Fuck." Then, with open outrage, "When did he do *that?*"

Jimmy made a reluctant noise into the bunk. As the red blotches across his back made sense, Dorian felt herself gasp as well. "That—that . . ."

She was on her feet, bile choking in her throat. "*How* did he do that?"

The medic twitched and gave her an eye white. Jimmy made another noise. Then, when her silence demanded more, muttered into the bunk, " 'Twas the bottle. The full one . . ."

A champagne bottle. Her stomach churned as she made out the weals, almost purple, right over kidneys as well as ribs. Jimmy tried to roll. The medic flattened his shoulder and said curtly, "I'll spray those with painkiller. But they'll need to check you at Emergency."

For kidney damage. God, the damage a full bottle of champagne could do, right there, wielded by a knowledgeable, strong, truly malevolent hand.

"But how the hell did he manage—!"

Jimmy half opened an eye. "I told ye. He wasna crazy . . . where it mattered. He had the girl . . . when I came in."

He shut his eyes completely. Against the pillow in the glaring light his profile looked harsh as battered stone.

"He said, Move . . . an' I shoot her. Then he dragged her round behind . . . an' hit me. Wi' the gun barrel. Fair over this."

His elbow half moved toward the rib dressing, and the medic drew in his breath.

"After that . . . I wasna fit for much roughhousin'."

Bastard, Dorian bawled silently. "But your back?"

"After. When he talked about . . . Brodie."

He stopped. Folded his lips. Their set said, I don't need, I don't want to remember that. For anyone.

Brutality, Dorian raged. Cunning, tactics, to disable and keep you disabled, he had a good idea, if he gave you a chance, what you might do. And an excess of vengeance. Before the final cruelty, to hurt you in the best way he knew.

The siren wound suddenly down. The ambulance slowed and she caught the bunk edge as a turn began. The medic said, "We're coming in."

He pulled up the blanket as well Jimmy's gown, then clambered into the driver's cabin. As he disappeared, Jimmy opened his eyes to meet Dorian's, this time in plain bewilderment.

"I dinna understand . . . y'r time. Yanks. On the field, they were . . . hard men, aye, plenty of 'em. An' trigger-happy. But no' like this. Is it all o' ye? Or just a few?" His eyes half dilated. "The polis—they dinna seem crazy. Or George, even. Is it just Yanks?"

"Oh, Jimmy." She clenched his hand in hers, wanting to throw her arms around him, to protect him, this once, as he had protected her. "I don't know, I don't think it can be all of them, I've met Americans and they weren't—"

Like P-A, she thought suddenly. Like all of P-A, even Reinschildt doesn't seem to have an inkling of the moral impossible. Any concept of something he shouldn't do.

"Some Yanks," she said, "yes. Probably some of us. I don't— understand it all. It's not just being in the army, or part of a megacorp. It's—the way some of them get."

He was quiet for a long moment. Then he said, "Aye," on that long-drawn note of resignation. This time it went to the edge of suffering.

"I've seen somethin' like it . . . on the field. In Erin." He stopped, and she knew they were both thinking about his wrecked parlor. Paddy Wild. "But here . . ."

He shut his eyes again. Then he almost whispered, "There's some things . . . about y'r time. I dinna think is worth the . . . the . . ."

The machine miracles, the glittering technology. Computers and ice cream and the Internet—and Laura reaching hospital, justice insisted, in time for modern medicine to save her life.

A deeper pain cut at her heart. She bent her head and hung onto his hand as the ambulance's turn pulled her away from him, and blinked back slow, almost impersonal tears.

Penned outside Emergency, she had time to picture all the possible calamities beyond the physical. Kidney damage, throat damage? But what if they ask things he can't imagine? Allergies? Are you a diabetic? Tetanus shots? If they want to take an X-ray? What if he doesn't just expose his ignorance, if he panics as well?

She bit her tongue and wriggled inside Anne's skimpy beach wrap. It's almost worse waiting damp and chilled and adrenaline-drained than it was hot and filthy and dust-grimed in the Ben Morar offices.

Until the young woman in floppy blood-spattered surgical blues strode up, saying, "You're with the Baringal people?" And she could only nod, the heart jammed solid in her throat.

"We had some tricky work with the shoulder blade, but the lung looks okay. She's taking blood. No definite prognosis for the percentage recovery yet. But she's stabilized. We're shifting her into the ICU. Family, or family representatives, can see her in a day or two."

Masses, was all Dorian could think. I promise. Every Sunday, to the end of my life.

"And—and—" She got it out before the surgeon turned away.

"The other case? Some airway inflammation. Very bad kidney bruising, but the damage should be only temporary. We're keeping him for observation tonight." She took another look. "You can see him, before they put him to sleep."

Jimmy looked paler than in the ambulance, fully gowned this time and settled firmly in a hospital bed, the white sheets bleaching even his hair. But his eyes focused when she pushed through the curtains, and the stone wall melted in open relief.

"You're all right." She slid down on the bedside and he tried to make a little room for her before their hands locked. "Oh, God . . ."

"Whisht, girl." It was barely a whisper, but however bedraggled, the expression was intended for a smile. "Have ye no' learnt yet . . . I'm hard to kill?"

"Oh, I know." She tried for lightness too. If you're really all right. If you haven't damaged your kidneys. If you can get over the other scarring, can live and manage to forget . . .

Holding hands was not reassurance enough. She tried to reach an arm over his chest, and he was cooperating more than willingly when footsteps came down the night-hushed ward. Instinctively Dorian drew back. A moment later the curtains shifted and Childers slid neatly inside.

He was still in uniform. He too looked tired and drawn. The aftermath of a big, dangerous, not entirely well-ended operation, Dorian thought, hardest on the one in charge. But he nodded to her with his usual scrupulous courtesy. Before he came to stand at the foot of the bed.

"You're okay, they said."

Dorian eased away. Jimmy managed to pull himself a little straighter. With a wariness she could hear, he said, "Aye."

Childers scanned him. The official face corrugated in an incipient frown.

"You mean, barring a hit on the head." Jimmy managed a sort of inclination. "And a good few places else. Over the kidneys, they said."

Jimmy dropped his own eyes. In a moment he muttered, " 'Tis supposed to be all right."

"When was that?"

"In the house. When he was . . . talkin'. He hit me a time or two."

"You'd have jumped him, otherwise?"

Jimmy's lashes flicked up and down. "He knew I couldna, wi' the kids." The set of his mouth retorted, I'd have tried.

Childers' own mouth compressed. "Breathing trouble. Possible kidney damage. He could have shot you at the door. Maimed you. Beaten you to death. It's sheer luck—and your dumb Irish stubbornness—he didn't finish you anyway."

Jimmy's eyes flew up. But then a reluctant twitch came at the corners of his mouth. "Dumb," he said. "Irish. Aye."

Very carefully, Childers breathed in.

"We got the perp," he said. "With no other deaths, and only one dangerous injury. The security guys are okay. Stunned with a Taser, tied up and gagged." Remembering those cocoons in the laundry dusk, Dorian felt her breath ease out. "We can put a cap on it with the media. They don't have pictures, they won't get names. I'll give them a press release tomorrow. In a day or two, the papers'll be done. The case itself is open and shut. Coroner's court. Mopping up. You've saved us a lot of—time. And work."

Jimmy stared at him, first incredulous, then, abruptly, with increasing wariness.

"And so help me," Childers said very quietly, "you ever do anything like that again, son, anywhere in my jurisdiction, and I'll paper the courthouse with your hide."

Jimmy's head reared back. There was more affront than shock in the down-the-nose stare.

"You didn't just preempt a command decision, or lay the whole operation wide open to a misconduct charge. You risked four lives. You deliberately stirred that bastard, with no psych skills, no siege training, no idea what he'd do. Then you risked yourself as well. With a good chance, after your goings-on, that he'd shoot you the instant you walked in. Leaving the whole shit heap to fall on us."

Jimmy's chin had come out. The stone wall matched Childers' glower.

"Not to mention," Childers said evenly, "Ms. Wild."

"I told ye I wouldna—I *couldna*—let her go in there!"

"And how would she feel, if you'd never come out?"

Jimmy's mouth flew open. And shut. The caught breath slid

away. Then he averted his face.

Childers stared at his profile. For a moment, Dorian detected something that might have been compunction. Even a hint of sympathy.

Then he said, "If one of my officers did what you've done, I wouldn't just discipline him. I'd throw him off the force."

Jimmy's head shot round. "Then 'tis lucky," he flared, "that I'm no' polis, aye?"

"*Aye,*" Childers snapped.

Both of them glowered. Dorian cringed. But then something in the clinch altered. The eyes, the body language slowly began to signal comprehension. Mutual outrage, mutual apology. A wry, rueful, almost amused accord.

Childers knows no one else could have done it. Jimmy knows Childers had to chew him out for it. But all the same, Childers is grateful. And Jimmy knows—admits—the chewing-out was justified.

Then Childers shifted weight and said with a piercing look under his eyelids, "Though as for what you really are . . ."

Jimmy's hands shut on the blanket. He took a breath.

"Ye said it. Dumb. Irish . . . sirr."

On the exact border, Dorian thought, her own heart thundering, between apprehension and reluctant respect.

Childers watched him, under those veiling lids. "Irish," he said.

Don't let him take that track. He's far too clever. Don't let him start thinking, start to guess.

"And carrying a concealed weapon. 'Borrowed' from a security agent. I should have your hide just for that."

"I hired him." The words shot out of Dorian's mouth. Childers looked at her and she babbled, "I hired him, so he had to have a gun."

She tried to hold his eyes, and failed. He looked back at

Jimmy, watching him now with near hunted intensity, almost crouched in the bed.

Childers' frown gelled. Dorian felt to her bones' marrow the instant when that scrutiny paused. Considered, abandoned purpose. Turned, slowly as a hawk changing its scan field, away.

Then Childers said, "I understand you've had some problem with your passport. We'll take Ms. Lewis' word, at the moment, as your ID. You'll almost certainly be asked for evidence at the inquests. On Brodie, as well as Sorenson. So don't leave Ibisville at present, Mr. Keenighan."

Sounding almost subdued, Dorian thought with his heart probably thumping harder than hers, Jimmy muttered, "Aye. Sir." And Childers turned to her.

"Ms. Wild, I believe your car, and both your belongings, are still in Blackston. The hospital helicopter can fly you up, tomorrow morning. If you drive back down, you may be able to pick him up, if the hospital's satisfied with his condition. And bring him some, ah, undamaged clothes."

Involuntarily she shot a look at Jimmy. But though his hands were tense, the dark stare was sufficiently composed. I can cope that long, it said.

"Thank you, Superintendent—"

"We'll drop you home now, and pick you up at, let's say, six-thirty A.M. By seven-thirty, you can be on the road."

"And check here by about nine. That would be very kind."

She saw nine o'clock go up on Jimmy's mental chart as Childers moved to usher her out. But damned if I'll just leave him like that.

She took two quick sideways steps and leant to kiss him, close above the line of beard. "I'll see you tomorrow. Behave yourself, if you can, till then."

She had done her best to make it overtly deadpan. He took the message, and understood it was for Childers as well. The first glint showed in that dark stare as he bent his head and murmured, "Yes'm, ma'am."

I can't believe, she thought, as the police car pulled into the motel parking lot, that it all looks just the same. Blackston, crisp and still cool on an early September morning, the park green, the dust all laid. Monday, when we met Dani in the restaurant, let alone Saturday, when I first checked in, seems a century away.

As far as my flat, coming home last night. Wondering if I'd sleep, even then. Still wondering, when I woke after seven hours' sheer oblivion. But at least I can function, today.

With what she told herself was a misguided pang she fitted Jimmy's scanty belongings into the rucksack and gathered her own. Downstairs, the receptionist accepted her credit card, turned it over, and frowned.

"Dorian Wild, yeah?" Dorian felt her heart roll. Will I hear Sorenson, now, every time someone says my name? "Can you hang on a moment? Got a mate really wants to catch up with you."

With startled thoughts of the media Dorian asked warily, "Who is it?" and the receptionist shifted her gum to the opposite cheek as she reached for the phone.

"Name's Tanya Wainwright. Worked out at Ben Morar." The flick of eyelids spoke volumes about small-town grapevines and small-town sophistication, which stifled outcry about the hottest news in town. "Something she needs to tell you, she says."

Tanya. George's secretary. The one link I couldn't find. The one person at Ben Morar who might have confirmed Chris's call.

"Tell her I'm in the restaurant," Dorian said, hefting bags.

Tanya was small and quick-moving with glossy brown un-streaked hair, demure in the Blackston version of a law-firm secretary's suit, Dorian guessed: crisp white blouse, navy pleated skirt. She slid into the opposite chair saying, "Ms. Wild, hello, no coffee, thank you, I'm headed for work. Cara said you were at the Park, she remembered your name from the news. I saw Tom Ralston a while back. He said you were asking about Chris."

Even though Dorian had thought herself prepared, the name was like a blow over the heart. After a moment she said, "I was, yes."

Tanya leant forward. "About whether Chris was sacked."

Half holding her breath, Dorian said, "Yes."

"Well, I can tell you. I saw Chris after Tom did. Probably I was the last person to see him—at Ben Morar. When he finished clearing his office, he came in to check off."

She stopped short, taking a breath. "He always came to check off. He was a good guy . . . I don't mind telling you, I know you were his girlfriend, but I had a soft spot for Chris."

Across the table their eyes linked. In the moment's pause filled with distant crows and teacup clatter, Dorian thought, Another epitaph.

Tanya nodded as if she had spoken aloud. "And I remember what we said. I always remember," she said it without emphasis, "what people in the office say."

Not just for efficiency, Dorian thought, or for gossip. As a point of pride.

"He came tearing in, the maddest I ever saw him. I've seen Chris fly off the handle and yell to raise the roof, but that day he was just white. He came up to the desk and he said, 'I'm off, Tanya. Off for good and bloody all. You've been a mate, and thanks for it. So long.'

"And I said, 'Really sorry to hear that, Chris. Will there be a reference or anything?' Cos if there was, I'd have to type it. And chase Richards for the copy as well.

" 'No!' he said, and started sort of laughing. 'No—reference, you out of your head?' And I said, 'You mean they gave you the boot?'

"And he said, 'They never had bloody time. I told 'em both to stuff their—job. To put it up their—behinds—and shove.' "

Tanya, Dorian found detachment to think, was as mealy-mouthed as Jimmy at times.

Tanya was also wearing a small but definite frown. "The next bit's what I really remember." She dug a pink nail as long and elegant as Dani's into a paper napkin. "I knew he'd had a brawl, and I didn't know—I didn't care—who was wrong. So I said, 'You'll pick up another job, no worries. You're a good geologist, Chris.'

"And he said, 'To hell with geology. I mightn't ever do it again.' "

Dorian felt her own breath catch. *This* I never heard before.

Tanya was nodding. "That was a real teeth banger. I mean, geology, he wasn't just good at it. It was Chris's life." She read agreement and nodded again. "I said, 'You're kidding. Come on, what else would you do?'

"And he looked out the door and said, sort of not listening, 'Dunno.'

"Then he stopped. Then he said, like he'd just thought of it, 'Oh, I just might go and join bloody Greenpeace. That's what I might do.' "

She stopped too, and blinked.

"Then he kind of pulled himself up. He said, 'See you, Tanya. Don't let the bastards grind you down.' He always said that. And he blew me a kiss and—went."

Leaving us to sit here, blinking at the memory like a pair of owls.

Dorian collected herself, too. She sounded only slightly husky as she said, "Thank you, Tanya. Thanks very much. I . . . I'm really glad you told me." For giving me, she could not get out, one more little piece of Chris.

Then the present came back. "Could you—if it came to a court case, would you be prepared to testify, that Chris told you he resigned?"

"Court case? You bet. I'll be more than happy, after those bastards sacked me for some pip-squeak Yank 'administrative assistant.' Screwing up files and losing phone lists and typing like a schoolkid." Her smile held a hint of fangs. "But I know what was in those files when I left."

There was a little pause. Then Dorian said, "No letter of termination for Chris?"

"No letter of termination. And I'll swear to that too, if they turn one up."

"McFadden?" said the woman on the hospital enquiry desk. "ICU?" She consulted her screen. "Condition's satisfactory. No visitors today."

Dorian let her breath out and tried not to feel let down. Of course nobody can see her yet, she's probably still doped to the eyeballs. "And a Mr. Keenighan?"

"Male medical ward?" Dorian shrugged. "Overnight observation? The doctors'll be finishing their rounds, if you want to go up. The ward'll have the latest news."

"Keenighan?" said a nurse at the ward station, when Dorian pinned one down. "Room fourteen. Kidney damage check, no blood in the urine." Lord, Dorian thought, I hope a female nurse didn't come for *that*. "Yes, the doctor said, he can leave as soon as his clothes arrive."

Jimmy moved, if not painfully, at least with extreme caution. He was still pale too, and noticeably tense, even having achieved the refuge of a fresh set of sneakers and jeans. They were in the car before he wanted to talk. But as she pulled into the stream of townward traffic he said, "Where're we goin' now?"

"My place." The inflection, part apprehension, part exhaustion, made Dorian want to lean over and pat him. I know this is getting too much, you're alone in this unending deluge of strangeness, it's not your world. "I thought, you might like to just—take it easy for a while."

I can't take you to Chris's unit. Not yet. I wouldn't leave you solitary, ever, in some hotel room. But I hope there isn't another fuss about sharing. Not just now.

Her peripheral vision caught his own sidelong glance. The wry little twist of the mouth. "I'll no' make a fuss this time," he said.

He did not want to talk about the hospital, beyond, "They gave me somethin' fearsome last night. Put me out like a coalminer's canary." And, "Those nurses. No decency at all!" But when Dorian opened her unit door, thinking, I don't have to worry, now, if my own place is what I'll find, he halted in the living room, with a long, encompassing stare.

And then dawning wonder, as he took in the TV, the stereo, the James Brown, the other furniture that to Dorian felt almost invisible. Before he said, "An' ye live here? All by y'rself?"

"It's only a unit. I know it's quite small . . ."

"Small?" An indrawn breath. A little laugh. "In Dungannon this'd fit half our house. An' seven to live in it. This—'tis fit for a manager, this."

Depositing his bag in the spare room, apologizing for desk and files, touring the bathroom, I can't believe I'm doing this, she thought, as if he's just another guest. But when she said, "If you give me your dirty clothes, I'll take them down with mine and run a load through the washing machine," he turned round short and gaped.

"A washing *machine?*"

Then nothing would do but a firsthand look. By the time she

had bloodied clothes quarantined, his original trousers carefully segregated—"Those're first quality moleskin, ye'd never toss 'em in wi' a white shirt!"—stain remover applied to collars and cuffs, detergent added and the machine filling, he was, if not entranced, at least beginning to thaw. "Ye'd be the most slovenly washermen in creation—ye dinna scrub a thing!" But as they started up the stairs she heard him murmur, with a backward look, "What Bridgie'd ha' given for one o' those."

"I need groceries," she said, upstairs. What on earth, at home, does, did he eat? Apart from mutton stew. He should rest, but this is probably safer. "I don't know what you'd like?"

The fruit and vegetable section of the local supermarket brought him up in his tracks. When he could speak again, he breathed, " 'Tis like a Sidhe feast, under the hill. Fruit out o' season. Magic." He half dared to touch a mushroom. "Where do they get these . . . out *here?*"

In Australia, Dorian thought, rediscovering history's gulf. For his time, fairy food. You might pick them, wild, in Ireland. But not in Blackston. Not even at the height of its wealth. Recklessly, she filled a bag and took some of the first strawberries as well.

But before they reached the checkout he was looking thoroughly dazed, and Dorian added potatoes, then, dubiously, pumpkin, then cereal and steak to the staples on her own initiative. They had just manhandled the bags into her kitchen when her cell phone went off.

"Dorian?" Dani looked immaculate in an ice-blue suit, but lines showed around her eyes. "The hospital said—Jimmy—was discharged. Are you—both of you—all right?"

Not just home, safe, physically as well as could be expected, Dorian filled in, but coping on the other fronts. Dealing with the memory, if not yet able to forget.

"I think we will be." It wouldn't be Dani to gush about

nightmares and ask if you had sedatives. Dorian reprised the hospital verdict on Jimmy, knowing she need not report on Laura. Dani nodded, with a visible tinge of relief. Then cleared her throat.

"I've told Anne to take compassionate leave, till next week at the very least. But with her and Laura both away, we're having a pileup in here." The gray stare needled Dorian's face. Inspection, not demand, she realized. Dani's never going to say, I'm sorry, I wish I didn't have to ask this. But if I don't look fit for it, she won't.

And I'm a junior partner. A member of her firm. She's back at work herself.

"I could come in for the afternoon," she said. "From two o'clock? I'll need a bit more time here." For Jimmy, she let her expression add, and Dani gave a quick nod.

Experience told Dorian, now, that the slight relaxation round Dani's mouth was relief. "Call by my office. I may have some updates, by then, from the police."

"I'm sorry," Dorian began apologizing as she clicked the phone off, and yet again her mind jammed at the sight of Jimmy, jeans and T-shirt, beard, cowlick, dark, formidable stare, tall and startling but no longer a temporary vision, in her living room. "I didn't want to go out, yet."

Not yet. I wanted to let you learn some of this world with almost the only person you can freely talk to. To keep you company, at the very least. But he was already waving a hand.

"Herself's in the right o' it. Wi' the three o' ye away they'll be drownin' in there . . ."

It tailed off. Dorian put the phone down and reached him before she thought. Her arms pulled clear of his waist, dropped from his back. "Oh, damn!" she broke out, fielding him somewhere round the hip bones, unable to control the shaky, only-half-amused laugh. "You're such a mess!"

"Aye." But the little catch of breath was also the intent of a laugh. And his arms came round her close and firmly. "But ye're no' a mess at all."

The embrace, the reassurance we couldn't manage in the ambulance, the hospital. Flesh and blood's reality check, as when Brodie died. You're here, alive. Safe.

"Anyhow," she said, as they slowly untangled, "you can sleep while I'm out. And there's the TV, you know how to use that. And CDs, I'll show you how to play those. There are some films, but a lot more music." She read the look on his face. "Okay, I'll show you that. But you have to rest some of the time! I'll get dinner, when I come home."

He had been very definitely drifting toward the stereo, but that brought him round. "*I* can cook quite fine, I'll have ye know." The fake dignity wobbled as he scanned the kitchen. "Or peel taties, if nothin' else."

"Okay, you can peel spuds, if you must." We sound like a married couple. We sound as if we'd been doing this for years. We sound the way I used to with Chris.

That dark spike of a glance up under his lashes had read too much. "I'll no' touch anythin'," he said, too quietly, "unless ye choose."

"No, it's . . . okay." I can't say it yet. That Chris used to come here, that Chris would cook for me. That it's not something, yet, I can replace. "I'm sorry, I didn't mean to sound . . ."

"Mo cailín. Will ye stop sayin' that?"

"Saying what?"

He was suddenly close beside her. His palm brushed, lighter than a breath, down her cheek.

"*Sorry.* Ye didna ask me to come here. Or make it happen. An' whatever's come of it, 'tisna all your fault. If I'm bent up like a Donnybrook brawler, I went lookin' for it. Both times. An' if 'tis—'tis all strange, an'—I'm a stranger—I can bear wi' that."

"Oh." But the little flaw of desolation in that last sentence had filmed her eyes. "I know all that. But still . . ."

"But still." A too careful pause. " 'Twas his place, too. An' ye've no' forgotten." Another pause. Then, more than carefully. "I'd no' want that . . . m'self."

If I were Chris. I wouldn't want my lover to forget me too soon. Whatever that meant to—his successor. And, she realized with a shock, I am thinking that.

But if you forgot Chris so quickly, she translated the rest, you'd do the same for me. And I wouldn't want to find you easily consoled. For your sake, for how I think of you, as much as mine.

She blinked the tears down and looked up into his face. They were still standing very close.

"Yes," she said, careful in her turn. "Chris and I—were here. And he did cook, sometimes. But"—she had to pause, to pick her way through the delicate, fragile maze of words—"that doesn't mean . . . you have to behave like it's a, a museum. That you can't—won't—be at home—belong here—too."

Is that message too blatant, she thought, as their eyes held. Too soon? Does it spell out too quickly what we're both, what I know we're both thinking, does it upset your customs the way I've done so often before?

He lifted his hand and again, very lightly but less briefly, cupped her cheek. Then he said, so softly that despite the words it verged on tenderness, "Show me how this 'music' starts. An' then off to work wi' ye. I can peel taties by m'self."

Dani appeared around four, when the flood of preliminary work on reclaimed or transferred cases had ebbed far enough for

Dorian to think, If I don't have coffee, I'll die. As she inwardly moaned and set the cup aside, Dani said, "I've just had Andy Childers on the phone."

"Oh?" Dorian tried to look alert and concerned. *I can't* ask if they've made it up. "Oh! Was it advance stuff about, ah . . ."

"It was." Dani slid gracefully into the client's chair, declined coffee with a tiny head shake, and folded her hands. There was a sleekness about her, Dorian thought suddenly, despite the lines at her eyes. "Preliminary reports. They'll do a media release in about an hour. In the meantime, they've turned up Sorenson's phones. He bought a new one yesterday. Then he left the other in his motel room. Charging, message bank on. That's how they missed it when he moved."

Their eyes met, and Dorian knew the information was as close as Childers, or the police as a whole, would come to an official apology.

"They did"—Dani's tiny fastidious grimace added, At least *this* worked—"manage not to destroy the call records getting into these."

Dorian forgot her coffee. "They found records! Who of? Not . . ."

"Reinschildt, yes." In anyone else it would have been a purr. "The police faces are a little flushed, actually. It turns out Sorenson was bugging their wavelength. He knew almost as much as they did about Ben Morar, and its aftermath."

She's in fucking Blackston, yeah. You throw her on that po-lice chopper and fly. That recording the bitch made in the rocks with Ed.

Dani's look said, You're not surprised. Do you know the rest?

"Jimmy told me, in the ambulance. That the records were just bait. He was after me."

Dani nodded once, too.

"Bait for Harvey, he said. I think that's Reinschildt?"

"That's what the calls suggest." If Dani were a cat, she would

211

have groomed her whiskers. "I think he left them there, deliberately. As a sort of insurance, perhaps."

"Eh?"

Dani very nearly smiled. "There are two calls to Reinschildt. In the first, Sorenson's almost ropeable about Brodie. You told him to fix it, he kept yelling, and he got himself—censored—killed. Now they'll hang the forgery on him too. And a good deal more, most of it profane, about Brodie being a friend and he wouldn't see him done down after he died."

"Jimmy said he kept talking about that."

Dani nodded again. "Reinschildt was going to hang up. Until Sorenson got to: You cut this call and I'll take it to the media. The stockpile, the Ben Morar suspension, the new mine, the—Chris's death—the lot."

Dorian felt her mouth fall wide. "Oh, my!"

"That stopped Reinschildt, yes. He said, What do you want? Sorenson said—Andrew played this to me—I'll get you all the copies of that model. And the contract. And the recording with Brodie. Reinschildt said, after a while, How'll you do that? Sorenson told him, Never you mind. You want the model or not?"

Dorian wanted to groom her whiskers too. An unsolicited, officially approved recording. I bet Sorenson did leave it on the phone. Insurance, yes. If he went down, he was going to make sure Reinschildt had a good chance of going too.

"Reinschildt hemmed and hawed a few times. Tried to find what Sorenson planned. Sorenson just kept saying, Forget it, you get the model or I go to the media. Which do you want?"

Between a rock and a hard place. Reinschildt himself. At last.

"And eventually Reinschildt said, Get the damn records, then. It was quite clear, he was thinking exactly what we did. There's no way to be sure he had them all. He started in to give Sorenson instructions, and Sorenson said, Whoa. I want a few other things first."

Dorian stared.

"Some P-A resources," Dani said, on the verge of smugness. "He said, I'll need a car, and I want it parked at the pullover by Bluewater." Dorian twitched, not needing to exclaim, it's only five kilometers north of Baringal. He'd take the police car that far, and change. "And then, in Cairns, at the airport, I want the P-A jet. Fueled up, on standby, from five P.M. tonight."

"A jet!" Dorian could not control the yelp. *Bigwigs from Brisbane . . . with a private jet.* "Then he meant to skip the country. Jimmy said he reckoned he had a fifty-percent chance of getting away—and he wanted the company *jet!*"

"He thought big, you must admit." Dani's tone held a judicious hint of valedictory respect.

"My God—what did Reinschildt say?"

"Reinschildt puffed and panted of course, spluttered about justification and cost and company risk and where was he going, anyhow? Sorenson wouldn't tell him. I'll give the pilot a flight plan, he said. And don't say the plane's not there or you haven't used it before. Or how'd Ed come in?"

Brodie. Brodie flew in from somewhere. On the company jet. The forgery, mending the dyke at Ben Morar was that important. To Reinschildt, to P-A's Pacific sector. Maybe to the company overall.

"When he got to that, Reinschildt folded. Okay, he said, okay. I have to sort this out. Give me the rest of the day, I'll get back . . . Sorenson said, No, Harvey, Mr. Reinschildt, *sir.* It's eight A.M. here now. It don't take all day to deploy a jet. You call me by ten A.M., or I call the TV station. They know about Ben Morar, they're all hot to trot. A big story like this."

Dorian could not help the whistle. "Lord!"

Dani herself half smiled. "He did have the nerve." She refolded her hands. "So then Reinschildt said a few nasty words, and hung up. Two hours later he called again."

Sylvia Kelso

Dorian drew in her breath.

"Okay, he said, okay. You get the jet, you get the car. We get the model and contract copies, you can burn the rest. If we miss those copies, I'll personally see someone finds you, whether it's the South Pole or Nicaragua. And you'll be finished. Understood? And Sorenson said, okay."

Nerve. What it must have taken, Dorian thought, to sit there, those two hours, gambling on a man like Reinschildt's playing true, calling you back, not just finding another eliminator on the spot. Not arranging some other double cross—and all the while, thinking ahead, knowing the risk, seeing the opportunity window narrow, where any delay, even an accident to the jet, would increase the chance of the cops catching up. All this before he could start the real thing. He didn't just have nerve. He must have been made of ice.

And planning the rest, like an SAS commando hit. Ropes, fluorescent vest, maybe a clipboard to play meter man, the gun in a concealed holster, another car, the second phone, the Taser for the security men. It must have been like a one-man military operation.

That's exactly what it was. As Ben Morar would have been.

And Jimmy and I threw a spanner into works like that.

She sat back and drew a long, long breath. Then she could feel the openly gleeful smile spreading, as she said, "So, can we go after P-A now?"

The smile glinted back at her. "Nine-fifteen tomorrow, I have a cancellation," Dani said as she stood up. "See me in my office. We'll lay out the draft."

214

CHAPTER 9

I forgot to mention Tanya. Dorian stopped short at her unit door. I was so lit up about Sorenson, and finally getting a handle on Reinschildt, I clean forgot to give Dani the case's new, other plank.

Tomorrow, she decided. Tonight I've other fish to fry.

The door swung open, and music poured out at her. Orchestral music, reaching a climax, its finale delivered by a single instrument. A violin.

Jimmy was on the couch. Hunched over on the couch, straining forward as if physically pulled into the nexus of the speakers, where the violinist was concluding his note. Lips parted, eyes . . .

If he looked like that when he was going to kiss me, she thought, I'd be in ecstasy.

The note ended. The unit rang to piped applause.

In a moment, as if released from a spell, Jimmy slowly straightened up. Then she moved and he whirled round and grunted as some injury twinged, and as he slithered back into the cushions, Dorian placed what the music had been.

Beethoven. The violin concerto. When he listened to anything but rock and folk, Chris liked the contradictory austerities of Bach and Satie, but her mother had given her the Beethoven concertos at university. Their romantic extravagance was part of her mind's furniture. Looking at Jimmy, she thought, Not like this.

After a minute, he slowly shook his head. Then without embarrassment wiped the edge of a hand under his eyes. Then he looked at the speakers and whispered, "That . . . 'tis a miracle."

It's only a stereo system, she had the sense not to say: an average stereo, a popular CD.

"Didn't you have Beethoven? Or at least, classical music?"

He looked up, and produced a half-strength snort. "Concerts, aye. Out o' tune pianos an' amateur fiddlers. An' songs fro' the music hall."

"Oh." No records back then, he'd only ever have live music. A poor family in Dungannon, and even if he could afford concerts in Blackston, what sort of music would reach the fields? No wonder a good reproduction of concert-quality Beethoven sounds like Orpheus.

"That was—" He got out of the couch. Now the expression was simple awe. "T' hear that wee man play. But the music . . . ye can hear the bones o' it. All the architecture. The harmonies." He shut his eyes. "If I do see heaven, I'll no' be chasin' angels. I'll've heard 'em here."

Damn Beethoven. I'd be in heaven, if he looked like that at me.

Then he opened his eyes and drew himself back to mundanity with a tentative smile. "Mo cailín . . . I beg y'r pardon, I was. I was . . ."

I know where you were. She dumped her briefcase and tried a smile of her own. "That's okay. You just better have peeled the spuds, though. Cos I'm dying of hunger, and I've got some *news.*"

"Oh." The look was very near consternation. "I didna . . . at least . . ."

"What's happened?"

"The taties." He looked as near as he could to shifty. "Horrible great lumps, they was, only fit for skelpin', an' then about as tasty as glue. An' down in the Gates o' Babylon I saw—"

"The what?"

"Ye know, the grocery place. The Gates o' Babylon." His mouth folded. "Grand as a Sidhe market, an' every temptation the de'il ever spawned—"

Dorian burst out laughing despite herself. "You mean the supermarket? Okay, okay, what did you see?"

He gave her an uncertain look, then gestured to the kitchen. "There was new taties, small ones. Nice an' clean. So"—with a certain defiance—"I went down an' got some, ye see."

"You went out? You got in and out of the . . . you remembered the way? But your back. Your ribs. The key! How did you . . . ?"

"I had money, what ye paid me, an' there was a key on the shelf," he gestured kitchenward again. "An' it didna hurt, I needed the walk."

Wits, I said. More than wits, to cope with a supermarket and somebody else's key, to assert his own idea of decent food, and—he can live in this world, if he has to, without leaning on me.

"I did sleep, a good while." He was growing outright conciliatory. "An' I found the steak, in y'r ice chest, an' put some peppercorns on f'r relish. Ye can cook whenever ye want."

"Okay." She managed to collect her own wits. "I'm just amazed you could walk that far. Let me put this stuff away."

While the steak sizzled and Jimmy silently annexed the vegetable preparations, she pulled a bottle of Wolf Blass from her top kitchen shelf. There is something, she thought, to celebrate. A double something. I wonder if he's ever had a decent red before?

"Australian wine?" He took a dubious sip, and surprise became astonishment. "This . . . this is . . ."

Not as good as Beethoven, she thought, and managed a smile.

217

"They may not be Scotch—ah, whiskey—but we make pretty good wines." Another score for our time. She lifted the glass. The toast came back, from her grandfather's day. She did not have to say she was thinking of Reinschildt, she had poured out that news over the cooking. "Here's confusion to our enemies."

He looked first grim, then suddenly amused. "Aye. An' here's to the king over the water." He passed his glass across the water jug, and she almost got a full smile. "If ye're truly wishin' to be old-fashioned, that is."

By the time they stacked the dishwasher—"ye wash *dishes* wi' a machine!"—the red had sent a glow through Dorian's veins, and from the backchat they were both finding funny, she guessed it had reached Jimmy as well. "D'ye have a machine to wipe y'r noses too?" He came round the counter, still smiling, and looked down at her. "An' what's m'lady's pleasure now?"

Pleasure. She looked up at him, thinking yet again how tall he was at close quarters, and the dimmer light of the table lamp traced the line of that lower lip, relaxed in a half smile, soft and close as in her motel room. Pleasure. She felt her ears buzz. Damn that Shiraz. I'm within an inch of grabbing him.

Grab a man with bullet creases and kidney bruises. Oh, that's a really good idea.

He had stopped smiling. Between them, the silence sagged.

"I—uh. Oh, lord, the washing! It's still on the line!"

She found the laundry basket, they clattered downstairs, both talking too loudly, laughing too much. After a small dispute over who carried the basket, they clattered back. "Here you are," she said piling his arms with jeans and trousers and T-shirts, "I'll find space to hang those shirts, soon as I fix my stuff."

Why on earth did I say that, she cursed herself, eyeing the spare-room doorway. I could have just said, Put your gear somewhere, I'm ruined, I have to go to bed, goodnight.

No. I couldn't. Not tonight. Not with him.

He must have stowed almost everything in the rucksack. Given his own space, his arrangements were more Spartan than neat. Small areas, shared, she thought. Dealing with that from birth. Her own voice echoed in her ears. "There's hanging room in here."

She half expected a demand that the shirts be ironed first, but he did not comment. He had become abruptly sober and noticeably quiet.

"I did make the bed up, those are clean sheets."

He straightened, just across from her at the bed foot. She tried not to shy out the door.

Do I say, Shall we go out? See a film? Heavens, try not to be completely ridiculous.

His hands were empty. He was standing wholly, abnormally still.

"I guess . . . we could, uh, put on some more music?" She just managed to bite her tongue on, It's too early to go to bed.

He said nothing. The silence grilled her like heated iron. It's not just that he's hurt, she cursed as ancient scruples resurrected, he's in my house, in my world, with nobody else to rely on. If I, if I *exploit* him—if I say, Come to bed, and then, one day, he, I, we don't want each other—if he hasn't gone back to his own time—what's he going to do?

I don't know, the rest of her mind retorted tartly, but if you don't say something Real Soon, it won't matter what you do.

"I—ah—" No. I *can't* say, Do you have everything you need? "Mo cailín."

His voice was still slightly husky, but it had softened to that rubbed velvet undertone. He did not move, did not try to touch her. But the inflection was palpable as a hand.

"Mo cailín." A little breath. "Dorian. Will ye come to me?"

She had turned before she knew. He met her eyes, and held them, though he was going red.

"I'd ask ye—if, if they do it here—tonight, I'd ask ye . . ." He dropped his eyes suddenly. "This night, to, to share . . . like the hotel." The little outward movement of both hands supplemented: I know I'm a man and not supposed to need comfort, companionship, but tonight, I do. Victorian scruples or not, I want someone near me. Near as sharing a bed.

And he'd have the right as well as the need, after what he's been through.

Then he drew another sharp breath and lifted his eyes.

"But if I did that—if ye said, Yes—if ye were here . . ." Now the red was deeper, though he would not look away.

"I know I wouldna—I couldna—leave it at . . . *share*."

Dorian felt her own breath stop.

He looked in her eyes, and set his jaw. "I know I'm . . . no' canny about . . . women. I know"—the red darkened—"ye might no'—I might no'—give ye—what ye'd want."

Stop, Dorian's hands said involuntarily. Don't apologize, don't feel shame, I'm almost sure you're a virgin, but you don't, you *don't* have to excuse that to me. "Jimmy . . ."

He had understood enough. The tension eased from the lift of his chin. Then he braced himself again, though now the tone hinted at wry, almost self-mockery.

"An' then, I know . . . I still havena a whole skin."

You made a promise, in that utility room. First, you said, grow a whole skin.

His lashes flickered suddenly and rose again.

"But a' the time, in that wee pool, I was thinkin': Mo cailín told me, Yes. An' I willna give that sod best—I canna die, I willna bluidy die . . . before I can—before she can . . ."

He held her eyes with open defiance, despite the reviving blush. "If I have to go back, I couldna bear that, either. I . . . ah, the way I'm feelin' now, I willna live to mornin', if I—if we—if I canna first say, Yes, to ye."

The pause seemed to stretch, lengthening, endless, like that eternal second as a drop of honey poises on the rim of a jar. In all the world there was nothing but this room, holding the moment, cupping the light, caught on his face, lost in the darkness of that stare.

Then Dorian found she had moved. Was stepping forward, and her hands had come out because his had already shut on them. And then let go, as she kept moving and his arms closed round her instead while her own arms circled his neck and she was thinking with satisfaction as their mouths met, At least I can touch you *there*.

Uncounted time later they came up for air. This time, she thought, still pressed tight against him, you didn't pull away. But when his grip changed, suggesting rather than drawing her toward the bed edge, she found she had hung back.

"Not here." It's just a single bed. I could catch your sore spots before I even know. But his body language brought her eyes up, to meet a more than apprehensive look.

"No' . . . ?" In your room, the gesture completed, in the bigger bed that I've seen for myself? Not there?

"No." He knows what I mean. I know what he's thinking. It may be my bed, but it's the one I shared with Chris.

His eyes had almost dilated. The look, close to panic, said, Not anywhere in the flat, then? Not yet?

Not here, not there. Inspiration struck. "Bring those pillows, will you?" She kissed him briefly and headed for the linen cupboard, spare pillows, spare, clean sheets. Tossing out the first one across the big rug in the living room, she said, "Here."

With a rug on carpet, even kidney bruises should be okay. She drew the last corner out smooth, and straightened, and without surprise found him close enough to embrace again.

They stood face to face at the sheets' edge. Her heart was bumping. I bet, she thought, his is too.

Because it won't just be sex, for either of us. For him, it's got to be the first time, if not physically, at least with all his feelings engaged. And for me . . .

It'll be moving on. Saying good-bye.

Really saying good-bye, to Chris.

The side glow of the table lamp limned the dark glints in his hair and beard, the eyes' deeper dark, the expression. Stern, concentrated, almost austere.

Is he saying good-bye too?

She held out her hands. Wordlessly he took them, but he moved no closer than before.

"I have to ask. Before we . . ." Before we pledge ourselves, in the ties of flesh and blood. "Is there—was there—anyone in Blackston? Anyone . . ."

Anyone who could be damaged, if we do this, in ways we can't, any longer, damage Chris?

He took her meaning. It was in the shift of his face. Then, just visibly, he shook his head.

"The fine girls," he said, "the managers', the owners' wives, the daughters . . . I'd watch 'em, aye. Passin' the *Miner.* Comin' an' goin', wi' their pretty clothes an' their parasols. But they were no' for me."

Not for a poor man, even a working man, she thought, feeling the lump return in her throat. Not the pretty, expensive girls, like the ones in the pageant on that Blackston street.

"The others . . . there's no' many decent women on a field. Even writin', I never made more than five pound a week. An' there was Ma, an' the girls. An' the house. Took the three o' us to manage that. But Bridgie. I couldna have . . ." Have denied her that. "An' ye canna—ask a woman to marry, wi' no place to call her own, an' less than five pound a week."

Amid so many who could have offered so much more. And only marriage would have done for you.

"Otherwise?" He gave his head another tiny, dismissive shake. "Shebeen drabs an' washerwomen? Or over to Gards Lane, an' the dance-hall Chinese?" The twist of the mouth was less fastidious than pitying. His eyes came back to her, dark and very still. "No. There isna—there wasna—anyone in Blackston—rememberin' me."

"Okay." She had to swallow before it would come out. His face moved a little too. Anticipation, perhaps, perhaps apprehension at last. She looked up and said a little too fast, "Just one other thing. I know, in your time, they, um, wore clothes everywhere." It had been part of folklore as well as history, the Victorian insistence on nightgowns, nightcaps, even on a wedding night. "But here . . . here, we don't."

She watched him work it out. The eyes widen, the apprehension become plain anxiety, and suddenly, a struggling shadow of that puck at the corner of the mouth.

"Ye mean . . . ye want us both to . . . ?" Strip off? Shock and inburnt modesty's reflex, disbelieving, halfway to scandalized. And then more than the shadow of a laugh.

"Mo cailín." The grin would not stay smothered. "I'm thinkin', the best o' that bargain'll be mine."

"I'll risk it." Suddenly she could feel her own mouth curve. "I told you, you have too low an opinion of yourself. Even when you're full of holes." She saw him in the utility room, those long spare muscles, that cream-smooth skin. "Besides," she made it carefully demure, "it can be fun."

"Fun?" For an instant scandal almost prevailed. Then in that dark stare the glints flickered. The youthful hell-raiser, the street boy. Teasing, recognizing, taking a dare.

"Show me," he said.

★ ★ ★ ★ ★

"Well, now your shoes are off, I can do this." She tugged gently to undo his belt, and he twitched. "And this." She undid his jeans button and as his elbows clamped instinctively, began easing the T-shirt free. When his arms relaxed, she worked it up over the rib dressing. "And . . ."

For a moment he stared back at her expectant look. Then understanding broke. He took the hem from her and began to draw it over his head.

She looked at him in the half-light, and he looked back. Nerves, tension, mild defiance, fading as he read her face. *You weren't lying. You do find me beautiful.*

If beautiful was a word he'd use for men. She gave herself a mental shake and moved closer, feeling for the jeans zip, at first trial the source of some comment and not a little near ribaldry. When she started to draw it down, he made one jerky motion, and consciously stopped. She drew the zip full open, then began to slide jeans and briefs together down his hips.

Denim crumpled round his shins. Gingerly, he drew his feet clear. Disdaining—not daring?—to look down. Holding her eyes, as if he dared not look away.

And he trembled, nervous, responsive as an unschooled blood horse, she thought, as she settled her hands, carefully, delicately, round his naked hips.

Too fine for satin, too soft for silk. Her fingers spread and caressed almost involuntarily, and he drew an audible, thickened breath and said huskily, "Is this 'fun' just for ye?"

"Oh, no." That involuntary smile had caught her own face again. Feeling demure, and reckless, and more than wholly desirable, she drew her hands back and shifted her shoulders a little. "Not if you can manage buttons, that is."

The tailored office shirt fastened with a procession of small ones down the front. She had expected fumbling, clumsiness.

But his fingers were quick and deft and almost too fast—till just between her breasts they slowed abruptly. The rest he opened with a care, a lingering, that was almost ritual.

He lifted his head from the task, and that dark stare gleamed. "Easier than fishin' out scrambled print," he murmured. "But I'd no' want it done *too* soon."

She caught her laugh back and tugged a lock of suddenly accessible cowlick as he began to ease out the shirt. He frowned over her skirt's unbroken front. Then his hands closed on her shoulders, she revolved obediently, and with a little satisfied sound he found the clasp at her waist.

A look over her shoulder, his warmth palpable against her skin, his cheek laid a moment against her hair, and he understood where to approach her bra. The snaps undid. He slid the straps off her shoulders. There was a little, precipice pause. Then his hands clasped her shoulder points again.

Even in half-light, the feelings were clear in his face. I don't, she thought, have to be jealous of Beethoven now.

In a minute or two he remembered to start breathing. He murmured something in Gaelic. Closed his eyes. Opened them. Whispered, "Mo cailín . . . can I . . . ?"

Can I do as you did? Can I touch?

She took his hands and drew them to her breasts and felt him shudder to his foot soles as his skin met hers.

"This?" he said, fitting the word between long shaky breaths, eyes searching hers, fingers sliding, tentative, questioning, into the top of her briefs. And she worked her hands up his back, feeling her way between bruises, and felt his spine bow as if her touch weighed like a boulder, as she said, "That too."

"Dhia," he said, now wholly breathless, on his knees, face against her midriff, hands slipping, shaping, caressing, over her loins, her haunches, her thighs. "Oh, Dhia, ye're so—so—the shape—the feel o' ye—I never knew—I never dreamt—"

Don't dream, she wanted to say. It's real this time. If you never had this before, if you spent thirty years lacking, missing the mere physical pleasure as well as the emotional bond, the surcease of loneliness, the laughter, the joy, you'll have it, full measure and running over, now.

She slid down on her own knees, drawing her hands down his ribs, his thighs, then between them. As her hand found him he gave one gasp and lost his breath altogether. She managed to focus on his face, eyes glazed, that lower lip meltingly soft, undone beyond desire. She kissed it, again, before she pushed him gently back on the sheets and said, with a last reach for composure, "Let's try it this way, for now."

So at the very least, she told herself when she drew both his hands to her breasts and finally slid a knee across his thighs, you're not going to blow yourself away before you even know what you've missed.

Dorian woke, and smiled before her eyes opened. At the unaccustomed give of living-room rug under her hip. At the tenderness of beard rash in familiar places, at the weight and warmth next to her. At the delicate susurrus of breath, lighter than a spider's step, on the newly explored territory of her ear.

" 'Behold,' " he said, under a whisper, " 'thou art fair, my love; behold, thou art fair.' "

She rolled over, luxuriously, inside the arch of his arm. Her heart gave a small, unfamiliar twinge at the look in those eyes. Keeping sight of the topic, she said, "What's that from?"

The look vanished in a narrowing glint of smile. "Ah, ye heathen. D'ye not know the Song o' Solomon?"

"I don't think so." She found another stray lock of cowlick and exerted pressure. He slid obediently down, his cheek coming to rest somewhere above her left breast, and they both sighed.

In a moment he murmured, "Now I know why the priests talk against it so. Sin an' temptation. Aye. The widest gate o' Hell. An' I'd sell my soul for it, did ye ask me, right now."

"I never meant to mislead you that far." He gave a small but full-power snort and other considerations revived. "Did I hurt you—last night?"

"Which time?" Then the grave, one-eyed stare melted in a smothered laugh. He sat slowly up, and began taking stock.

"I canna tell y'r bruises from the others, but there's still skin on m' back. Though ye've torn those pretty hospital patches clean off. I think there's blood as well as—other things—all over the sheets. If ye'll teach me to use that 'washin' machine', I can see to that."

"You can wash as well as cook?"

"We hadna much choice, after Bridgie . . ." He let the rest slide into their mutual quiet.

In a moment she said, "If you do that—take the sheets off my bed too."

Wash them too, she saw him understanding. As a statement. A symbol. That even if the bed's the same, it's no longer under Chris's taboo.

Oh, Chris. Will I ever finish saying good-bye?

"I made him a promise," he said abruptly, looking at his hands, "last night."

She drew one of his hands toward her and let that answer, What?

"I said, I'll never try to replace ye. Or ask her to forget ye. But I'll take care for her . . . the way I think ye'd want. Whatever I have to do."

"That's . . ." She felt her eyes swim. His hand closed on hers, and she drew it against her cheek.

He'd have liked Jimmy. They'd have liked each other. The same ironic humor, the same ability to laugh at yourself. The same courage, I think.

Oh. I didn't tell Jimmy either. Tanya. I know why Chris left Ben Morar now, why he told George and Reinschildt to stick their job. And I still don't understand.

She let go Jimmy's hand and turned on her stomach, chin in palms. "Yesterday," she said, "I found out something else—something new—about Chris."

He listened without interrupting. Except that after a few sentences, his hand settled in the curve of her back. Fingers spread, unmoving, in the intent but not the distraction of a caress.

"Tanya couldn't figure it out either," she ended. "Why would he—how could he—have just, just decided to give up geology? His career? His life?"

After a long moment he said, "What's this 'Greenpeace,' then?"

"A big environmental protection group. They campaign, they have blockades and demonstrations. Just about P-A's complete opposite. And Chris was a company geologist."

Another long pause. Then he said slowly, "That, then, wi' her—was that when he made up his mind?"

"I suppose—no. No, wait. Ralston. Ralston said . . . that morning. Chris was giving the publicity guy the specs of the new mine. Ralston said, he just stopped. Then he said, *I don't know why I'm doing this*. And he walked out. Next thing he'd fronted George. So that's when he decided. Because after that they had the row."

Ranting and raving like a rabid greenie. Beside her, Jimmy sat motionless. Traffic rumored remotely. Apart from a fitful door slam, the apartment block was almost quiet.

Jimmy's thumb shifted, a tiny, absent touch against her skin. She craned around. He was staring before him, a deep crease between his brows.

"D'ye know . . . it minds me o' the Road to Damascus," he said.

"The what? Oh." Of course, he'd have the Bible at his fingertips. The apostle Paul, Mosaic zealot, Christians' persecutor. Struck down by God on the road to Damascus. Every belief reversed, spun from Mosaic to Christian fanatic, in one blinding slash of light.

Her scalp prickled. She rolled to see Jimmy's face, and saw her own near-awe reflected back. Maybe it wasn't God, but to experience an illumination, a transfiguration like that . . .

She sat up too, to touch his shoulder, the comfort of warm, tangible flesh and blood. He looked sideways with a brief, comprehending smile. I've never felt anything like that either, it said.

Then he visibly changed focus. One of those butterfly touches on her cheek, before he turned her wrist to see the watch face, and grimaced. "Why ye canna use a clock wi' hands . . . D'ye know, 'tis the half o' eight already? Must ye go to y'r 'office,' or"—the awe had become a distinctly secular gleam—"d'ye think, another wallow in sin . . . ?"

"Sin . . . half-past *eight!*" Dorian nearly catapulted up. "I have to see Dani at nine-fifteen!"

"I think that'll do," Dani said. "List our evidence first, yes. That we know about the Ben Morar job suspensions and the compensation swindle. Also the proposed forgery. That we have evidence about a P-A employee involved in Chris's death. Withhold anything about Brodie's bag, and Tanya's evidence as well. And of course, George's efforts with the yield figures. We have an obligation there, and it'll be a separate investigation in any case. Do point out that the police have given us access to some recorded phone conversations with Sorenson, which indicate P-A's direct involvement in a hostage situation."

She sat back a little in her office chair. "Reinschildt may think he can blow off the swindle stuff, and claim the forgery was only intent. His barrister can discredit the stockpile recording. But he can't dismiss the Sorenson calls."

No, Dorian thought, scribbling numbers in her notes and consciously not baring her teeth.

"Mention that at this point, we have no desire to approach the media. Not before the police investigations close."

Carrot for the donkey. With a glimpse of stick.

Dani turned a gold-and-fluorescent-purple propelling pen to and fro. Her eyes had an absent, inward look. Then they turned to Dorian, gray as steel and twice as cold.

"Then list what we want. As we've agreed, our first objective is to clear Chris. To have it publicly spelled out that he was not sacked from Ben Morar. And, yes, say we want a public disclosure of Brodie's part in his death."

The haggle point, Dorian thought.

"You can also mention we require personal immunity for everyone involved, on our side, from any further—attentions—by persons employed by or connected to Pan-Auric."

Dorian nodded. Let's not mention, yet, the possibility of a damages suit. For Anne and the kids, if no one else.

"If stopping the mine is our highest priority, then it won't hurt to make a preliminary statement of intent. Put in the part about, information indicates the new mine, as currently projected, will be historically destructive as well as environmentally hazardous. We will be taking advice."

Formal notice of a lawyer calling on specialists in preparation for mounting a case. Dorian felt her spine creep as at a trumpet call.

"I think"—Dani glanced at her watch—"I can leave you to set that up. I do think we should consult before it goes. Check my schedule with Jo." I'm lucky to have had this long, Dorian thought, this much of a senior partner's expertise. She said, "I'll be as fast as I can," and Dani nodded. Then her eyes flickered up.

"I imagine you'll want to see Laura too. They were expecting to allow visitors tomorrow, the last I heard. I wouldn't—yet— try to talk to Anne." Dorian nodded, trying not to look as sick at heart as she felt, and Dani set down her pen.

"Dorian, I suggest you see Laura in the morning, and then go on to Blackston. There's something I want you to check."

Dorian tried not to stare. Tomorrow is Saturday, but . . . "I thought, the caseload?"

"It won't take long. Though you might want to go alone."

She read Dorian's face too quickly and permitted herself a small, far-too-perceptive smile. Yes, it said, whatever you've been up to, it shows. The smile vanished.

"I want you to go through the old cemetery," Dani said.

Dorian had yelped before she knew it. *"What?"*

"The old cemetery," Dani said patiently. "Where Jimmy's sister may be buried."

Dorian could only stare, trying not to cry, Do you think I'm a ghoul?

Dani rapped the pen on her desk and the gray seemed to lighten in her eyes. "Think, Dorian. If you're right about this alternate history thing, if there really are two Blackstons—then there should be two of the people as well."

The Anneke Silver collage seemed to loom out of the wall, its pale-trunked trees bending like lathes. Dorian knew her mouth was sagging, and could not pull it shut.

"You didn't think it through?" Dani stared at her, eyes still sharp as laser points. "They might have this Ned Kelly, and we don't, but your ancestor must have been in both, times, or whatever they are. Else you wouldn't both know the story about the hat. We know Jimmy, and his sister, and her husband, were in the other time. But there's a picture of him here as well."

Doubles. You're saying, doubles. Not just alternate history. Alternate people.

Two of Paddy Wild. Two of Jimmy. Two of—

"No! No, that's impossible!"

The pen went down with a snap. "You have a man here from eighteen eighty-six, walking, talking, stirring up gunmen and bleeding genuine blood. What's more impossible than that?"

"It's just history—alternate history!"

"History *is* people, Dorian."

"But two—two of him—of Paddy Wild—of—!"

Dani's jaw stiffened. "Two of you, maybe, yes. Two of me."

My God, Dorian thought. She's already figured this as well. The uncanny, the bizarre, the instinctively denied idea that she's not the one and only Dani Lewis. That somewhere, there's another one of her, in a—world? That differs in just one or two small ways from this.

"I can't imagine how the timelines, or whatever they are, got crossed. But you have to admit the evidence. If this about Ned Kelly is true, then Jimmy hasn't just traveled forward in our time. He's come from another time. Or place. Somewhere almost here, but not."

Dorian got her breath. It took her as far as a winded "Uh."

"Our Jimmy," Dani said calmly, "seems very fond of his sister. So there's a least a fifty-percent chance the other was too. And that means a chance he might have stayed in Blackston. If you can find Bridget's grave, you might find his as well."

Dorian felt her mouth fall right open. Then her spine began to creep in earnest and she nearly backed out the door.

"I can't do that!"

"I said, you might do better to go alone."

"But, but—" God, beyond the sheer gruesomeness of hunting a grave for a man alive, here and now, a man who'll be looking at the grave of his—double? A man I've just—my God, what can she want?

"I don't understand! What's it matter if there's a—even if I could find—" Her whole back squirmed. "What's the *point?*"

Dani actually rolled up her eyes. "If we find a grave for Jimmy in this whatever it is, then we know there's also a birth date. And with that, we can find the original birth certificate."

Dorian tried again not to wail, I don't understand.

"At least, the young man in Hong Kong can access the records." Dani had grown cool again. Surely, that look said, you'll get this point. "And once given bona fide certification, I'm pretty sure he can jigger the date."

Dorian wondered if she should catch at the doorjamb. Then all the pieces came together like a firework going off.

Jigger the date. Like I did, when I told Jimmy what to say to the cops. Produce an up-to-date birth certificate. And with that, and a JP's signature, you can apply for a passport.

Jimmy can apply. If Dani's hacker is as good as she seems to think, that's the ID problem settled overnight.

Dani nodded, coolness thawing to the verge of a smile. "There'll be a lot of paper trails to manage, yes. Parents' names, addresses, and so on. But once those are in place, all Jimmy'll need is a copy of the certificate for the British Consulate, and the usual contact names, and photos with a JP's signature."

Then she smiled outright and added sweetly, "And, as you know, I happen to be a JP."

A hacker who can plant fake identity details in a national— the British national system? Dorian's head swam. And swam again, with gratefulness.

"I don't know how you had time. I haven't even *thought* about IDs since—" Since Baringal. "I never even got that far with the double history thing! I hadn't . . ." Then all the shock coalesced in one thoroughly unguarded *"Why?"*

Why have you put yourself out, expended not merely office hours but thinking time, the most valuable resource for Lewis and Cotton, on my, on Jimmy's affairs?

Dani pushed the gaudy pen once more across the desk. She sounded supercool when she finally spoke.

"Lewis and Cotton originally involved you with the Ben Morar case. You might say"—a dawn shadow of a smile—"since you met at a firm party, that we involved you with Chris." She pushed the pen again. "And now we owe—Jimmy—as well."

Because without him, Dorian thought, you could have had three junior partners not merely injured, psychologically damaged, but dead.

Happening simultaneously, that might have destroyed the firm.

Dani lifted her eyes. "In one way or another," she said quietly, "Ben Morar's cost you a great deal. I think it's only fair, that you get something back."

Dorian took a second to work it out. Ben Morar cost me Chris. And grief, and peace of mind, and the mayhem with Brodie and Sorenson, and then it gave me the other traumas as well. Shooting someone. Watching someone die.

So Dani's going to see I keep something out of the mess. That, if she can manage it, Jimmy stays with me.

As the shock subsided, she found she was having to bite the inside of her cheek. Damn it, the woman's a whited sepulcher. She's not doing this for Lewis and Cotton. She's a raging sentimentalist!

"Thank you," Dorian said, trying for steadiness. "I, I see what you mean about the cemetery. I'll get up there tomorrow. As soon as I've seen Laura. I—I do think I'll ask Jimmy—if he wants to come."

Across the shining lake of desk Dani's eyes examined her, and she hoped devoutly not to blush. Then Dani said, so neutrally it was blatant irony, "You'd be the best judge of that." She gave herself a second to observe Dorian's confusion, then lifted a hand and reached for a folder, and Dorian eased shut the door.

This time when she came in, Jimmy made his best attempt at a leap from the couch and reached her in two strides—to pull up short for a suddenly anxious scan of her face. And then reach out both arms, with a smile she had never seen before.

"Ye didna tell me," he said, when they finally let go, "about this feller Yeats."

"Who? Oh. The poet?" Dorian managed to deposit her briefcase, although her other hand had an inexplicable need to stay locked in his shirt. Why on earth are you talking about poetry, when all I want is another kiss-and-hug like that, more of the luminous reassurance in that smile: I didn't dream it, you did, you do care for me.

And then, maybe, we might think a little about bed.

Not now, she scolded herself. There's dinner and the Blackston thing and that incredible theory of Dani's to tell him, and he's got stuff for me as well. About my old English textbooks, if nothing else. "What were you doing," she asked, unslinging her laptop, "with Yeats?"

"Ye dinna have much to read but law, or the sort o' thing I've already stuffed m' head wi' in the library. So I thought I'd try some poetry." His face was lighting again, if not to a Beethoven glow. "He knows the old stories, Cuchulain an' Maeve an' Oisin, an' he's a fine ear for a rhyme. At least one I've a mind to read ye." Enthusiasm changed to something that made her own pulse speed up, before the other word recurred.

"Library? You've been out? You've been in the town? You went to the . . . !"

"After the washin', there was nothin' else here. An' I wanted

235

out. To see the place again. 'Tis a fine huge change." He sounded almost complacent, if not admiring. "So I was in the promenade, what is it, the mall? An' I saw the sign, Library."

"So you spent the morning—the afternoon—there?" She was torn between consternation and mirth. I should have known. A small North Queensland city wouldn't daunt somebody who migrated clear to the goldfields, he probably thinks it was pretty quiet in comparison.

"Aye," he agreed, with definite complacency. "They gave me a library card."

"Jimmy!"

"Be easy, mo cailín. All they wanted was an address. So I gave them"—a little pause—"the one ye gave to me."

Chris's unit. The next pause held, before she recovered enough to smile. "So you towed home a ton of library books? No. Then what did you do?"

"Ye're learnin' me too well." But it came with a smothered smile. "I walked out in the 'mall,' aye, an' found a wee ballad singer. Wi' one o' y'r guitars. The sound was fine, but the tunes! He was moanin' like a drunken cow."

"Oh, no! Don't tell me. You thought you'd have a, what is it, a jam?"

"A session, aye. No' quite." The look turned wistful. "If I'd m' fiddle I could ha' shown him things." He brightened. "But he says he's a mate wi' one he doesna play, an' if I come down the mall o' Sunday mornin' they'll be there."

"Jimmy . . ."

The bright anticipation checked. The anxious look that succeeded it twisted her heart.

"I don't want you stuck in here," she said, walking back into his arms. "But you will, you will be careful?"

"Aye." It was quiet and earnest now. "I know, mo cailín. I know." Then a faint chuckle shook him. "I've been cautious,

236

aye? I wouldna go wi' him down the pub." His arms tightened a little. "I said, when ye came back, I needed to be home."

Home. Can that—could that possibly be true?

How can it be?

She shoved the thought away. He's here, and I have him for as long as this lasts, and if we're happy, forget what else is hovering.

She tightened her arms, and let him go. "I'm going to change. No, I do *not* need help—yet. Since you've spent the day roystering, you can get the veggies ready, and then there's half a bottle of white in the fridge. And I've some things you'll want to hear."

He was not much interested in the Reinschildt letter. " 'Tis all legal, Herself'll no' need me teachin' her strategy." The idea of a fake passport got attention quick as his comprehension. But her first stumbling attempt to expound the doubles theory brought him bolt upright on the couch.

"Ye mean—ye think—God an' the saints!"

"It makes sense." She was just beginning to digest it herself. "If you have Ned Kelly, and we don't, but we both have Paddy Wild—well, maybe it is double histories. And if they have some things in common, they must have people in common too."

His mouth was more than at half cock this time. "Then ye. An' me. There's more of us? There's another o' you, somewhere ahead in my, my, whatever it is—an'—"

He stopped. Then he said, very quietly, "An' there *was* another o' me. Over, back, across whatever this is—here."

"It mightn't be the case at all, we might have this all wrong, I don't want you to go up there and find—and find—"

He eyed her carefully, before he put his glass down and took hold of her hand. " 'Tis proper uncanny, aye. An' a set-down too. To think ye might no' be the, the only one. But mo cailín, think. If ye had—have—a double, she canna be up there. 'Tis before y'r time. An' if there is another o' me—he's no' alive now." He frowned suddenly. "D'ye think, that's why I can be here?"

"I don't know." She swallowed, unable to confess the shiver of pure dread that went through her, reasonless, blood-deep, at the thought of confronting even a duplicate grave.

He did not reply. His brows had corrugated deeper. He was staring at nothing in a way that suddenly reminded her of Chris, caught in an analytical question's warp.

Then his mouth suddenly set hard, he made a quick little withdrawing motion. And an even quicker shake of the head, before his attention leapt back to her.

"No. We dinna know. But dinna ye want to know? If it *is* so? We can look. In the graveyard." It was purpose, if not enthusiasm. "We can find out."

"And if it is?" She did not want to say, Could you face Bridget's grave? Again?

He paused a moment. "Ye're thinkin', could I see where Bridgie . . . ? Aye. But . . ."

Another long pause, and she had a definite sense that he had set aside some other, crucial consideration. Then his eyes came round, and he said, "If 'tis true . . . we can get the birth certificate. An' try for a passport. An' then . . ."

He looked deep in her eyes and she understood the rest: And if we ever do defeat P-A, and for some reason I don't, can't go back to my own place, I'll be able to stay, legitimately.

And I'll have you.

Their eyes locked tighter than their hands. The pause seemed to go forever. Before they both undid their fingers. Then he got off the couch and offered her a hand and said quietly, "Come ye an' say what we'll eat. But if ye go up there tomorrow, mo cailín—I'm goin' too."

"Ten minutes," said the nurse at the ICU's double doors. "She's stable but still not very strong. Over there."

Laura's face looked almost as white as Jimmy's had the first night. But as they came up her eyelids lifted, and despite the sunken, dark-rimmed eyes it was the basis of Laura's smile.

I'm so sorry, Dorian wanted to say. I never meant this to happen. Not to you. She bit it back fiercely and leant over to kiss Laura's cheek, to squeeze her left hand. "You sneaky bag," she said, "you've landed that doozy of a Castelloni thing on me after all."

The smile brightened toward real. "Thought you'd slide out, didn't you?" It was a half voice, but the hand tightened on hers. Yes, it said, let's do the shop-chat and trade friends' abuse, as if everything was usual. At least to start. But Laura was already looking past her, to Jimmy, tall and silent at Dorian's back.

"You're okay." It came on a soundless sigh. "I was so scared. I thought . . . I thought you'd . . ."

That the crowning touch of nightmare wouldn't just be watching you beaten, but thinking, knowing you dead.

Jimmy came up to the bedside. Laura made a faint motion of her hand, and he bent to take it in his. "I'm a hard man t' be rid of," he said.

It came with a glint of the amusement he had given Dorian, but with a different undertone. Survivors, she thought suddenly. She was there. She went through it. She knows, in a very different way, what it means.

He gave Dorian a glance, seeking permission, she guessed, then settled a haunch on the bed. Dragging up a chair, she was in time to hear him say, "Will I tell ye the rest?" She opened her mouth, and shut it again. This is a story, she understood, that survivors need to share.

For most of the way to Blackston they were both very quiet. Not far from the hospital, Jimmy asked, "Can they tell, yet, if she'll be right wi' that arm?"

And lapsed back into silence when Dorian could only say, "I don't know."

The road turned pink, the Blackston hills appeared. Jimmy stiffened in his seat. He's seen it from the air, Dorian thought, but it's the first time he's approached our version from the ground, from his old perspective. And it has to look so different.

It was eleven-forty. She asked tentatively, "Before we—did you want some food? Something to drink?" And he looked across at her briefly and shook his head.

Dorian had been to the original pioneers' graveyard once, with Chris. She half guessed her way down Landers Street toward the railway, distracted by Jimmy's sudden tension and occasional quick motions that suggested distress. At a stop sign before the tracks, she dared to ask, "Is it your back? Is something hurting?" and he gave a brusque shake of the head.

"No' in m' back."

"This here," he said, when she waited. "This was the center. O' the reef. O' the mines. The Solitaire. The Worcester. St. Patrick's. Bonnie Dundee . . . Victoria. The Queen." He swept his gaze round the wide shallow dip scattered with houses, sleepy little streets, big, flourishing trees. His eye stopped on a row of boulders across a street end and his mouth pulled in a far-from-happy smile. "That there . . . 'tis all that's left o' the Solitaire. Block, Deeps, Consolidated. All gone."

The smoke, the dust, the machinery, the frenzy of men and animals, the din of stampers and locomotives and poppet-head winches, the rattle and thunder of falling ore . . . her spine chilled at the memory. The shift whistle's moan. Banshee, she imagined, a past's silent mourning, and drove carefully over the railway line.

"An' this was Queenton." He sounded at once sad, angry,

and resigned. "Better yields than Blackston, once." Again the sweeping, dismissive glance over idle emptiness, and then a look that said, Drive on.

But when they reached the top of the old graveyard, he said nothing at all.

A couple of acres, Dorian estimated, squinting into the hard midday light. With a dilapidated gate, and a tumbledown two-wire fence, a long treeless spire-pocked slope sinking to the ridge's foot. Out here, nobody watered the grass. The earth stretched brown and ragged, desolate except for the remnants of graves.

I don't want to get out. I don't want to walk around in that. I'd forgotten just how bad it looks. And what it must seem to him . . .

She turned instinctively, reaching for an arm, a knee. He was staring before him, that look of appalled disbelief still on his face.

Then he said, barely audible, "D'ye no' tend it at all?"

"I—it—it's the old cemetery, it, there hasn't been anyone buried here since, since the nineteen hundreds—" Oh, my God, that's the near future to him. "We don't, I mean—" I can't say, It's just a tourist site. "It—it—there isn't—"

There isn't anyone left who remembers. Anyone who loved them. Anyone who cares.

"I'm sorry." She could barely hear herself.

He turned his eyes across to her. He looked composed now. Too composed, that withdrawn calm of the moment when he had rejected her money, her food. "In Erin," he said, "even the old yards—they dinna forget."

I'm sorry, was all she could make her eyes say. Again.

In a moment he drew a long breath and said, more than heavily, "Aye." Then, like an old man, began to clamber out of the car.

"Your hat?" Guessing the sun would be ferocious, she had bought one in Ibisville. He clapped it on in silence and headed for the gate.

I can't ask, do you remember where . . . I can't ask, I can't say anything. She took her keys and bag and trailed silently at his heels.

He held the gate for her. Closed it behind them. Looked ahead, and stopped.

Dorian had forgotten the worst of the desolation. Not just the tumbled or broken monuments, the cracked or illegible headstones, the empty spaces where graves might have been. The worst was the ones with neither name nor monument, mere rectangles of anonymous stones.

Beside her Jimmy drew a sharp, shuddering breath and said, "Quartz."

"What?" She jerked round despite herself.

In the shade of his hat brim, his eyes looked pure black. Pupils dilated, she had time to think, before he caught his breath in a jagged little mockery of a laugh. "God be wi' us! Quartz!"

Dorian could only stare.

He turned to her. He was pale even under the tan, and his mouth was set in a kind of wounded smile.

"It wasna like this," he said harshly. "It was brown, aye, most o' the time, an' dry. But there was monuments, all white an' bright, an' iron fences, an', aye, places wi' new, new ground broken, an' places wi' stones no' laid, an' now an' now there'd be flowers. But"—his mouth compressed savagely—"they didna put down *quartz.*"

Dorian dared not say, I don't understand.

" 'Tis the ore," he almost snapped at her. "Fro' the mines. Whatever was left before they struck lode, or when they stopped workin', the poor stuff, the useless stuff—they've taken the dry stone an' put it round the graves!"

242

"I don't—I don't—"

" 'Twas what they came for. Gold—or the chance o' gold. An' y'r fine forgetful folk've left 'em quartz!"

He took her by the elbows. He was trembling very slightly, with that distress on the edge of rage.

"D'ye no' find it a mockery?" He narrowed his eyes into hers. "That men—an' women, an' children—should come here, wantin' gold, an' die, an' lie here—an' their graves be trimmed wi' dross?"

Gold seekers. Dreaming, hoping, searching, dying. Buried under a travesty of ore.

Her neck, her back, her stomach all shuddered together and she pulled away from him as the dust and the roar crashed back over her, the stockpile's lethal rock cascade, Brodie vanishing, buried, entombed, in a pyramid of stone.

"Mo cailín. Dorian." He had her by the elbows but his voice was normal again, quick and anxious and alert. "What is it? Are ye all right?"

"Brodie," she managed, gulping, hanging onto him, trying to tell herself, It's the sun. "He was—buried under quartz."

For a second he went perfectly still. Then, in an oddly expressionless voice, he said, very softly, "So he was."

They stood in absolute silence through a tiny draw of wind, under the battering sun. Then he released her elbows. "Aye," he said, on a note of more than resignation. "If ye come lookin' for Eldorado—ye can expect a deal poorer comeuppance, I suppose."

"Oh, Jimmy." She wanted to catch and hug him and burst out, Let me make it up to you, let me make you forget.

But it's not my place. This mightn't be his world—his history—but it's his time. Not mine.

He touched her cheek with a knuckle's back. Then he said, still in that too-quiet tone, "Bridgie was over here."

Halfway down the slope, to the left. Dorian tried not to look at the monuments or to read headstones, most of all not to notice the nameless graves, or the ones so small they could only have been a child's. Jimmy too, she thought, was trying not to see them. Was navigating steadily to the one place he remembered, blotting out everything else.

In case they carry a name he remembers. That wasn't here when—he last came.

He stopped. She managed not to walk into him. He did not have to speak. The set of his shoulder had already announced, Here.

There's a headstone. Thank God for that. Sandstone, it looks, small and low, and probably not expensive, but it's there. No iron fence. Quartz—she tried not to shudder—quartz as a border, but a headstone. Fairly legible.

"Bridget Burke," Jimmy said. His voice had gone husky. "Beloved wife of Patrick Kevin Burke. Eighteen sixty to eighteen eighty-five."

He doesn't have to read that. He can remember. It's what—the other gravestone said.

A long shudder went down her backbone and she had to hold her hand back from his sleeve. But he had taken a couple of steps nearer, bending over the grave.

"Patrick Burke," he said shakily. "Husband of Bridget Burke. Eighteen fifty-eight to nineteen oh-nine."

He didn't forget her. He didn't marry again. He was buried with her, when he died.

She blinked tears away, thinking, If you have to find your own past, or even a double of your past, it must be a consolation to find one like this.

Then her tongue seemed to stick in her mouth. I can't, I can't say, Is there another? Do we look around? I can't stand beside him and search for his own grave.

Jimmy had straightened up. Removed his hat. Bent his head, and was silently reciting something. In a moment, he crossed himself. Dorian hastily bent her own head, though she did not dare mimic the rest.

He put his hat on. Then he looked round and that mouth corner pucked, but not with amusement. "Will ye look to the right?" He glanced along the slope. "If—'tis here—'twill be close. In the same row, I'm thinkin'." The compression of the lips added, or what passes for a row. "I'll try this way."

Dorian gulped and moved. The sun leaned on her shoulders, the glare struck up at her from the quartz pieces, glittering grayish white, from the arid ground.

Next to the Burkes' grave—how weird to think that—came a big, stone-paved family plot, with an almost intact granite spire. Next to that an empty space. Her heart bumped. Beyond that, a nameless stone rectangle. Oh, God, what if it's one of those, how can I know, how can we tell? She looked desperately around for Jimmy, and stopped.

He was standing quite still, looking down. In the all-but-horizontal vista, he seemed even taller than usual. He had worn his original trousers and white shirt. The dark and white leapt at her out of the monotone landscape like a new monument.

She did not notice how she reached him. Nor did he glance around. Trying not to take hold of him for her own reassurance, she followed his eyes.

Right next to Bridget and Patsy. I could have guessed. No iron trim either. More quartz fragments. A very simple stone, little more than a marker, perhaps six inches wide. Sandstone again, the letters barely visible.

J.M.K.
1856–1908

CHAPTER 10

They were halfway to Ibisville before Jimmy spoke again. The words dropped into that silence like pebbles down an unplumbed well.

"What happens to the souls, d'ye suppose?"

"What?" Dorian's eyes shot sideways, even on the Burdekin high-level bridge.

"The souls." He did not look at her. "If ye're a double, that is."

"*Souls?*" Dorian's concentration tilted. There was a lay-by beyond the bridge. She pulled in and stopped and swung to look fully at him. "Jimmy . . . ?"

He turned toward her, but he did not reach out. He still looked remote, in more than physical distance, as he had when they left the graveyard. The way Chris would look in the throes of calculation, she thought. But this isn't just a matter of intellect.

"The ones that're doubles." He was frowning again, that deep cleft between the brows. "If ye're a double . . . ye have y'r own body. So when ye die—d'ye have y'r own soul? Is there— two o' ye—then too?"

Dorian caught in breath for, I don't know, and, Does it matter, and stifled both.

"Because if ye're a double—ye're the same *person*—"

He looked directly at her, and there was more than anxiety in that peat-water stare.

"The Creed says, I believe in the Resurrection . . . o' the body. So there'd be two bodies, aye? But if ye're only one person . . . is there two souls?"

"I—" Theology was always beyond me. I have to take the Creed on trust, let alone the Trinity. "I don't—"

"Think." He said it with the first hint of urgency. "If there's two o' ye, why shouldna there be more? An' if there's more than two." A shudder went through him. "How'll God deal wi' the Resurrection, if heaven's runnin' over wi' duplicate folk?"

Dorian gulped at the bizarre image herself.

"It doesna make sense. God can do anythin', aye. But surely, He has to make sense?"

Logic hitting faith head-on. This is beyond me. I daren't say anything. This is more important than finding the grave. It's more than life and death, to him.

"But—if there was only one soul. An' the bodies're just duplicates—"

Dorian's belly clenched. Occam's razor, the splitting blade of logic. Far better sense than a heaven full of multiple Jimmies—or even half of them in Hell. Duplicate bodies. Just one soul.

Then what happens when they die? The duplicates who weren't reincarnations, who lived at the same time, but with separate personalities, separate lives?

She could see the terror in his eyes. I believe in the Resurrection. But what if the Resurrection doesn't mean recovering *my* body? What if, in a divine economy, I'm sucked into some common soul with a single flesh?

She stretched out and caught at him as if he were slipping over a physical cliff. "That can't be right! God wouldn't do that—!" God's supposed to be good beyond all uncertainty, not just omnipotent but wise. Wise means kind. No kind god could do such a thing.

God isn't *supposed* to do things like that, his eyes answered. But out there in the cemetery is a duplicate's gravestone. Can trust withstand the strength of fact?

"No." She spoke in pure denial. Then theology itself rescued her.

"Listen, we don't understand it. But we're not God. We don't even understand the two histories or whatever they are. But God must." She took another breath, reaching for the terms of a faith that had slid outside her own reality. "God made them happen, or they wouldn't exist. So God has to know how they work. And, they'll have a reason, and, and God will've figured out the souls thing too. It'll make sense, to God. It just doesn't, it probably can't, to us."

She hung onto his hands and tried not to hold her breath. That's the best I have. The best I can do to knit your religion to a cosmos that even this glimpse reveals as so much wider, so much more complex than the Christian view: a single world, a linear history, Eden to start, Resurrection at the end.

I've cost him his world. I can't lose him his faith as well.

His eyes had locked on hers. She was vaguely aware of the yellow sign behind him, with the warning icon and the words *Danger. Crocodiles live here.* She held on to his fingers with all her might, praying, she thought it must be: Let me get him over. Don't let the crocodiles get him. Just let him get over safe.

He let his breath slide out on a long, long sigh and his fingers turned over, clasping on hers.

"Aye," he said, the extended cadence that could signal grief or resignation and now spoke, if not of hope, then of an impossible conundrum possibly resolved. "We might no', maybe we *can* no' understand it. But 'tis there. An' if 'tis there . . . it must make sense to Him."

I'll let the pronoun pass, she thought, giddy with relief, what's it matter what sex God is, so long as this hasn't shattered your faith in one. So long as the crocodiles missed you. So long as you can still believe.

"Okay." She held on for her own sake, trying to breathe more easily. Damn it, I thought P-A was the worst danger. Physical things. "Okay."

Slowly, that stare lightened. His eyes regained mobility. Then he gave a tiny nod.

"Aye. I've always thought . . . we dinna—we canna—we should have the sense no' to try figurin' God's view, from where we are. Even the, what d'ye call 'em, theologians."

"Mmm." Dorian dared not add more.

"An' this: the two times, the histories, the two—of us all, maybe. Aye. If we—I—can trust Providence for—bein' here—I can surely trust Providence for that."

He did it. He walked over that half bridge of cliché, and now, it'll be all right.

She still could not speak. But he smiled very slightly and tightened his grasp, then let go. "An' now ye've pulled me out o' the pit fro' Darwin an' his like," he said, overly straight-faced, "ye can drive on. 'Okay'?"

"Fink," she said, reduced by relief to kindergarten levels, and pulled back on the road.

Silence resumed, but she could feel it was easier. Jimmy had slouched a little in his seat, one knee up against the dash. But he only spoke again as they met the panorama at the top of the range.

"D'ye suppose the lives are the same?"

"Eh?" The road was nearing what Dorian always thought of now as Chris's curve. Hayed-off grass, gray-green leaves, twisted-rust bloodwood trunks scooted past, blue-smoke coastal distance opened beyond. "Which lives?'

"The doubles." He sounded almost academically curious now. "I suppose it doesna matter for them, like Ned Kelly an'

Fitzgerald, that're—singles." A pause. "That is, if they're no' doubles wi' some other—history. But for us that are? If he"—he did not have to nod back to Blackston—"lived fifty-two years . . . will I?"

It was still detached, almost pure speculation. Lord, she thought, working into the next bend, he really doesn't care when he dies. The only thing that worried him was about his soul.

"I don't know," she said. Would I want that, if it was me? To know my years' span, ahead of time?

"Or if ye do change—histories—does that change everything?"

"I don't . . ." There was a semi slugging uphill and a stupidly impetuous four-wheel drive trying to overtake it on the bend. She clamped on the brakes and swerved half on the shoulder, slammed a furious hand on the horn, added a finger when she had one to spare. The hell with how long I might live. Can God cater for lives cut off by terminal idiots?

If I'd died then, would my double—doubles—have died too?

Lord, there are just too many questions. Only God could answer them. "I don't," she said, pulse still galloping, eyeing the oncoming traffic as for an ambush, "I don't know."

There was a moment's pause. Then he said, too meekly, "Will I whisht then, an' let ye deal wi' these eediots?"

"Oh, Jimmy—drat you!" She could not help but laugh.

"I'll beg y'r pardon, mo cailín." When he spoke again the hidden amusement had subsided. "But ye canna blame me for wonderin'."

Not after seeing your own name on a gravestone, the recorded span of your double's life.

She managed a fleeting pat on his nearer knee. "I couldn't help it either. It's just . . ."

"We canna tell, no. Or at least . . ." But there he fell silent, his mouth clamping, if not into total rigidity.

At least what? She thought. In our own timelines, we can't tell? But we might, if we jumped like he has. About our doubles, anyhow. Maybe about himself. If he goes back, if he lives to fifty-two, as the year approaches, he'll be thinking, wondering . . . I don't think I could stand that. I'd sooner the future as it is. Better uncertainty, than knowing the day of your death.

And if he *could* tell, irony added darkly, if he goes back, and it does happen, there's no way he could pass it on to you.

But if he stayed here . . .

She shut that thought down as it surfaced. Here or there, I don't want to think that he might only have another twenty or so years.

She said, "There's a petrol station up ahead. They have good coffee, if nothing else."

They were both still sober, if not somber, when they reached Ibisville. Past two P.M., Dorian thought, wanting a shower to shuck the abrasion of dust and sun she always felt on her skin after a Blackston excursion. And we could do with lunch. Then I should get in to L&C, even if the news about the grave can wait. But when she said, "I could put in a couple of hours at the office," Jimmy lifted her chin on a finger, and said firmly, "Ye look like a ringtail possum in daylight. Forget y'r office. Off wi' ye for an hour or two an' sleep."

"If I need it," she attempted defiance, "so do you."

He considered her a moment. Then the mouth corner curled. Demurely, he said, "So long as ye mean, just sleep."

"I mean, just sleep," she said firmly. If his eyes were not sunken, there were shadows under them. "Tonight we can, um, consider other things."

Both mouth corners twitched. But he followed her to stretch out on the bed.

When Dorian woke she had rolled from the pillow to bury

her face in Jimmy's shoulder. Unfamiliar T-shirt, familiar, ridiculously persisting scent of wood smoke, grown man, impossibly, even yet, Sunlight soap. His arm was curled above her head. When she woke, it slid down her shoulders to hold her there.

"Mmm," she murmured, stretching like a cat in sun.

A rumble under her ear answered, "Mmm."

And I bet you know exactly what I meant. She let her cheek move in a smile.

"Mo cailín." The voice was soft, but the inflection said, I have a serious question. She murmured, "Mmm?"

" 'Tis no' easy—'tis no' manners to say this . . . but have ye thought—we're no' married, aye?"

Sleep went on a blink. She did not try to lift her head but she knew he had felt her tense.

"If I get pregnant, you mean?"

His muscles suppressed a flinch. His voice was steady. "Aye.

"I'd marry ye," he anticipated her, "before it happened, I'd marry ye if it never happened. But—" His fingers closed gently in her hair. "Ye know—that might no' be—a help."

Because once—if—P-A's settled, who knows what the reality fold might do? We might intend, we might actually marry, and me find myself left here pregnant. Alone.

Dorian climbed on her elbows to see his face.

"I know you'd do it." That was beyond question. "I know it mightn't—be possible." I won't think about that. She took a deep breath. Let's skip Women's Rights and whether I'd choose to marry. The rest is bad enough. Lord, how's a nineteenth-century Catholic going to react to news of the Pill? "But . . . it mightn't be necessary."

A pause. Then he said, unwontedly earnest, "Isna that—trustin' a little to luck?"

"Ah—not in this case. You see—nowadays—we have, um,

proper—birth control."

There was another pause where she felt her heart beat. His eyes had half crossed, as they would at the twenty-first century's harder body blows. Then he gulped, and said the last thing she expected. "D'ye mean, like Harriet Martineau?"

"Harriet *who?*"

"Martineau. Ye know, the suffragist. She talks about 'voluntary motherhood.' 'Tis what ye mean, aye? Bridgie read her somewhere. When she an' Patsy got arguin' she'd fetch out Martineau—an' Patsy'd turn blue an' yell about self-control bein' a fine thing, if ye werena a man."

"Oh." Oh, lord. Temperance and Chastity. Thank heavens for Mum's feminist history. "That's what they used to say men needed, wasn't it?" She just controlled the giggle. A fine thing to preach on the Blackston field. "No, this doesn't need self-control from anyone. I can take pills, or, or use a device. Or"—she took another deep breath—"you can wear something too."

Explaining condoms put both their straight faces over the edge. Jimmy lasted longest. But when he turned delicately purple she prodded his intact ribs and he collapsed in his genuine guffaw.

"A rubber lifesaver." He wiped his eye corner carefully. "Do I—do *I* have to, ah, put it on?"

"I *can* do it." She tried for blandness. Their eyes met and they collapsed again.

When they sobered she had to ask the other question. "It doesn't worry you? It being—in your time—against the church?"

He turned his head to meet her eyes, and his fingers curled again in her hair. "Aye. The church is—was—against it." A long pause. "But now—'tis different. An' . . ." He stopped, turning his face away. Under his breath he added, "Even in my time. Bridgie. She couldna—*we* couldna afford a child. An' 'twas hard. So hard, for both o' them. But especially, wi' the priests, an' confession, for her."

A short-funded couple, already sharing a house with a brother, with the demands of family in Ireland on their backs. And then the pressures of religion to weight a husband's, as well as her own desires. How on earth did she survive?

"Bridget must," she said impetuously, "have been an amazing girl."

There was a little pause. Then he said quietly, his eyes directed over the bed end, but not with any forbidding inflection, "Aye."

The silence held. Before he shifted his fingers again with the little murmur of pleasure he often made at touching her hair, and smiled at her, the light waking, like sun on peat water, deep in those dark eyes. "But as for ye, mo cailín sidhe. If ye havena used this 'pill' or y'r 'devices' already . . . then"—the gleam turned distinctly wicked—"ye might show me the other way, aye?"

I made a promise, Dorian groaned, dragging herself out of bed short of seven A.M. Every Sunday, I said. Mass. She tweaked a lock of hair from under the other pillow and mumbled, "Cathedral's got early service. Up."

Do we worry about confession, she wondered, as they scrambled down the back hill path to the Catholic cathedral, beside the cutting atop the next street. I can skip it, but Jimmy's got a lot on his plate. Apart from unmarried, contraceptive, repeated, unashamed sex. But when she hazarded, "I'm sorry you missed confession," he gave her that quick wicked glint and shook his head.

"Fine help 'twould be, after dallyin' wi' ye all Saturday night." The grin flickered in and out of existence. "Be easy. I'm no' takin' communion. I'll find mysel' a confessor for the thing wi'

Brodie. As for ye." The smile this time made her heart skip. "I'm no' confessin' that."

Breakfast over, she said reluctantly, "I really should go to the office. I have to draft that letter to Reinschildt, if nothing else." But this time he scanned her and gave a quick little nod. "Away wi' ye, then. An' dinna worry about me. I've"—already it was anticipation for music, she thought, if not Beethoven—"m' own fish to fry."

Around one o'clock Dorian thought, Okay. I've done the letter, I've caught up on Laura's cases, for a Sunday, that's enough. A small guilty thought appended, Especially this Sunday. She stamped it down. He's probably not even back yet. If he met his "ballad singer," it would be in the Sunday markets, maybe they've gone busking. Or to the pub. He's probably not back. But she hurried to the parking lot, and up to her own door.

Music flowed out again, not orchestral this time. A single violin, glancing and flittering with lazy accomplishment over a tune whose lolloping rhythm she could identify as a jig.

She shut the door. The tune found closure. Jimmy swung round on her straight-backed dining chair and beamed at her across the violin under his chin. "Did ye ever hear a sweeter tone?"

Dorian started to laugh. "You—! You've got it away from that poor man in a single morning, and he'll never see it again!"

"Ah, d'ye think me a thief?" The grin robbed it of sting. He came to his feet, laying the violin carefully back in its case. " 'Twas a gift. I've had it twelve months, he said, an' I'll ne'er play it like that. Ye're welcome, take it for as long as ye're here."

"Oh. Then that's okay." She overrode the little falling pause. "It's a good one, then?"

"Aye, a little beauty." He was torn between her and the music, she realized with an inward smile. "Maybe no' as sharp 'twixt notes as mine, but a lovely tone."

The hand hesitating over the laid-down bow supplied her cue. "I bet you haven't eaten anything? Well, entertain me, maestro, while I dig out something for lunch."

"Ah, but wait!" The bow went down in earnest. He rounded the kitchen counter with something near a bound. "The market, we went buskin', they call it, aye? An' the fruit, the greens, 'twas better than y'r supermarket, I couldna say no."

A pawpaw on the counter, golden ripe. Two pawpaws, avocadoes, tomatoes, a lush hydroponic lettuce, a half dozen of the bristling red sea-urchin fruit called ramjams, potatoes, silverbeet, fresh and dark as malachite. "Heavens, Jimmy! Even in the market, this must have cost . . ."

"Ah, but we went *buskin'!* An' they havena heard a proper fiddler, these folk."

He was yanking things from his trouser pocket. A clatter of coins, a flutter of notes. "D'ye see that?" With blatant satisfaction. "We made the better o' forty o' y'r dollars each."

His own money, earned in a true market. A drop in the bucket of expenses, but it's his. Independent of me.

She said, "That's great," with all her feelings' truth, double pride in the achievement, the music, pleasure echoing his. His smile reflected it back. He understands. I don't have to say, Thank you, for the fruit. For the gesture that says, I'm determined to contribute. Or spell out anything else. She brushed his cheek and said, mock-demanding, "Music. I'll get lunch."

Monday we posted the letter, Dorian counted mentally: registered mail, special delivery. A couple of days to reach Reinschildt, maybe three if he's overseas. That's Wednesday. Today. At least a couple of days before you can expect him to respond.

There can't be anything back earlier than the beginning of next week.

She sighed and wriggled in her office chair. Jimmy's got the violin—fiddle—and the library and heaven knows who else he's likely to meet downtown. Next thing I know he'll have hired on with a rock band. Or a construction crew. With the bruises settled, idleness is chafing him, the way I expected. No word on the inquests. Hardly major work to see Laura every day. There's nothing definite about Anne. I could get him a bicycle. Start teaching him to drive. I could . . .

Ask Dani how her hacker's going. She reached out, still with some trepidation about calling Dani outside total emergency, for the phone.

"It's more complicated than I thought." Dani sounded crisp, but neither impatient nor irritated. "My contact says, with the original date and place of birth, he can do a genealogical trace. Fix the original family. You did say Jimmy had no brothers? To keep the name, then, we have to find a collateral line. Then he, or they, will follow it down into the nineteen eighties. Once they find a bona fide family in the right time frame, they can produce a certificate."

"A"—Dorian moistened her lips—"fake certificate?"

"Unless they're lucky enough to find a family with a son who died young."

Not impossible, Dorian thought, for that time and place.

"That," Dani was still talking, "will take time, and money, naturally. I've told him to go ahead with the research. But after the certificate's arranged, we have a choice. The application can be made in the UK, or overseas. In the UK, all you need is the birth certificate and certified photos, same as here." Dani paused a moment. "If someone in the UK signs the photos, though, someone complicit with the process, we have another opening, if these people chose to blackmail us. And then there's the visa. And the Australian entry stamp. They are obtainable. But they'll cost."

The pause warned Dorian. "How much?"

"For the passport and certificate, we're looking at six thousand US dollars. With the visa and stamp, probably five hundred more."

Dorian suppressed the grunt. Two months' car payments, maybe three off the unit. I can afford that, her heart replied without hesitation. For Jimmy, I could afford a lot more than that.

"Okay," she said. "It'll take me a few days to put it together. How soon . . . ?"

There was a much longer pause. Then Dani said, "Lewis and Cotton will contribute—"

"Not money." Dorian did not have to think. "You found the contact, you're taking the risk with that, you're prepared to sign the photos. For Lewis and Cotton, the risk's more than enough."

The pause came again. Then Dani said, "We can discuss that later. The alternative is to apply from here, through the Consulate. We still need the birth certificate, but we don't have the photo problem. On the other hand, there will be queries about a man of thirty applying for his first passport from overseas. The story could be riskier than the UK application. The contact does have a contact in London who'd pass it without questions."

But when it came up for renewal, the same questions would turn up, and the hacker could have the same hold on us.

"Maybe we should wait till we see if they can sort out the certificate. And I talk to Jimmy."

"Yes. I'll keep you posted."

There was another abrupt pause. Before Dorian could speak Dani said, "I've seen Anne."

Dorian's heart jumped. "How is she? How are they? The

kids, are they okay? Is she taking more leave?"

"I've told her to take two months' leave. She's adjusting as well as you could probably expect." God, Dorian thought. "She and Sam are both in therapy. The children are having worse problems, I think. Anne's talking about taking them away altogether. A house on the island for a month, perhaps."

"That sounds a very good idea. For all of them." Blood on the doorstep, the echo of blows and terror in the living room. "I'd like to catch up before they go—"

"I wouldn't do that."

Dorian's words died in more than shock.

"Anne will send you a message herself. But the gist—she knows what happened isn't your fault. I accepted the risk, she said to me, back when Chris's message turned up. But accepting a risk isn't the same as seeing your family carry the consequence. Dorian's my friend. She's still my friend. But my kids are my kids. I don't think I could face Dorian yet, and not"—Dani paused again—"not blame her—or do worse than blame her—for what's happened to them."

Dorian tried to swallow. Her mouth felt numb. Anne, her mind said stupidly. I haven't just hurt Laura. I've hurt, I've lost Anne. My longest-known, the second of my best friends.

She bit hard on her tongue as tears swelled in her throat. You don't need to bawl in self-pity. Compared to Anne, to Laura, to Jimmy, what have you lost?

Chris, retorted her mind, unanswerably.

And if you have Jimmy, it added, there's no guarantee you won't lose him as well.

But they aren't Anne, my workmate, a mainstay in the grind of daily business, not just off time's pleasures and delights. They aren't my *friends*.

"Dorian," Dani said evenly, "I think this is temporary. I know it's very upsetting. I know you'll know better than to try to see her, to make any sort of protest. I do . . . understand. And I'm sorry, too."

The Terminator. Who never talks about emotions, if she is a raging sentimentalist.

"I do—I do understand," Dorian said shakily. She pushed tears away with the side of her hand. "I won't try to—talk to her before she asks. When you see her, though. Just—if you think it'll be okay, give her—give them my love."

She had barely been home five minutes before she realized Jimmy was watching her. It was hardly another five before he cornered her in the kitchen as she turned from pouring an early glass of red.

"What is it, mo cailín?"

There's no point in trying to say it's nothing, it doesn't matter. He'll know why and how it does, almost as well as I do myself.

When she finished talking, gulping back more tears, he sat very quiet beside her on the couch. Then he slid an arm round her shoulders, and drew her close, and said nothing at all.

Because there's nothing to say, she thought, staring into the James Brown's serene, impregnably indifferent bush. He knows he had a part in it. He knows I didn't mean it to happen. But it's happened, and there's nothing anyone can do. It's one of those things, like death and taxes, that nothing can help.

He doesn't even have to tell me that.

She sniffled a little, setting the glass aside. Leaning into his solid warmth and weight, she thought, How long will I have this kindness to rely on? This sympathy?

She slid her arms round him, tightly. As he grunted a little, half amusement, half surprise, she said into his chest, "Am I cooking dinner? Or are you?"

★ ★ ★ ★ ★

We could go to the movies tonight, Dorian considered, in a momentary lull about four o'clock on Friday. I'm stopping at five, and to hell with the backlog. We can see Laura tomorrow. Later tomorrow. Just this once, I'm going to sleep in.

Her mind had slid to possibilities beyond sleep when Mrs. Urquhart's phone rang. A moment later she leaned out of her cubicle.

"Ohh, Dorian? There's a Mr. Reinschildt asking for you."

"There's a *who?*"

Dorian's heart tried at once to jump out her mouth and dive in her stomach pit. It's too soon, he couldn't have got back before next week, what do I say, what'll he say, I need Dani, I thought he'd write—oh, heavens, I'm not ready for this!

But he's on the line. Now. For you.

She gulped desperately. Took in four huge breaths. Told herself, If you can shoot George in the leg and mean to shoot Brodie in the back, you can handle Reinschildt on a phone. She straightened her collar. Trying to sound steady, she called, "Put him through."

The line clicked. The holoscreen stayed blank, and the echo of Sorenson chilled her blood before a male voice spoke. "Miss Wild? Miss Dorian Wild?"

"Yes?"

"One moment, Mr. Reinschildt's calling."

His secretary. She shuddered as if her spine had been iced and just managed not to speak.

The line clicked again. A second voice repeated, "Miss Wild?"

"Mr. Reinschildt."

Finally. The Pan-Auric Vice President. Brodie's Fix It. Voice to voice if not face to face.

The holoscreen came up.

Reinschildt's hair was silver-gray as Brodie's and almost as short, but she could tell it had been styled, not cropped. The eyes were blue too. An echo of George's Marlboro stare, though the bones were anything but picture perfect. Heavy brows, a hint of lantern jaw. A stare like an X-ray machine, with more than X-ray penetration. Money, status, power. Cold, not in animosity, but with power's indifference.

"Miss Wild, I'll be in Cairns on Sunday between ten A.M. and four P.M. There's a conference room at the Miramar. If you arrange a time with my assistant, I'll discuss your letter then."

American accent, but not Brodie's. Or Sorenson's. Generic newscaster? East Coast? Ivy League? That tie, the coat says, both. So does the calm assumption I'll drop everything to be there when he says. Seagull manager, commented an irreverent Net joke. Flies in squawking, eats, shits on everything, flies out.

I should say, I'm busy on Sunday. Or, I don't live in Cairns.

No. The point is the meeting, not scoring points to keep your ego up.

"That would be acceptable." But some conditions have to be made. "I'd prefer to have my lawyer present." Because sure as God made little apples, you'll have legal big guns with you.

The holoscreen went out. The cold clipped voice said in her ear, "Bring your lawyer, Miss Wild. Bring whoever you like."

"Iceberg," Dorian said to Laura's half-anxious, half-excited stare. "East Coast, wealthy, I-never-notice-underlings iceberg. We're all just shit under his chariot wheels."

Jimmy gave her a startled look. Laura spluttered and held her shoulder dressings. "Oooh, he did get to you!"

"Of course he got to me. Reinschildt. In person. On the phone. Yesterday. I thought he'd send a letter or get legal advice, or take months to get back at all." Though for Jimmy's sake, she thought, I'm glad he didn't do that. "Now I have to hare up to Cairns on Sunday—I bet he flew in on his flipping private jet, he's going to munch and crunch us in a couple of hours and whiz off to Vanuatu or Honolulu. I should have made him come to Ibisville."

"You *are* pissed." Laura was grinning, at least half the old wattage. "Sorry, Jimmy." She had picked up his taboos quite early. "Us lawyer women, when the pressure comes on, we always swear."

He gave it a perfunctory smile. His eyes, Dorian knew, were still on her.

"Well, cheer up, Dor. It may be Reinschildt in person, but you've got the Terminator." The grin revived. "Reinschildt's munch and crunch might end up as spit out, or choke."

"I hope so." Dorian tried to sound cool for Laura's sake. Then her eyes caught the wad of bandages, and she thought, Laura. Anne. Sam. Della and Jonathon. Her teeth clamped and the berserker rose inside her, colder, more implacable than Reinschildt's voice.

"He's got a lot," she said, "to answer for."

Laura looked up sharply. Then she glanced at Jimmy and said, "Hey, you better go with her. Otherwise she'll put another bullet in someone. And I bet Reinschildt'd bawl a lot louder than George."

She spoke with deliberate lightness. Jimmy answered evenly, "I am goin'," and did not smile at all.

Notepad, biros, laptop, hard copies of relevant documents. Agenda notes. Dorian recited the usual court-appearance checklist as she marched at Dani's shoulder up the Miramar steps. CD of Chris's phone call, Brodie's interview, George's interview—the list went quite awry. CD, specially acquired from the police, don't ask how, of the Sorenson–Reinschildt calls. Copy of Chris's will.

"Aquamarine Room," Dani announced to the first reception-

ist in the marble-floored foyer, more extravagant, Dorian's skit-
tering mind remarked, than the usual Miramar wedding cake.
"We have a conference booked for eleven A.M. Under Pan-
Auric, I believe."

"We'll fly up," Dani had announced. As Dorian finished, "I
said I'd bring my lawyer, could you represent me? I know it'll
be Sunday, but—" Dani had been reaching for her phone. "Jo,
book me two seats to Cairns Sunday morning. Can you get us
in before eleven?" At Dorian's movement Dani's eye swung
back. "Make that three seats," she amended, reading, by appar-
ent telepathy, the look on Dorian's face.

If Jimmy survived a daytime flight upcoast in an Otter, Dorian
told herself, he'll cope with a Miramar elevator. The doors
closed and she surveyed them in the mirror wall. Jimmy in
white shirt and his fawn Blackston trousers, with the adamantly
demanded addition of a tie and business shoes. And I went for
decorous in gray-and-pencil-blue-striped shirt, but Dani . . .

Dani was wearing fuchsia, a spectacularly collared dress vivid
as an orchid, matched by her lipstick, the polish on her nails. It
must, Dorian thought, struggling with just too ready laughter,
be the Lewis equivalent of a gauntlet. Or perhaps, a raspberry.

Outside the conference room Dani stopped. She glanced up
at Jimmy and said, "You have reason and right to be here, but I
want your promise on one thing. No matter what happens, unless one of us asks, you don't intervene."

Dorian watched him think it through, that stare unblinking.
Not quite the stone wall. Not, she devoutly hoped, obduracy.
But if he digs his toes in, there's nothing either of us can do.

"You did the right thing," Dani said evenly, "with Brodie.
And with Sorenson. But this isn't a shooting situation. Dorian
will lead the interview. I'll intervene if necessary. But wildcat
break-ins from the sidelines may send the whole thing out of
control."

Dorian crossed mental fingers. Dani waited. After another moment Jimmy inclined his head and said, "Aye, ma'am. Ye know y'r business. I'll no' speak unless I'm asked."

Just visibly, Dani let her breath out. "Thank you," she said, and knocked twice on the conference-room door.

It was smaller than Dorian had expected, with one broad window looking to the distant beach. Sunlight and palms and one of Cairns' lush tropical green hills traversed rapidly across her vision and disappeared as she focused on the table inside.

Long, polished, boardroom style. Upholstered chairs. Three men getting to their feet on the right side. *Reinschildt's stringers,* said Chris's voice. Secretary and at least one lawyer, she amended, younger man, white shirt and tie, older man, three-piece suit. Reinschildt between them, equally anomalously suave. Armani, doubtless. In Cairns, so suitable. The irritation gave her nerves an edge. She said, "Mr. Reinschildt? I'm Dorian Wild."

"Miss Wild." The tone was as cold as the upright stance. No offered hand, not the barest nod. "Harris Charles, my legal adviser. Don Paglio, my assistant."

"This is Danielle Lewis. My legal adviser. And this"—she tried not to pause—"is my security consultant. Seamus Kee-nighan."

When she and Dani concocted the title Jimmy had struggled not to laugh. "He'll know I'm no' such!" he had protested. And Dani said, "Dorian hired you. He'll know who you are. This'll remind him why."

Whatever he knew, Reinschildt never batted an eye. But she saw the shift of more than recognition in the younger man's stare.

Dani's own shift warned Dorian, Keep moving. Don't wait for them to offer you seats. It will be occupation of a vantage if they do. She came up the table's left side. Facing Reinschildt across it, she thought with shock, He's small.

Shorter than Chris was. No taller than I am. About five feet five. Next to Jimmy, a perfectly suited, exquisitely groomed, tailor's manikin.

And I'd best not let *that* show, she thought, setting down her briefcase, laying out the weapons of legal war. You can give him the opening speech, Dani had said. You've already begun the offensive. This is his response. Let him set out his hand, if he will.

Reinschildt waited for them to settle. Then he touched the piece of paper topmost before him and said, "You have evidence to support these claims?"

No title this time. Dorian refused to let her teeth set. The berserker was already imminent.

"We have evidence, yes."

The cold blue eyes regarded her as if she held a poker hand. Wait, she could hear Dani saying. Don't offer anything. Make him ask for it.

"Legally valid evidence?"

"My adviser considers so."

Another grapple of eyes. Then one perfectly shaped fingernail touched the paper edge.

"My legal advice is that Pan-Auric has the freedom to suspend operations at any mine legally under its control. For any length of time. Further, Pan-Auric has no legal obligation to pre-advise the public about possible compensation, for resumptions of any land not freehold, within an officially granted mining lease."

We don't know if the Mining Office have granted this lease, Dani had said. If he brings it up, ask to see. But if they have it, don't get involved with the ethics of compensation. Leave that to me.

"Do you have proof of ownership? And of a valid lease?"

Reinschildt gave a slight nod. The assistant—secretary,

Dorian amended defiantly—slid a hard copy across the tabletop.

Dani intercepted it. Against the paper her nails stood out dark as wine, and Dorian saw even Reinschildt's eyes follow them.

Dani glanced through the pages. Nodded as curtly as Reinschildt. Slid the paper back. Said, "We'll notify the current lessees to take legal advice."

Reinschildt's face stayed empty but she fancied a tic flitted across the lawyer's cheek.

Dorian folded her hands carefully atop her own papers and met Reinschildt's gaze. We've stated the claims. It's your onus to answer them. Come on, she thought, feeling the berserker stir. Come on, manikin. Dance.

"You claim to have evidence that an employee of Pan-Auric was involved with an alleged homicide?"

It was the lawyer who spoke. Dorian answered to Reinschildt. "We have evidence that a Pan-Auric employee, Edward Brodie, held up Mr. Chris Keogh at gunpoint. Took his papers and laptop. And then sabotaged his vehicle. Causing an accident in which Mr. Keogh died."

I got it out without a waver. Chris's name, as if he was just a legal point.

"What evidence?"

Tell what you have, Dani had said. Don't show. "We have a recorded message from Mr. Keogh. And Edward Brodie's recorded admission."

The lawyer's poker face nearly melted. Reinschildt, still at freezing point, said, "Proof?"

Dorian laid her hand on the little heap of CDs. "We reserve the proof for prosecution evidence."

And that got to them, she thought, noting, as she had so often in court, the tiny lag and pause that followed a telling point.

Then Reinschildt said in that blankly chill voice, "Edward Brodie was requested to retrieve papers that were company property. Anything beyond retrieval of data was entirely his own initiative."

Dorian locked eyes with that blue stare and thought, Sorenson was right. She felt the rage rise in her own throat. You didn't tell Brodie to do it, but you didn't say, don't. You gave him another blanket order: Fix it. And now you'll rat on him to cover your own arse.

She said before she could help herself, "Do you have proof of that?"

"Nothing," Reinschildt came back, pure ice, "outside a court of law."

Which means he's going to swear it, under oath.

If he does jettison Brodie, Dani had said, and he almost certainly will, given what both Brodie and Sorenson have said about him, don't pursue it. There's no point in wrangling over that here. Just hit him with the calls to Sorenson.

"And Troy Sorenson's actions during the siege at Baringal beach were also undertaken on his own responsibility?"

The air tingled like a blizzard wind. I didn't think Reinschildt's eyes could get colder, Dorian thought, trying not to break out in goose bumps as she sat.

"Miss Wild." He hasn't sat any straighter, she told herself. It just feels as if he has. "I have taken legal advice on your letter. I'm authorized to make this counteroffer. Pan-Auric will publicly announce that Mr. Keogh resigned from Ben Morar, before the company was officially taken over by Pan-Auric. Pan-Auric will also sign an agreement that you, and the other persons you may stipulate as being involved with Ben Morar mining company, during the events at the Ben Morar mine, or at Baringal beach, will, on Pan-Auric's part, be held under personal immunity."

He did not read it off the page, but spoke direct to Dorian. The ice had thickened another inch.

"In addition, Pan-Auric will not pursue charges against you and Mr. Keenighan. For trespass, unlawful wounding, grievous bodily harm, aggravated assault, and manslaughter, if not homicide. Against both Pan-Auric and Ben Morar employees."

Be prepared, Dani had said. If he goes for the counterattack, to soften you up, he's likely to threaten you with everything you thought George could throw at you, and more. Don't let him see you blink. And don't let him know that George has already agreed not to press the shooting charges, at least.

"In return, Pan-Auric will receive all copies of the statistical analysis model Christopher Keogh designed while he was working for what is now a subsidiary Pan-Auric company."

I'll see you in hell first!

Dorian just managed not to bawl it aloud. She felt Jimmy jerk beside her like a jolted spring. She knew Dani's hand was poised to grab her arm. She bit down ferociously on her tongue and swore at herself, Don't yell, don't crack, don't show it, don't let him see he's got through.

Beside her, Dani's voice, more glacial than Reinschildt's, said, "Mr. Keogh willed the model to Ms. Wild. Mr. Keogh's contract with Ben Morar explicitly reserved it as his personal property. Pan-Auric has no claim."

Reinschildt did not bother to shrug. He did not even look at Dani. Talk, that posture said, compacted and heedless as a sentient boulder. You made your terms, now here are ours. If you don't like it, you know the alternative.

Dani did not speak again either. She's waiting, Dorian realized. Because the final decision is mine.

She took a little breath that seemed to go to her lungs' base in liquid fire. Then she said clearly, full in Reinschildt's face, "No."

The air was tingling again. Reinschildt was watching her, still with a complete absence of expression. It doesn't matter, that look said. You're no more than a minor annoyance, a pebble under the Pan-Auric juggernaut. We don't care if you give in to our demands or we just ride clear over you.

Then he said, "No announcement of Mr. Keogh's resignation? No immunities?"

"No model for Pan-Auric," Dorian said, unable to do it except through her teeth.

"Charges to proceed?"

The berserker broke loose. "Try it," Dorian said, and dropped her hand back over the CDs.

Reinschildt glanced away. Once, briefly, at his lawyer. Not to consult, merely to remind her, she realized, of the force he could invoke. God is with the big battalions, she remembered. Even in law.

Beside her Dani's fingers moved. Long fuchsia slashes curling on the papers like a visual jab in her ribs.

The other weapon. God, I forgot the other weapon. The one Sorenson used, the only one that Sorenson could use, at the end.

"Today's the twenty-sixth of September." She tried for chill and managed to sound slightly sweet. "If, by the evening of sixth October, Pan-Auric has made no announcement on Mr. Keogh's resignation, or has not contacted me regarding personal immunities—including the charges you threaten to lay—or given me, in writing, a statement that Pan-Auric understands Mr. Keogh's model to be my uncontested property . . . then I will have no choice but to contact the media."

She tried not to catch her breath as if the air had filled with literal ice.

"My legal advice is that we should then offer full disclosure of the incidents involved. From the court case over Ben Morar's faulty tailings dam, to the source of orders for the Baringal siege. Including"—she laid her hand over the CDs again—"the contents of these interviews."

The lawyer made something that could have been an aborted jerk. Reinschildt did not move. He's solidified from the core out, she thought. Ice, not human flesh and blood, in that blue glare.

Yeah, she thought, glaring back with shaky but furious defiance. Threaten me with the law, you bastard. But with the media, the news *is* power. The money'll be there for *me*.

And it won't matter if you sue me for defamation. By then, Brodie and George and Sorenson's recordings'll be all over the globe.

Try running *this* pebble under your juggernaut.

The lawyer twitched. Reinschildt shifted a hand and he stilled. Dorian could feel Dani beside her, frozen in a fury of fear and rage and exaltation almost as fierce as her own.

Reinschildt stood up. He leant forward, hands on the table, and spoke softly, but no longer indifferently, as she had with him, straight in her face.

"We've researched your friend. Mr. . . . Keenighan. He has no British passport. He has no Australian passport. He has no known address in the British Isles. He has no known address in Australia. He has no bank accounts, credit cards, driver's license, social security number, or—health card, whatever it's called here. He has no visa for or record of entry into Australia."

Dorian could only stare.

"But eighteen years ago, an IRA grass disappeared into a witness-protection program in the British Isles. His name was Michael James Keenighan."

Every shred of breath froze in Dorian's lungs. The blue eyes bored into hers like diamond drills.

"This is my last offer, Miss Wild. We will publicly announce

Keogh's resignation. We will waive the charges of manslaughter and so on. But if you don't return the statistical model to Pan-Auric, and sign an agreement ceding all rights in it, then withdrawing all obstruction to Pan-Auric's operation at Blackston, we will pass the information on Keenighan to the Australian police."

He leant a little closer. Dorian could not move.

"Then he'll be deported, Miss Wild." The voice dropped to a blizzard purr. "Most likely, to Ireland. His chances there, I guess you can figure for yourself."

He thinks Jimmy . . . he knows what we know. But he's found this other Keenighan. If Childers gets hold of that . . .

They'll send him to Ireland, as a known IRA grass. Oh, God, oh, my God.

Then something like a bolt of ice went down her own backbone. I may not know what to do. But I inherited the berserker. I'm the descendant of Paddy Wild. And *he* wouldn't sit here dissolving like a marshmallow. He'd fight for what was his.

"I will not answer that—that *proposal*"—she was amazed that it came out icier than Reinschildt's own voice—"without legal advice."

And Paddy Wild wouldn't melt into tears either. She straightened, and gave Reinschildt every ounce of her rage and loathing. I hope it is the proverbial blowtorch glare.

He took his hands off the table. "I'll give you twenty-four hours." The ice had thawed back to indifference. "Then call my assistant, and tell us what you'll do."

CHAPTER 11

"I can go," Jimmy said for the fourth time. "Ye dinna need me now. They'll no' try the hard men again. An' Herself'll sort the legal parts." Too deliberately, his voice firmed. "Ye dinna need me at all."

Dorian could not find the strength to reply. Slumping into the hospital visitor's chair, she thought, I feel like a sawdust doll. And somebody just let all the stuffing out.

"An' wi' me gone, ye can tell Reinschildt to—take a walk. There's nothin' he can do."

"There's plenty P-A can do." Laura squirmed on her pillow heap. "Everything Reinschildt threatened, and more. Sue Dorian for the model. Press those other charges. Sure, we could countercharge, but we're short a major witness, without you. If we blow it to the media, that could get Reinschildt charged—and sacked—and convicted. But bad press won't stop P-A. Not if they figure they can still get the mine, and the model, on the other side."

"It stopped Reinschildt."

"Because it was his hide on the line."

The hospital air-conditioning thrummed, blending with nurses' talk, patients' buzzers, the clatter of trays and trolleys and instruments. Dorian shifted her fists under her cheekbones and went on staring at the floor.

We can get Reinschildt. Her brain ticked yet again round the circuit that repetition had made a beaten track. We could, we should manage to keep the model. The will's there, the contract's there, we have evidence of P-A's other mayhem. The best they can do is appeal, and eventually some judge will throw them out. Though if it comes to a test of purses, as Anne said ages ago, they could drain me dry.

But the mine . . .

Oh, Chris. She blinked at the generic institution carpet. You tried to stop them and got killed for it. We've tried to stop them and we've hurt people, killed people, and done no better. Whatever happens to the model, there's still nothing to stop the mine.

Even if I lost Jimmy as well.

"Half a loaf's no use."

The words were out before she thought. But the other two turned as if she had produced an oracle.

"We need it all. To get Reinschildt. Keep the model. Not have Jimmy—driven away." That's if he *can* be driven, a sudden small cell of horror inserted. What if the fold really is Providence, and it won't open again till we fix everything?

"Most of all," she said, lifting her head at last, "we have to stop the mine." Because that's what this is really about. Not what happened to Chris, whether he lived or died. Stopping the mine. That was his priority.

Laura shifted on her pillows. Long friendship deciphered the drop of her lashes clearer than words. Sure, Dor. Getting Reinschildt's a good bet. Keeping the model's doable. Losing Jimmy may be unavoidable damage. But the mine?

Jimmy got out of the other chair and turned to the window. As he stared up to the near flank of Mount Stewart, tawny grass haying off under the Nile green leaves and white trunks of poplar gums, his profile echoed Laura's response.

"We *have* to do it! We can't—!"

She stopped. In the silence, the hospital noises merged into a sound track, a long-drawn, unending rumor of defeat.

Dorian dropped her head back in her hands. So I've spelled out what we want. I've known that all along. It doesn't bring us any closer to getting it. Oh, damn the model, she thought bitterly, it's never been anything but trouble and destruction. Why'd Chris ever invent the thing? Why'd he have to make it work at all?

For a moment she thought even the air-conditioning had stopped. But the words fell into that small, perfect hiatus, clear as rain descending in single drops.

Suppose the model *didn't* work?

Jimmy and Laura were both staring. Jimmy had swung round, Laura half sat up. Neither spoke. She saw them through a bubble of crystal, remote as another world.

The model only worked, her mind went on, thought cutting clear and lethal as shards of crystal, after Chris made that last adjustment. Before that, it never found anything.

Suppose it was readjusted, so nothing showed again?

The one time would look like a fluke. Nobody but me has a copy. It couldn't be cross tested anywhere. Nobody has results that worked from it, except Pan-Auric.

Suppose . . . it was coming more slowly now. Deliberately, steady as running blood. Suppose they had the model back. And they ran the tests again. The same tests Chris ran.

And nothing came up?

I can't do that. Every cell of her body rebelled. That model was Chris's darling, his greatest achievement, his life's work. It, he, doesn't deserve to be doubted, discredited, ruined. Warped into a lie. I can't do that. I can't.

But if I don't?

Oh, Chris. Would you—will you ever forgive me, if you know?

She had stood up without realizing. Jimmy's hands closed on her shoulders. Across Laura's suddenly uncertain "Dor?" came his too-soft "What is it, mo cailín?"

She wiped at each eye with a finger. Then she turned, slowly, wondering if this was how assassins felt before they struck.

"Suppose," she said, "we give them what they want."

They both gaped.

"Hand over the model. But drive a damn hard bargain. Announcement of Chris's resignation. The immunities. Freedom to protest the mine."

Laura's mouth opened in jetting outrage. And shut.

"What're you thinking, Dor?"

"As a haggle point"—Dorian's mind was still moving, cold and steady as water in an Arctic cave—"we could even concede, no media."

Laura's eyes went to marmalade-colored slits.

"Then suppose," Dorian's voice almost wobbled, "when they try it out—the model doesn't work."

Beside her Jimmy jerked. The hiss of his breath supplanted words. Laura took a second longer. There was a definite waver when she spoke.

"You mean—jigger it. Chris's model. Deliberately."

Dorian bit the inside of her lip. "Yes."

"I know," she said, in the poleaxed quiet. "It's—unthinkable. But what would happen, if we did?"

It was Jimmy who spoke first. Shock had lowered even that deep voice.

"The tests. The assays willna match. If they run a check, 'twill come out wrong." The note rose like a startled bird. "The field'll no' be there!"

"Oh, my God!" Suddenly Laura was half whooping, clutching her shoulder and bouncing in the bed. "Hide in plain sight! If they use a jiggered version they can look till their ears turn blue!" She tried to throw up her arms in a victory clutch. "And if they can't find the field, they won't start the mine!"

Jimmy grabbed Dorian and spun her round with her feet right off the floor. He was laughing too, the concussions jerking her through his ribs. "Ah, mo cailín, ye're more than Sidhe. Ye're a bluidy genius!"

"They can't have checked." Dorian leant on him, wiping at her own eyes, half sorrow, half wild relief. "Chris had the model, they had to buy on his results. We'll have to make them run it again. Maybe a scare. A rumor about the model being—unreliable. Maybe"—her brain was turning over now like locomotive drivers—"somebody important, hinting in public?"

"That LTU geology guy," Laura put in. "The one you said checked the results for Chris."

"Yeah, maybe. Though that would mean telling him the truth." Dorian's euphoria chilled. "He mightn't agree. And if he tells P-A . . ."

"Sound him out. If he feels iffy, get someone else." Laura swept on with her usual ease in overleaping problem points. "But how'll you jigger the model? Do you know anything about stats?"

"Not really. I guess just change a figure or a variable. With anything that delicate, it ought to be enough."

"God, yes, probably one thing'd do." Laura's voice slowed. "Wait, though. It's on the CD. There's a date and time on files. If the latest date's way after Chris—finished with it—P-A'll smell a rat."

"We could just delete it. Send the CD back." Dorian's own brain caught up. "No. CDs: even if you wipe the file, the data stays on."

Damn, she thought, as the flow of possibility narrowed into technical swamps. There has to be some way round this.

"We could make a new copy. Say Sorenson broke the original."

"Mmmm." Laura too was wearing a heavy frown. "But how'd

you make the copy, then? And you could still have held a copy back."

Dorian sank into the chair, cursing silently. A great idea, it would have been.

Laura had slumped. Suddenly she shoved half upright again.

"Wait, wait. This Net fanatic I know, he told me once. Yeah! Listen, Dor, you know you can change your computer's clock? If you do that, and make a file, it'll show the altered date." Dorian gaped. "So we change your computer's clock. Put it back to—the day—Chris would have had the CD last. Open the final file. Jigger it, save it. There's no way P-A can tell it's not the original."

Dorian turned it in her head, almost not daring to hope. "And there's no way," she said slowly, with chagrined memories of wrong buttons punched on her own files, "they could get the previous version back."

"No!"

Dorian allowed herself a sip of hope. "Except . . . I'd really like someone who knows what they're doing to alter it. What if we just do something minor, and it still works? Or they can fix it again?"

Laura frowned. Then her eyes gleamed. "If Chris kept some duds, we could give them an older version." The gleam faded. "No. We can't get the true one off. And even a dud might let somebody figure the next step. We can't just sell P-A a dummy. The model," her voice slowed, "has to go out of sight for good."

For good, Dorian thought. That means, erase the model itself. As if Chris never invented it. All his work. His reputation. His achievement. It won't just be the model we wipe out. It'll be Chris as well.

"Dor." Laura was not effervescing anymore. "Dor—I don't think we—I don't think I can do that. Not to Chris."

"Ye're forgettin' the Road to Damascus," Jimmy said.

When they both turned, he looked at them with something like surprise. "What the wee feller—what Chris said, himself. *I don't know why I'm doin' this.* An' then he went tearin' off to stop the mine. To fight wi' both his managers. Throw up his job. An' he said—to y'r office girl—maybe he'd never do geology again."

Laura's eyes went wide. Dorian nodded. "Tanya told me that. George's secretary."

"An' I thought, 'twas like the Road to Damascus." Jimmy's own eyes darkened. "When ye said this first, I thought, 'twould be worse than shootin' him. But if he said that . . . if he was goin' to throw it all over, no' just that job, but geology . . . maybe, himself, he'd never have wanted to use the thing, the model, again."

Or have anyone else use it. Could Chris have made such a transformation as that?

Dorian looked back on Tanya's words, Ralston's words. Her own memory of that phone call, Chris saying with white fury, *Find me a good environmental lawyer.*

"No," she said, with slow but with increasing surety. "He mightn't have used it. He mightn't even have wanted to publish it."

"I guess," Laura agreed reluctantly. "But we'll have to discredit his work—not just say it didn't work, we'll have to *make* it not work." Her eyes glistened. "That's so unfair, after he got it all up, and then—"

Then he got killed for it.

Killed for the model, or to stop the mine?

Dorian took a deep breath. "He willed me the model," she said. "He saved the disk for me. Palantir. He made me his executor. Whatever happened—he expected I'd take care of things."

And I promised I would.

"I know it's—a terrible price. It's—maybe higher than what

we'll get for it. But . . . when he died—Chris's—last project—was to stop the mine."

She blinked again, seeing that last dream image, Chris fading into the eucalypt grove. Into the shadows and colors of the earth. His life's work, its knowledge. His oldest, deepest love.

"And I do know . . . when Chris made up his mind what he wanted . . . he didn't ever count the cost."

There was another falling silence, in which she thought, with surprise: I've just made him *my* epitaph.

Then Laura nodded, and wiped her own eyes. And Jimmy shifted his shoulders and said quite simply, "Aye."

"It's—an idea." Dani gave a three-sixty spin to her propelling pen. "*Quite* an idea." Slowly, her mouth began to curve. "Poetic—justice—you could say."

A jujitsu scam, her beatific expression glossed. P-A's might extorts what they've wanted and it costs everything they did it for. They've already bought up Ben Morar and taken the new lease. They'll be left with a defunct old mine, a nonexistent new one. And a model that doesn't work.

"There are no other copies extant?" Dani came back to earth. "You're quite sure? Chris's laptop? Reinschildt smashed that, Brodie said. Anything in the office at Ben Morar? Just the one version on the CD, that Chris smuggled out? The one you have—had?"

"The one I put in the bank, yes."

"Then it went to Baringal." Dani's brows flexed. "All the copies you made went to Baringal. And the ones Sorenson stole were there. So they're all in police custody."

"Oh," Dorian said in blank dismay. "Damn! I could have told Reinschildt that, too."

"We might yet." Dani's mind was moving at its computer speed. "They'll be evidence. But the inquests should be pretty soon." Her hand moved toward the phone and stopped. "I think I can do something about that. We only need one disk for this? The original?"

Childers, Dorian thought. Don't ask what tale she's going to spin, what leverage she'll use. And then felt another pang on her own account.

"No," she said slowly. "I think we have to hand over the lot."

Chris's own disk, with his hand-printed title. But it has to go. Reinschildt, at least, will know the significance of "Palantir." And the rest have to go too. We'll be sustaining one mighty lie, we can't support a second one. We can't hedge.

"If you do that," Dani said, "you'll virtually destroy the thing. It can't ever be published. Or passed to the industry." The tone added, You have thought of this?

"It couldn't ever be published," Dorian answered as steadily as she could, "anyway."

When Dani kept looking, she added, "I think Chris mightn't have minded that."

She summarized. Dani listened without interrupting. Then she nodded once and said, "He was a good man."

She continued, "It'll be best if I do the haggling. Reinschildt won't show in person, so neither should you. So. If they get the model, we get Chris cleared. The personal immunities. That covers any criminal charges. And the threat to Jimmy. And we stay free to contest the mine." She frowned a little. "I think we have to go for that, or later, they may smell a rat. We can demand, as haggle points, disclosure about Chris's accident. We'll also cede, if we have to, word to the media?" Dorian nodded. "Very well. I'll contact Reinschildt's secretary tonight."

"We do have to make P-A rerun the model," Dorian said. "I thought we could start a rumor it was unreliable. Or maybe a public comment. Say, from an LTU geologist. One of them checked the results for Chris."

"Possibly." Dani's brows pleated. Then the frown became a small, Mona Lisa smile. "Leave that to me."

Dorian could not help the questioning look.

"I'll brief Moira," Dani said.

"She's been very upset," she went on blandly, "about George. Not just his getting shot, the whole forgery and swindle thing. But he's still an—old friend, I'm afraid."

So if Dani tells Moira there's something fishy about the model, in a legitimate briefing—almost—Moira will feel herself bound to pass it on. And George will blab it to P-A. Whether it's to get back on their good side, or because he thinks I'll owe him a favor, or to get his revenge on them.

Dorian could feel herself mirror Dani's half-feral expression. Dani gave the pen another twirl, and paused.

"It's more than likely, when the results crash, that they'll ask a second opinion. Dorian, did you say Chris checked with a geologist? George at least will know that." Now it was a definite frown. "I think you'd better locate and advise him. It's risky, but it's safer than leaving him in the dark."

"But what if he won't play along? It'll be his own professional opinion on the line."

Dani considered. Then she said, "If he gets that far—tell him what P-A did to Chris."

"Yes." Dorian just bit back, You're the one who's a genius. Yes, fellow feeling as a geologist ought, at least, to guarantee the double cross's security.

"We may still need a public channel," Dani considered. "If there's no action in say, a fortnight. Maybe"—her eyes narrowed in another beatific look—"an interview, on TV or in the paper. Where the geologist drops it in, apropos of something else."

Dorian could feel her own blissful-demon smile. "I'll get onto it now."

"Mike Somebody? Who works with mines? Drill-core analysis?" The voice of the Earth Science departmental secretary came briskly over the line. "That's probably Mike Brubeck. I'll give you his number. You're in luck, he was on a field trip over the weekend."

"Chris Keogh? Yes, yes, I knew Chris." Mike Brubeck's voice was resonant, with an occasional stammer before the topic caught his interest. "Yes, I did check some core results for him. With his new model, yes. You need to talk about them?" A pause. "Well, I've got a spare hour, tomorrow afternoon. Two P.M.? Okay."

"So if you're worried he'll pull the plug, make it a trial run." Laura wriggled her good shoulder and pulled a face. "Jink a copy of the model. Ask him to run it on Chris's data. Tell him you're checking its validity as a part of probate. Then if it's really jiggered, let him tell *you*."

While Dorian turned it over, Jimmy gave a smothered snort.

"Double-headed penny, ye spalpeen? Tails, it works, an' ye don't tell him anythin' more? An' if P-A ask, he'll honestly say the first time was a fluke?" He snorted again. "Heads, it don't work, so then ye tell the truth?"

Laura laughed aloud. Dorian began, "But I don't *have* a copy . . ."

"Dani." Laura waved her good hand expansively. "You've got till two o'clock tomorrow, yeah? Get her to twist her pet policeman's tail. All we want's one copy, for now."

Dani can probably do it, Dorian conceded. Dani will do it if I ask. I could call when I get home. "But what if it flops, and I tell all, and he still won't play?"

"Like Dani said. Tell him what P-A did to Chris."

A choice of evils. If we don't brief him, he may simply tell P-A the model worked when *he* saw the results, and that'll point them straight to us. If we do brief him, and he won't play . . .

She stood up with a jerk. "I don't think we should try to trick him," she said. "I'll tell him the story, and take it from there."

And if there's trouble, let's hope Paddy Wild can get me out.

"I remember you, yes. Chris talked about you. And you were at . . ." Mike Brubeck let the rest trail off. At the funeral.

His room, Dorian thought, was the typical geologist's bower-bird nest: papers, rocks, books piled on every shelf and every spare inch of floor. He perched opposite her before the overloaded desk, a weathered, bearded man with a monk's tonsure of red-gold curly hair, in LTU casual academic gear of sandals, long shorts and T-shirt. This one said, "Resist Reforestation: Stop Strip Mining." Deciphering that, she felt a first twinge of hope.

She lined up her evidence on the desk: a copy of Chris's will and the contract, her phone with copies of his message and the Brodie interview. The CD that Dani's secretary had brought at midday, labeled "Palantir 3," but not in Dorian's hand.

"This is Chris's stats model," she said. "Chris willed it to me." She launched yet again into the tale.

"Now," she wound up, "in spite of the will, and the contract, the megacorp are trying to blackmail me to get the model. They're threatening to attack my friends."

A bit of stretched truth, but in essence accurate, she thought, trying to read his face. It looked notably blank. She drew another breath and plunged.

"So . . . I'm planning to give them the model. A version that doesn't work."

His eyes shot up to her face. Narrow, blue, creased deep in crowsfeet. In another ten or twenty years, she thought, Chris's eyes might have looked like that.

"I know," she tried for steadiness, "what that model meant to Chris. What it might mean to the industry. But—I don't think, by the time he left Ben Morar, he cared about that anymore."

She laid out the other evidence. Tanya's, Ralston's, Chris's own words. The ongoing silence dug at her confidence. "I can only do what I think he wanted," she heard herself beginning to sound harried. "And this isn't fair to him. But it's the only way I can see."

She stopped. Those are the facts. He's a scientist, he should be able to make a decision without persuasion as well.

The building rumored with footsteps, distant voices, the faint growl of air-conditioning. Like Ben Morar, she thought. The office at Ben Morar, all that fuss outside, and inside, a duel with one person's judgment, one person's belief. That time, I was hoping to get past with minimal truth about one incident. This time, everything's riding on it.

The silence stretched. Her nerves stretched. She looked down at the crowded desktop and tried not to bite her lip.

Mike Brubeck said, "Do you want me to change the model for you?"

"Oh!" Dorian's head flew up before she could help it. "I hadn't thought—" She got a hold on her wits. "Firstly, I just wanted to brief you. About the plan. In case P-A checked back with you."

"And what did you want me to tell them?"

He still sounded thoroughly noncommittal. She glanced at his T-shirt to encourage herself.

"Well, if you said it was working when you saw the results?"

"That makes them suspect the version they got back?"

"Um, yes. But I didn't quite know how to—what you'd want to say, that is, if . . ." I left that blank, she let her expression finish, for you to settle, if you did decide to help.

He shifted in the far-from-ergonomic office chair. His voice echoed a little in the cluttered room.

"If Chris himself wanted to stop the mine. And if the company tried to shaft him, alive *or* dead . . ." His voice deepened a halftone, and there was a glint—of anger, she decided—in the blue eyes. He tapped the CD on the desk.

"If the company contact me, I'll tell them to send me a copy of their model and Chris's data, so I can run the results again. If they actually send it, I'll give them the results."

Dorian felt her back muscles twitch like a startled cat's. "But what will you tell them? How will you explain . . ."

Despite the beard, she saw his cheek muscles shift.

"I'm working on a book," he said. "It's called, *Real Rocks.* It talks about the difficulties of reading core-logs and other samples, because rocks in the real world aren't anywhere near as simple as in textbooks. And geologists—even the best geologists—can make mistakes."

And you feel the way I do, about traducing Chris. But you'll do it. Even if you might end up looking mistaken yourself.

From somewhere at the bottom of a suddenly dry throat, Dorian found her voice. "Thank you," it said.

For the first time he glanced full in her eyes, and she thought, It is anger. Almost as strong as my own.

"I never actually got a look at the model," he said. "I'd like to see the real version, just once."

"You would?" Dorian heard her voice go up, excitement, gratitude, relief, and he gave her another direct look.

"I should be able to change it fairly easily. I work with stats models all the time."

"Oh." Dorian sagged against the straight-backed visitor's chair. I'll get to "thank you" in a minute, she promised. You won't say a word about this, will you? is almost certainly superfluous.

"But you know, the, the date on the file will be wrong—"

"That's okay, we think we know how to fix that." She tried not to babble. "If you can just—change—this one copy, and show me what you did, I can, we can alter the others and then . . ." The stale, slightly antiseptic air seemed to sparkle like vaporized champagne. "Then . . ."

His eyes flicked to hers and away but she thought a match to her own expression lurked behind the beard. He took the CD, holding it carefully in a hand as weathered as his face. "I should have it ready," he said, "in, in the next couple of days. I'll call you to pick it up."

"The coroner's dismissed need for an inquest on Sorenson." Dani's voice came crisply over the phone. "Police action, clear cause of death. But there will be one on Brodie. This coming Thursday, two P.M. I've told P-A they can't have the models till the police release them. I've told Andy Childers that even though that copy let you move on the probate, we'd really appreciate having them all back as soon as possible, for security. Against P-A." The sheer blandness of her voice was an italic. "He'll play ball. He wants this inquest over more than we do. If we pick the copies up in person, we could have them as soon as Friday. That means"—her voice was just too even—"we could courier them to P-A, Saturday."

Dorian found she had been holding her breath. She let it out, slowly, and loosened her fingers round the unit phone.

"Mike, ah, said he thought he'd have that report for me, in a couple of days."

In a moment Dani said, "Good."

I bet Brodie sounded like that with a target in his heat scope, Dorian thought.

"If we get the copies off to P-A Saturday," Dani was going on, "I could brief Moira, perhaps, Monday afternoon."

That gives me Friday evening to jink the models, Dorian calculated. Say two, three days more for P-A to get them, and Moira to gab, and P-A to rerun the tests. If they're going to contact Mike, they could do it by the end of next week.

"So in a fortnight . . . we might know."

"It's a reasonable round figure." Dani sounded as nonchalant as Dorian tried to be.

A fortnight. Just a fortnight, and it could all be coming to an end. P-A run their wonder model again and their mine disappears. They check the results with Mike and he says, Hey, geologists can make mistakes. Even Chris. Even me.

Then what do they do?

The obvious, she told herself. They curse and foam at being led up a garden path. They take stock and allot blame. With luck, heads will roll. Reinschildt's especially.

Then they do the economical smart thing. Cut their losses. Drop the lease. Close Ben Morar. Pull out of Blackston for good. What else would they do?

So Chris'll have what he wanted, whatever the price.

And then?

Her pulse fluttered suddenly and her eyes rose without volition to Jimmy watching her across the dining table, the fiddle set upright on his knee, as he waited for her call to end.

She snatched thoughts and eyes away. "Okay," she said. "That sounds—pretty good. Uh—they'll notify us, me and Jimmy, about the inquest date, won't they? Officially?"

"You should hear tomorrow," Dani agreed. "I'll be at the inquest, naturally."

As your lawyer. Dorian nodded, mutely, into the holoscreen. It's really pointless, she thought, to say "thank you" again. Then she took another look at Dani's face, the razor concentration, the faint but predatory smile, and thought, she's the Terminator. She's enjoying this. She should be thanking me.

The screen blanked. She put the phone up. She had thought she moved normally, but in a minute Jimmy set the fiddle aside and came round the table to her.

You always notice, she thought, turning into his arms. I don't have to signal, you read the signs beforehand. Like Chris used to do. She shut her hands in the T-shirt that said "Earth Is Not a 404" and thought, does he know it's a Net joke? If a double-edged one. Our earth may soon be a lost Net page for him.

Her hands clenched. I won't think about that. "Did you get that about the inquest?" she said into his chest.

"Thursday? Aye." He sounded quiet but not daunted.

"They won't ask much. The real stuff's in the police statements. And we've already given those."

He made an affirmative noise. His arms settled more closely round her, and she pushed her nose into his shirt, his still anomalous personal scent, his body's warmth.

"If everything works . . . you mightn't have to wait much longer . . . at all."

Oh, damn, I wasn't going to talk about what might happen, let alone how waiting's been so hard on him. "I just meant—I didn't—"

"I know what ye meant." He still sounded quiet. "I've been thinkin' about that, mo cailín."

Her throat shut. She clutched handfuls of cotton and shut her eyes.

"Laura. They're about ready to—what d' ye say?—release her? 'Tis near enough to a jail. You remember she said, her sister's no' comin' after all, there's a crisis wi' her kids? An' Laura sayin' she'd have to get a nurse around."

"I remember," she said, when he paused.

"Aye, well, I thought." Another pause. "Mebbe . . . we could have her here. There's that other bed," he began in the gap. "An' she'd no' need a nurse. I could see to her. I'm no' run off m' feet. An' I have done—somethin' like that. Wi' Bridgie."

She did not have to fill in the rest. Before, while Bridget died.

Oh, Dorian said silently, breath catching like a pain. You're thinking about someone else, and I'm here worrying about me.

"Yes," she said, spreading her fingers for a wider round of T-shirt, lifting her face. "Yes, that's a great idea." At the least, this time your patient should survive. "She might even pay attention, when you tell her what to do. And if you're busy, I don't have to worry you'll run off with a builder's crew." His half smile was wry as hers. "So I can concentrate on work."

He was watching her closely. "Ye'll no' mind?" he said.

"Mind? Oh." A third in the flat, someone to trespass, however tactfully or reluctantly, on our privacy? She did not have to work for the grin. "Not unless you want to make *really* passionate love on the living-room floor?"

"No!" The splutter was a laugh. He shook her lightly, hands either side her face. "I'll stay to the bed." The smile narrowed wickedly. " 'Twill make a change, no' bein' odd man out mysel'."

It has changed things, Dorian thought, pulling the outer door shut on Jimmy's Tyrone burr, on Laura's familiar spontaneous laugh. Even one other person shifts the dynamic of a, a group, a situation, however welcome that person is.

But Laura really is welcome, she decided, as she started down the corridor. Not just for herself, or for giving Jimmy an overtime job. I know that's a blessing, simply from how much easier he is. Talking more. Laughing, too. It's good for us, as well. How long would it be, alone together, with the mine thing hung over us like another stockpile, before we lost the honeymoon glow? Started scratching, picking at each other. Maybe got tired, overexposed.

No. I don't think I'd get tired of him.

But he might get tired of me.

Or maybe not tired, just distracted. Carry over into daylight those times I've woken to feel him awake beside me, lying so straight and still. A stillness of more than memory. The tension of a frustration close to fear.

Thinking about his mother. The girls. Left without word, without his and Bridgie's help. And Patsy. With a house to pay for. With Michael. Whatever craziness that might bring.

Anything that takes his mind off all that is good.

She pushed the eighth-floor button in the Perpetual Insurance lift and remembered half wryly how she had once feared coming in here. It seems nothing now. Not after Ben Morar, and Baringal, and meeting Reinschildt face to face.

And already it's Wednesday again. With the inquest almost a week past, its worst hurdle the coroner's struggle with Jimmy's accent, that turned every question to a miniature interrogation. That must have tried him as much as another tiptoe through the minefield of what to say, what to omit. About the whole Ben Morar incident.

But he managed. A very perfect stone face, taciturnity just not reluctant enough to kindle suspicion. No wonder, when he came back to sit beside me, I could see his shirt cuff, the angle of his jaw, damp and slick with sweat. Despite that very co-operative coroner. I bet Childers had something to do with that.

But the rest went smooth as oil, the cops handing over the model copies Friday, Mike Brubeck phoning Thursday night. So I could pick up his disk on Friday too, with a little printout of the part I had to alter on the rest. And spend the evening over that. Yet another good-bye to Chris.

Before Dani mailed them Saturday. Direct to Reinschildt, flitting somewhere round Port Moresby, via P-A's own courier system.

While we dawdled away the weekend, settling Laura in, going

down the markets, watching *The Lord of the Rings* on DVD. All three of us carefully avoiding any mention of the real battle, of what was going to happen, Monday sometime.

The last hurdle. She pushed open her office door as her mouth dried. Not quite the last, but the last phase of the struggle started, oh, God, I hope so. The closing of the trap.

"Oh-h, Dorian?" Mrs. Urquhart leant out of her cubicle with a more than usually oily simper. "There's a Mike Brubeck wanting you."

Dorian's stomach somersaulted. She managed, "Thanks, Gloria. Is he still on the line?"

"Oh, yes, he just this moment rang."

"Ah, ah, hello, Dorian, this is Mike Brubeck. I thought you'd want to know. That parcel arrived all right. Chris's books."

Dorian sank down in her office chair with the phone clamped to her ear and every finger tingling as if she had touched a jellyfish. Her mouth said, "Hello, Mike. I'm glad to hear that. Today?"

"Yes, in the morning mail."

Dorian's heart bounced somewhere against her palate. The code words. He's said the code words, the code we arranged, in case P-A's security is still as good as Sorenson's and they're paranoid enough to tap my phones.

She managed an almost-casual tone. "Thanks for letting me know, Mike. I hope the books'll be useful. Ah, keep me posted, would you? As, ah, executor."

There was a little somehow different pause. Then he said, "Sure. I'll let you know."

Dorian clicked the phone off. She was suddenly catching at breath as if she had run a sprint race, muscles twanging fit to fly out of the chair. It worked. It's working. Moira's told George and George has blabbed to Reinschildt or someone and they've run the model and . . .

Now they've contacted Mike and asked him to retest.

She dropped both hands on the desk and bit her knuckles to keep herself from jumping round the room in elation or in sheer fright.

It's started. They've taken the bait.

"It will work," Laura insisted, dragging the couch cushion further under her arm. "It *is* working, Dor. Jeez, what else do you want? P-A've called Mike. He'll run the dud and give them the results. It's Wednesday now. They could have them back by Friday, and then the rest'll happen. It has to happen. What else can they do?"

"I don't know." Dorian wriggled in her own couch end and tried not to bite her fingernails. "Oh, I know, we've planned it all, it's going like clockwork." Her stomach let off another flight of butterflies. "I keep thinking, it's too easy. It's all too good."

Laura rolled her eyes. But Jimmy, ensconced between them, glanced sideways at Dorian, then reached out and pulled her toward him, into his shoulder's coign. Glancing up, she caught his profile, very calm in the TV screen's half-light. Perhaps too calm. The way he looked, she thought suddenly, waiting with the gun, in that motel room. But he had already returned his eyes to the TV, and was enquiring gravely, "D'ye tell me these Star Trek fellers think they've flown to the *moon?*"

Last Wednesday, Dorian calculated, P-A called Mike. Till Friday, at least, for P-A to act on his answer, and who knows if their management work over weekends? Besides, they'd have to consult on something as big as this. We can't expect any sign of a reaction yet, she lectured herself as she opened the Subway Jason had brought her, as usual, for Monday's lunch.

And of course it's stressful, the whole thing's such a gamble, so much is at stake. But P-A have taken the bait. The really tricky part was getting them to retest. Once they got that far, the rest was, is inevitable. Laura's right. You just have to wait.

In Mrs. Urquhart's cubicle the phone shrilled. Dorian's nerves jumped even before Mrs. Urquhart called, "Oh-h, Dorian? Ms. Lewis is wanting you."

Dorian's stomach curdled. "Now?"

"She said, yes, if you could."

Dani was behind her desk. Very much the senior partner, Dorian's nerves assessed, encased in a steel-blue suit to emphasize her position, the desk between them like a barricade.

With Childers standing beside her, his police uniform a shade lighter than Dani's suit. And a uniformed constable or sergeant behind him, arms folded, posture tense if not uncomfortable, the gun on his hip very visible.

"Dorian," Dani said. It was definitely the Terminator voice. "Superintendent Childers would like a word with Jimmy. As his lawyers, I've requested that we be present. Can you postpone your appointments and bring him down to Ibisville Central? Now?"

Dorian's breath stuck. Police station. Childers. Now. God, what's happened, what can they want with Jimmy, has something else turned up about Ben Morar, about Baringal?

Or is it the model? Has the whole scam blown up?

"Dorian?"

Dorian jerked wits and muscles together and managed not to croak, though lunch seemed to be coming back up her neck.

"I'm sorry. Yes. I can get Jimmy. I'll call him . . ."

"Ms. Wild, I'd prefer that you just pick him up." Childers sounded as bleakly official as Dani. He made a half gesture behind him. "Sergeant Pattel will escort you. Bring you through the station and so on."

Escort me. Dorian felt her knees melt. Not just get me through the red tape. Escort me home. So I can't call Jimmy and warn him, I can't coach him on the way. Whatever this is, they don't want him to know beforehand. To be warned. To get a chance, they must think, at escape.

The sergeant was moving. He'll walk me right back to my office. She shot a frantic look at Dani and Dani's steel-cold stare answered, Don't argue. It could do more harm than good.

Or did it mean, Dorian wondered, ice filling her stomach, There's nothing you can do?

"The *polis?* The station? Now?"

He dropped his voice on the last word with a reflex glance behind. Laura, Dorian thought, looking up at him through the unit door, trying to make her eyes convey warning and support and panic all at once. She's probably asleep.

Jimmy's eyes swung back to her. Slid past to Pattel. His whole body seemed to compact. He glanced briefly down his jeans and wear-creased T-shirt and said it with a lack of expression louder than a shout. "Will I come like this?"

We couldn't even write a note for Laura, Dorian fumed. Damn the stupid subordinate, does he think if I got in I'd have climbed over the balcony or something? And for what? What in God's name, her scrabbling brain demanded yet again, can they be up to, with precautions like this?

Pattel directed her into the police car park. Directed them both, with the perceptible absoluteness of an armed escort, to stay in the car till he was out himself. Aimed them at the back entrance of Ibisville Central, through the metal scanner and bag X-ray, into a maze of officially bleak, once-sterile and now-overused corridors. Gray paint, cream paint, cryptic door signs and name tags slid past Dorian in a blur. All her consciousness was concentrated on Jimmy, moving so quietly, far too quietly, at her side.

Thank God, she had time to think once, that he doesn't still have the gun.

They turned a corner. Childers and Dani were waiting at the first doorway beyond.

Interview room, Dorian guessed. Second floor, so no window exit, if there was a window to try. Plastic table, plastic chairs. Video camera high in one corner, the telltale mirror flash of a one-way surveillance panel along the opposite wall. The institution cream paint was grubby and the atmosphere was thicker than the dirt. Tension, stress, menace. Certainly, fear.

Dani sat one side of the table, and beckoned Jimmy before the police could intervene. As he sat, Dorian pulled another chair beside him. At least, with us so close, he knows he's got help, her brain said foolishly.

Childers did not demur. He came round the table and sat down himself. Pattel stood, unobtrusively obtrusive, in front of the door.

"Mr. Keenighan." Childers' voice was as noncommittal as his slight-but-evident frown. Not a hanging face, Dorian assessed, but certainly, more than the usual police mask. More like a deep, almost nervy wariness.

"Mr. Keenighan, about this passport of yours."

Dorian's hands were on the table. She clenched her mind to keep them loose and drove her feet against the floor instead. Not Baringal. Not Ben Morar. Worse. Infinitely worse. And we haven't had time to brief him, time to think of anything, now we can't act at all.

Jimmy lifted his chin. He looked Childers in the face and answered as evenly. "Aye?"

"If you have an Irish or British passport, it's not on record." Childers let the sentence end drop, neutrally. It was still less accusation than wariness.

Jimmy waited. Childers waited. Dorian tried not to clamp teeth in her lip. Oh, damn and blast the pair of them, will they stall until my nerves break down?

Childers chose to end the deadlock. He said, "What *is* your nationality?"

Jimmy swallowed, almost invisibly. Dorian knew why it was sticking in his throat.

"I'm fro' County Tyrone."

"That's in the north? Northern Ireland?"

This time it was a nod. Childers said, "Your passport's British, then."

Jimmy produced another nod.

Childers studied him. Dorian thought inevitably, sickeningly, of that moment in the hospital ward when he had come so close to this same topic, and chosen to turn away.

Childers said, "Are you actually James Michael Keenighan?"

Dorian felt Jimmy jerk as if lightning had caught him in the spine. The knowledge flew at her like another lightning blast. *P-A*. They know what they've lost. And whether or not they suspect the truth, they're getting their revenge for it. *They've* told the cops.

Her eyes went sideways. Jimmy sat rigid, very upright. But she caught the glare in his eyes, and was cravenly glad not to be in Childers' place.

Jimmy opened his lips. He said, as if the word were molten. "Aye."

In a moment, Childers said, "You don't ask why I want to know?"

Jimmy said nothing at all.

Childers eyed him. Jimmy had looked down. He sat perfectly still, and Dorian thought suddenly, This is neither innocence nor guilt, it's experience. The real stone wall. The silence all beset prisoners learn.

That must be plain to Childers too.

But I can't say, Talk. I can't say anything. There's no place yet for a lawyer to intervene.

Childers said, "You have a British passport, in that name?"

Slowly, lashes lifting by fractions, Jimmy looked at him. Then he drew up both hands and set them on the table, palm down, the long fingers spread, curved if not loose.

A signal, Dorian thought as her mouth dried. I will not attack you. I am unarmed.

"I *had* a passport." He spoke very quietly now. " 'Twas in my name. My own name. But ye can ask what ye please—sirr. I canna—I *canna* tell you how I came by it."

Oh, heavens. Dorian tried not to gulp. What sort of a gamble is this?

Childers was watching him now like the proverbial hawk. Their eyes locked. Jimmy's profile said with quiet but stone-set obduracy, That's all you'll get from me.

Dorian dug toes into her shoes as the ramifications sank in. God, let this work. Let Childers take it as some government security and assume Jimmy really can't say where he got it, even if he isn't the IRA grass, let Childers take that look at face value and trust him, Dani, us, far enough to let it go.

Childers was still staring. Now it had become an open frown. Then he said, "*Are* you IRA?"

Jimmy gasped. Then he came out of the chair with a sound half snarl and half scream and flung himself forward over his hands on the tabletop.

"*No!*"

The chair went on its back. Childers was on his own feet. Pattel sprang forward and checked with fist clamped on his gun.

"I was *never* one o' them murderin' sods! Aye, I lost m' head wi' that bla'guard in the stockpile, an' did stupid things wi' the other one, an' mebbe m' hands were never lily-clean, but I never shot a man i' the back—or blew someone up or—no!" He strained over the table, breathing hard, blazing in Childers' face. "*Never!* D'ye hear?"

Childers said, "I hear." He made a hand signal. Pattel drew slowly back, though he left his fingers on his gun.

"Right," Childers said. He looked round and gestured again. Sit down.

Jimmy gave him one last glare under his brows, and righted his chair.

Childers stayed on his feet. In a moment he said, "Not lily-clean?"

Jimmy growled in his throat at the tabletop.

"Irish," Childers said. He sounded almost dispassionate. "Used to rough stuff. Fast on your feet . . . or he'd have nailed you, at that mine." A tiny pause. The next words came like a slingshot. "Done that sort of thing before?"

Dani moved and went still. Head lowered, Jimmy twisted a hand on the tabletop.

"Aye," he muttered at last. "A time or two. No' like that." It came with the slightest shiver. "I was just a gossoon. A brush wi' the troops, aye? A wee bit stone throwin'. Callin' names."

Dorian could see Childers fitting it together. Northern Ireland, the Troubles, adolescents, the wild kids, troublemakers, teasing troops—*streetboy,* she heard Brodie say. And they *were* British troops. She tried to keep the hysterical bubble of laughter buried. Just in the wrong century . . .

Childers' shoulders had relaxed. He pulled his own chair round and sat.

"Look, son," he said. "If you're not IRA, and you are James Michael Keenighan, just tell me. Did you have this passport at all?"

Dorian felt her heart stop. He's swallowed it. He'll accept Jimmy's not IRA, he'll take the rest as Jimmy set it up. It's just the passport. Oh, Jimmy. Can you concoct another tale like that?

Jimmy was very near wriggling as he sat. He sank his head lower and did twist his fingers, the picture of a minor lawbreaker, constrained by equal parts sheepishness and guilt.

"I do have—I *did* have it, sirr. Only . . ."

"Only?" Childers said after a moment.

" 'Twas in m' pocket." Jimmy muttered it into the tabletop. "I went fossickin' down a hole. An' old diggin', wi' water. A creek, aye? An' it fell out."

He plaited his fingers tighter and finished almost under his breath. "No' six months ago. Up in the Peninsula."

Childers sat back. For an instant his face telegraphed understanding, exasperation, involuntary mirth.

"Then why didn't you say so?"

"Ahh." Jimmy let out his breath. "I didna . . . I wasna . . ." The slight wriggle, the duck of the head spoke volumes. A proverbial shady character, already known to the police, who will take any evasion to avoid more visibility. "I was goin' to tell them . . . at the Consulate."

Not quite explosively, Childers breathed out himself.

"Okay," he said. "Whatever's going on with—whoever passed that information"—his eye flicked to Dani and said, not at all romantically, I know *you're* involved—"I don't want to know. You've done nothing illegal on *my* pitch. Just get yourself a new passport, and you're clear with us."

Jimmy's head came up. He looked directly in Childers' face, and the stone wall had vanished. He said, still almost under his breath, "Thank'ee—sirr."

Childers heaved to his feet. Jimmy moved. Dorian struggled to follow, her knees, her every muscle dissolving with relief.

It's over. Jimmy's got himself clear. With some inspired lying by omission, and some judo use of Childers' own assumptions,

and the more than truth of that cry about the IRA. The cops
won't touch him now. P-A did their worst, and failed.

CHAPTER 12

They left through the station foyer, Jimmy walking between Dani and Dorian like a VIP in his wedge of satellites. Except Dorian's hand was locked firmly in his arm, and she could feel the damp of his skin, the tiny tremor of muscles letting go in the wake of supreme effort. Extreme fear.

And brilliant ad-libbing, she thought. To get ambushed like that, and turn it around with bare implication and inspired guesswork, and walk out free. She tightened her fingers in a surge of possessive affection, and murmured, "You should have been a barrister."

He made a low sound in his throat. Amusement, understanding, weariness. They reached the steps. Dorian looked out in the open street and thought, Home free. At last.

Then the triumph segued into rage.

He shouldn't have had to do that at all. P-A had their damn model. They gave assurances. They *promised* the immunities! Then they threw Jimmy to the cops. Not to fix anything, they never even contacted us first. From sheer—bloody—vindictiveness.

She glanced across at Dani, and in the shade of the ancient tamarind tree outside the station Dani's own eyes had a glint like whetted steel.

As they turned for the car park she said, "As soon as we get back, I'll call Reinschildt's secretary. Tell him that since they broke their undertaking, that cancels ours. Now we'll go to the media."

Jimmy let out a yelp. Dorian gulped. Then the first impulse to compose a war dance faltered. "Um," she hazarded. "We weren't exactly honest with *them?*"

"They got their model. That was the bargain." Dani's voice was still precise and cool, but her glance seared. "And if we let this pass, they'll know we fooled them. What do you suppose Reinschildt will do then?"

He'll be sure we've still got the real model. He'll try to get it back. More violence and mayhem, more spying and attacks and break-ins and . . . more people hurt, killed. Dorian's spine shrank. Please, God, no more. I can't take any more.

She gulped, thinking, Dani'll despise me for a wimp. She looked up. And Dani, cold amid that blaze of anger, said evenly, "I'm your lawyer, Dorian. I'll take care of it."

"Honesty, hell!" Laura was as angry as Dani and far noisier. "If P-A'd been honest they'd *have* their mine! And they'd've offed Chris and got away with that as well! But they were just too greedy. So now they've had their way, and if they try to kick about it, they deserve whatever they get!"

She flopped back on the couch and Jimmy roused at her grunt. "Whisht then, ye pepper pot." He swooped for a cushion. "If ye stir that shoulder, ye'll be getting' y'r own desserts."

"Can't be worse than that bloody physio." But though Laura let him ease the cushion behind her, Dorian could feel the direction of that frown.

"Dor—Dani's right."

"I know that." She tried to suppress the sigh. "I just—hoped it was over. That they'd sign off and go away and—"

And we could go back to normal. Laura could get better, and Anne might come back to us, and I could just be a lawyer.

And Jimmy . . .

Her mind shied from the last, far-too-sensitive corollary. She put down the champagne that Laura had insisted was the only fit celebration. "I'm going to start dinner. Whatever they do about Dani's ploy, we'll find out soon enough."

"Reinschildt's secretary took the message. He's out of Port Moresby. Up-country at some mine." Dani paused like a couture-dressed avenging angel in Dorian's office door. "I expect him to contact me today." The black waisted jacket with its thread-fine pinstripe made her eyes paler than ice. "I'll let you know."

I don't want to know. Dorian managed a nod without shutting her eyes, and Dani was gone.

But a bare three hours later her voice came coolly over the office line. "Reinschildt called in person. He's spitting chips." The little pause said, A good number of them on me. "It boils down to, Hold that media release, we can talk, give me twenty-four hours. I have to consult."

"Consult!" Something like irritation stabbed through Dorian's miasma of reluctance, of painful anticipation, of incipient fear. "Who does *Reinschildt* have to consult?"

"His CEO, I presume."

A byte of memory snapped into Dorian's mind. Jess in the Paragon bar, talking about Pan-Auric. Trouble with a Panamanian gold lease. The CEO's reputation. *Aaron Thorpe can play very rough.*

God, she thought. That's all we need. Not just Reinschildt, a bigger shark on our tails.

"Okay." She worked for quiet, for coolness. "Twenty-four hours."

"I can so use a laptop," Laura was protesting from her usual couch corner. "Left-handed, with the mouse on the couch arm.

Think I'm a complete lump? I need some recreation, Dor. Rest, eat, physio. When I get out my shoulder'll be useless, yeah, cos I'll be as big as a house!"

"Okay, okay." Dorian retreated on the kitchen. "Play Spider-man or Solitaire or whatever. And if you drop the mouse I won't pick it up!"

Jimmy glanced up from a half-peeled potato and her momentary irritation, the endlessly hovering storm cloud, lightened yet again. Her arm went automatically round his waist. She leaned into his chest, and he made a little welcoming noise, shifting to support her better. I remember you peeling spuds in your own kitchen, she thought. I didn't know, then, how you'd addict me to that look, that slow, sun-on-peat-water smile.

They were in amiable dispute over potatoes duchesse—"why Frenchify good taties wi' all that glop? Isna a dab o' butter on the jacket good enough?"—when Laura called out.

"Dor?"

The tone shot Dorian round the counter with Jimmy at her heels. As she flew for the couch he leapt to the unit door, kitchen knife still in his hand.

"I Googled Pan-Auric." Laura still sounded half breathless. "Look what I got."

Dorian took her eyes from the face that matched that voice, and looked at the screen.

News article. The usual blurry picture, tropical vegetation, a presumably battered vehicle, another traffic accident, is this important? "Laura, what—"

"Road Violence," the headline proclaimed, "in Papua New Guinea."

Road violence, PNG? Pan-Auric? "What do we have to do with—" She stopped on a gasp.

Reinschildt's in PNG.

Dorian threw herself on the couch and almost snatched the

laptop from Laura. "Let me see."

She felt Jimmy lean over the couch back. She hardly noticed. The small print seemed to spring out in her face.

Papua New Guinean activists are presumed responsible for an ambush this morning on the Lae to Highlands road. A four-wheel drive carrying personnel from US company Pan-Auric's Denga gold mine was halted by a roadblock, then attacked by men with stones and clubs. Two Australian employees sustained head wounds and a broken arm. The third man, an American, fired a revolver, and wounded at least one person. The attackers dispersed, but the fourth passenger, another American, had already been pulled from the vehicle and sustained a blow to the head.

Mine employees answered the men's radio SOS, and the wounded were ferried out by helicopter. The American victim is now in Port Moresby hospital. A spokesman said his condition could be described as coma, but would not offer a prognosis. The victim is believed to be Harvey Reinschildt, Pan-Auric's Pacific Sector Vice President.

The Port Moresby police chief said incidents between locals and mine personnel have escalated in the last twelve months. "We will be on patrol," he said.

Pan-Auric has declined to comment on the incident.

The silence spread and deepened till the unit seemed to resonate with it, as if a stone had fallen in a well. Or a mine shaft, Dorian thought. Images skittered madly over her mind, dripping tropical greenery, that vehicle tilted in the ditch, a surge of figures, flailing arms. Clubs. Clubs and stones. Stone Age, tribal warfare. Did a stone get Reinschildt? Gold country. Another piece of quartz?

The laughter rose so sharply she knew it was hysteria. She drove her hand into the cushion and jerked round on the couch.

Just as Laura said sharply, "Jimmy, what's wrong?"

He was still leaning to see over their heads. But the pose had frozen, and his face was the color of porridge, with a sudden tremor in the mouth. As she scrambled up he straightened. And then he crossed himself.

"Dhia." It was smothered in his throat. "I did pray—I canna say I didna. To be rid o' him, aye, but . . . sent away or somethin', no' . . . no' . . . oh, Dhi-a."

Schooling and superstition together froze Dorian's blood. If he did pray . . . if we're really in the hands of Providence?

"Jimmy, cut it out!" Laura snapped.

As they both jerked round she gave them her best courtroom glare. "I don't care what you think about Providence or coincidence or karma if it comes to that. It'd take more than you to set this up. You saw the report. They have trouble like this all the time. And if Reinschildt did"—she caught up the falter—"if he does die, maybe Providence had enough of *him!*"

She glowered. Jimmy stared. Then, slowly, his shoulders relaxed.

"Aye," he murmured. "I'm bein' presumptuous. 'Twas just"—he glanced back at the laptop—" 'tis come so awful pat."

And it's such a thunderbolt, it's hard not to think about the hand of God. And be appalled, revulsed, at what God, it seems, might do for us.

Dorian felt her own neck creep. But Laura snorted and pushed the laptop with her good hand. "Come and get this off me. As a nurse, you'd make a great reporter. Thickheaded, superstitious Mick . . ."

Dorian nearly gasped. But to her amazement, Jimmy snorted back and came round the couch. "An' ye'd be the perfect patient, ye daft carrot-topped Presbyter." He scooped up the laptop. "An' ye kickin' the bee-skep to start." He glanced at Dorian, with a half smile as forced, she realized, as Laura's cheerful brutality. "Mebbe, now, we can start dinner again?"

" *'Twas* so pat, though." She knew Jimmy had not recovered, even before they went to bed. "We're needin' a way to stop them, an' now this."

"Coincidence needn't mean, um, purpose." Dorian could not come closer to saying, Providence. She rolled to get her head on his chest. "Not that sort of purpose, anyhow."

She worked her hand into his armpit. He sighed, and then murmured heavily, "Aye."

Resignation, if not acceptance. Dorian moved a little closer. He eased his fingers into her hair. Then he said, too casually, "What d'ye reckon happens now?"

Dorian moved her own mental horizon from the past. "I guess—it depends how independent Pan-Auric's sectors are. If the Pacific's a self-contained unit, it—Blackston—that whole thing will probably stop dead. Until, either Reinschildt gets back, or—"

Or he dies, and someone else takes his place. And the whole circus has to start again.

She groaned inwardly. Let it just be over. I don't care about the damn mine any longer, I just want us *out.* Laura better, Anne back, Lewis and Cotton normal, Jimmy . . .

She pushed her face hard into his neck. "Sufficient unto the day." She dredged up the Biblical quotation, knowing he would catch the sense. Time for P-A's evil when it comes. And the other evil, as well. She kissed him over the pulse point and felt it quicken. Then his hand slid down her back and he said into her hair, almost fiercely, "Aye."

They slept in Saturday morning. To hell with the caseload, Dorian thought, turning over somewhere around six o'clock. Just this once, I'm going to sleep as long as I like. So it was nearly ten before she meandered out, to find Laura on the couch, glumly doing physiotherapy exercises, while Jimmy dismembered the weekend paper on the countertop.

She mumbled. Laura mumbled. Jimmy gave her a little smile and a raised eyebrow that said, Slugabed? She groaned and nodded and he slid over the coffee pot. Dorian took a long swig and settled on the stool next to him. As she reached for a section of paper, the phone rang.

"Oh, damn!" She lurched up again. Flicked *Screen* from what was now instinct, and Dani's private office number came up.

Her heart bumped. She pressed *Answer,* and Dani looked out of the holoscreen.

"Dorian." That precise voice held a thread of emotion. Surprise? Excitement? "Look at this."

She held it up for the scan. Fax, Dorian decided, pushing the screen to maximum magnification, making out the series of figures along the foot. Handwritten, but with a logo at the top.

Her heart stopped. The logo was dark-blue and gold, a square capital P superimposed on a golden A over an image of the globe. Underneath, smaller capitals said, International Mines.

"Can you read it?" Dani asked.

"Wait . . ." The handwriting was black and tall, sweeping tails and tops, close but not cramped. Intelligible, as those who pass orders learn to be, but unmistakably individual.

Ms. Dani Lewis, Lewis and Cotton, Ibisville.

Pan-Auric Mining will in future maintain all immunities contracted for persons involved in the incidents at Ben Morar mine and Baringal beach.

Pan-Auric will not respond to any media releases Lewis and Cotton or their clients may issue on these incidents.

The company is closing down Ben Morar mine and will void the Blackston lease.

It was signed. A big signature, slashed but not sprawling, expanded, Dorian thought, to dominate rather than fit a contract's signature space.

"Aaron J. Thorpe."

The holoscreen trembled faintly, so the words seemed to iridesce. Tiny rainbow edges. Like the colors, Dorian thought stupidly, around a piece of gold-bearing quartz.

Dimly, she heard Jimmy's grunt. Then Laura, clear and gleeful as a trumpet. "They're pulling out!"

She tried to answer. Only the words remained, staring through stupefaction's fog. Close down Ben Morar. Void the Blackston lease.

"Dor! Dor! Wake up! Wake up, will you? We've won! They're pulling out!"

Habit spurred Dorian's muscles: answer, move, else Laura'll get up or do something crazier. A voice mumbled, "Yes." Too big, she thought vaguely. Too much. Everything you ever wanted, all tipped in your hands at once.

Jimmy's hand closed on her shoulder and a hiccup of feeling went through her, vivid as a stab. She swiveled on the stool. He was almost smiling, but his eyes were anxious. Under his breath he said, "Mo cailín?"

"Yes." She could make her lips move, for him. Her mind moved too. It's over. It's all over. We've stopped the mine. Chris didn't die—we didn't wipe the model—for nothing.

Pan-Auric are pulling out.

"Dor, who's Aaron Thorpe?"

Her eyes focused. The fax had gone. Dani was staring out of the holoscreen, and it was Dani who replied.

"Pan-Auric's CEO."

"It came right from the top, then." Laura's voice flickered near to awe. "And handwritten as well. Jeez."

Handwritten. From the top. Jimmy asked me what they'd do now and I said, *Depends on the company structure. It might stop till there's a successor. Or till Reinschildt comes back.*

But it won't matter now if Reinschildt does come back. The CEO's overridden him. Thorpe's written the communiqué himself.

Thorpe. A megacorp CEO. With minions at his fingertips. Would he write in his own hand to one pipsqueak law firm about one mine in one sector of his juggernaut?

"Give me another look."

Laura stared. Jimmy's hand shut. Dorian hardly noticed, staring at the screen where the blue-and-gold logo stared back.

Reinschildt has to have said what he suspected. That we jiggered the model before he got it back. And probably he told— had to tell—Thorpe what he did about it. Dobbing in Jimmy to the cops.

And Thorpe's overridden that too.

Her brain seemed to cleave under a succession of lightning strikes. Thorpe didn't back Reinschildt over betraying Jimmy. He's said that. And he's taken the whole Blackston–Ben Morar thing under his own command.

They quarreled. It came with lodestone certainty, true as magnetic north. Thorpe stuck at something in Reinschildt's plans. Reinschildt wouldn't back down.

What happened then?

Her hand was over her mouth. The hair rose and hackled clear down her neck.

"What is it, mo cailín?"

Jimmy's hand rocked her slightly, anxiously, but she had no time to reply. She was staring down the lightning's illumination with blood congealing in her veins.

What happens then is that Reinschildt gets himself knocked

on the head and ends in a coma in hospital. And might never come out.

Aaron Thorpe plays very rough.

Her brain careered on like a toboggan out of control. You could arrange an ambush up there, easily. The locals are already up in arms. An unscrupulous company man would know how to contact them, to bribe, inflame. That sort of thing's happened for years in the US. With their union struggles, with their Mafia. Oh, God. Oh, God. Could Thorpe really play as rough as that?

To double-cross his own subordinate, cohort member, friend for all I know—to actually eliminate him?

And I worried he'd be after us.

He doesn't give a damn, her mind postscripted with icy clarity, about us. He won't accept the immunities for our sake. Or for honor or decency either. It's the company. Reinschildt had already cocked up, with Brodie, with Sorenson, and he was making matters worse. Maybe he was determined to have the model, or the mine, maybe he was obsessed with getting back at us, but it was all going to escalate. And P-A would carry the can.

What's a defunct mine, and a useless stats model, and a suspect new lease, and a vice president's life, against that?

You'll never know, she told herself. This fax is the clearest signal you'll ever get. Maybe he didn't "put Reinschildt away"— Jimmy's phrase came vividly back—but he's reversed Reinschildt's whole policy. Scuttled his project. Affirmed the agreement Reinschildt broke.

An executive decision. Clear the company of a minor slur. Then cut your losses—however high they come—and get out.

The others were all staring at her, Laura silenced, Dani's look eagle-sharp. Jimmy's eyes were far too dark. He knows, she thought. He remembers Brodie. And Sorenson. He's seen this lawlessness, this callousness, firsthand.

He'd believe it could turn on its own kind.

It's all supposition. You could still call it coincidence. A hysterical bubble of laughter burst in her throat. Not the hand of God, just the hand of Thorpe. But you'll never prove it, so why tell them? Leave it as luck, coincidence, our hotshot efforts, David's mighty sling stone. And Goliath just seizing a chance to commandeer control, rather than making it.

"Yeah," she said, and drew a deep breath, shaking her head a little. "Sorry. I just—can't quite believe it yet." She forced a smile for Laura. "But you're right. We've won."

Laura whooped. Briefly, astoundingly, Dani smiled. She said, "Yes." The cold pale stare added, There's more you're not telling me. But for now, I too will let it go.

Dorian nodded a little. Dani nodded back. "I'll see you Monday," she said, and the screen blanked out.

"Jimmy, get that orange juice," Laura was commanding. "And Dor, open that other champagne. Jeez, if it's only ten o'clock and I can't get out to a pub, we can still celebrate!"

"Yes," Dorian said, clambering off her stool. "Okay."

And there is cause, she thought, staring down into the orange juice's golden heart, feeling the champagne's supercharge burst in her blood. We did block the mine, we did save Blackston. We didn't betray Chris. We did stop P-A. An international megacorp. And we stopped it in its tracks.

No. Somberly, another part of her mind contradicted that. We didn't stop it. In New Guinea, in Panama, somewhere else, Thorpe's juggernaut'll keep right on going.

Mûmak. The word came back from *The Lord of the Rings* books. The enormous war elephant that ran amok in an ambush, plunged out of the fight, off the road, and away into mystery. We didn't "stop" P-A, any more than Tolkien's soldiers did. We just turned the mûmak aside.

But surely, for us, that's enough?

She lifted the champagne flute. Laura followed suit. Jimmy smiled at her and said, "I'll gi'e ye another toast. One the Keelies use in Glasgow." He tilted his head. "I say, 'Here's tae us.' An' ye say, 'Wha's like us?' " He paused. They chorused it obediently. "An' I say, 'Dam' few, an' they're a' deid.' "

He raised his glass. As the champagne bit into her own sinuses Dorian thought, Chris.

And not just Chris. Brodie. Sorenson.

Aaron Thorpe.

Paddy Wild.

Jimmy and me, if it comes to that.

She took another mouthful and felt the bubbles rise in her blood. Damn few like us, indeed. And a good thing most of them are dead.

Jimmy laughed and triumphed with Laura, but after that he grew gradually quiet. Pottering round the flat, coping with Laura's euphoria as well as her disabilities, Dorian tried not to notice. Determinedly, she limited her horizon to the past. We've won. Jimmy's safe. P-A's pulling out. That's enough.

By the time they went to bed he had grown outright abstracted and she was consciously determined not to ask. I know what it is. What it has to be. The same thing I'm thinking. It's over. P-A's going. If this is what he came for, it's finished.

So, is the fold going to work?

Will I wake in the morning and he just won't be there?

She turned over with a lunge and fastened an arm over him, and he caught his breath in a grunt. But then he turned and with equal fierceness locked his own arms round her.

He's still here. Dorian thought it the moment she woke. Still beside me, the familiar length and weight and warmth, the little snuffle as he breathes, the weight of his arm, lax in sleep, over my waist. I'm not thinking past that.

When they came back from Mass he hooked the fiddle case over his shoulder, and raised his brows to her. She said, "I think I'll stay in. You have fun," and he nodded, and did not try, this time, to persuade her to come.

It was late when he reappeared, a good while after two o'clock. As he came inside, Laura looked up. And then said quickly, "Where's the violin?"

There was a sudden, lapsing pause. Then he moved across and began to empty his pockets as usual on the dining table. "Ah," he said, carefully casual. "I gave it back."

Dorian stood halfway between lounge and counter and felt her lungs shut as if crushed.

He looked up at her. His eyes were dark, and somber, and unflinching. Almost, but not quite the stone-wall face. The words echoed between them: *take it for as long as ye're here.*

Dorian turned and went into her bedroom, and shut the door.

In a moment it reopened. Jimmy shut it quietly behind him, and came to her.

Dorian walked into his arms as she had so often and as they shut round her the ice broke on one paralyzing stab. How often have I asked myself, how long will I have this? How long will he be here?

And now I know.

She pressed her forehead into his shoulder. Wood smoke, sweat, Sunlight soap. He spoke softly, painfully, into her hair.

"I dinna *want* to go." His arms tightened convulsively. "Ye know that. But—I canna stay."

Not even for me. Not even for us. Not with your mother back there, and the girls, and Patsy, and everything else that encompasses. Not when your part here is over. And back there, left without a word, are other people. Dependents, responsibilities. A whole other world.

"I know, I made him—Chris—a promise. To see to ye. Always. The way he'd want." His voice was very quiet. "But . . ."

But I had other pledges. Prior pledges. Priorities.

She caught her breath down and strangled the incipient sob. I won't cry. It's hard enough already. For both of us. We always knew this might, this would have to happen. If it's come now, at the very least, I've had him for a while. I wouldn't be without that, whatever the cost.

Dorian lifted her head. Wiped the heel of a hand over her eyes, and said, finding she could refuse to let her voice wobble, "How do you want . . ."

His grip tightened, and released. He put his hands up, arms still round her, to clasp her shoulders, and she looked up into a small, definitely wobbly smile.

"Mo cailín," he said under his breath. Then he drew himself together and said, "I thought—we could mebbe go to Blackston."

To the *Miner.* To the likeliest way, the road we both went. Through the *Miner*'s door.

In a moment Dorian said, "Okay."

The horizon rose and fractured, the pink granite road pointed straight to the line of little hills. Beside her in the passenger seat Jimmy moved slightly, and let out a long silent sigh.

The fold hasn't worked already. I thought it might, Dorian thought. But thank heavens, that at least, if he has to go, it seems he can do it in his own time. His own way.

He was wearing the clothes he had come in, with his few belongings back in the pockets. His watch, his money, the battered miner's right. He wouldn't take anything else, if I could give it to him. It's probably right. What use would modern money be, or even something as simple as a Mag-Lev flashlight?

As for antibiotics and sneakers and shirts that don't have to be ironed . . .

She stopped herself. Don't think what might happen to him, in the normal passage of years. If he's going to die of pneumonia, or tetanus, or TB, or some other thing we could have helped. What he'll do, in those intervening years, how he'll explain this hiatus, what he'll find in the *Miner,* in his own house. How he'll cope with Paddy Wild. If he'll still be a Union man.

If he'll marry, one day.

She jerked her mind ferociously back to the road and started working out the quickest way to Landers Street.

They parked in another side street. On the brief walk to the corner the October sun battered them, ricocheting from buildings, burning through the spasmodic wreaths of dust. Even in this modern town, with such little wind, with these acres of bitumen, it's like a furnace, Dorian thought. What'll it be like where he's going, as hot as this or hotter, and no electricity, no iced water, no air-conditioning?

She jammed her mind down again. They came round into Landers Street. The *Miner*'s building was halfway down the block.

At eleven o'clock the street was virtually empty. They headed down the sidewalk. Dorian's sneakers were almost soundless. Jimmy's work boots crunched.

In the *Miner*'s entry he checked and turned to her. They stood looking into each other's face.

I can't say anything, Dorian realized. There's nothing to say, if I could get it out. This is destined, inevitable, it's morality as well as what's probably some kind of natural necessity. And if it isn't Providence, it's fate.

He moved his hands. She went to him and he clenched her to him so hard she lost her breath. She locked her own arms round his back, trying to memorize the shape and weight of him, those long spare muscles flexing under her hands. She turned her face up, and with all the moment's passion, all its desperation, they kissed.

Then he let her go. Said, almost inaudibly, "Mo cailín." He added something in Gaelic, that ended in "Dhia." Touched her cheek, and turned on his heel.

His boots crunched on the steps. The glass door swung open. And slid shut.

In time, Dorian found the sun beating on her neck. Sweat beaded her forearms, light bucketed up off the street. There was a char-grill under her hat.

And I've been standing here—five, ten minutes now?

It hardly needed confirmation. But something sent her forward, in her turn, to the steps.

With her hand on the door she checked. *It worked for him. What if it works for me as well?*

For a second she wavered. Then a surge of something she could not analyze, terror, hope, sheer recklessness, drove her hand. *Let it work, if it wants. If I do go after him, I won't care.*

The door swung back.

The *Miner's* front office was a long high-ceilinged room, chill with air-conditioning. An old-fashioned stair, wooden treads, banister and newel post, rose halfway along one wall. Some kind of papers filled shelves opposite and behind. Between stair and door was a counter manned by a yawning girl.

And no one else.

CODA

I swore I wouldn't do this, Dorian thought, as five little hills
rose over a ridge in the pink granite road. Never mind a bare six
months later. I swore I'd never come here again.

Like the road, the rigorous light and the long upland horizons
remained. But at the end of March, after a moderate Wet, the
air sparkled, the land was sheened like the fur of a healthy
animal, lemon-green acres thick with rich, seeding grass.
Everything's the same, she thought. And it's all different.

As it is with me. I have what I asked. Laura's okay, if her
right arm will always be a few degrees stiffer than the left. Anne
and Sam have sold the Baringal house. Anne's back at work.
We're nearly friends again. Dani and Moira have reverted to
senior partners. I'll never hear if Dani and Childers are still an
item, or how far it's gone. How far it went. I'm just a lawyer
again.

And the ache's still there. Closer than skin, a part of me.
Never admitted, never forgotten. What can words do for loss?

She slowed for the town outskirts and thought, without heat,
Dani didn't so much talk as engineer me into this. Coming into
the main office that day, with the girl behind her. A tall girl,
with tanned skin and blonde hair almost as unruly as Moira's,
and a truly casual choice of gunge-green blouse and polyester
skirt. The outdoors idea of big-meeting chic, Dorian remembered thinking wryly, as Dani said, "This is Dorian Wild, our

319

leading junior partner. Dorian, this is Evelyn Cox. She's a geologist."

As if time were going round again, through that three-years-past Christmas party. Dani saying, "This is Dorian Wild, one of our junior partners. Dorian, this is Chris Keogh. He's a geologist."

So she had been off balance even before the surname connected and the floor seemed to rock slightly under her feet.

"Ah—ah—where are you from?" she managed, and when the girl said, "Sydney, originally," she could not hold back the rest. "Oh, I thought—Cox is quite a famous name, up here, on the old goldfields—and you being a geologist—"

And the girl smiled happily, unbending, and answered, "Yeah, that was my great-great-uncle. Richard Cox. He found the big Blackston mine, the Solitaire." She looked for comprehension, and, reassured, grew more technical. "He invented what they called deep mining." A hint of shyness. "Kind of a role model, when I was a kid."

And Dani intervened smoothly, "It's about Blackston that Ms. Cox is here."

"I was working for this US company, Pan-Auric." Settled into the corner sofas, Evelyn relaxed enough to keep talking unhelped. "They were doodling round with a thing at Blackston. Takeover of a small local company." You know the story, her tone added, blithely unaware of how Dorian's head spun, how she was thinking, Dani, damn it, how could you do this to me?

"There was some talk about a really big field, but it never came off. I was up in the Gulf, but I went through Blackston just before they closed down, and they had a file with these results."

Dorian's lungs seemed to contract in her chest.

"Core-log data, you know?" Evidently their faces said, Yes, well enough. "And . . ."

She teased her lip. "And, well . . . there was something odd about them. But the local guy, and the bigwigs up the line, they'd all had a look and said, No go. And the office johnny was going to throw them out. So I picked them up."

Very slightly, her exposed ears had flushed. "Nobody wanted them, after all. I took them away and looked through them again, and I thought . . ."

You found Chris's results and you saw what he saw. And you ran some other tests and you thought . . . oh, God, oh, God. What did you think?

"I couldn't make them go anywhere." Evelyn relaxed again, half smiling across the table. "But it made me think about Blackston. It's kinda—romantic, you know, for me? The Solitaire and my great-great-uncle Dick. So I ferreted round a bit. Found a few other surveys. Some went really deep."

Dorian tried to make her face convey civil interest. Do you really turn blue, her wayward brain enquired, if you hold your breath?

"And I found the end of the old reef. The Solitaire. It's way the hell down, but"—she had sat up, and her voice quickened— "you don't have to go in from the top, in the town, like they did. There's an old mine across the railway, the Walsingham, a shaft they turned into a pit. I looked at the contours. You can go in by adit and tunnel, and the pit's already so deep the gradient's workable. Then it's only half a mile to the reef."

When neither spoke she wavered, then collected herself. "And the core-logs are really pretty good. I showed them to my senior at, um, this other place. He reckons it'd cover the cost of access, then pay out for maybe two years."

Not Chris's mine. Far too deep. Not that momentary El Dorado that we had and lost. She didn't have the model. Without that she hasn't—she couldn't—Dorian found room for a prayer of gratitude—have uncovered that.

"So I went out there and, um, looked around. Because—well, I'd just left this other company." For reasons, the tone hinted, not all to their credit. "And it seemed to me, if it was a new mine, and on the Solitaire, the locals should have a chance to, ah, invest."

Dani's face was inscrutable. Dorian tried not to catch at the side of the couch. Oh, God. God help us all. I know what she's going to say next.

"So I asked around, and there was this guy who used to run the old Pan-Auric mine. Out at a place called Ben Morar. P-A wound the company up when they left, and he was under some sort of a cloud for a while, but when I explained he caught on right away. He was really keen."

The voice faded into burble while Dorian tried not to shut her eyes. God, how could you let this happen? Not just let her find another Blackston mine, but send her straight to George?

Who'd jump on a new El Dorado with his teeth and all four feet. Who'd think this time, he really had found the answer to his prayers. Who'd probably get the locals to fund it and go in with him. About one of their own, people never really learn— they'll probably make him CEO!

And this bright, eager, young woman will get *her* fingers burned.

Do him justice, another voice said. At wind-up the dividends from Ben Morar must have been very low. If he kept out of court over that, then it's Thorpe's doing, not a miracle. But it has to be low tide with George now, and if that means low tide for the other investors, it means Beryl and Connie as well.

"So there'll be a meeting," Evelyn was saying, bright and upright on the couch. "To float the company, in Blackston, this coming week. We've sent out the notices and everything, George—Mr. Richards—has seen to that. There's been a lot of interest and people are saying they'll come. So I thought, if we're going to draw up company constitutions and stuff, and then get down to employees' contracts—I better think about a lawyer. My own lawyer," she amplified, looking from one to the other. "There's a guy in Blackston the company'll probably hire. But—well—"

Not so downy as she looks, Dorian thought. She's heard George's reputation, and the Marlboro charm hasn't bowled her over after all. She wants someone independent, outside Blackston's ambit, to protect her interests.

"And this mate of mine said Lewis and Cotton got her through a really nasty divorce."

This is credentials to deal with a mining company? Dorian stifled it, along with the almost hysterical laugh. We dealt with Ben Morar, didn't we? From the very start?

"So, Dorian, I suggested you'd be the best person, with firsthand experience of gold mines and of Blackston, to help Evelyn out."

Dani's just-too-even voice was adding: *Are you listening? Pay attention here.*

"Ah—yes. Ah . . ." Dorian groped madly for an out. "But with Mr. Richards . . . don't you think, um, Ms. Cotton?"

"No," Dani said, quite mildly. "I don't."

That steel-gray stare added everything else. Moira knows George, Moira is senior, yes. Moira's a rainmaker. You know the rest. For this job, the worst possible choice.

"I'm sure," Dani went on calmly, "you're the best person to deal with Mr. Richards. Especially with this."

Because you know him, Dorian filled in as she tried to smother a very inapposite laugh. You know each other as few people could, you having put a bullet through his leg. And he'll know what I know about his shenanigans, and what I can do with it.

You know how I feel about Blackston, she telegraphed back.

How could you do this to me?

"I have," Dani said, "every confidence in you."

She means it. She expects I can put personal—loss—aside. And use personal experience, to operate as a thoroughly professional lawyer. For this bright, determined, cautious but not disillusioned girl, to keep George from slipping one single scam under the net.

Because that's what it means, to be a lawyer.

Dani said, "Evelyn is hoping that our representative will attend this inauguration meeting. With her client."

No, Dorian thought, panicked, I can't go back. Not Blackston as well as George again, not see those buildings, walk down those streets. Not remember, what I've been trying so hard to forget.

But Dani's look expected assent. Refused to admit anything but assent. Dorian tried to sit up straight and produce a firm if wordless nod.

It was almost worth it, she thought, stowing her briefcase in the car, trying not to burp up the beer a grateful Evelyn had urged on her in the pub. Just to see George's face.

Before we did that very formal reintroduction, all "Mr. Richards" and "Ms. Wild." And I sat down with Evelyn on the dais of the Saint Columba Community Hall, while he rose to address what will be the Walsingham Consolidated mining company's shareholders.

Because she carried it, that bright, enthusiastic, knowledgeable girl. It hardly needed George to puff her off as Dick Cox's descendant—"Dickie Cox," corrected an irreverent Tyrone accent in her head. Her presentation, and her patent expertise, and the way she talked about the new mine, eager but not foolish, carried it all.

So now they have a company. With the constitution set up,

under two lawyers' supposedly eagle eyes. The local guy was quite happy about that. He knows George's reputation, I think. But like the rest of them, he wants to see the town prosper. And he wants locals to do the job.

This time, George won't get a chance to invite in the megacorps. When the mine folds, it'll fold honestly, and nobody will get their fingers burnt.

She slid into her driving seat. She had parked along Church Street, in a business lot that must once have held another big old house. Shutting the door she looked right automatically and her eyes met the green of Lister Park.

No. I didn't go near the Park Street Motel. I didn't go any further than this down Landers Street. I declined drinks with shareholders up at the Stock Exchange, and I steered Evelyn away from the White Horse. It's all over. The fold opened, and the fold closed, whatever its reason, and it's all done. I could walk down there, and be safe.

From a cross of the timelines, maybe, as Dani called it. But not from myself.

She switched on the ignition. With both hands on the steering wheel she recalled Laura's words, down the Sand Bar the previous week.

"Sure, he's gone." She had spoken very quietly, for Laura, staring out to sea. "But you won't let him go, Dor, until you go back. See it all again. And really—really know it's true."

"I don't have to see it to know it's true," Dorian had retorted stiffly, and Laura had looked at her with something like pity and answered, "Yes, you do, Dor. Because till you do that—you're never going to move on. You'll be stuck . . ." She had blinked quickly and looked away. "So for Chrissake, go up with this wunderkind geologist and put the whole of—of the other thing behind you. So I can say I've got a mate again. Not a flipping ghost."

Dorian edged the car out to the gutter. Then she looked left.

The miniature poppet-head of Saint Columba's bell tower looked back at her across Landers Street intersection, bright in the sun. We went down there. The first day I took him to church.

The tower shone palely, wood never darkened by smoke. Behind it the sky was pure as only a defunct industrial town can leave it, snowy late-March clouds afloat in pellucid blue.

Not the Blackston he remembered. None of that's here now. What is it you fear?

Abruptly Dorian put the car in gear, turned left, and drove up the street.

I'll show you, she inveighed silently, to Dani, to Laura, to a host of unspecified listeners. You want me to do the purge thing, do you? The trip down Memory Lane, the great New Age meet-your-fear-and-conquer-it? Okay. I'll park the damn car halfway up Landers Street and I'll walk right into the *NQ Miner*. I'll do the whole thing, and you just see how much use it'll be!

She found a park hardly a block away, outside an ornate front that had once been a jeweler's shop. She slammed the door with decision, put on her hat as if she were Napoleon, and stalked back up the street.

Two-thirty in the afternoon, the meeting over, it was almost empty, sun-heated, somnolent. But within twenty paces the heart was bumping uncomfortably in her chest.

What if it *isn't* over? What if the fold—what if the fold's still working, and—this time, when I walk in the *Miner*'s door—

Don't be a fool, she berated herself. Nothing will happen. Nothing can happen. He—Jimmy—went away, and the fold shut. The celestial as well as the earthly books are closed. Just do this and tell Dani and Laura you did it. Then they'll shut up.

And one day, you actually might forget.

Into the entry. A modern concrete gate jamb. The glass-fronted door, with the ornate nineteenth-century script, at the head of the four stone steps.

She put her foot on the first, and the door above her darkened. Someone was coming out.

The door swung back. He filled the opening, a tall man in a dark, old-fashioned three-piece suit, half his face masked under an old-style felt hat. A beard obscured the rest. In his left hand he gripped a positively antique traveling bag.

The other hand held a violin case.

He looked down, she looked up. She had time to see the eyes, dark as peat water above the cedar-red of sunlit beard. Time to feel her heart jerk, the tongue stick in her mouth. Then he gave a half yell, half gasp that became a strangled "Mo cailín . . . !" and cases went flying as he took the steps in a lunge and she was in his arms.

She let go at last. He still had her by both shoulders, as if she might vanish between his hands. Her own fingers were locked in the lapels of his coat. He looked down at her half laughing, almost incoherent, the face of a man dazzled beyond wildest hope. There were tears, clear in the sharp sunlight, on his cheeks.

"Mo cailín," he said, shakily. And then, "Oh, a cailín mo chroí." The laugh was half a sob. "That means, m' darlin' girl . . ."

"Oh, Jimmy." Her own tears threatened to escape. I don't think I've said more than Oh, Jimmy for the last five minutes. Unless it was some other inanity like, You came back.

"You came back." She said it again, less fact than incantation. "You came back."

"Aye." His ribs spread against her fingers with the depth of the sigh and then his arms clamped round her again. "Ah, Dhia, I could only hope . . . I prayed. But I never thought—if I got here, I never dreamt—"

That you'd be here, as I walked out the *Miner's* door. That we'd encounter, in that very first moment, face to face.

It's the fold that did it. What else, she asked herself, joy breaking now into laughter, could it be?

She shut her own arms again and pressed herself into him, catching the familiar throat-stopping smell through the heated wool of his coat. Sweat, wood smoke, Sunlight soap. The tears welled up, overflowing like the mirth. He's back. He's back now, and I'm never going to let him go.

From the street came an apologetic cough. A voice hazarded, "Excuse me?"

"Oh, lord." A local woman, by her dress, half embarrassed, half amused, hesitating at the gate. "Sorry, sorry," Dorian babbled. She took another handful of lapel and pulled Jimmy forward, into the street. Into my world, right into my world, and this time, if the fold opens, it'll have to take us both.

He moved to follow, then checked. As he turned, stooping, she remembered his impedimenta, and exclaimed with new delight, "You brought your violin!

"Your own violin, oh sorry, fiddle, I mean." She could feel herself babbling again as he straightened up. If he brought that it wasn't chance this time. He meant to come, and he meant— means—to stay. She grabbed the traveling bag and staggered at its weight, and the other question was out before she thought. "But what are you *doing* here?"

He looked at her, just a fraction uncertainly. Then, at whatever her face said, he smiled.

She blinked, dazzled by the joy. The open tenderness.

"I was comin' back," he said. "Aye."

"But. But—" Then at last she recovered the mundanities. "We can't stand here, someone else will run into us, come on"— this too was a silly delight—"my car's just up the street!"

"Last time 'twas a hotel. Now 'tis that car again. Ye're ever draggin' me off . . ." He's not thinking what he's saying either.

The sense is in the tone. Every word a caress. He hefted the violin case. "An' a good thing, too, I'm fair perishin' in this coat."

"Take it off." She flopped the bag down, ready to pull it off herself. And the rest too, if I don't control myself.

He shucked out of the coat. Automatically shot the cuffs of yet another white shirt. She led off and checked. "No, wait, there's a café in here."

A rare old-style Blackston café, no tourist re-creations, cheap plastic-topped tables and metal chairs, strictly functional. Not even table service. She ordered tea at the counter, and as she set the cups down had to pause a moment to let her eyes linger on him, deliriously, lovingly. He's here. He's actually here.

"An' ye mean to take bite an' sup wi' me as well?" He was still grinning too, as if he could not stop. Do you think, that look teased, you need to enchant me over again?

"Oh, indeed I do." She sat down and his hand reached involuntarily to hers. Their fingers locked. Let it happen again, she thought, the way it did before but not quite the same, as it has with the mine and Evelyn Cox. Let's drink tea as a stopgap, like we did in the motel room, and I don't care if we look silly as a pair of newlyweds. This time, the rest will be different.

She took a gulp and set the cup down, drawing a long, releasing breath. "Now," she said, "what were you *doing* back there?"

What had you planned, walking through that door, dressed to kill, with your violin in one hand and what feels like your life savings in the other? What did you intend?

He too drank without letting go of her hand. Then he said, "I was leavin' Blackston, aye."

"Leaving? But . . ." She stopped.

"So I put on m' fine clothes, an' took the fiddle an' m' gear." Faintly, he smiled. "An' m' miner's right, an' "—a meaningful look—"m' birth certificate. An' I said, I'll bid 'em fare thee well at the *Miner.* An' walk out that door. An' if I dinna go—where I will to go—I'll walk down the station, an' I'll take the train."

"But, but to where?"

He lifted a shoulder. "To Ibisville. South. If 'twas the train— 'twouldna have mattered where."

But it didn't have to matter. The fold worked.

Their eyes met and held as they had so often. Now neither of them had to smile. Smiles, laughter, were the first moments' overflow. This, said his grave but not somber look, this is contentment. Consummation. Joy's truth confirmed.

"But," she said after a moment, not sure how to broach it, "but—why?"

You went back to Blackston, by intent. To Patsy. To the *Miner,* and your job, because otherwise you couldn't have helped your mother and the girls. That was the world I took you from. Why, having got it back, at such sacrifice, would you want to leave?

He looked down at their hands, and the lingering light in his face darkened to something like his old somberness. Then he said, "D'ye know the tale about Oisin's return?"

"Oisin? He was Sidhe, wasn't he? A great warrior or something?" She groped after scraps of child-sized Irish myth.

"One o' the noblest, aye. An' he went away, some say when Saint Patrick came. Left Erin. Went to Tir-nan-Og."

The Land of the Young, the pagan Celtic heaven. She made an assenting noise.

"An' after what seemed a day an' a day, he'd a notion to go back. So he rode his fine Sidhe horse into Erin . . ." His voice checked and broke oddly. "An' 'twas all changed."

She looked sharply up into his face.

"The old Sidhe duns, the great holds, were gone. All the land was different. But he saw some weaklin' folk tryin' to work a boulder out of a road. So he rode up an' leant down to help, an' they mazed at the shinin' o' him, the gold-clad warrior, like an angel on his silver horse. But when he heaved up the boulder wi' his hand, the saddle girths broke."

Dorian took a sip of breath and stopped.

"An' the horse an' the gear vanished. An' there in the road was a wee wizened old man."

He bent his head a little, drawing in his own breath.

"They took him up, an' he told them his name. An' they were mazed in earnest, for, said they, 'Ye call y'rself Oisin, an' him one o' the Fair Folk. An' the Fair Folk've no' ridden Erin this last thousand years.' "

Dorian's throat shut. She could not speak. He was silent too. But then he looked up and held her eyes.

"Oh, God." She caught his hand in both of hers. It wasn't Tir-nan-Og, but I did take you out of time, didn't I? I took you away and when you came back the clock had jumped and everything—everything—had changed.

"Oh, Jimmy!"

Did I cost you your job, your friends, the rest of your family? Your place in life, in the web of history? Did I send you back, like Oisin, to a world that never knew you at all?

"Mo cailín, mo cailín . . . shhh." His hands cradled hers. " 'Twas no' like Oisin. For the one thing"—his lips curved, though his expression held more than amusement—"he lost Tir-nan-Og an' Erin both. Me—I've come back."

"But—!"

"Aye." His shoulders set a little. "It wasna a thousand years, then. But it was—five."

"*Five . . . !*"

"Whisht, girl, whisht." One hand slid up to cup her cheek. Don't blame yourself, said that gentleness.

"Oh, Jimmy." She could feel her own voice break. "Oh, God— just tell me, what . . ."

"I was lucky—some." The voice was carefully meditative.

"Danny Sheehan, that was senior compositor, he remembered me. I couldna tell him what—I did—but he vouched for me—to the new man."

So you still had your job. But . . .

In a moment Dorian dared, "New?"

He looked in her eyes and gave a tiny nod. "Dinny was gone. Retired, the year before. By then . . . dead."

People came to settle at another table, the reverberating clang and rattle of metal chairs, crockery on a clothless tabletop. Gone, she thought. Dinny. Your boss, mentor, sparring partner. The heart and soul of the *Miner,* however often you quarreled. Gone.

"Patsy . . ." He read her look and nodded hastily. "Danny gave me the address. Patsy'd boxed up m' stuff. I knew, he said, where you was gone. Away wi' the fairies, sure, to that bhan sidhe o' yours. She'd put a glamour on ye. But I knew, one day, ye'd come back."

Dorian's hands relaxed. Who cares what Patsy thought of me, he was still there. Safe. Then the words made sense.

"Address? He wasn't—at your house? No. No, of course, without you—" And without Bridgie, he couldn't afford the rent. I cost Jimmy his house as well.

"But he was okay? And Michael? They didn't . . ."

His hand tightened on hers.

"Patsy," he said too evenly, "kept his wits. They parted company well back. But Michael . . . he tried to set a gelignite charge. Down the Solitaire shaft."

Dorian felt her whole body jerk. "Oh, Jimmy . . . !"

His mouth had pinched. He did not look up, but he kept her hand in his grasp.

"It killed him, aye. An' the papers talked about crazy men, saboteurs. They wouldna call him a Union man. They wouldna say *why.*"

Dorian knew better than to offer some anodyne like, He'd probably have done it, even if you were there. She did tighten her hand in his grasp. "But the Union?" She groped for consolation. The wee workin' man's group, memory said. "That went on? That was all right?"

"Aye." Wryly, his mouth corner pucked. "They were foundin' a workers' paper when I got back. Chock-full o' young firebrands. They didna"—the casual easiness faltered—"remember . . . have much need o' me."

"Oh, Jimmy!" If you want to see if you're indispensable, her grandmother had used to say, put your hand in a bucket of water and take it out. "But—but—" She swallowed and broached her own concern. "How did they make out with . . . Paddy Wild?"

He looked up under his brows. "They didna make out. He'd had the de'il's own row with Dickie Cox. Mebbe two years before. Taken himself off the field, wi' a blast o' sulfur an' a curse. I reckon, he started y'r folk for South Australia then."

Dorian felt her breath ease out. Gone. No longer there to balk and hound you, to wreck your house and maybe beat you up as well as your friends. Not there to salt the wound with memory of his descendant, time and a world away.

"Patsy told me all that." He glanced at her and smiled faintly. "A whole night the man couldna stop talkin'. An' . . . he'd some letters. From Ma."

"Oh! He wrote to her? He let her know—you'd gone?"

"An' she didna believe it either. Nor all his talk about sidhe. 'That fool boy's gone after his fool gold again, an' in his own time, he'll come home.' "

She tried not to blurt, But the money! The money you and Patsy and Bridgie used to send? How did they manage, without that?

He was smiling again, but this time she could feel the effort.

"But by then, they didna need me. Caitlin an' Molly, the two next after Bridgie, they'd both wed. Caitlin to a flax factor in Dungannon, Molly to a feller in Rock. An' . . . the last letter. Ma said, I'm to wed again m'self."

Dorian felt her mouth fall open. He produced a really effortful smile. "A Gallagher. Another o' the local fellers. Widowed lately, an' known Ma all his life."

At the other table, spoons rattled and two boys had begun to quarrel over a milk shake. Dorian sat mouse-still, torn between emotions and not daring to loose any of them.

"Aye," he murmured. He had dropped his eyes again, and the lashes hid their look, but the line of his mouth was clear enough. "At the worst, wi' the four o' them still growin', an' nothin' but charity to fend for them . . . I couldna help."

Involuntarily her fingers moved. She felt his attention come back. He shifted his own fingers in response, and took a sip of tea. By now, she thought irrelevantly, it's probably cold. That touch had said, It's over with. Whatever I failed to help, or left undone, the chance, but also the need, is gone.

But when he looked up, irony lingered in the curl of that mouth.

"I canna tell," he said, "what . . . Providence—meant by that. It doesna seem enough to say, 'Twas for the best wi' them. Or even, 'Twas for the best wi' me. But mebbe"—the twist deepened—"a wee matter o' pride for a man, thinkin' he can keep his kin, let alone save the world single-handed, doesna concern Providence."

"Oh, Jimmy." She took his hand in both hers and clamped it tight. "You *did* save the world, you know that. Maybe not single-handed, but where would we have been here, without you?"

She held that darkened, weighted stare. "And if things were okay with, with your family—mightn't that have been Providence too?"

The stare began to weigh like veritable stone. Then he sighed, and yet again, eased back in his chair.

"Mo cailín . . . ye give things the damnedest turns." The corner of his mouth moved, but it was toward a smile. " 'Tis no wonder ye're a lawyer."

"Well, to say it was bad that they managed without you—that *would* be flying in the face of Providence."

She held her breath at the double irreverence. But in a moment the smile grew genuine.

"Aye, ye're a fair heathen, still. No, I'd no' do that."

The boys at the other table had stopped quarrelling. Broken chips and plastic forks littered the floor, but the mother was gathering her belongings to leave.

"Well," Dorian said, trying for brightness. Damn, this is supposed to be happy. He's here, he's safe, I've got him back, the family was all right. "Anyhow, you and Patsy could get another house together, and . . ."

He looked straight up at her and her heart bumped. No. Finding Dinny gone and Michael dead and the family okay wasn't the worst.

"We could ha' done that," he agreed, softly. "But ye see— Patsy'd married again."

That stone in the graveyard. Bridget, beloved wife of Patrick Burke.

In this world, he remembered her.

"Oh, my dear." She shut her hands fiercely on his, letting th touch speak for her. I understand, I feel it, I know exactly h and why that was so bitter. Precisely because of what you fo over here.

His fingers answered hers, and relaxed. At the other tab family had risen to go.

"Aye," he said, to the tabletop. "He had the right. 'T human that he—bein' left like that—losin' both of us .

335

That he move on, as the family did. That he build another life.

He lifted his head again and drew in a long slow breath.

"All that," he said, as if she had asked it aloud, "was part o' the thing." His eyes spelled it out. I went back, at such a cost, and it wasn't needed. All I found was superfluity and disillusion. With Patsy at that disillusion's core.

"But that wasna all." His voice changed suddenly and his eyes opened on her, the full impact of those peat-dark depths. "The rest was here, mo cailín. Rememberin' ye. Everythin' about ye. Rememberin'—us. Lyin' in that cold bed o' nights . . . I remembered, aye. I couldna forget."

He took her hands in both of his, leaning forward over the table, taking in a long, long breath.

"So I said, They dinna need me here, any longer. An' my heart's no' with 'em the way it was. Maybe it's all different over there—maybe it's no' my time an' I'll always be a stranger. But"—suddenly the deep voice darkened to fierceness—"that's what I *want*."

That was what really mattered. Not what I left behind, but
· I was coming to.

leant forward too, their hands clasped between them, like
˙ teenagers, she thought, in a fast-food shop. Like a pair
'er mind sharply amended. Plighting a troth.

ʏy." I sound like a teenager. All but breathless, on
ʳs, whether grief or joy.

ₑlf speak clearly, slowly, with all the feeling she
ᶜ you knew how I missed you . . . how glad I
ʰted, too."

ʰers. His lips parted. He leant forward
ɳ, and then caught himself. "Ah!" It
ʰth. And then the sun-snatch of a
, but I canna—no' here . . ."

Not kiss you. Not how I'd want to, as pledge, as affirmation, as the prelude to real love. Not here.

The other table was empty. The café had subsided into mid-afternoon quiet. "Let's go, then," Dorian said.

Like birds in the same flock, they were on their feet together, gathering luggage up, moving. Free hands connecting before they had to think. The joy bubbled up again so Dorian thought, I'm not walking, I'm floating. I could dance across this floor.

Only in the car, headed without question for Ibisville, her left hand caught on Jimmy's knee, did her haze of euphoria open beyond the present. Then she found the words bubbling up too, unpremeditated as everything else.

"Now we can go ahead and get that passport, I'll tell Dani, we can decide what's the best way. And once you have that . . ."

Then in the legal sense at least, you're really here. A valid civil entity. Safe.

He squeezed her fingers. Her tongue ran on of itself. "You can get a bank account and a credit card if you want, you could buy out Chris's unit if, if you wanted a place of your own. You can learn to drive. Get a license. Have a car." Independence, she felt without need for consideration, so you needn't ever feel fettered to me. Except for love.

"Very fine indeed," he said, the irony softened with amuse-ment. "An' how'll I pay for all that?"

I don't say, You can be my kept man. You'd never stand for it. She wriggled her hand to mark expansiveness. "Oh, you could do anything. The newspapers. You could be a reporter. Or write that book. Or"—she managed to flick yet another look at him— "join a rock band, after all."

He was smiling, she had time to notice. Amusement, gentle rather than acerbic. But the set of his chin said he had already shaped, if not chosen, his own way.

"Then what do *you* want?"

He stared ahead, and the amusement faded like a sunset into thoughtfulness. Then he said, "There was another reason I thought—mebbe I'd get back."

Dorian let silence return, What was that?

"Back—in my time—I kept thinkin'. About here. About all the—fine things. The computers, an' the medicine, an' the cars, an' "—his brows quirked with something near the old irony— "the supermarkets, aye?"

His voice went serious. "An' the better things. The birth control. The laws to save the blacks, an' the Chinamen. The suffrage. You an' Laura, workin, earnin' your wages. Bein' lawyers. Women's"—his voice italicized one of her terms— "*Rights.*"

He turned a little in the seat. " 'Tis very fine, mo cailín. An' yet—there's things wrong still. The hard boys. The lawless ones. The ones that dinna care." Brodie, she thought. Sorenson. Thorpe. " 'Tis worse, somehow, seein' that here, than . . . where I was."

Because the machine glitter's so seductive, Dorian deduced. The bad side of humanity looks twice as dark.

"An' ye know—we didna really stop Pan-Auric. The mine, aye, but no' the company. We just turned it aside."

To have her own thoughts come back to her stopped Dorian's mouth.

"So, makin' ready . . . I thought, another reason it might work: If Providence sent me here to do a job—it isna over yet."

Dorian found a wide verge above a creek bridge, and pulled in. The bush enclosed them, the road shrunken to a margin, a limit to the silence on rippling miles of growing grass. Her voice sounded overloud.

"Jimmy . . . what is it you want?"

He turned fully, holding her with that dark, earnest gaze. "I'll earn m' bread however it comes," he said. "But what I want"—

and his half smile said, parenthetically, Besides you—"is to do what I did before. No' to be a Union man, not now. But no' to leave things—to the bad."

Land League, Irish Home Rule, Unionism. You want to be—to remain—an activist.

The stare was growing darker. "An' I know," he said, very gently, "that ye never wanted all this with Ben Morar. Pan-Auric, an' all the trouble. Ye'd be happy . . . just bein' a lawyer."

Solving domestic cases, making my living. Except for elections, never considering politics. Sinking back into the old life, the one I wanted so much. The safe, familiar, unexacting life of somebody who takes things as they come.

Except I didn't want to take things as they came, I tried not to, to the bitterest end. It took you to raise the berserker, even at the point of shooting George. Even after losing you, I'd have let myself slide back into that passiveness. It took Dani to kick me out of the cocoon, and send me off to Blackston. If she hadn't done that . . .

She shivered and clamped her hands on his. Okay, she said silently, Whoever's listening. God or whatever you are. I promised once to go to Mass. If I got Laura and Jimmy back. I'll promise again. If this is what Jimmy wants, I'll do it. I'll remember what it can mean, to be a lawyer.

"Okay." Her voice was solemn as it had not been in the café, when they had made what she knew now was a personal pledge. "You want to work to, to change things." You don't, she added silently, want to stop with enough for yourself. "Um. Did you have anything in mind?"

A car, two cars, a semi roared past on the highway, and the slipstream bucketed the dancing stretches of grass. He looked out at it, with pleasure, with, she realized suddenly, a look of protectiveness.

Then his hands relaxed. Easily, moving to eagerness, he said,

"I reckon the wee feller—I reckon Chris already told us." Very softly, he added, toward the window, "An' I'd no' forget."

He turned back to her. " 'Tis the worst o' this time. No' just Pan-Auric. Them an' their ilk're the leaders, but there's nobody's hands clean. Never mind y'r wars an' politicians. The worst is what y're doin' to the earth."

He was watching her face. "I thought it myself, that day by the park. Comin' home from church."

When you said, *Some things are better here.* This is. It's not a desolation, or a mine site. It's protected, cherished land.

But this is a town where it no longer matters. Where the juggernaut's already passed.

She raised her brows. He smiled at her and spoke with a warrior's anticipation, with no doubt of her understanding. Taking her reply on perfect trust.

"So, I'm thinkin', first thing . . . we'll go an' join' y'r Greenpeace, aye?"

ABOUT THE AUTHOR

Sylvia Kelso lives in North Queensland, Australia, and has been telling stories for as long as she remembers. She has previously published three fantasy novels with Five Star: the well-received *Everran's Bane,* its sequel, *The Moving Water,* which was a finalist for an Australian Aurealis genre fiction award, and *The Red Country.*

Sylvia Kelso lives in a house with a lot of trees, but no cats or dogs. She makes up for this by playing Celtic music on a penny-whistle, and is learning the fiddle as well.